Passacaglia

An Analytical Novel
David O. Scaer

-The Fourteen Seventy-
Roanoke, Virginia

2014 *David O. Scaer*

*All Rights Reserved.
Published in the United States of America*

in 2014

by
*-The Fourteen Seventy-
Roanoke, Virginia*

Printed in custom-modified UglyQua font

Library of Congress Cataloging-in-Publication data

Scaer, David O.

Passacaglia / Scaer

10% *of proceeds from this novel will be donated to
-Les Amis de la Cathédrale de Nantes-*

Passacaglia

'[F]ugal technique significantly burdens the shaping of musical ideas, and it was given only to the greatest geniuses, such as Bach and Beethoven, to breathe life into such an unwieldy form and make it the bearer of the highest thoughts.'

—Erwin Ratz, *Introduction to Musical Form*

'I,I,I,I had much grief, in my heart, in my heart. I had much grief, etc., in my heart, etc., etc., I had much grief, etc., in my heart, etc., I had much grief, etc., in my heart etc., etc., etc., etc., etc. I had much grief, etc., in my heart, etc., etc.'

—Johann Matheson in 1725, parodying Johann Sebastian Bach's declamation in cantata *Ich hatte viel Bekümmernis*, BWV 21 (The New Bach Reader, 325)

Qu'as-tu donc créé, O Louis, Roi des Francs?
Un royaume saint, sans blême? Un empire—
—Si, Roi, tu arrives à le garantir—
Sinon, la guerre civile à tes flancs

Prenne dans tes terrains de jeux d'enfant,
Cendres, supplices, et privations... pire
Encore : toute une génération, Sire,
Vouée aux flammes, la France brûlant.

O Louis, où en est ton règne ? La perle
De ton œil perdue, tes champs verts marbrés,
Tes troupeaux, ta ville aussi ne tienne

Plus ; tous tes saints trésors, comme des merles
S'envolent. Car ton Ciel, si près
De toi, se perd. Si est ton Aquitaine.

O Louis, King of Franks, what thing have you wrought?
  A kingdom, a holy empire? A nation
  If you can keep it. A devastation
  If you cannot, a civil war throughfought

'Crost your late-liv'd playground, your life-love brought
  To ashes (flayed to ribbons), starvation,
  Deceit, confusion, a generation
  At war, a home aflame, a nation fraught.

O Louis, where's your kingdom now? Your vineyards,
  Your green marmorated fields, your seven
  Flocks all leveled, cities burned, bishops slain?

They might's well be gone, flown 'ways like black birds
  Flown like prayers away. For your Heaven
  Is lost to you. You've lost your Aquitaine.

Sometimes you've got to kill a sturgeon several times

The Fat King of St. Denis tore free of his basilica, driven from the old mausoleum by his own blood flooding torrents through his ears, driving driving driving toward the Island wild with fury, his heart wild and red, his heart forging claws to tear free of its ribcage, so great was wrath in him.

He had mentally killed his son a dozen times before he ever saw the boy's dainty little masque that day. (The last time, he had strapped him to his altar at St. Denis, the altar where he could see his own face frozen in sculpted death, and he filleted the boy with his own sword.) The Fat King smiled to himself.

You have to strike the sturgeon hard enough to release the roe, but not quite hard enough to break its back

'Oh, Father' was the boy upon seeing him.

Oh Father broke his boy's nose with the heel of his palm; his years of quietly mortifying his common sense (*drinking-in* the loft of pale lovely words of light and charity and Jerusalem issuing forth from the lips of good Abbot Suger) were instantly lost in the hot sting of his palm withdrawn, his son's canine still embedded in his bloodless fat.

Sturgeons are bottom feeders, he won't be needing that tooth anyway

'Give me that sodding heir, you lifeless bouse. Roe for the table, or I'll make you steak.' The Fat King's teeth were all there, all nice and yellow-variegated, and still good enough to chew his child like cheese. His other palm didn't yet have any of his son's teeth in it, and it in turn cracked The Young King's palatine bone.

Dainty sodding bottomfeeder, full more of mud and slime and corruption than pearls

Love is the primitive conceit maintaining that one person is somehow less hateful than all the rest. Hatred is equally primitive, but as its opposite, is hotter and more perfect. In its heat, hatred had somehow made the Fat King's sword lay forgotten in his robes, Salic laws unbent by the double crime of regicide and infanticide.

'*Heirs! Is that so very painful...?*' And his fists rained down upon his son, and they were heavy as bags of sand. 'You've got simply to split that squirming little being down the middle like a trout, and pinch out as much of your family's glory within her as she can stand. Do I have to bring in a priest to bless the happy event yet again?'

You should never be king. You have no sense of the arc of years. You should've stayed a monk. You don't deserve Aquitaine

And Aquitaine loved her Eleanor, and Eleanor her Aquitaine, and the Young Louis was soft and limp and capable only of making her drooze out sad sickly daughters, as able to wear a crown as they were of carrying stone. And the Young King Louis hated them as much as he hated Eleanor, and all of his monk's training under lightfilled Suger was lost when his fists grew hot with the memory of his father's, and planted fear and hatred into Eleanor.

And the annulment occurred.

* * *

The Romans had martyred Denis a millennium earlier, chopping his head off in one stroke. *Iron-meets-skin-and-bone-and-gristle,* and Denis' blood had sprayed out over the Mount of Martyrs.

But the story is better than that, and has as its next chapter Denis *getting back up* and picking back up that head of his and beginning a slow, plodding march, a dead man carrying his own head around. And from his mouth issued gospels and revelations, and warnings to the Romans of their impending judgment, and words of regret and grief and love for the people of Paris. 'Gone are my days among you at the thermes, and gone are my careful friendship and watchfulness for you, my Lutece flock, my Parisii darlings.' And although his mournful lips never said to follow him on his long, bleeding pilgrimage, the Parisii did anyway, and watched in horror and wonder as the headless, dead-and-yet-not-dead martyr collapsed—finally bloodless, finally lifeless—in a still clearing in the midst of a dark grove of canopy chestnuts.

The monastery and basilica grew up on the martyr's dark, oily soil, and the kings of Paris began coming here to commune with their people's saint.

And Hugh the Capet lived in his own century, and would name his son *Robert Your Future King*, and made him sacred during Christmas Mass, when *Your Future King* was aged fifteen years. And then, realizing that he and Robert were now in their essence both Kings, Hugh enacted his patron saint's own ending, and, a stumbling man decapitate, spoke gospels and revelations and funereals, groping about until he reached minster, and began digging his sepulcher.

And one day my body will run bloodless, and it and my garrulous head can just tumble on in

And the Future King quartered then on the Island, and waited for his father to die so that he could nudge him into the open ground, and in his turn become like his father, and in his turn begin digging his own grave next to the people's saint.

And so it went: a Capet electing, in his own lifetime, his son to kingship, and withdrawing then to Denis' side to await resignedly the inevitable, and the son conducting the business of the Parisii from the Island. And when elder Capets die, younger Capets move off the Island to dig their graves next to their mouldering fathers. And become in their turn Capetian saints.

* * *

The Fat King had loved his elder son first, and better. And after shortly, when Philippe was man enough to see the fat man's fancies as they were, he became the old man's foil, the bearer of new tidings, the inventor of fire and bringer of young lovers to table and a man full of words and the kind of spirits you can't get in the monastery, and his words were a challenge to the Fat King, making him cringe a little, making him little a little. And the Fat King loved him for being the King he couldn't be, and for making of the kingship a *leaper*, a *biter*, rather than a low slow lumbering slumbering, stupid *sturgeon* like himself.

The Young Philippe was ferocious and devout, and vowed to one day go the Holy Land to cover himself with heroes' ribbons. The Fat King envied him his passions and prowesses, and the furnace of ambition that lit him from within.

The Fat King squinted his eyes into smiling.

For the King had had his heir now, in this lean and proud Philippe. For he now knew that he himself was now immortal, his own blood forever in the Kings his Philippe would sire. For now the fates of nations has swung like a pendulum into the light.

For now.

* * *

How could bridges be any more sacred than this one?

Philippe The Young King had been a flurry of robes like an aerie of crows, a concert of hooves' clatter crossing from one side to the other.

On either side a chasm, up ahead an Island sanctuary, while back behind: a languorous labyrinth

Philippe had read of Theseus in the maze—and although the Island was the only city he'd ever known and the bridge to it the only bridge he'd ever crossed, he felt certain this one was as glorious as any labyrinth in mythology, as great an interstice uniting the known with the unknown as any other. His father, it was true, had already crossed over this one, flown over his own bridge, from the Parisii's Island to the sacred chestnut grove with its shrine to the Saint-Denis' minster looming a sacred shadowed limbo leading headlong to eternity and nothingness—it was as if by crossing this bridge away from the Island, you were crossing from life into death, and by crossing *the other way,* well...

And so Philippe would ride to beat Hell nearly every night across that bridge of his father's, out toward the *world beyond,* a crazy thrust right up to the edge of Everything, a young man's insane impulse to cast himself bodily through the night of his worst fears: of tipping over the edge, and teetering toward—even *into*—Nothing. And as yet a bachelor, the shuddering obsessing fear of losing himself, of drifting away into the darkness, would turn over in his turbulent mind, and the desire to flirt with annihilation would become, within just a few hours, a rending need to calm the fire if not in his heart then in his loins, and risk everything in some stranger's bed. The old bridge was a bit of a labyrinth itself: being the only new land the Island had seen in its history, the Parisii had seen fit to tilt one ramshackle house against another, an unknowable concretion of houses and barely-houses, all sharing three walls and some part of roof with three or more neighbors. And the tiny streets spread through the houses on the bridge like a propagation of veins in Philippe's hand, and this dark place would welcome its dark son.

And the gates would crash to the pavers every night at one, separating the bridgecity from its Island for the remainder of hours, abandoning it to the wolves and fiends who seeped out of the marshes and hollows. And Philippe, each night, would tear himself away from another woman, and find the horse no commoner would dare touch for fear of losing his hand, and mount just in time to fling himself back through the gates and find himself back among the Known, among the Safe.

* * *

Then there had been the night that the darkness took her child back to herself, and all that came to an end.

All they knew was that Philippe's horse was all alather through the gate by the sounding of Matins, and no rider aboard.

They had found Philippe by morning light. All the scribes were allowed to write was that he had so badly broken his limbs, he would never reawaken.

For the life of him, the Fat King couldn't remember his second son's name.

Not Philippe

'Spring *Not Philippe* from his cloister.' Wherever that was.

Not Philippe. He had forgotten how much he hated his second son.

The boy's given name was eventually found to be something like Ludovicus, and the Fat King began savoring lengthy murders of his second son, if only because they really were mirror images of each other: the same *name* even, and the elder Louis—the Fat one—constitutionally unable to abide hearing his own name profaned by otherwise well-meaning men summoning his *son*, cast about for some other name they could use on the runt without having to have his own person insulted constantly. He'd break the boy of his vow of chastity of course, and all the other vows, too, so even 'the monk'—which the Fat King snarled in the height of derision—began to seem *mal a propos*.

The Fat King—*sixth of the name*—refused to call him *Seven*, either. The number seven, the Lord's number, was worth more than that. And besides, 'the monk' had broken his vows and would go straight to Hell anyway, no sense of adding to the irony.

Eventually, the taciturn boy would become 'the sturgeon'.

At least a sturgeon is good for some roe. You hit it hard enough...

And a new order of obedience came to be.

* * *

The sturgeon was—*eventually*—good for some roe.

Auguste came into this world a bluish and sickly boy, the very image of his father the sturgeon and his grandfather the Fat King, and come to think of it his mother, homely foreigner named Adelaide. All signs pointing to the perfections of the fathers before him.

But Auguste was different, too. Confused stories about his uncle swept through his memory, some great fiery hero of the ancient past, and 'Philippe' stuck to the pale chilly fry like some kind of profane challenge, pushing his God-given name aside with casual elbows. They say his grandfather had beaten his father blue until they saddled the boy with the dead uncle's name: ridiculous tales, as his grandfather had died years before Auguste—*Philippe* Auguste now—had seen the light of the cold northern sun. They say that his grandfather had hated his father for how much they looked and acted and spoke like each other, and they say he had loved his uncle—*Philippe Auguste's namesake*—in his father's stead. They say, too, that his grandfather had lined up Eleanor for his uncle and not his father, and that *things would be different* if only his uncle had lived.

And this part of the tale he has no trouble at all believing.

* * *

And Philippe Auguste has had an interesting day. He turned fifteen today, and was made sacred today (whatever that meant), and for that matter, he now realizes he is married.

And it is night. And Isabelle is beneath him, and she seems ridiculously young to be absorbing the kinds of cruel acts Philippe Auguste was ordered to perpetrate upon her as many times as possible.

Perhaps he is distracted by the girl's cries. Perhaps it is too warm in here. Perhaps he is nervous about the blood pouring from her. But his mind is wandering.

Damnation. He's lost his rhythm. And the girl is sobbing silently, and he knows that there is much riding on this, and he's getting riled up at having trouble concentrating.

Damn

He circles his eyes up to the headboard. *Think!*

Champagne. Blois. Ardennes. And for a time he is feeling a bit more confident again. *Chartres. Beaufort. Artois.*

Artois. He was told the girl brings Artois to him as a gift. She has never seen Artois, doesn't seem to care what it is or where it is or how many people live there or how many other kings' lands Philippe Auguste might have to cross to go and see Artois for himself. And then there's the fact that Artois is *his* now—*he doesn't quite understand that concept either*—and that he was also given everything that had been his mother's too, which is a list he finds more of a singsong melody than anything he can possibly picture as real 'things'. *Champagne, Blois, Ardennes...* Somebody had made him memorize all the various and sundry 'lands' his father was going to leave him when he died—he'd had mnemonics for all of them that were just as long as the list itself—and he knew at least that they were trivial little ragged bits of territory: a village and a few farms here, a sturdy stone house with some land there. It's impossible to list them all now—*after all, this is his wedding night*—but he knows they're there and he knows they're his. But if he were one day to try to locate them all by marking them on a parchment, they would form a measles across the ragged, craggy old face of the landscape.

'*Measles across the landscape.*' No rhythm there.

Damn. Not again.

All he can think of for now is that he is fifteen years old, and has, grafted into his very name, precisely forty-two titles, one for each one of the forty-two parcels of land—most of them God-forsaken, several (he is told) exactly worthless, all at untold distances, all of them small enough to throw a flat stone across—belonging to him. And he'd need to be a sparrow or a ghost to visit all of them, darting invisibly over the dozens of borders separating him from his pitiful little constellation of potagers and fly-teeming marshes. Hell, even his little Island citadel wasn't entirely his: he was just one meager baronet among a half-dozen great, horned bruisers with their mobs of mercenaries, swarming the eastern end of the Island...

And now he is out of bed, with Isabelle left huddling in her tears and blood.

If I am allowed to exist at all, he thinks, *it is surely by virtue of the mobs' simply failing to notice me yet*

And when he thinks of the impotent spangling of Capet holdings—pathetically far-between, completely unable to offer one another protection even, completely unable to even speak to one another—he is reminded that each and every one of those sad little farflung 'domains' (what else to call them, 'fields'? 'gardens'? 'yards'?) is as surrounded as his little Island is, surrounded by hard-shouldered, athletic, exquisitely well-armed and well-organized menaces.

What I need is...

Isabelle is squirming and wincing—she has given up weeping, and is now a mass of salt-streaked cheeks, swollen eyes, and Lord, how Philippe would love to get himself some kind of powerhouse of his own... catch The Big Fish instead of scooping up all these small-fry domains nobody else wants.

For God's sake: Artois? Where the Hell is Artois?

Too bad Aquitaine's gone.

Aquitaine is long gone indeed. And Philippe Auguste's father is in his cold cell at St. Denis' monastery tonight... he may as well be in his cold crypt, so much he undid Philippe Auguste's wellbeing with his chasing away of Eleanor, beautiful Eleanor.

What I need is...

There's nothing in Philippe Auguste's imagination that quite equals her. When he thinks of Eden, descriptions of that distant, shining prize—*more land than a hundred Artois', full of rivers so laden with fish you can walk 'cross bank to bank feet dry, calico hillsides blanketed over with vineyards and throughpierced with wine cellars... Beautiful and healthy and white... ô Aquitaine, watched over by your thousand towers, guarded by your high walls, your heart sleeps sound tonight, does it not?*—flood his mind.

What I need is... Aquitaine

He circles...

Aquitaine with her ammonitic peaks. Aquitaine with her rushingrustling forests sighing. Aquitaine with her dappled Atlantic sands, her salt-capped waves and her dusty grapes—*for God's sake, all those grapes and orchards and wheatfields!*—and her stout limestone churches. Aquitaine and her dancing, healing rains to rinse the smell of sweat and sweet from his body. Aquitaine and her Eleanor, that long-lost Eleanor, Eleanor and her cruel, haughty glare and her steely voice that made nations of men. Aquitaine and her Eleanor, that restless huntress who had besotted his slow, cold, dimwitted father.

Forget the other forty-two titles

Aquitaine would make an outstanding forty-third

And he came, hot and freely.

Eveillé dans mon lit, l'ange vint à moi
   Disant dans le noir, à moi, honni, plein
   D'horreur, fatigué de mes travaux vains
   Moi si faible, mon cœur rempli d'effroi

'Ne pense trop où tu es, ni ne vois
   Trop le fil qui t'y amène si loin
   Des rives. Ton secours n'est pas ton choix.
   Attends, dors, comme tu te le dois.

Tu es jeune. Le jour t'apporte son pain
   Et la nuit son vin. Manges-en et bois
   Et ton courage reviendra plus sain.'

L'ange me vint une seconde fois,
   Me toucha, et dit: 'Malheur ! ce chemin
   (Course si fâcheuse) est trop long pour toi.

The angel came to me. Awake in bed,
  Darkness surrounding me, filling me through
  With horror and shame, and cold fatigue knew
  Me in my weakness, heart thrashing with dread

'Try not to think where you are, and the thread
  That brought you here. You are already far too
  Far from shore to swim back yourself. Rescue
  Is not yours to knit. Wait, sleep, rest your head.

You are young. The day will heal you. Once fed
  With night's turning wine and day's cautious bread
  Your life will return, your years are still few.'

And then twice she came and touched me and said,
  'This journey (this endless course you led,
  Your wearied path) has been too long for you.'

*\ *\ *

A man with a wide neck thundering *christs* down upon him.

'Quit your shouting. You're in my house, and the girls are asleep.'

The preacher had shoehorned himself between the young man and the narrow door. Vicus recognized the tactic.

How dare you try to trap me in my own home

And yet the preacher's neck continued swelling wider and wider, struggling around the word, 'Christ! Christ! Christ!'

They should leave a letter or two out for when people misuse the name of saviors, just to let people know that it is not God Saves, but Man Curses

He couldn't think of the title... *tetranym?*

No, that's not quite it

Words for the four-letter acronym for the *I Am That I Am* swirled roundabout him.

Tetragrammaton. That's it

And in Vicus' mind, he began to hear the man bellow *Crst crst crst!*

Is this what an exorcism's really like? He tried to imagine it.

The afflicted man sits or kneels before the baptismal font. The assembly gathers in a circle behind the afflicted man. Most merciful God, we confess that we are captive to sin and cannot free ourselves. We have sinned against you in thought, word, and deed, by what we have done and by what we have left undone.

And the preacher railed on and on.

I don't know. I'm not feeling it

* * *

The rehearsal had run long. Garcia Lorca's *Blood Wedding*, and he was playing the part of Death. A bit part—the irony that Lorca's Death was only a cameo was delicious to Vicus—but that was how Vicus would best have it. He hated performing, and the only reason he'd even signed up was that the theater was an old abandoned one, with a ragged old curtain embroidered with some scene from a Watteau painting, and somebody had figured out how to jury the old radiators, and you could warm your hands by placing them among the bars if you weren't too bothered by the risk of sweeping through a half-century of cobwebs.

The director—what was his name again, *Deudon?*—had vetoed the all-too-instinctive *Death-as-Grim-Reaper* reflex and had opted instead for something closer to a confidence-man ethos. But Vicus had nothing in his tiny stash to fulfill his director's wishes. He did have an old coat and tie with him—for the life of him, he'd never know why he had ever packed such a thing, as he'd vowed never to be caught in a suit again until they stuck him in a pine box—and now, he was feeling constricted by the tie around his neck and weighed down by the clammy weight of the old wool duster he was thanking his stars he'd remembered to pack, too. It rained year-round in Nantes it seemed, and although the duster was waterproof enough, the latest iteration of Rain had morphed into some semblance of rainsnow, great heavy flakes falling hard like grains of pumice and clinging to the wool with a new tenacity the duster was unable to fully account for. And although the wool wasn't damp per se, it was now... *heavy*, and the weight of water held within its fibers was a thermal mass, a bulk of Cold that lapped up any warmth that seeped from Vicus' bones.

Thank God for old radiators

And everything evolves slowly in this dark space, and Vicus realizes he knows all the other actors' lines before they do, and he hates their weird pronunciation of Lorca's words—probably the anonymous translator's fault those words just don't sit under the tongue.

And even though he is only twenty, he realizes that his joints are aching from the cold, and he begins dreaming of ways of getting his long bones in between the rungs of the radiator. When he makes his first attempt, his patella is too wide to fit. He rests it against the radiator anyway; the knee in his one pair of good slacks dusted gray with soot.

'We'll get to Death next rehearsal.'

And Deudon (or *Doudon* or *Dieudonné*, can't remember which now) is looking sheepish for dragging Death into this cold theater without even having him try out his lines, and invites him—*drags* him—to the Jupiter across the street for a couple cognacs.

Unaccustomed to the strength of the distillation, Vicus sucks its flavor from sugar cubes.

* * *

'Do you honestly believe this is the *easy way out*? If you do, you're far stupider than I thought…'

Thank you

The wide-necked man had been leaning far forward, perched on the lip of the chair in Vicus' living room, but now at these words, he leaned back, a satisfied mug over a satisfied paunch.

Just when did you screw up the chutzpah to take a seat?

The room was half-lit, a few ticks colder than comfortable. A few feeble Christmas decorations still dangled hangdog over the front door window, January neglect. A clock over the piano murmured. Vicus noticed the girls' tea set near the dark tv, some washcloths for tablecloths.

Silent night holy night

His blanket and pillow were jammed into the couch's corners. Seeing them, he at once felt a pang of embarrassment: his sleeping situation was out there, out in the open, out there for the world—stranger and preacher alike— to see. But then he remembered that no preacher had been invited, and Vicus felt something like a grim, gritty *fuck you* coming on. This was still his house, still his couch, still his living room (for a time at least), and uninvited guest was really just another name for intruder.

Preacherman wants to show up to folks' places uninvited, preacherman'd better get used to seeing shit like this

'Now you tell me how you can break your vow to God so easily.'

'I don't feel like telling you anything. It'd be one thing if this were a courtroom...' His voice trailed off: no point in finishing. Preacher didn't want to know the answer, he wanted to prove he was right. Vicus found himself staring at his toes.

At least my feet don't need to know they're right...they just need to know they're feet

Copper in his mouth, dead ringing in his ears, coral a great concretion in his gut. He remembered all those warnings about the symptoms of the first onset of heart attack: airless chest, tightening muscles in the neck, diaphragm a sharpened steel rod. *Vow to God.* That word *vow* sank through his spiraling guts. Had he known promising anything to God could cost him like this... His lips formed over words he didn't know how to say.

Who am I to bear it?

'What?' Preacher leaned out over his perch again. Not to hear but to challenge the very breath that issued from Vicus' lungs. His words were sharp, yellow, hard... bone words, tooth words of transparent enamel, words to violate the airspace surrounding Vicus, to invade his very logic. 'What did you say to me?'

Vicus hadn't realized his mind had gone audible. In the hushed, heated conversations of his inner world, he guessed he should be ready for anything to seep out.

'I said, *Who am I to bear it?*' Vicus was surprised how tiny his voice sounded to him.

'And what the Hell is that supposed to mean?'

The man's voice was rising again. It was unclear to Vicus if people thought he was particularly deaf, or particularly dense, or both. The preacher spoke louder.

'*Who are you to bear this?* Did you really just ask me that?'

'I'm not so sure I was asking you. Just asking, I guess. Not even that.'

'You really think this is the easy way, don't you?'

None of your business what I'm thinking

* * *

'It's called *Departure from Cythera*. I think. Cythera was the island of Venus' birth.'

The cognac burned transparent flames in him. And Vicus was seeing the director in something approaching adequate light for the first time. Deudon was a divine wreck, a joyous crash victim. Vicus remembered something a theologian had written one time: that artists are like charismatics, only more stupid; it's like they don't know not to be sad about things. The bartender was evidently used to seeing Deudon here and for some reason didn't seem to mind the man's filthy persona or loopy conversations. Cythera a case in point.

'It's what they call a *gallant* painting. Or an imitation of it I guess.

A tapestry of a painting. An *ekphrasis*. And then they say Watteau *found the Lord* one day and decided to burn all of his paintings, thank God he didn't have access to all of them any more. *Cythera* was already in private hands, he couldn't get to it and burn it to ashes.'

'I hate it.'

'You do?' Deudon said this without bothering to even look away from his drink.

Vicus could picture the old theater curtain with great clarity. Knots of slick shiny nobles, a man's hand at each woman's back, wandering wistfully in disordered clutches toward the harbor.

'A bunch of aristocrats with nothing better to do than... *cavort*. Damn them.'

'They're not cavorting. It's very symbolic. They're departing forever from the island of Venus. You don't cross back, you know. Love is that way.'

The cognac was sitting in heavy, and the Jupiter was overwarm after the icy theater.

'Well then leave me out. The only philosophy those happy souls—and I place Watteau firmly in the boat with the whole lot of elite travellers—seem to have time or brains for is whether or not Love will last...'

Vicus pushes his coins onto the counter. They defy his struggles to lift them from the smooth surface. He damns his close fingernails. Finally he slides them toward the edge with the side of his hand and into the ashtray, and they castanet in drily, coins for his cognac eyes.

* * *

The Jupiter was in the old St. Similien neighborhood—dark and grey and brick and ashes, a scaled-up city-block-sized radiator with barely enough juice to keep your bones from creaking. And Vicus—Deudon's Death, the dark, haunted Charon of Nantes—pushes off from the bank. St. Similien was farther from his own neighborhood—a rundown mill quarter—*you've become very mundane, haven't you?*—than he had yet been, this late, and buses weren't running anymore, and it was snowing harder now, real snow and not that bluegray indecision that had soaked him earlier.

And he heard the great big molecular flakes strike his ears, louder than his footfalls, and the cognac fought back with hot blood into his reddening earlobes. And he really didn't know where he was, but he knew that just by going vaguely uphill he'd be unlikely to stray too terribly far away from true line. Félibien was his road, and it was long and straight and easy, and all he'd have to do was be attentive to the streetsigns—it'd take real bad luck to somehow miss the crossing.

And after what seemed like an hour or a second, he sees the market, a wide ugly square called Talensac, which pinches closed at its upper end into Félibien, and so he knows he's nearly there.

And he realizes he is very drunk.

And he sees all the other old drunks drifting across the sidewalks crisscrossing Talensac. And he doesn't know the poet, but somewhere in Vicus' head the poet was convincing enough to remind him of his ancient verses: *she cultivates in him yet another melancholy...*

> *...A heavy accretion of flattery mingled with complacency*
> *And caresses ripe and fragile petals*
> *All anchored in his soul like jagged blocks of coral*
>
> *His pride rears up as a silhouette*
> *Seizes upon the absurd obstacles that cross dizzyingly before him*
> *And to throw himself down*
> *Bursts open*
> *To spend himself:*
> *A broken wave upon a jetty*

And the drunks all waver on through his tunnel vision like listing galleons, and

Vicus has half a mind to find a good doorframe here, too, and spend the night *a broken wave upon a jetty* in his cognac haze.

Felibien eventually sights him down, and a mile long of streetlights is a string of pearls leading him home. The drunks are behind him, but the impulse to find a nice quiet dark corner in somebody's garage near the water heater is still there.

Do you think if I fell asleep out here, I would wake up before I froze to death?

Finally deciding to jog through the slowmotion snowfall, and the only cars are the rare police cruisers, stop-motioned each streetlight, tires whisking white noise away in Doppler shift. Gravel grinds wet white sparks under his shoes, and the landlady has left the door unlocked and the blinds open for him.

* * *

'...And I know you've not once thought of your children!'

Time for you to stop yelling at me, and show me you've thought of my sleeping children too

'Do you think this is going to be easy for them?'

Come to think of it, I don't seem to remember you ever offering me your care.

Unless you call tonight Pastoral Care

'How could you ever give them up?'

Who's talking about giving them up?

* * *

Like captivity, labyrinths are as labyrinths do. Félibien is about the only straightline east-west in the whole city, and south of that line—the zone reaching all the way to the Loire—is a true labyrinth, all seven-pointed star-shaped intersections with spokes pointing into the darkness, goodluck finding your way, and the pigeons eat all your breadcrumbs before they hit the dirt. Your only hope is the hardware shop that's always closed, the center for Breton arts with the joyful mournful keening pipes finding seams in the stone, the long line of antique shops with the colorful goblets and the manuscript leaves paling in the wide windows *thank God they all aim north*, the Boulevard Guist'hau with its centerline planted with sycamore and the peeling bark and honey leaves mouldering to tannins in the gutters. Beware the rumbling old man who haunts the staircases in the gated street, the one with no streetlights—he'll mumble unspeakable abuses in his terrible voice that tickles the subacoustic—and beware the dark cobble walls near the old school, where ferns grow out from what must have been a Gaulish fortress, thrown together in anticipation of Hadrian's own masterpiece, and where the street is so dark you wouldn't know if the rumbling man was after you until after he had slit your throat.

The long walls of the seven-sided prison (which some fool had had built in the center of town) are, to Vicus' mind, the center of the labyrinth, and guard the night from the monster of human instinct in uneasy, heavily-mortarred truce. They grow no ferns, grow no moss: they are sterile stone, unscalable by anything resembling life. And your footsteps echo twice as loud here in the dark slanting shadows of the streets, and you wonder if there are inmates in the yard just inside that wall, smoking in the cold air, warming their hands by a 55-gallon drum and hearing your footsteps and plotting to kill the man they prove to be the owner of those loud footsteps that sometimes plod and sometimes stroll.

Sound—*here*—is a different phenomenon than it is in the rest of Nantes. Somehow the bell of old Saint Clement, through some trick of the narrow streets playing subtle with urban acoustics, can be heard here, four miles away as the crow flies, a slow plodding cadence arcing over the Erdre at St. Pierre and meeting your own cadence, and together they sift over the walls of the city prison.

Vicus, having heard that old, sad melody dozens or hundreds of times as he hurries past the prison at the center of Nantes' labyrinth, could play it out for you on the next piano he finds: *e, g, d... e, g, d...* But it would make his heart quicken as it does every time he hustles past this point in the labyrinth, worrying about the glum souls captive within, locked in stasis. Barely able to keep their hands warm, stamping their feet in place.

We've come a long ways from Cythera

Freedom and captivity. That was where his head was. The silken, sly, slothful men and women of Cythera... well, they hardly qualified as human beings at all, but instead they were paper flowers, or taffeta draperies... And as such, they broke Vicus' heart, this portrait of false people, this posterizing of... *wretched meaningless love,* this parade of pennants, satin standards for *idleness* and *frivolity* and *superficiality* and *elitism,* meaningless all, infuriating all, all manner of human social pathology that made Vicus regret—viscerally regret—being even vaguely identifiable as *being like them.*

The net of memory of his life—the aching in his temples—the dark intersections with the seven directions—the nights in the cold, wandering the deserted streets of the sleeping city—the sharpened corners of broken cinderblock laying just behind his sternum, herding his breath into crowded corners, pressing it against the huddling, shivering memories, all jumbled and sharp and fragile: blades of plateglass shattered, devilish points and terrifying, curving razoredges, all intersecting, all superimposed, touching and sliding across one another, sometimes smoothly and silently, sometimes grating toothedge—the net of memory ensnaring him yet again.

The city is wide, and the streets too often left unmarked—some leading to civilization and safety, some leading to black, highwalled cutthroat alleys: dead ends.

And the cold night: terribly, terribly long.

Le mauvais œil soit toujours avec vous
   L'ire de tes pères soit visitée
   Sur toi jusques en perpétuité
   Justice divine pende du cou

L'on relâche et dans tes villes des loups
   Des bandits des landes en l'obscurité
   Une toux pour ton poumon irrité
   Et pour le cœur d'infini courroux

Mais viens tout près, viens tout doux l'angelette
   Guide-moi aux chemins de tes cités
   Où le malheur ne me prend ni me guette

Soulage-moi qui crains calamité
   Protège ce cœur qui tant regrette
   Des années perdues l'immensité

The ancient curse is upon us: the sin
  Of the father, to sixth and seventh son,
  To the sixth and seventh generation
Falls, and falls on us. Let justice begin.

Amok run wolves the city walls within.
  Forests haunted by murd'ring frontier Hun.
  Another cough for your tattered lung.
For your heart, more ire than has ever been.

But come, my sweet angel, come sweet and near,
  Guide me through your streets and alleys as one
  No longer enslaved by threat or by fear.

Companion in my calamity's tear,
  Protect this heart, this heart come undone
  In the immensity of this last year.

* * *

There had been a family friend who on a whim bought a tiny fetish for him in dense, dark hematite. A steely armadillo, found in a Cherokee gift shop.

'I have no idea why. Just seemed like you.'

And so he had pocketed it, and it would find its way into the liner of his coat and surprise him each time he threw his coat over a chair. Dark cold leaden hematite knocking a sharp divot into the frame.

Gotta be careful you'll put out a window with that

* * *

He had wandered over the border with Italy—and back—a few dozen times that year. It was no big deal. There was no wall, no fence, no nothing. No Italians with machine guns demanding his papers in the one direction, no Frenchmen with machine guns in the other direction, either. No checkpoint, no gate, no sign. It was just a deserted one-lane road that sinewed among the olives, way up in the Piedmont. A few times, he had gotten distracted with a tune in his head or the Med shining crystals up at him or a pebble in his shoe, and before he knew it he was on the other side, easy as kiss-my-hand.

He remembered at those times something perfectly useless someone had told him: that you could always tell which side of the Loire you were on just by looking at the houses. It seems that houses on the north bank all have slate roofs, all steely grey. And houses on the south side all have clay tile roofs. And inasmuch as he noticed such things, he knew this to be true. How a whole half of France had known what the norm was would remain a mystery to him— it was surely a question of housebuilders and roofers-tilers or slaters—having incumbency on one side or the other, living for generations and generations among slate- or tile-roofed houses and simply never asking the question why.

But at least the Loire was a real boundary, and you would never accidentally wander across distracted, a song whistling away at your pursed lips until you finally noticed all the slate roofs. The crossing into Italy was really only a watershed. He had tried once or twice to figure out just where folks *became* Italian or *became* French, but you couldn't look at people like you could a house, and besides, near the border someone was just as likely to be bilingual as not, and there were more subtle shadings than nationality, too: people speaking Ladin or Provençal or a half-dozen other patois that he couldn't get his ears around.

Eventually he would alight on the idea that there was really some kind of overarching frontier mentality, common to both sides, both nationalities, and that the only way to find out which side of the line he was on was to squint his eyes and perceive a sort of gradient, one in which his own alterity was acceptable or unacceptable, a calculus by which he himself would be analyzed and judged (by his height or his stride or melody of his accent, or the way he smiled at strangers, or some other measure he could not guess), the Italians seeing him with welcoming eyes, *seeing him as a guest,* and the French looking upon him with distrusting eyes, *seeing him as a foreigner.*

And this way the border was not so much a line in the sand as it was the way the wind blew, the wave of the flag, a quotidian, a dynamic, a treaty renegotiated tacitly between him and the girl on the bicycle, the man with the hoe, the old couple sitting, the old woman knitting.

This old woman believes I have a cold, dark heart

I must be in France

* * *

Cherokee is a real place, an Eden, a home-planet, and the Cherokee derive their name from that place—that place they lost—and so saying *so-and-so is Cherokee* is to refer to a whole history of life in that place, and the wholesale loss of that place, and that place's loss, too, of its people, of its *self.* They say that when the white man moved in, the second thing he did—after deporting the Cherokee over the horizon to a long and bitter period of diaspora—was to raze the sacred orchards at Kitua, with all their crow's-egg apples planted roundabout with sorghum.

I have no business being here

It turns out to be possible to graft one apple tree with a matchstick-sized brin of a second apple tree, transforming it from the one variety into the other with a few well-planned, well-placed nicks of a razor blade's subtlety. And after a season, the two varieties have joined so completely, knit their fibers together so intimately, it becomes impossible to tell where the one organism ends and the other begins; you might find a few bits of old grafting wax, or a few traces of clumsy razoring, or on the odd chance, a disjunct where the two varieties of apple grew at slightly differing rates, but beyond these meager signs, the chimera would go undetected.

And when Vicus had heard that the Cherokee had somehow gotten their hands back on their same land, nestled in the same sacred Cherokee *val* from which they had been driven a century and half previous, and when he heard they had somehow gotten some sacred crow's-egg apple stock—weedy volunteers that had pushed up next to the foundations of an old schoolhouse—and were planning on having a valley-wide session of apple-grafting to the end of rebuilding their sacred grove, one tree at a time, he had been quick to pile family and gear into the car and thread his way through the Blue Ridge to find Cherokee. It'll be a long road for a short payoff.

* * *

They have sunshine in their skies that they don't have in their hearts

A typical Saturday at 18 rue de la Liberté, across from Place Magenta at the threshold of the pedestrian zone, 06000 Nice. It is chilly and clear in October, and the floor-length windows to the street are open, and the white walls and parquet floors shine. Smell of pine cleaner in the air, too pungent. The radio murmurs notes and words and static, the station having wandered with no one in the room. There is a tiny kitchen here, and the appliances seem narrow and toylike. Steam rolls from the transom above the door to the tiny bathroom.

Vicus now in his towel, his skin pink and hot from the shower. He imagines the warm moisture blazing from his skin in the cold air of the living

-Passacaglia-

room, roils of vapor curling off him like smoke, if only he could see it with some clever interferometric backlighting. The futon is his only real furniture, the only furniture with upholstery, and it tilts back to reveal his wardrobe. T-shirt and jeans, t-shirt and jeans, t-shirt and jeans. Coffee singing, cupboards bare.

In hindsight, maybe he should have known that private comforts made public are considered profane in this city. But the shopkeeper across the street looks up and sees him t-shirt and jeans, barefoot, mug of coffee between his hands, face to the sun, wet hair; he catches her eyes narrowed staring suspicions at him.

* * *

His fingers burn from cutting into too many grafting sticks, the folded metal corner of the razor blade a repeating insult to skin after hundreds of grafts in the cold morning. He is sunburnt, his forehead hurts, shining. Sunshine and concentration. He peers under his glasses at another new graft taking shape; he and an elderly Cherokee man have been having a silent contest to make the tightest one. Although his competitor hasn't said a word in a half-hour, Vicus knows the man is enjoying himself immensely.

Vicus concentrates harder. He senses his wife has positioned herself to occupy the corner of his peripheral vision, standing there as a challenge and watching, waiting to catch him the moment he looks up. He decides never to look up.

* * *

Cimiez is the former Cemenelum, and when Cemenelum ceased to be (somewhere in the fourth century), Cimiez became nothing more than a name on a map. The modern Cimiez is worthless, meaningless tripe, with streets named for princes of Wales and other non-notables, whose villas bubbled to the surface in times of excess, stucco'd monuments to the beau monde cloving the slopes of Kamanalon hill.

Construction struck a new road through the heart of Cimiez, and laying its foundations, workmen began finding cut stones layered across beds of gravel; stone courses with the unmistakable twelve percent crowning of a Roman road.

Dig down six feet anywhere in Cimiez, and you find old Cemenelum and its thermes, its *decumanus* oriented perfectly east-west. The presence of the *decumanus* and its perpendicular *cardo*, together with the monumental baths and a glorious Antonia (depicted as Venus) found on her back, all point to Cemenelum being a major stopover between Rome and the Narbonnensis along the Via Julia Augusta. Dig deeper and you'll unearth an arena for 5,000 men… And emerges the picture of an entire *oppidum*, a stronghold, a warehouse fortress built to overlook the old Greek *Nikaïa* and her trading centers nestled in the curve of the Bay of Angels…

And from this point, historians are evoking the *Cohors Ligurum* mentioned in Tacitus, the prefecture of the whole *Provincia Romana*.

It was as if the Cimiez roadbuilders had known it was there all along.

* * *

Sundari is bored, and it is Vicus' fault.

'Why don't you grab some sticks and a blade, you'd be good at this.'

Her fingers had made a handbag in the car; she had grumbled into the night in the hotel, her fingers putting in a zipper and building a luxurious liner out of one of the girls' scarves.

'I don't want to.'

'Why not?'

'I don't like the way you dragged me all the way here, and now you're ignoring me.'

'No, you're ignoring all these people around you. You should see the face you're making: you're turning everybody off.'

'You drag me down here, and all you can talk about is *these people*.'

* * *

They call Nikaïa *Nice* now, and it is a big city to cross on foot, and the climb toward Cimiez is unusually steep, and even in the crisp October air, Vicus is regretting that sweatshirt he put on.

It is a profanity, that whole zone between Massena and the foot of the Kamanalon: plexiglass pharmacies and plexiglass bus stops, and a little higher up than the pharmacies, where plexiglass gives way to stucco and chalk, the palms are really just tokens of Riviera-ness, just little pockets of lurid *luxure* jackhammered into squares in the sidewalk by the suite of lawyers renting at such and such an address and they have their gardeners shave them carefully into unnatural pineapple shapes, claiming the leaves will otherwise stain their cars' finish, but really only because the lawyers' suite across the street does the same and has long ago forgotten the reason why.

It is Saturday afternoon, and the sun is heating up the back of his neck and making his scalp tingle with sweat, and he bunches his forehead against the headache he didn't realize he had for the last twenty minutes of walking.

* * *

'You spend all day in the Garden of Eden, and all you can think about is the dirt?'

'This barn isn't very clean, you know.'

'It's a *barn*, for God's sake.'

'The girls are filthy.'

'They are not. The girls are *outside*. There's a difference, you know...'

'And look at your hands.'

He shoved them deep into his coat pockets, embarrassed. 'What about my hands?'

His right hand wrapped around the little hematite armadillo fetish he had forgotten was floating around in the liner.

* * *

Cimiez—*Cemenelum*—is ribboned off for some reason.

Damn

The sidewalk is radiating heat up through his soles, and the blue of the sky is buzzing menacingly like an arc lamp. Cemenelum is recessed into the flesh of the Kamanalon several yards, though, and it's beginning to dawn on Vicus just how much the heft of soil surrounding the excavations is somehow be attenuating this horrible weight of heat bearing down on the earth, and on his head.

That ribbon is hanging limp in the sun, a yellowed palm leaf giving up its turgor.

It is not a site very well guarded, is it?

It occurs to him that this 'Cimiez', this 'Nice' that's surrounded it, both have been burbling and simmering into their perverse existences for seventeen centuries, while proud Cemenelum has been gathering dust, literally gathering dust, becoming gray and lost and forgotten, while the greater beast has been prowling with its whipping tail, everywhere else but here. Cemenelum hasn't needed 'protection'—from the greater beast, or anybody for that matter and from Vicus least of all—ever since Caligula drew breath. That ribbon is a mockery to the weight of years, to the persistence of this place, to the tendency for stone to rest quietly against stone.

He slips across that threshold.

* * *

'You know, you're right. You shouldn't have come.'

'Now you tell me.'

'…Because you could've been just as unhappy at home. And I and the girls wouldn't have had to watch you set your jaw for the last ten hours, and withstand all your complaints about how dirty the dirt was, and listen to all your slights of the people around us, and your slights of us for that matter. You have no idea how tiring that is.'

It is dark, and the headlights' glow is simply insufficient to illumine Sundari's face, but he won't look at her anyway because he knows he'll just see her jaw set and her lips narrowed against her teeth and her eyebrows in that arching circumflex she had mastered, and the light will do nothing but make her skin seem grayer, and he had fallen in love with the flush of her cheeks a decade ago and the questioning wrinkle in the center of her forehead and the quiet music of her words, and now and now and now if he sees her again *just now*, the ashen pallor of the headlights will make her dead to him, and if he just stares straight ahead he won't have to live with the memory of what she is like *now* into time immemorial, and he can just concentrate on the lively, silent scenes of their first weeks of married life.

Just don't look

Just concentrate straight ahead

* * *

The old Cherokee making apple grafts with him that day had finally been coaxed out of his reticence.

'What do you know about armadillos?'

The old man was taken aback by the seemingly random question.

'You mean those critters always getting killed crossing highways in Texas?'

'Yeah.'

'Nothing except that, I guess.'

'Thanks.'

And they had gone on working. A few minutes later, the old man spoke up again.

'Armadillos will put up with just about anything, you know.'

* * *

'I shouldn't have come.'

'Like I said, Sundari.'

Just let the road lead

She continued. 'I shouldn't have come. At all. It was a mistake to marry you.'

* * *

And he is crossing a Roman road in a Roman garrison town on the highway leading to the fringes of an empire.

And it is cool here, and he can smell something like iodine faint in the air, and he knows the Med is just a mile distant.

His steps click in sharp echo on the road. The *sempervirens* cypress have thrown this place into shade, and he pulls his sweatshirt from around his waist and bundles it on.

He finds the crossroads of the *decumanus* and the *cardo* and sits in the crosshairs. When he stretches out on his back, he sees the Roman sky; in his peripheral view, the baths and their high circles, arches drawn tight; if he cranes his neck, stacks of dry clay pavers—ready for the next section of the *caldarium*—come into view, and a few elongate bricks with them, holding the stacks vertical until they can get the wider tiles into place above them. Straight up, blackbirds swing through on otherworldly arcs.

They had found the sculpture of Antonia Major, her stare stately and distant, within a stone's throw of this very spot. He could only imagine the man's heart who first laid eyes on her, the ultimate payoff for crossing a Roman road.

He tries to imagine what other Venus might still be waiting to be unearthed here, her eyes to the rare heavens, her gaze seeking eagles, a Roman eagle at that, an eagle long-departed, an eagle where Vicus could only see starlings.

Venus des oliviers, Vénus du Piémont,
   Vénus à l'étoile, Vénus la merveille,
   Vénus la si pâle, Vénus la vermeille,
   Vénus des orages, Vénus des vallons,

Vénus des frontières, Vénus des larrons,
   Vénus des hors-la-loi, Vénus des malsains,
   Vénus des réchappés des prisons du destin,
   Vénus dans les ombres, Vénus du pardon,

Vénus qui se penche me chuchoter à l'oreille :
   'Ne t'en fais pas,' me dit-elle, 'Je veille
   Sur ton rêve, et mes lèvres sur ton front.'

Et saisissant mon bras, et sans même un son,
   Elle découvrit d'abord l'un puis l'autre sein
   Et y posa délicatement ma main.

Venus of the olives, Venus of Piedmont blest,
　　Venus of the morning star, Venus the aurore,
　　Venus blushing midnight, Venus pale dawn wore,
　　Venus of the valleys close, Venus at storm's crest

Venus of the frontier, Venus the bandits' guest,
　　Venus of the troubled heart, Venus no man's land,
　　Venus of the fugitive, Venus of the banned,
　　Venus of the shadows, Venus of the distressed,

Venus, lean in to me, Venus my heart implore:
　　'Calm your heart, and still your mind, and may no more
　　These dark thoughts assail your dreams, troubling your rest.'

And uncovering first one, and then the other breast,
　　She reached over then to me, taking my arm, and
　　So delicately, against her heart, pressed my hand.

***

I've thought about you so much, El. Even dreamed about you. I've peopled my cities with you for a century—for three, for four, for a half-millennium—looked for you in the line at the market, the standout in the coffeeshop, the one roasting chestnuts on the corner, handing out flyers for charity, pulling curtains from backstage. I've called for you in mazes and in public squares, but not knowing your name, people just cross the road from me, signing themselves, nervously turning their collars to warn me away ward me off.

I sat on the steps of the theater for a whole winter once, every day making the same trek, a bag of pastries in case you came along.

I heard your steps echoing crazy in the old city, and although the geometry of buildings and corners thwarted my ear, I stopped and waited for you to turn onto my sidewalk, cross the road toward me. I caught sight of your coat, the hem of your skirt as you ducked into the subway, I've heard your voice as you buzzed to your friend in the tenement. 'It's me.'

They knew you by your voice, the pronoun a useless calling card, your voice all they needed to know, and so I memorized -It's me- and its melody, wrote its meandering mode, its mesmerizing shape into the creases and folds of my days and nights. And the wind whispered reminders, and the moon fell across me to give me blue sleep filled with your -It's me-.

And in my dream, you're at the mezzanine with the ice cream, the whole universe consisting of your dripping cone and your lips chasing the drops. In my dream you're sipping breakfast in the morning sun on the terrace. In my dream you're just done with exams, your head thrown back in a gale of laughter in the dorm room window.

I think you may have seen me, too, El. I think I caught you watching me once or twice: commissary, New Years, train station. I waited too long at the head of the line at the bank just to jar you into revealing yourself, I made that same old joke asking for coffee at the register, I reached across you for the sugar.

I was the one offering my umbrella at the taxi, the overpolite man crossing in front of you at the concert, Please pass the salt with my stranger's accent to get you to say something, just give me a sign, a touch, a sigh, a smile. And now I see you before me.

Thank you for your letter.

* * *

The city hasn't given me a convincing sign of life yet. When I close my eyes, I don't get some eyelid image of the city like I'm supposed to, with sunlight slanting chaos through and against glass, cascading shrilling shattered tourbillions of reflection and refraction. I don't see old newspapers blowing around the abandoned streets, or vapor billowing from beneath the trains, or pouring from holes in manholes. Those things, as you know, would imply present (or recent) habitation by living beings.

Instead, the lasting impression this place leaves me is the cold: I close my eyes actually, and hallucinate the wind billowing through my shirt and freezing my coat into something closer to a construction tarpaulin, stiff and noisy, a damp sail tied to with frozen ropes. The wind here can take the life from you, wick it away into the white wind, heavy with the Atlantic today.

Your message found me in my room, a few minutes before midnight. I am booked into a single, on the corner of the hotel, with glass meeting at the corner above my desk, and the weather had been trying to break in and when your note arrived, it was as if there was finally some life appearing in this angle of the seventh floor. I'm a little fossilized myself, you know, and the thought of life, and light, beacons and lamps trying to melt through icy glass panes was disorienting, and it flooded into me like new hot blood into an old joint. Because truth in advertising I am a dry old carcass, dry and dusty for my forty years, far older and wearier than I have a right to be. Truth be told: cold, noisy stiff canvas was made for keeping the snow from reaching the dead floors of abandoned warehouses, for covering holes in graveyards.

But I don't want to talk about the past. Let's talk about you.

***

Thank you for sending the pictures.

And I can say in all honesty that I still don't know what you look like.

These women are all so varied; I can tell they're hypothetically the same person, sure, but (God love you) how light can be so fickle as to give me such discontiguous fractions of your person like it does is beyond me. This one here is a confident, candid woman with a straw hat; this one is a daydreaming sylph in a stand of sunflowers; this woman here is an ethereal beauty in sepia profile, looking for her longtime penpal or lover coming off the gangplank. The stunning young lady with her arms wrapped around her young daughters at the beach, her hair pulled back from her sunkissed forehead. The woman with the laughing eyes, her hand fluttering to her mouth to hold back a wave of giggles. Serenity in the half-light among the flowers and ferns, the knowing grin built of confidence and irony distilled from a lifetime of warstories untold. The student in the arms of a vast tree in Barcelona, her figure dissimulated beneath a flowing honeyamber sweater. Bravery and inscrutability in the studio, spotlight beams and lens flares, eyes dark and smoldering. Blanche Dubois on stage, the kindness of strangers, love or lust? I'll settle for kind.

It would be just as helpful—it would be a damnfairsight more helpful in fact—if you would just take a picture of your hand or something, so that I could imagine you a painter or diva or writer or teacher or prophetess or monarch or seamstress, so that I could just fill up the room with a hundred more yous, each one some new essence of you, each one some new persona built over the armature of your skin and sinews and bones, the collected tissues and vessels and musclememories prototyped against a whole lifetime of being who you are.

Or have I hit a nerve? For I have been parsing your words now instead of your photos, trying to tease your person out of the interstices separating them, one from the next, and I think I might have better luck wringing your tone from your pen than your personality from your postures and gestures. You were, after all, Blanche onstage, and you love the camera as much as it loves you. But can you be so many women on paper?

The equivalent gesture, I've decided, is to send you some music. I am a tenth-rate composer, a tormentor of music rather than a musician really, and an arrogant arrogant man at that, and what can speak of me best if not my opaque, lifeless, complicated little fantasies, musings more than musics, darkness made alive and drawing breath? It should tell you everything you need to know about me.

Receive, then, this little piano fugue, Rachmaninoff meets Bach meets Vicus, at once angry and ironic, at once windy and sullen, at once broad strokes and narrowlidded sardonikon. It is decidedly backward and passé, and even recalling its composition, I somber even now into perverse nostalgia for lonely walks in lonely places during lonely times, knitting hermetic melodies in the harsh creases of my forehead. It is a profanity, my composition process: a lonely game of pickup sticks, an effort of mathematics rather than of imaginings.

Hell of a lullaby for my El. I apologize in advance.

* * *

I'm drifting around my room like a ghost, looking for you. I have read and reread your letters a hundred times already, trying to find you hidden in the economy of your words. You are here in this room for all I know, dissimulated amongst the curtains or the confusion of hotel bedsheets, I would never know, so changeable and diaphanous your image is.

I will keep looking. I would be a damned fool to be sleeping in the same room as you and not try to find you and tangle up our limbs together here in the dark of seventh-floor-corner. The wind is whistling outside, and the stoplights are all blinking blind and dumb on the corner below.

But it is warm and dark inside, a forbidding kind of safety here, true, but safety nonetheless, safe for lovers and insomniacs.

* * *

All white and light and architecture, like a visible fugue. You are asleep on your side, your head is on your arm, the curve of your hip sculpted matte white skin. I see the length of your spine, the vital curve of your waist becoming your buttock becoming your thigh.

My hand finds you here in this white place, without waking you, my hand touching you as if to memorize your shape, to make my palm alive with the contours of you.

You stir.

And when you roll to your back, my hand slides naturally to the delirium between your thighs, and you wake. Your eyes don't look away; instead, you challenge my eye: to bring pleasure to you while keeping my gaze locked into yours.

* * *

No one has ever thought to actively look for my heart, not even once, not even me; its membranes have never been anything but membranes, and yet they keep me alive, pounding away insistent as the day I was born, as if for some more mysterious purpose well beyond that of pumping blood. No one has sought my heart out, no one has thought to sound its depths for the nature of its purpose, but it thrashes away anyway, just as if it were Important.

There's nothing special about it, except to me.

Times have been hard, and as a result my heart is... well...

El, the easiest way to put it is this: I think about all those angles in complex spaces—a church vault's apex, the recessed spot under Pieta Mary's veil, the corner in the room above my bed, places where the light never reaches naturally—I think about all these places with something truly akin to pity, as my heart knows it is their double, their kin, their brother. There is nothing inherently inaccessible about these places, not really, but in truth they represent coordinates where natural light has never fallen, where people have only looked when they had misplaced something, when they had something to prove and no other place to dig it out of.

My heart is one of these places.

No one, poet or philosopher, has adequately told me 'what it's good for' in their cold analyses of The Good Life, and certainly no theorist has ever bothered to ask me. Most probably they would scent on to some clinical, phenomenological purpose for my heart, as if its job were to feel (and sometimes suffer) rather than to do, as if it were the radar rather than the fleet, a heart built to perceive rather than to be.

And if that's what it is destined for, even then it has seen so much, felt so much, lost so much.

I could wallpaper a room with the collected boarding passes accrued during my various travels, and fill a thousand books with the transcripts of conversations I've had with strangers in libraries and cafés; I can tell you of a hundred different times I've sat in some improbably distant place and simply went into record mode, memorizing the light and the sound and the swirl of people. And the trace of those privileged instants is still intact, and helps me live Then when I cannot Now. What then if my heart is the sum total of all its experiences, that entity that emerges spontaneously from the flood of inputs and throughputs, never once the source of wisdom or kindness or meanness or spite, but slowly, blindly blinking awake in this seemingly neverending trek, slowly becoming the route, slowly acquiring the attributes of my hosts—the wisdom, the kindness, the meanness, the spite—accrued during its long trajectory? It's not like I lack for adventure or broad horizons (or for memories of horizons for that matter).

Why then this scream of desire? What has my heart lacked all along?

It seeks and seeks and seeks. And all it wants is to be sought. It wants not so much to be worthy of seeing, of judging, perceiving, remembering and feeling—it could use a bit of peace and quiet, now that I think of it—but instead aches to be worthy of being the object of somebody's desire.

Of your desire.

Because in my whole existence, that would be an experience unlike any I have had.

Why would a woman like you ever want a heart like that?

* * *

But who knew that all these travels to the ends of the world—seeking—would bring me back to this seventh-floor-corner on this cold morning, your letters all gathered up safe into my jacket, something like hope in my eye? For it feels like five hundred years since I've felt that. Strike that: it has been a half-millenium since I've ...felt.

I will be travelling again over the next few days, returning to find my kids again. And although the way is long, I figure if I write a single alexandrine for you every seventy miles, I'll have built a passable sonnet by the time I arrive back home. A single syllable every five miles, and I should have enough time left over for some kind of holorithmic Envoi, or at least a colorful title or something.

On the way, I will be passing closer to you than I ever have been since we first found one another. What will it take to keep my course from deviating, and reading you your Highway Sonnet in person? Will you feel my proximity as I pass by? The subtle pressure of my hand at the small of your back, blinking tired eyes as my fingers brush your hair back?

It obviously doesn't work that way. Because if it did, you would right now be arching your back in the pleasure my fingers beckon from you.

* * *

I'll admit—now that the damage is well and truly done—that the music I sent wasn't exactly what you thought it was. Although I never actively try to be standoffish, there is that reflex in me, an instinct to fire some shots across the bows of people I care for, long for, fall for, and hit them with something hermetic and inscrutable. 'Oh yeah? There's this fugue of mine, this one here.

Deal with it.' And their reply—always some sort of confusion or hostility—gives me some new raw excuse to become even more standoffish, to turn my nose up at them: 'Vicus, you're ahead of their time,' 'Vicus, they're ahead of your time,' 'Vicus, the room isn't yours, you'll never reach them.'

Can I reassure you that this wasn't my intention with you at all? It is only an ingrained reflex: 'send El your fugues/your concerto movements/your very sullen preludes, she will hate them as a matter of course, and as she says so, you will take her distaste as a shorthand for her future hatred of -you-, and then you can clearly perceive her intent toward you, your complete incompatibility, and you can end all this preemptively.'

But El, I don't want this to end. I don't want to cut this off preemptively, saving myself before I get hurt. I don't want you to leave. I don't want to chase you off. Because I think we stand a chance of being perfectly compatible with one another, perfectly good to one another, perfectly good for one another.

I leave for you, then, as a good-faith token of goodwill, this little Prelude for flute. It is dark, and high, and upright (probably a reasonable analog for organelles of my own psyche kept encrypted for too long), and it kept my head busy for several days as I walked around the campus, late nights at University, my head given over to its contours, my ears and lips and mind singing away in a rakish piccolo, haunting the old brick arcades of the University with my stately c-minor.

And in the interest of full disclosure: I no longer whistle for the sake of whistling—I am too old and dusty for that, and my bones creak too much and my forehead knots up too much for me to whistle credibly much anymore. I whistle in order to fix a pitch into live sound.

Yet this little Prelude is no simple mathematical construct: instead it occupied me fully those nightly walks, and unreeled its melody into my quiet nights meditating and writing, and into my sleep; really, it is near and dear to my sleeping and wakeful heart, and represents me as I long for you these anguished nights.

For it is no longer mine, but yours, and it cannot be otherwise.

Consider this music then as tonight's Lullaby, and consider then with sadness and pity this: the heart of the man who wrote it as it tries to find you, seeking you in order to bring this gift to you. It is his heart's gift; maybe one that can bring yours a bit closer to mine.

* * *

Long days driving; long nights awake.

My thoughts drifting toward you as I make way; a dozen-hour polyphony of left-brain navigation, right-brain sonnetry, head all at once becoming the road before me, head having next become the exits competing with my chosen trajectory, each exit a real exit, a road leading to escape, a flight from the weight of the dozen preceding years. Years preceding what? Preceding my life.

My life could truly begin if only I just deviated, just once, from this highway, and never arrive home.

Wow. I can't believe I just said that.

* * *

I'm home. I shouldn't be here. I worry about what picture you might ultimately draw of me.

I am sending you one. I am weary, my eyes have the weight of years, the narrow pupils of rainmakers, the mordant pinpoints of concentration, don't close don't close don't close even a second you'll only sleep an hour. I comfort myself telling myself that greater souls than mine have had this same years-old fatigue closing down over their features, maybe worse even, it's not so much my wrinkles as it is the transparency of it all, as if you could see my heart breaking a year ago, a decade ago, the weight of years anything but invisible.

You will soon learn that I am an extraordinary insomniac. What fool cannot sleep? The night has its teeth in me by the turn of midnight, and tires of me by one. I'll usually have a dream—a narrative, a long unswerving rail to follow—by that point, one that scares me awake. Always the same theme: an insoluble dilemma, an unanswerable riddle, Hold these wires together and if you let them part for even a second...

A hundred ways of it going wrong, only one—one—of it not plunging off into the chasm.

How my head can play such games with me when I can't answer back, set up a whole house of unspeakable violence in my way, and wait until I can't defend myself to spring it on me. -Pie Iesu, ne me perdas dia ille-

Why my dreams overnight can't be of simple farmsteads on distant hillsides, dusted with snow and a plane of hearthsmoke in the morning stillness, a cabin in the woods, only the shade of a cabin, only a scent of cranberry and candlewax, maybe reading or poking at the fire in the chimney? What would it hurt if I dreamed of drinking a cup of tea—Scarlatti playing in the background—with a beautiful woman across from me? What harm could there be in this? That she might beat me in Scrabble, that my tea not have enough sugar?

I wonder if you would ever join me in such a place? Or are you too much a city girl?

Until then, I keep dreaming of holding back the Apocalypse with my two wires together, the whole rig jackknifing over the cliff. Dreams that scare me awake, heart a cannon fired upon the great white leviathan, terror held just within, released when I finally drowse far enough to let the wires go.

If I could only spin up the initiative to actually do something during my hours awake—something other than fret that is—I could do something great, I could be someone great, four or five more hours in the day than most of humanity. And the added weight of that new responsibility—what, too lazy to work at three in the morning?—hardens my eyes a mite further. And you end up with pictures like this one.

What do you worry about at night, El? Maybe a check that hasn't cleared yet, maybe an incautious word at a pushy daughter, maybe something else?

And look at me, suddenly the sad elitist of insomnia—what, you don't dream of the impending End of Days?—I'm sorry, I can be such a jackass when I'm tired like this. And honestly, once the demons have scared me awake and gone away to haunt other souls and I've calmed down a little, I'm kept awake by a song lyric, or a witty insult I failed to fire off while the argument was still hot.

I'm telling you, I think it'd be much smarter if we were in the same bedroom when one or the other of us is wrestling with it. Even better would be if we just dreamed the same dull, happy dreams together, too, and hand in hand put off the Rapture for another night. Come, then, and meet me in the cabin with the smoky chimney on the quiet hillside, and you can beat me in Scrabble.

* * *

To you then, dear El, and to you alone, my heart remains an open book, a public document, a broad melody; it exists to exist and for no other reason. It seeks you daily and nightly, it is restless and grey, it is troubled water.

* * *

What relief, what pure, broad, uncheckered relief it was to hear your voice just now. The timing could not have been better. My God, your voice, the first time! My ears are still ringing, resonant with ...you. I was so nervous, the hours before calling. I pace, I write, I stumble over words, I blush clear into my forehead.

Perhaps someday you'll explain to me the origins of your accent—

I heard your melodic lilting laugh; it reminded me of when my youngest is concentrating—busy on a drawing, tongue just visible at the corner of her mouth—you can hear muttering all manner of little hmms and hrmphs, little sputnik beeps and whirrs, telling you there is much happening just beneath the surface.

I awoke just now, wanted to write you while it is all still fresh.

Woke with something of a vision of you, holding me in the dark... The first words to say it are in French; they are simple, they are clear and unadorned:

Tes mots qui cherchent mon cœur
La vision de ton visage qui me hante
Ta main qui cherche la mienne
Ta voix derrière ma nuque
Tes bras qui serrent ma taille
Tes jambes autour de mes hanches

Your words that seek out my heart
The vision of your face haunting me
Your hand that seeks mine
Your voice at the nape of my neck
Your arms around my waist
Your legs around my hips

I want to experience this kind of intimacy, this kind of warmth—simple, clear and unadorned. The thought of napping—all tangled up in you, legs and arms all threaded through like braids in a ribbon, threads in a tapestry—is delicious to me. Forget the erotics of it, it is still the nec-plus-ultra of comfort, of contentedness. Ravish me, El, with some tandem napping...

* * *

I don't know how much time or thought you've ever put into the study of musical forms; I myself have done altogether too much of both for my own good; I pride myself with having actually dreamed out new forms, marveling at their architecture upon waking, marveling how a mind as slow-witted as mine, as dumbly engrossed in himself as I am, can somehow unstay his mind enough to see new forms, born recognizable and vital, born into this world unique and free, arching out of the ooze and mire of my most sullen mind and defying the clawing mathematics of stricter, nearly physical forms, nearly crushing in their vital mass—fugue, canon, others. I remember once, adrowse on the floor in my grandmother's house, with the sound of her shoes shuffling along through in the darkness next to my head in the middle of the night, and with my eyes closed in half-sleep, and hearing the rhythm of her steps as she haunted the house with her sleeplessness, my mind began to tease patterns from her footfalls and assign at one remove mathematical values, at another remove, durations, pitches, intensities. Soon, swimming in the flood of these dark, purposeful, purposeless numbers, an entire mass for choir and orchestra would emerge, singing an ancient-sounding melody—freely invented, too, by my sleep-deadened mind—spinning it out in a hundred new directions, my mind a battered old loom turning out yards and yards of new cloth, tapestries of troubling intricacy, built of the basest threads, footfalls of my insomniac grandmother.

In my conscious mind of course, in the here and now, in the cold flush of dawn, there would be no way for me to invent on that level, to that length, with such drama and control and fire. My own footfalls are too cautious, my step is much too plodding for novelty to spark into being. I speak slowly because I think slowly, and I daydream nearly sullenly. A beautiful melody—the creaking of a wellworn door on its hinge, the melody of a lover's voice—always locks onto old rails by light of day; only in my most somber improvisations at the piano, only in my pinwheeling reveries brought about by drink—or night—or love—can I press old bricks into new shapes.

In my everyday I am a slavish worshipper of form—and not only musically, but linguistically, culturally, religiously as well. There's something in which composers—well, maybe composers like me, amateurish, controlled by forms (not like the major composers, themselves -controlling- forms)—often find themselves ensnared, and that is when they begin a composition, an imitative composition, where one melodic idea is parsed for its shape and mathematics, those loose geometries becoming shortcuts for higher, stricter calculus. Past experience—memory—becomes a fool's heuristic for the predicament of the present... Novel melodies—contours and quirks all but unknowable to plodding souls like mine—squeeze into stiff old shoes. 'This... will be a canon two-in-four with a free tenor'—the mere fact that it is nameable is evidence enough of its failure.

(Old Janequin used to sign his name with the added title -Pecunia Deficinibus-. 'Crushing Debt Janequin'. You can imagine how he fairly groaned to slip out from under that old name's burden, and with what jealousy he pursued some other title, -any- other title, anything but the old one: maybe 'Composer Ordinary to the King' this time. 'Organist of the Chapel Royal'. 'Artful Dodger'.)

I have been many things to many people, El. A man with an accent. A quick-witted man. Young, and old, and a transient no fixed abode no forwarding address. A Rabelaisian, a romantic, a realist. A man very alert in the eye, a sparrow's darting mind. A man moody and grey. A neo-baroque, a postmodern, a medievalist. Upright, cunning, treacherous, upright again. And each time somebody pegs me—'I know you're a Galilean, you accent betrays you'—I will shift and weave... and emerge something else, something new. I slip clear of the wreckage of the old self; what was once canon has now, imperceptibly, morphed into sonata, and that (by God) has escaped musical notation entirely to shapeshift into a hendecasyllabic plea for a lover's most intimate gifts.

El, you can't even begin to know the title I have dragged with me for the last years.

Trapped by, trapped in, trapped.

Today, at noon, haunted and hunted by the demon of my own identity, chased out of my last refuge, pursued to the last crag of the last cliff, I took the only step still available to me.

I balled up that old canon I didn't even realize I had stumbled into, wadded up captivity itself with its cruel, crushing, choking chains.

Sweet El, whose voice I now know. Tomorrow I emerge having crossed this road, a new man, stride enlivened, strangely different, a man with a brand new divorce.

And tonight. I will mourn, a keening, complex passacaglia of ruined dreams.

L'aube illumine à l'heure l'échafaud :
   Le jour fixe, ce dernier jour déverse
   Son ire sur le pécheur qui traverse
   La plate-forme au tambour du bourreau

Le dernier jour se dresse, hors du clos
   Des cendres noires de la nuit adverse
   Et atteste le péché qui transperce
   L'homme souffrant sous le faix de ses maux

La nuit est maîtresse soulant charruer
   Le jour son esclave, qui accore

La nuit profonde, que l'obscur décore.
   L'aube même n'arrive à l'atténuer

J'ai tout le temps du monde, temps à tuer ;
   Le temps est long, regret plus long encore

Dawn's an hour off, the chosen day has come:
   The witching hour, the working hour, the day
   Of wrath, when guilty man shall cross away,
   Climbing tipping gallows at hangman's drum

The last day rise up (at trumpet's sound) from
   The night's ashes, and waking, shake them 'way
   And testify the sins that held him sway
   And give account for all their wicked sum

Night is day's Mistress, pricks day with her quill
   The day's night's slave to carry out her will

Dark is the deep, and long is the night
   (Truer yet by the glare of morning light)

And I've got time to spare, and time to kill
   For time is long, but mem'ry longer still

***

The most mundane form of insanity?

Vincenzo Peruggia was certain that the sun was a hallucination, rising from the Ligurian Sea before Sainte Maxime first in sandstone, then ribbons, then admiral fanfare; finally, risen over the horizon after an hour's dawn, Chaucer's 'fresh flowers, white and red'.

Believing you're the Messiah

Peruggia watched as his wine cork tumbled in curious curlicues on the compartment floor; the train bumped and heaved in the haze of morning.

If only this dawn would last forever

He held the open bottle up to the window, looked through the wine at the mounting morning. The wine's color matched the sky's tint exactly; Peruggia marvelled at how he could see the sunrise through the pinard with no distortion.

The cork turned drunkenly, and as the train lurched again, escaped out into the hallway. Peruggia thought about jamming his finger into the bottle's mouth and chasing down the cork. But there was only a half-bottle left, let the cork go where it wants. He kicked the compartment door closed.

Nothing rattles, nothing shines

He looked at his suitcase, *the* suitcase, brass corners, seated across from him—he wasn't really alone in his compartment, was he?—and he felt in his heart something of a longing, and across from him was the object of his longing, the Bride of Christ.

He remembered the bottle of pinard with thumb over it; with the compartment door closed, he couldn't see the sunrise anymore. He held his bottle up, looked at old Brass Corners through it.

The pinard would taste so much better now.

* * *

It really came down to a misunderstanding, a *malentendu*, nothing more, nothing less. Had everything been clear, none of this would have happened, none of this would have been necessary.

You can't go on romanticizing it, you know

They say Giovanna had been a pawn, that she was just another cog in the machine, but Peruggia knew better, Peruggia saw more clearly, Peruggia saw with the long view, saw with the eyes that sifted evidence, Peruggia could scent right and wrong, and always fell on the side that was right.

Everybody wants a martyr

More than that, there are even those who seek to build martyrs, manufacture them from whole cloth: no fewer than three monasteries had seen Saint Michael touch down and found them; and now Naples wanted her own Joan of Arc, and chose as her beloved *pucelle*, Giovanna of the white gorget and the *fleur de lys* scepter.

It takes just a moment to mung it all to Hell, it takes men of action and clear eyes to set it aright

Peruggia's eyes narrowed as the last of his pinard disappeared into his stomach.

They did well to strangle her

* * *

The Church has its favorites, and you can play with that fact as much as you like, that is, until somebody catches on that you're playing both sides.

Peruggia tried to picture Giovanna, and was having trouble seeing her in the light of day… and she certainly didn't look anything like a royal to him. Sure, he had seen miniatures of her in history books, but how much could you tell from that? How tempting, instead of garbing her in all the regalia—Hell, artists can dress her however they like—to see her covered from head to toe in dark blankets, huddling in a mostly-dark upper room, all the trappings of 'royalty' (whatever that meant) absent… Giovanna trying to stay warm, amusing herself at some sort of hybrid chess match, playing a hundred pieces at once over a giant irregular patchwork quilt, only vaguely understanding what the various pieces were, what they represented, maybe not exactly stupid—far from it—but naïve and in over her head, ignorant of the conventional ways those pieces might move…

Just wait till you spot my knight and my bishop in cahoots riding in close formation, just wait till you see my king ride across you in broad gallops

And in his mind's eye Giovanna would make a move on her giant crazyquilt chessboard with her great fictional game going on, and then flutter back to her weaving, chuckling feebly at the designs she had made—weaver, chess player, they were all the same in her dim mind—and wait for some new caprice to catch her fancy, and she'd move her men all over again.

And each time Peruggia thought about Giovanna bemusedly trying her hand at Statecraft, men would burst through in his mind's eye, and scatter the pieces with their wet boots.

* * *

Peruggia never gave Giovanna the chance to speak during these visions of his.

Once or twice, she would uncover her head, unwrap herself from all those shrouds and sheaths, and he would see her face, all shoulders and bust and her expressionless eyes neither here nor there, completely neutral, a woman kimberlitic, purest carbon for eyes and iron ore for hair and lips, heavy clay skin breastswhiterthananegg… she was surely from Mars or the depths of some limestone cavern, the Lethos flowing slowmotion leadedglass, inert grottoes deadly with transparent concentrations of some heavy gas toxin preserving her forever, her eyes heavylidded, anoxic, unfused, unfocused.

I'm sorry, what did you say Love?

He would taunt her like this whenever he thought she might have somehow become reactive, whenever she looked like she might become something other than a prime number, something other than a dusty star alone on the horizon, something other than a mute beaked narwhal in an isolated break in the ice, a bowsprit, a white china cameo.

What, nothing to say? Hmm?

He imagined she might one day try to push an apologia past her frozen cautered lips, that she might one day be tempted to mutter 'In the future there'll be someone who understands what I did, I'm sure of it, I'll die for it.' He was always sure to cut her off before she could utter a word: he would violate her mouth with his own power his own manliness his own virtue; he would press her uvula to the back of her throat, she would choke on him before choking on her own words that was for sure—

I don't give a damn if she's bright or dull, she'll be taken over by my hot, living being

—and as he thought these things, he would feel the fire climb limb by limb up within him, something of a challenge, *I-know-I-am-but-what-are-you*, something of a Jacob's Ladder current of electricity that would take him over, a soulless subsonic hum, making his breath catch in his throat, making him more than he was.

She'll gag on me before she can explain herself

And he would strike her breasts with the heel of his hand, just to hear her moan disarticulate tones.

I can't hear you he would taunt her again and again.

And still he could see thoughts weave words beneath the divine arch of her eyebrows, something about 'They will one day write books that make my own brave life's chaos make sense. There will be future memory of me...' But then he would strike her again, and the unwritten unsaid words would become worlds forever unvisited.

Don't close your eyes, don't turn away

* * *

Her husband had died folded over an assassin's blade. They had brought her to trial—*ordeals to try the lady with, pricks and spurs and fire*—they somehow missed *her*, failed to take *her* when they prosecuted and hanged the perpetrators—but she would stink of his blood anyways after that.

She had found asylum in Avignon, where the rival Antipopes sat, and sidled up to the corrupt men born of French crown blood, nephew bishops named by powers rivaling her own, crowns rivaling her own wayward crown, thrones threatening her own tipping throne.

Let her prop up the Antipopes, let them bring ruin to her as they do to themselves in their heresy

And Peruggia imagined her reign a wallowing rowboat full to the gunwales with great inertias of seawater, and the Antipope Robert the Genevan, crowned illegally at Fondi, with his foot pressing down—hard—on the rails of her foundering craft...

They say she opened a brothel in the Papal courts in Avignon, they say she opened it to serve all the corrupt crown princes worshipping at the feet of the Antipope.

And when he saw her in his mind's eye, there she was, seated in her carriage with its high velour walls embroidered with scenes of some kind of Paradise or maybe some kind of Hell—*Elysia*—scenes of hard unreal beauty, a more beautiful reality than was allowed to exist in this world of ours. And the velour would shift and toss as Giovanna's carriage bumped and lurched,

-Passacaglia-

and like the panels of the curtains jostling for plumb in Peruggia's train compartment, the landscape would come disjointed, the east from the west, like buildings out of phase with those just across the street from one another, where windows face into alleys and gardens. At Giovanna's back, an Elysian scene of troubled clarity, smoky hues of greens and blues and ochres, scenes of the smoky aftermath of a Florentine earthquake.

And every time the carriage jumped and lurched (as it sped incongruously to the Antipapal brothels invading Avignon's tile-and-stone squares), Giovanna would suck in her breath, gasp sometimes, a nearly inaudible yelp of surprise. And each time she was tempted to pull back one of her sfumata velour curtains, with their unreal scenes of dramatic cliffs and an anonymous footbridge over a cold stream, pull them back and tell the driver to take it easy on her damn his eyes, she felt her uvula being cruelly pressed to the back of her throat.

Peruggia's thumb was so deep in the neck of his bottle of toxic red pinard, he feared for a moment he might not ever get it back out.

* * *

The train has turned now, and the sun is glinting in through the heavy glass, etched with age and neglect, sea salt from the Bay of Angels. Its light is hard, and yellow. Peruggia is squinting, regretting to be awake at all.

The curtains are old and won't reach across the whole way now, and there are sharply-defined triangles of light jabbing through to him like Judgment. Peruggia holds his bottle up to the gaps in the curtains, and his whole world prisms into paintings of blood.

* * *

Clement had been more Overlord than Pope, and he had his business to watch over, and he knew that chaos within invites chaos from without, and when he thinks about it, he realizes he's feeling a sudden sense of welcome washing warm over him, a hearty invitation to endeavor making Naples his business, and he thinks he just might indulge himself. And he knows it is sinful to enjoy this sort of thing so much, but there it is: the prerogative of Popes is a thing not to be trifled with, and Antipopes are coming out of the woodwork anyway and need to be harassed like stray dogs, like beasts that steal into cities and make mayhem. And the Neapolitan girl, she wants to show her head? Be ready to lose it.

Peruggia closed his eyes, and saw Clement in his glory, marble bust old Roman style and all, fat as three men, his eye leveled to the horizon, ready to make merry cutting down all the Church's enemies like forests.

It won't take long, will it, Holiness?

And indeed it took but a stroke of the quill, and Giovanna of Naples became a heretic.

* * *

She surely didn't know it as it occurred, she was running anyway, undoubtedly knew nothing but the noise of the road, the fear of having governments upon her shoulder. It's not as if suddenly you cease being able to feel your limbs or reflect visible light... It was a strenuous act of *power at distance*, this pronouncement of anathema, and demonstrated on Christendom's bright stage the real geometry uniting Clement to Giovanna... and Clement to the rest of the world, for upon his declaring her a heretic *latae sententiae*, the power of Papal law came to bear immediately and in all time, and anybody allowing her to contravene this law would themselves become accessories to her heresy, subject to the penalties the law provides, and those penalties were nothing to scoff at.

> *Wherefore in the name of God the All-powerful, Father, Son, and Holy Ghost, of Blessed Peter, Prince of the Apostles, and of all the saints, in virtue of the power which has been given us of binding and loosing in Heaven and on earth, we deprive Giovanna di Napoli herself and all her accomplices and all her abettors of the Communion of the Body and Blood of Our Lord,*

> *we separate her from the society of all Christians, we exclude her from the bosom of our Holy Mother the Church in Heaven and on earth, we declare her excommunicated and anathematized and we judge her condemned to eternal fire with Satan and his angels and all the reprobate, so long as she will not burst the fetters of the demon, do penance and satisfy the Church; we deliver her to Satan to mortify her body, that her soul may be saved on the day of judgment*

That last detail was mere nuance, mere formality (as no one was really looking out for Giovanna's soul—that was somebody else's problem); and when the bishops all read these words aloud and threw their lit tapers to the floor of the basilica, she probably felt nothing more than an odd emptiness in her heart...

* * *

You pushed

She pushed back

Peruggia spoke to Clement across the centuries, pitying the woman's inability to accord the man his proper due, pitying the man the gravitas of his authority over her. He knew that the rain fell just a little harder, just a little colder, upon Giovanna, who could blame her for clamoring for shelter in such times? He watched her as she clattered into the square before the Antipope's palace in Avignon, with its silvery stone buttresses and its proud towers.

What gives you the right to walk right in?

But she was a ward of the Devil now (now that Clement had decided to send her to Hell), and surely godless Antipopes had thrown the doors even wider for the woman who ran their brothels and sown chaos among the real sons of Peter.

* * *

The morning hills of the maritime Alps were coralescent with stucco'd manors. Nice was coming up. And Peruggia's train slowed further; he could hear the regular street crossings far up ahead as the engine smacked her wheels against some new regime of rail-over-pavement; the sound dopplered toward his car as each new bogey struck the crossing.

He looked at his watch. Seven-thirty. The train will be in its siding soon.

Bottoms up

He lowered the window and pitched his empty bottle into some *Niçois'* backyard.

* * *

He saw Giovanna in the courts of the Antipope Robert of Geneva: far from kneeling, kissing the ring, approaching with utter deference, she was at his great table, both Heretic and Heretic Pope alike leaning over the same great ebony table of his, with Giovanna's great quilt chessboard draped over the corner casually, the persistence of lunacy. She had peeled the great patchwork from her own shoulders, she had been wearing her own chessmatch with her own invented rules to keep her warm in the cold rain of Avignon, her assortment of Miscellany Rules that must have made sense to her alone, her and anybody else caught *in flagrante* in unholy pacts with the Devil. And she was showing the Antipope her plans, now that she was damned.

There was a look of calm desperation on her face. Peruggia could see her detailing her strategies on the tips of her fingers; too far away to hear, he wished he could block her speech with his very flesh, bring tears to her eyes with cruel jabs at the back of her throat, distract her from her anathemic courses by violating her mouth and lips again.

This giant table should be put to higher use than drawing up plans unholy to Christendom

But unable to hear her, he was unable to thwart her. All he could hear were the deep tones of the Antipope, somehow reassuring in their depth.

'But *mi Donna,* you have no heirs.' And although grammatically a protest, Peruggia could hear the Antipope feeding new strategies to the pale clay-colored girl with the mere tone of his complaint. And Giovanna's eyes narrowed, she bent to play another piece on her chaotic chessboard.

'*Mi Donna,* such a move will surely be seen as treachery. Naples is Clement's fiefdom, what right does, what right do *you* have to...?'

But Giovanna was already moving more pieces, strong sweeping moves, the desperate chessboard of fanatics.

Don't you know the rules to this game?

The Antipope stood back, surveyed the board. His finger between his teeth in intense concentration, considering the tilting, folding chessboard as it devolved before his very eyes. Finally he broke his concentration, stepped to the darkness at the edge of Peruggia's sightline. Peruggia could hear him pouring wine, still speaking to Giovanna.

'You do realize how much you're counting on a future generation to vindicate you, don't you? You do realize you will never live to see this come to fruition, don't you? You do realize you're giving it all away to a stranger, a *foreigner* at that, do you not? You will double Clement's ire, you will throw *so much more oil* onto the fire of his anger...'

He returned to the table, visible once more in the pale light of Peruggia's imagination.

'It is nonetheless brilliant, and fascinating, and forbidding.' The Antipope's nose dipped into his goblet. He set the goblet down on the edge of the chessboard. 'I can sic the Pharisees on this right now if you want; they'll have it drawn up in ten minutes.'

Peruggia burned to stuff the heretic's mouth with meat, with sand, with hay, with anything, anything to keep her from answering. But when she nodded wordless assent, the Antipope turned to summon his lawyers.

* * *

Peruggia could barely steady himself. The train was in the terminal roll, and the filthy grey stone buildings of the trainstation district of Nice were an insult to him, and the rails rocked the train to and fro, and that last draught of pinard was flooding his veins now. He stumbled to the door of his compartment; when it wicked open, he spotted his longlost cork tumbling past drunkenly. He had half a mind to grab it and chuck it out the window, too, try to hit Nice in the eye.

And he can smell Nice now, too. And here he'd been thinking that Paris was the filthiest city in the world.

He always liked the sensation of stepping off onto the quay while the train was still rolling, and he pushes past the other passengers gathering their things, obstructing his way, moving far too slowly for him; and now, holding onto the outside of the train, one foot on the running board, one dangling out into empty space, ready to cross the gap on the fly... and the wind would feel so good after all that time in that hot, enclosed compartment. And the horizon is shifting and tilting, and he has to make a special effort concentrating on the smooth pavements of the platform now advancing upon him—*Don't want to fall under the train and onto the rails now, do you? Commit commit commit*—and he is in flight: crossing over, crossing over.

* * *

'I took the liberty of having every witness we could find brought in. Clement will lose his mind when he hears of this, and will challenge the legitimacy of this document in a hundred different ways.' It seemed as if there were a hundred people in the room now, from pages to lawyers to painters to nobles to the Antipope himself. 'If they could sign their name, I had them come.'

And The Document was written out decuplicate, and it was read aloud to check each copy for errors.

> *To all those who this writ do see or hear, or will see or hear in the future: that this day, April the Fourth in the year of Our Lord Thirteen Hundred and Eighty, GIOVANNA, Queen of Naples, Countess of Provence and Forcalquier, Queen consort of Majorca and titular Queen of Jerusalem and Sicily, and Princess of Achaea, does solemnly adopt as her real son LOUIS OF ANJOU, the second son of King John II of France and Bonne of Luxembourg, Duke of Anjou, Count of Maine, Duke of Touraine, and bestows upon him all the rights and privileges due her name, and upon her decease, bequeaths upon him the titles, lands and powers formerly belonging to her, namely that at the event of her death, he will become, in addition to his present titles, titular King of Naples and Jerusalem and Count of Provence and Forcalquier. Signed and witnessed to this day...*

'Are you sure you want to do this? It can't be undone.' The Antipope chuckled darkly.

'Of course, that's the whole beauty of it...'

* * *

Peruggia strode on broadly toward the terminal, gradually catching up with the train that had overshot him by a hundred yards. The sun was just breaking over the terminal, luminous yet not luminous enough, and the glare of the sky sickened him to his core.

'Monsieur, Monsieur!'

The conductor was calling down from the train.

'*Si?*'

'Don't forget your luggage, Monsieur!'

And the little man heaved Brass Corners over the gap before Peruggia could think to react; thankfully it hit him in the chest, knocking him back a pace, and all he had to do was let his fingers find the edges and hold on.

When it dawned on Peruggia what he had almost left in his compartment, he staggered to the bushes and vomited.

-Passacaglia-

Ici, la longue marche et ici les armées
   Et ici encore, des soldats, chevaucheurs
   Et archers ; ici la tristesse, la clameur :
   Chacun y accomplit ses méchantes corvées

Ici, sur les cendres des maisons incendiées
   Les soldats triomphent ; ici, dans la fureur
   De la guerre on festine ; ici l'étrange lueur
   Des étoiles qu'on pause admirer, bouches bées

Je chercherai parmi les débris des marées
   Voyez, voyez comment sont venus les malheurs !
   Voyez le registre béant de tant de pleurs :

Ici on voit partout les débris des années :
   Ici on deult, Ici on vit, Ici on meurt—
   La scène piteuse, détresse dans mon cœur

Here the long march away, here heavy squadrons part,
   Here again the soldier strikes, here the rider rides
   And archers' arrows fly; fear and chaos resides
   Here, and here every man practices his cruel art.

Here, huddled, distressed, the widow hides
   From the great beast; here soldiers triumph; here at start
   Of war they feast, here the very sky is torn apart
   By flames of houses, here the blazing star divides.

I'll pick through debris brought in by the tides
   Beaches strewn over with the floods the tears impart;
   See how they almost cover up the gaping chart:

Here scattered all 'round the debris of years resides:
   Here they grieve, Here they live, Here in death they depart—
   The pitiful scene of such distress in my heart

And if you can't recognize your own children...

Havoise began every day by counting the stones in some solitary corner of Montreuil-au-Houlme minster.

...Then you should look for your silhouette in the face of your grandchildren

It was a richly decorated building—a constellation of buildings—and in the hour following *Mesoniktikon*, the sheltering sky of the enclosing cloister would be her clock, and the cut stones her Rosary. And she noticed that many of the stones held fast within the cold vaults over her head—the arcade of the cloister—were invisible at this hour of the night, and Havoise knew of their existence only because they provided the needed step from one visible stone to the next; sometimes she needed to theorize as many as thirteen or fifteen invisible stones arcing into the discreet blackness of the deeper vaults to cover the span, and only later by the attenuated light of day did she actually verify their till-then only hypothetical presence.

But tonight it is black as pitch in the deeper corners of those vaults. It is an accident of geometry by which the light of oil lamps here in the four-cornered cloister (light only dimly augmented by the blue glow of the dome of stars, each star a calculus of distant white sand) trips and falls between columns and pilasters of the arcade; Havoise can perceive a rhythm of six cut stones visible, six more cut stones in darkness; six stones visible followed by six stones only ideas, ideas real enough to hold together this arcaded building, ideas rough enough to hold up these dark vaults, ideas stout enough to walk under in safety.

And she perceived in that rhythm—the pattern of six in light, six in darkness—reminders of her own ancestors (the highs and the lows, the heroes and the rogues), and she knows that six is mankind's number, for on the sixth day the Lord made Adam and gave him breath, and Havoise knows that she herself was knit together in her mother's womb imprinted with that number six,

My life is one of the Marian mysteries

...And so as much as she hates to admit it, she is feeling at home under the six stones, with her memories of angels and mortals, demigods and warlords who have conspired, in mysterious lots of sixes—years, generations, beats of the heart—to bring her about, to make her a reality.

* * *

The *Mesoniktikon* begins at midnight; at first it was overtly punishing to have her sleep interrupted over and over through the night in order to shoehorn in all the various canon hours' worship as she was required to, and she had struggled and raged silently against the Vespers and Complines and Mesoniktikon and Matins and all... But now the Hours have begun to grow on her, and she realizes she actually has some sense of privacy (and, if she dares think it in this place where 'property' is a notion antithetical to the Orders, *ownership*) among the colonnades of the cloister at the hour of deepest night, after the *Mesoniktikon* has been rung definitively and the younger sisters have disappeared back in their cells. And so in time, Havoise began to retool her day to begin at the first tolling of the Mesoniktikon, recalling (to anyone who would care to question her) the words of Mark of Ephesus:

> *The beginning of all the hymns and prayers to God is the time of the midnight prayer. For, rising from sleep for it, we signify the transportation from the life of the deceit of darkness to the life which is, according to Christ, free and bright, with which we begin to worship God. For it is written, The people who sat in darkness have seen a great light.*

The cloister is silent, and Havoise is embarrassed by the brush of her clothing and the dry, irregular tock of her stick against the pavers as she moves about in this silent space. And there are saints here—men and women who have given their lives and fortunes over to the convent, to the faith—and they are cold and dry under their stone effigies, lying in state, stone prayers sculpted to show to the monaries faithful obedience even in death. And knowing that even these are the bodies of her own kin, here in the cold dry stale still emptiness of their stone tombs, she endeavors to walk even more silently, and disturb their sleep not at all.

* * *

The scriptorium was off-limits to anybody not working (or stoking the fire after dark), but the Abbess has always turned a blind eye to Havoise, who seemed sometimes to move about so slowly as to be invisible—and besides, what was there for a sleepless old woman to do in a convent but walk around in the cold cold cloister or pray in the church?—and no one doubted she did both faithfully, everynight moving like a ghost through the cloister or standing—silent as statue—at the rail of the chancel, somehow able to stand in place seemingly for hours, immobile, bent over her walking stick, her shoulders round like the dome of the sky; she nonetheless made an effort to put some stitches into the Tapestry every time she left the open cloister to warm her bones in the close, oilydark scriptorium (which she did probably three or four times nightly), and whenever sisters came in to stir the fireplace, they would make a point of finding Havoise in her little circle of candlelight, and in silent approval of her handwork, lay their hand on Havoise' round shoulder and lay a few new candles at the foot of her stand. And when Havoise points her shaking finger to the words slanting across the panel she has underway, it is always a silent request for the sisters to check her Latin.

And tonight is just like every other night, and when she feels the sister's presence at her side and the hand on her shoulder, her hand moves as if of its own accord to the embroidered letters, *Hic domus incenditur,* and the sister leans close in the flickering light and reads, her lips forming silent syllables, *Here they are burning down a house,* and she nods, and Havoise feels the sister's fingers tighten gently over her shoulder, and she knows the Latin is good and that she can continue to the next panel.

* * *

The monaries would do well to remember the sufferings of Mary as an example, as a portrait of perfect suffering and perfect obedience, and perhaps even pray that the Lord would cause them to suffer as the Mother of Christ had, such that their own suffering could teach them lessons of submission and obedience as well.

The Disputation was the mystery of the evening, and Havoise finds it a troubling leg of each year's lectionary pilgrimage, causing her to cross some of the more broken terrain of her memory, for the last several decades. Christ's *lingering* in the Temple to harass the doctors...? That made for good theology—establishing Christ's authority and legitimacy from the age of first manhood—but seemed a foul deal for Mary, who must have been out of her wits with worry once she realized her Son was not with her.

Havoise may have had that feeling before herself; she presses her eyelids together, and concentrates on forgetting.

It wasn't working very well. Tears well up between her eyelids.

But tonight, perhaps Havoise is feeling distracted; perhaps she is feeling disobedient and unsubmissive, but the directive *to suffer more* seems to be a burden more than a woman should be willing to bear, and bear in silent and perfect submission.

It is Epiphany, and it is cold in the open cloister, and the view of the stars in the frigid blue of the sky is suffering enough. She is through counting stones for the day, and sets her course for the scriptorium, where she will balance herself on her walking stick by the fire until her blood begins moving again, and then she will buy back that moment of warmth by sitting with the Tapestry for a time.

* * *

That star had spun through overhead—so sinister, so sinister!—a little sharper each day, a little brighter each day, burning hotter and greater and stranger daily. And as dawn approached in the East, the star, with its coma tresses of terrifying silver, would drowse toward the West, only to rise again next midnight, in time to terrify anew.

* * *

Rollo was a ghost, a demon, a sinister star arising at midnight at some random new point on the eastern horizon, a night visitor, his hair whiter than silver, fire in his eyes and white vapor pouring from his nostrils. And when he rode, crowns stolen from the heads of kings he had murdered rattled rings over his biceps, and when he sailed, he would hang one-armed over the bowsprit of his landing skiff, sword the other arm, waiting for the launch to touch the beach; he would literally hit the pebbles running, and blood would be streaming gaily from his sword within the minute.

They say he tore roofs from the churches of Paris to rebuild his fleets. They say he attacked Picardy fifty times in fifty years. They say his second-last official act was to personally behead a hundred Christians in the square in Rouen, then (as his last act) to gift the Rouenese churches a hundred *pounds* of gold to honor his baptism as a Christian king. They say his blood runs in the veins of Scots to the North and Grimaldis to the South, that every man, woman and child alive in Normandy today is 1/64th Rollo.

* * *

Falaise. Havoise remembers grey cliffs, the tall chalky crags and the great grey chalk keep of Robert that sits upon them. Falaise the sleepy Falaise, forever raining, forever grey. Havoise remembers the weavers of Falaise, the row, straight as an arrow, of six weavers' shops, and running from shop to shop to fetch supplies or bring food around. She remembers seeing her father in the upper room of their shop worrying over pennies, and writing, writing writing—this was the life of burghers in Normandy—and whenever she is awake at night and sitting in her little circle of candlelight, she thinks back to the days when she slept in the little nest her father had built for her and her sisters in the attic rafters, and she can hear her father counting coins—9, 1, 4, 7, 3, 6, 9, 1...—and she sieves the linen ground of the Tapestry between her fingers a bit more attentively, trying to remember the weight of the weave her father would make. And once a year she would accompany her father and the other weavers to the steps of Notre Dame de Guibray, her arms laden with the richest fabrics her father and his guild could make, an offering of simple tribute to their lord. She feels she remembers seeing Robert at one of these ceremonies, although her father had told her no such thing could have possibly occurred: Robert would simply send his men to retrieve the tribute, bring it back to the keep in their carts.

'If we were lucky, we'd never have any contact with Robert. *Ever.*'

Havoise remembers that her father had always called Robert 'The Magnificent' in public. But 'The Devil' behind closed doors.

Robert was the great-great-grandson of Rollo.

* * *

Havoise remembers the tanner's daughter from her earliest childhood. *Herleva.* The name narrowed the eye of every woman in Falaise. Havoise, too young to understand her elders' suspicion of Herleva, loved watching the woman's legs as she waded through the dye trenches, wondered at the rich colors her calves would adopt, and loved watching how her face would adopt an ecstatic grin, face to the sky, while telling windy wild tales to her fellow dyeing women, just before the punchline would fall.

Havoise was ignorant of the old Frankish etymologies of *Herleva,* never quite understood the resonances of the snickering distortions of her name, mostly expansions of Frankish *harlotta.* All she saw were Herleva's freckled apple cheeks, her long auburn braid, her muscular calves, her gales of laughter. She was beautiful. And Havoise stole glances at her every time she carried textiles to the dyers for her father, not afraid to just sit chin in hands hours at a time, watching Herleva march through the dyeing trenches.

And time and time again—too often to be completely random—there would be commotion, and the dyer women would clutch together, seemingly half out of fear, half out of revulsion, with lightning glances over their shoulders, up toward the crag with its keep.

'He's watching us. They say he can see for miles, they say he can see a mole on your shoulder.'

Havoise would try to follow their sightline, and each time, saw nothing: at the wall, or the gate, or the tower. Squinting, hoping to spot the ghost, the great-great-grandson of Rollo. And each time she would look back to the dyeing trenches, the women were already fleeing, the cold, colorful water swirling in their absence.

* * *

Mesoniktikon. Havoise knows the liturgy by heart—she has sung it, essentially identically each time, for the last decade—and she has to concentrate hard to keep alert, keep her head in the building. She find herself counting the blocks of stone in the church piers; at least by counting, bottom-up, her head, heart and eyes are drawn upward.

She tries to articulate for herself: if each stone—in this chapel, in her arcaded cloister, even in the close vaults of her cell—if each stone, whether regular in shape, or some oddity of form (the hyperirregular polygons for corners and points of vaults), if *each and every one of them* represented a human being she has known, a man or woman she has known of—not just mother and father, sisters and friends, but even *(or especially)* the mythological characters, the devils, demons and ghosts who won't die—where does she, herself, fit in to this great complex forest of stone?

She feels guilty for being unable to concentrate during the hymns, and she murmurs absently the melodies of prayers and orations.

I have lived—and will die—beneath and between the half-million stones of this minster

But now *Mesoniktikon* is over—she doesn't really know where it went—and the sisters file out, their footsteps echoing in the high, amber-lit chapel. Havoise would be mortified if everyone had to wait for her in her crooked, shuffling gait, and pretends to continue praying as the rest disappear. As quiet resumes in the building, she rises painfully and, with some effort, shuffles out after them.

It is snowing, and the glow of candles in the chapel, together with the wan light of the lamps set into the stone walls of the cloister, gently illuminate the great heavy flakes, and Havoise can see the shadows of the cloister arcades made real as they extend out into the snow suspended in ether, and she realizes that the stones that made up this minster shadow toward one another, as if silently acknowledging one another's presence.

The tombs of saints are part of the minster's masonry; they are paved into the floor of the chapel, they are made visible in sculpted likenesses out here in the cloister, and snow is filtering down out of the courtyard and onto their faces.

They will sculpt my face into stone one day soon

She makes her way toward the scriptorium. Although it is hardly *warm* in here, at least there is the fire to stir and it is dry here, too, and there are useful things to do for the rest of the cold night.

And the Tapestry is bundled strategically in the trunk at the foot of her work chair, and when she pulls laboriously at it, she has the start of next panel on her knee. And she is disoriented for a moment—there at first was only a mass of colors, a curve of embroidered ochre. Only when she saw her caption—*Here, the soldiers are fighting the Dinannais*—could she really orient herself. And she realizes that *Here, Now* she must begin a likeness.

Try to remember how he looked, how he was, try to remember the likeness of his soul

* * *

The day Herleva disappeared (they say), she had been in the dyeing trenches, and when Robert the Magnificent trained his eye on the women, she didn't run away as the other women always did, but instead, following some unnameable instinct, continued marching through the cold, raw water, raising her skirts an inch higher on her thighs.

Nine months later to the day, Rollo's great-great-great-grandson was born. His name was William.

Que lui profiterait-il, si loin du port,
  A celui dont le récif est le destin
  A lui sur ce pont qui balance, malsain,
  En péril solitaire ? l'orage son sort.

Du sel qui se crispe aux lèvres, par l'apport
  Du vent ; tonnerre qui tourne son sang en vain
  Et la pluie qui essuie ses larmes enfin
  Ses cheveux tout fauves dans le vent si fort.

Que lui profite la nuit de sa terreur ?
  Comment le sauver, perdu dans son erreur,
  Si loin de toi, quand seul, enfin il s'endort ?

Il ne me restera que toi dans mon cœur—
  Mets mes os à part, quiets, quand je serai mort
  Et garde mon cœur, ce qui reste de mon corps

Passacaglia

*What profits a man this far from land, in ships
   Bound for the reef's edge, bound for the sea's embrace,
   On this tilting deck, in this lonely place,
   Solitary peril here in the storm's grips?*

*The night's stormgale spray bring seasalt to his lips;
   The thunder in his heart make his hot blood race;
   The rain stream tears and blood from his face;
   His hair alive his limbs wild as the wind whips.*

*What profits a man the night of his terror?
   How could you protect him in his hopeless case?
   How can he be, so far from you, so far from grace?*

*My thought is of you borne away in my error:
   When I die, lay my bones in some quiet space
   In you my heart lives, recall its feeble trace*

* * *

A wise man turns his fatal flaw into his best asset

And so every Thursday morning, well before dawn, that heavy old padlock clock would scare him awake and he'd stumble around in the cold and dark for a half-hour. His brother had sent him When One Has Lived A Long Time Alone to consecrate his lonely little studio on 18 rue de la Liberté,

> *When one has lived a long time alone,*
> *One wants to live again among men and women,*
> *To return to that place where one's ties with the human*
> *Broke*

and every morning he'd remember that gift sardonically: he had nearly no furniture, and no reason to buy any, and his temptation is to take down a catalogue of all the eclecticism of his icebox alone, just pin it to the world to change it even a little bit, make the world even a tiny bit his with some record of his own mundane-ness. He'd even been tempted to take all the doors off their hinges—no reason for 'privacy'—just to be able to navigate the place in the dark, no lights, no sound, no worry, all mine.

And it is still dark when he triplechecks the presence of keys in his pocket, backpack on, the great tempered glass door, '18' stenciled at head height, and the Med air is heavy and hot-laden. He has no umbrella, he'll risk it, tough it out if it turns on him.

There's a good bakery in the basement of 32 rue Massena, in the pedestrian zone, it's right on his way, and they open up early enough to make it worth it to him. And the goods are cheap, and he has his ritual: a focaccia that's not too cheese heavy—five francs—two brioches at two francs each, and two pains au chocolat at three francs apiece, and wax bag, he sets heading for the University at Boulevard Herriot.

He always has the focaccia first—he doesn't exactly like it, only knows it's full of fairly energetic things that are likely to keep him from getting malnourished, and seats within it a wide enough variety of olives and peppers and dried tomatoes, lumps to keep him nourished intellectually: he thinks of Hubble and his crazy expansion model, raisins in bread on good days, and on bad he worries that his impoverished diet will kill his kidneys with rabbit poisoning—and then the focaccia goes down a little easier and he follows up with the brioche and the pains au chocolat, alternating, always finishing with a chocolate bread, buttery bottom of the bag structurally weaker and weaker, and you always program that last bite from the very first, leave 'em laughing.

* * *

'They're really good. Sweet. You should have one.'

Grapes.

'No, I'm good.'

Bricks and badly beaten hardwoods, not really two rooms, just a single long room with a wide set of French doors across the middle, a narrow-waisted kitchen, a bathtub, noisy neighbors, cinderblock shelving. University. A contract a tenement a rental.

'You should. They're really good.'

'Had enough, thanks.'

He loved the place for itself: a two-minute jog from the department, it's a top floor you know, and in what way isn't it a penthouse? He'd already surreptitiously fixed the lousy rental paintjob in the living room—the one half of the big room they called the living room—and his dissertation is a language all its own, spilling across borders and into the corners near his Grandpa's chair where he'd fall asleep. People would find their way in on Friday nights, people from his department, from her work teaching music, and the old maple table his Mom had given him was just wide enough for three couples if you were close friends.

'Try one.'

She was famous for building a meal out of nothing. *Rations to tandoori* he chuckled to himself, and all he had to do was find a bottle of red to wash it all down with, didn't even have to be all that good the rest of the food could stand on its own, and each time they would end up telling the story of how they met, how it had all worked out. Top floor made for the warm floor in winter, and folks would stay on, and wine would meld into coffee, and coffee into whiskey shots nursed for an hour, then two.

'I said, I'm good.'

He would spot her at the window sometimes, and he wondered what she had been watching before he came along. Sometimes his arms would be full of corrections and a few new books that should fill in the footnotes a little, and at those times he wouldn't have his head about him, would just look up and see her in the window up there like another thought staring at the top of his head. Other times, more alert, he wondered if she weren't in their window longing for a husband with a real job, who could give her something other than the handmedowns that had kept him alive all those years. Most days he'd try not to look as he approached, and he'd try to walk as he always had, as if no one were watching, and he'd be sure she had seen him shore up his stride into a more handsome one, but one day he'll fool her into thinking he hadn't known she was there at all.

'But I got them for you.'

He was embarrassed whenever she had a tray ready as he opened the door just back from work, and there was lassi or something homemade you couldn't ordinarily find in a little college town—*if the guys in the department knew what I was sipping right now, feet up, ottoman and all, I'd lose so much cred... 'What happened to your politics, Vicus?'*—but in his heart he knew it was sweet of her and the most she could give on a budget where two-thirds went to housing alone.

'I've had enough, and besides, they'll be too sweet, my teeth hurt.'

But other days—he would admit they were rare, but they were there—the last thing he wanted was a dish of homemade things: staff politics were steep and launched longlasting ripples, and between the continuous pressures of teaching and classes and budgeting and the dissertation that hung over him day and night for years, sitting in place would grate on him, and he'd find himself pacing or wringing his hands, and sometimes he would make up a story *the car looks like it's illegal let me repark it,* and everybody knew that if you tried finding a parking spot at this hour you'll be driving a mile at least *don't worry I don't mind the walk* but then that look would darken her features again. Sometimes he would relent and urbanely sip at the ginger tea that was already turning in its cup waiting for him, but other times he had actually felt his future threatened *the reason they take it so seriously is because the stakes are so low* and needed to feel the mindless rhythm of the march, and dream of what was behind that fence, behind that door over there.

And sometimes, the car really was parked illegally, and God help him if they got a ticket, what with their budget.

'Don't insult me in front of our guests.'

And the dinner parties would last all evening, and he'd pour on the charm as best he could, knowing there could only be this waiting at the end of the day: really good food, really good conversation about times gone by, some grim stripe of satisfaction at having done it, having made a good go at it.

'Which one of us knows better how hungry I am—me or you?'

The candles would burn down to the stump, and wax would infuse the fibers of the tablecloth. The wine is warm now, and its color is dying in the fading light.

'Then try just one.'

'You're kidding me, right?'

And she is on her feet, and her eyes were fire, and the guests are looking at each other, nervous.

'Eat one.'

'How many times do I have to...?'

And she is trying to force his lips apart and ram the grape against his clenched teeth.

* * *

The sky is threatening, and he is four miles from Rue de la Liberté. He's watched the same sunrise over the same scene—*Ligurian Sea, At Dawn*—every Thursday morning for who knows how long now, and he can think of a hundred times he's walked the whole trek backwards, just to keep it in sight. But today there's been some grave functional failure in the paradigm of Sunrise, and what should be a brightening in the sky has turned out to be nothing but a phreaking of the horizon in shape and color, and somehow it is all turning out green and ochre wherever it isn't just outright black, and it's clear it's all going wrong in the morning sky God help us.

This part of Nice is filthy—how tourists could ever believe this place is anything other than the very spot where France and Italy rub their loins together is unknowable—and the sea has become steely and glassy. Turn your back to it; head uphill toward Herriot; the campus is all Marshall Plan and will withstand the worst the Med can dish out; and without thinking about it he is inside the main hall, whose own green and ochre—a severe case of fluorescence winning out over incandescence in a rending, wrenching warfare of attrition—rival the building eastern sky, all chemical and radiological, like spent gunpowder, like burned concrete.

The French kids are already in the main hall; those with umbrellas are holding them dearly, and those without must live across the street.

He withstands the usual barbs and hooks left in his mailbox: *There will be a disciplinary meeting at noon regarding conduct issues involving you* is a standard hail, in the secretaries' florid pen skitter, and he balls it up, knowing that the problem is with the system rather than with him or even his caste, *it always Involves You since you're the low man on the totem pole*, and *it's all 'disciplinary hearings' because if we didn't have disciplinary hearings, it wouldn't be Thursday* and he has a few more chestnuts all lined up that he'll murmur to himself as a mantra to keep from losing consciousness during the noon hazing session. He has his lessons built, has had them for weeks in fact, has them memorized, the hardest part of the morning is finding enough space in the dark, tall hallways for his shoulders to fit through, and the failed interior lights are no longer augmented by the failed natural lighting from outside, and when the noise levels reach painful with student *barratin* and when every new kid pressing through the hall counter-current carries a different load of humidity and heat in on them, he knows it has got to be pouring out there.

The classrooms are all dark, stark places, sometimes with odd angles and random shapes—a classroom shaped like a cane, like binoculars, like a conch—and it is confusing to have to rely on the building's artificial lighting once you've gotten used to the light that spirals in, indirect, from the courtyard, through the frosted glass, from the skylight. *Why teach at all? If they're as distracted by this building as you are...*

He would spend the whole year deciphering the arcana of class codes: *A* for majors, *B* for minors, *C* for kids completely outside of the English section; generally, he loved his Bs best—they were serious enough to have their shit together, but not so very serious as to have already become divas about it. And he loved them as if he loved them: they had watched out for him in a hundred ways, and Vicus was flattered to realize they had no pretentions of studying English in some (probably vain) effort to be *really good* at it. Instead, there was some kind of cult of personality at play, and they poked and pried at him to figure him out, crack him a little, make him theirs for the year.

And if that isn't proof of friendship and esteem, I don't know what is

The 'disciplinary meeting' is as suspected: more a demonstration of the chair's failures than the faculty's, and the underlings—Vicus included—have all arrived at the blush of twelve noon, and the chair has sent word that she will be along soon, perhaps in threequarterhour, perhaps not, just wait for her, the meeting is essential. The chair's secretary is sheepish, and spends her time noting down who arrives at what hour and minute, and who gets up and leaves and at what hour and minute, so that further 'disciplinary meetings' can be scheduled.

Vicus cools his heels, and listens to Bach in his head, and wishes there were windows in this room.

*　*　*

'You know, I don't think that's very clean.'

Vicus hears Sundari before seeing her. The day is whiskey yellow—hot as Hell outside—and his head is thick with pollen, summer asphalt thermals and dusty windshields on a September afternoon. Thank God it's dark and cool in here.

'What isn't?' He's moving slowly: his head is still turning, his thoughts aren't in the house with him yet.

'That, um, that shed.'

That shed is the garden shed, the paraphernalia of a year's yardwork.

It's hard-cold inside, and his eyes are adjusting too slowly with the curtains drawn; he steadies himself against the counter, balances imperfectly to jackknife his shoes—heelheel—off his feet.

'I don't get it.' Still distant, heatdrunk, *gimme a sec.* The floor is good and cold through his socks in the dark room, tile exchanging his heat for theirs. Vicus' eyebrows ex to remember, *Newton's Law Which?* His head is still outside, still pounding from the heat.

'I don't think it's very clean.' Sundari's voice in the half-light of shades drawn.

His bag isn't off his shoulder yet and he's already got a glass in his hand. Icecubes pinch at his fingertips *got any lemonade?* until they pitch in and ring the glass. He cracks them with a draught from the pitcher, reloads, his larynx pulsing greedily until the second glass is down.

'What does that have to do with...?' The glass is in the sink and the hallway is darker than the even kitchen was, his fingertips help navigate. *Helluvaday*

'You touched it, didn't you?'

But he is in the bedroom, and he unzips his bag. Stack of papers out on the bed.

'Touched what?' *You wouldn't believe the corrections I've got*

But she's in front of him now, and suddenly his head is back in the room with her.

'That shed.'

'Yeah. Yeah? Yeah.'

'You *touched* that shed.'

He was missing the punchline and didn't want to say yeah again. 'I left the gas can out yesterday mowing, didn't want to leave it out overnight again.'

But suddenly she is a tempest of motion, rage over a lost penny or something, his papers fly and the coverlet is peeled away. Sundari is seething subsonic words through her teeth *make me slave away all damned day long* and Vicus' head is turning more than ever.

She is crying now. 'How *could* you?' Hot tears, *God she's radiating heat.* 'It took all day to dry these, now I have to do it all *again?* Just throw your junk everywhere will you...' She shoulders past him head down, rougher than usual, not even crossing eyes with him, not even speaking in his direction.

He doesn't dare move, doesn't dare whisper, doesn't dare blink, doesn't dare think. The bed is disassembled now and jammed into the washer, she's in and through the room to the bathroom and back to the kitchen and to the washer; somewhere in the commotion she's got a towel out and has snapped it loudly over the shower curtain, and she has a big sponge and a bucket out now and is washing down the hallway walls.

'Don't just stand there, *wash off.*' Side of her mouth.

He hasn't moved a muscle. 'Is this about the...?'

'*Yes it's about the shed* and about you giving me *even more* work to do,' but now she's pushed past him again and is stomping toward the kitchen, and when her footsteps approach again she's still on the same sentence, and she's crying even more now, '*I wish you'd just wash off and not touch anything else*' but she's gone again and he can hear her flatfoot toward another corner of the house.

He doesn't think, instead he *does*. He's afraid he's missed something really big, and as the water's running down his back, he doesn't even think to scrub. His first real thought is a question to himself, *Does she know I didn't roll in it, whatever 'it' is?*

The water is off now and he has his towel around him. Each step measured. He hesitates: she still at it? He sees the bed is cobbled back—old sheets, no pillowcases yet, washer's on—and he can hear her steps, loud and intentional, coming back through. She sees him standing there, towel and barefeet, but doesn't slow down a single beat. She's wiping off the windowsills now.

'You done dripping yet?'

Which he takes as his signal to move—all caution—toward the dresser and find some clothes. He's got his boxers on, and he's struggling a bit with the next step.

'What are you doing?' She's watching him gymnastics his way into a t-shirt, one hand always holding the wet towel high.

'The, um, *the towel*' he says lamely.

'What, are you *too stupid* to know what to do with a towel? Set it down and get dressed. *Throw it on the bed and get your clothes on.*' There is something oddly calm in her voice, as if she hasn't been here watching all this for the last twenty minutes.

* * *

He's balancing on one foot—not daring touch the bed—getting his socks on. There's a soul-rending scream from the bathroom, and in a flash, Sundari is back before Vicus. She's crying again.

'Where's the soap?'

He can't bring himself to ask what? yet again, and stands there dumbly. Somehow her question is supposed to make sense in this particular universe.

'I *said*, where's the soap?'

'I have no idea.' The one answer he can think of.

'*There's no soap in the stall.* What, are you too stupid to know to use soap? Don't you know *how* to use soap? *Or are you too stupid to know how to use soap?*'

* * *

He is astonished to get back out to the University steps and find the streets still dry: all those impressions of cloudburst achieved have only been prefatory, preambles only of major storms building just offshore in the Med, eight hours of tension building in the springs, and all the heat and humid carried through in the fibers of his students' clothes had only been troubling electrochemical precursors of the impending strike.

It's held off eight hours; I only need forty-five minutes more to get home

He had watched in corners all day to try and poach a forgotten umbrella—thinking the sky was already torn open—but to no avail, and the hike'll be intoxicating without one anyway, the running of gauntlets, the staying-ahead of it, the slipping-through, the artful dodge. Leave your bag in the office 'hind the counter.

* * *

His step is light stopwatch fever rabbithole, only four miles anyway, you'd stand a better chance of getting caught by storms waiting for the bus, didn't care a lot couldn't think of a reason why not, and the Med is sure odd today, really a pool of oil, surfacetensionslowmotion, the Holy Eucharist in some sort of fictional fractional gravity.

The storm is humming and churning offshore, an undigest succession of colors at once pearlescent, at once septic and sickly, hovering like the bogey man, the Devil himself the anti-aurora, a half-arch ready to collapse. House-o'-cards. Poison darts.

* * *

It's not like he didn't try, it's really not. A half-hour earlier and he'd have made it, but the weather is on his shoulder, it's starting to build a checkmate on him. At first he heard the drops hitting out in the Med, maybe a half-mile or more, a rustle of canvas, the old familiar rush of blood in his inner ear.

Thrush. Breath. Thrush. Breath.

And then the slap-drop of fat drops pop to the sidewalk, ionizing, volatilizing, a strange sketch of wet and dry on the sidewalk of the Promenade des Anglais. And before he can thank his stars for some kind of intermediate stage between the calm and the storm, there's a line of horses galloping in off the Med.

The wind has pulled his shirt from his belt. The wind tastes like seasalt. Vicus presses forward into the gale, his glasses awash, part rainwater part seaspray.

What is there to do except trudge on? And so he does.

But then he thinks about that last thing there. He stops, and looks around him. Water is streaming across him, through him. The sky is almost black. He realizes for the first time that he can hear nothing but the blast of wind, the roar of awnings beating helicopters in squadrons, and the waves have become nightmares of oily night.

There is a bench here, looking out into the deep, shifting menace. He clambers up, shirttails fraying, carefully shoves his glasses into a pants pocket.

Try not to think where you are

He sees each wave blasted off at its peak, each peak atomized to gritty astringent, and himself the convergence of all that spray and wind, each wave a new height, each wave a new presence, a new threat.

All I know is that the sea and the sky have me now

But each wave spends itself against the shore, against him, and he is arms-wide eyes to the churning skies, and he sees himself from the sea's view, the unknowable confluence of music and words and gales, so very human, so very alone: the only one here, the only one left, a man alone.

All I know is that my heart is still beating

His blood is in his ears, and his clothes are a sail, and his heart is a flag, his mind a flame.

All I know is that my lungs are still drawing breath

And the words are carried away in the storm and he feels his heart is free, and his mind is awash in darkness, thought-and-yet-not-thought, and his mind is the focus of much lightning, and the only words that come to him are borne away in the tides, and the wind tears his words away, not like pulling the air from his lungs, but like pulling dragons from a strong tower.

In love for the final day

The sand endures, it is just these bald waves' collapse you hear

Thrush Breath Thrush Breath

Heureux qui, comm' Thésée, perce son labyrinthe,
   Perce dans les chambres noires de l'inconscient,
   Et parmi les os des mystères, des sacrifices,
   Domptant cette obscurité, cette horreur sainte

Heureux, Thésée ! La tyrannie de mainte
   Année brisée ; la fin du monstre géant
   Achevée; maintenant glorieux, triomphant, hisse
   Vers ta rive tant désirée ta voile teinte

Mais où, âme perdue, est ta caution domptée ?
   Te revoilà dans ton quartier, tes rues étroites
   Ton jardin, ta porte, ta propre cheminée

Mais navigue, âme chétive, héros de si peu
   Ne regarde ni à gauche, ni à ta droite
   Mais va, marche, regardant tout droit, malheureux

Happy who, like Theseus, breaks into the maze
  Piercing into the black chambers of the deep mind
  Through the mysteries, among sacrificial bones
  Owning the very darkness, piercing horror's haze

Happy king Theseus! The tyranny of days
  Is broken asunder, the death of Minos' kind
  Achieved, and now covered in glory, your mast groans
  Your ship plying on, beneath your dark sail aways

But now where, you lost soul, has your bravery gone?
  Here you are now, your town, your narrow street in sight
  Your garden, your door, your safe hearth and its soft rays

Navigate now, you timid soul, you cog, you pawn,
  Don't you dare stray from your path, neither left or right
  March on, eyes front, eyes straight ahead, dead straight, always.

* * *

Have you no code, no voice, no enigma for others to recognize in the rhythm of your pace, no quirk of speech? What will they remember of the physical shape of your revolt?

Peruggia strode down Avenue Prince Napoleon with the strength of thirty men, swinging Brass Corners as if it were a movie prop.

See the wind cleave from the angles of my face—my chin, the height of my bones—like a shockwave, a wake

The city murmured its thrum *Nice is really a bestiary, isn't it? just a moat full of creatures, just an ark of humanity* and he had heard that Nice was the refugee center of the world but you'd never know it striding through erect as Peruggia here, angling on through like a soldier or a Pimm's poster all silhouette and tails: these folks were no ghosts, no shadows of former men, no noble laurels at all 'sfar as he could see from the man and woman on the street. But August is at its sharpest and the heat seems to rise up like a heavier-than-air poison filling a closed room, and he can feel his legs resist his Pimm's stride, and soon his stomach is melting out of column, too, and now his cheekbones have a deep red hot pressure encroaching, all needles and heat.

They told him that Prince Napoleon arcs down toward Massena from the station district, and the neighborhood leading to it, he knows, is shaped something like the vessels and vesicles serving his kidney—hairfine leading to narrow leading to broad leading to thoroughfare, and if the world makes any sense at all, there will be some sort of more-or-less-steep gradient leading from the whorehouses and moneychangers to the cheap hotels leading to the garret housing and so on; so far, he hasn't been able to perceive any sort of blood-brain barrier between the station district and the rest of Nice; perhaps the whole damned place is just a giant cheap hotel? But now he's starting to see familiar landmarks of commercial civilization—booksellers and cheap lawyers—and he realizes that he's been on Prince Napoleon all along.

Prince Napoleon is built like a road should be (this close to the heart of Christendom), would in fact be a splendid, wide avenue, but the Niçois have perverted it to a contentless wash of humanity knowing no boundary, respecting no conventions of space, human to human, and the sheer press of glistening, stinking human flesh against him, caroming against him from God-knows-where on every side—*here is the signature of the refugees finally*—is beginning to make his stomach turn out volumes of acid, and the heat intensifies in his cheeks, and he feels that shift in his esophagus: he is on the verge of losing that salutary volume of pinard that had kept him going all night long, *and come to think of it, what were all these people doing out in this heat on a Tuesday anyway?* and the rush of sound was like several duels unfolding around his ears all at once, a constant clatter of swords' edges hissing and glissing across each other, just a hard shine of white noise appealing to his every attention, every channel full, every sense plugged with new mudslides—demands and sly offers—*a whole beerhall city, isn't it? a whole nursery full of made-up names* and all he can think to do about it right now is to stride longer stronger and harder and swing Brass Corners around like a savage beerhall windmill and kill as many of these cretins as he can until he can reach the sea and rinse his damned jammed ears open, swim straight down bluegreen till his ears let loose and let the auditory sludge of Nice float free to pollute other shores.

* * *

The Duke is no powerhouse, it is true. But his energy! The boy could cleanse the whole world of contagion with that tirelessness, with that wiry physique, with that nimbleness

The Duke of Angoulême would simply not stop. His sword nearly outweighed him, nearly bending and tearing his arms loose from his shoulders like breaking through a beef joint, nearly tipped him over on his back like an ancient Olympian hero beneath the weight of it, like an old trébuchet tripping and bending, deciding whether to wind up and fire or collapse upon itself. His arms flexed hotly, sweat greasing his limbs in the light of the oil lamps in the dark chamber.

And the sword would lift laboriously, miraculously—*Strike! Strike!*

Strike!—and come crashing down again and again and again, clumsy in the boy's fatigue. The rug was holed to tatters from so many misses sailing past his sparring partners and divotting the floor; after a while they even stopped sharpening his blade, so dull and bent and ragged they became with his failed, flailed strikes that they couldn't straighten them out again.

It's hard not to love him, to admire him like a hero, to see our best selves in him

He was reaching manhood: he smelled like a stag in rut when he was near to the end of his exercises.

The stink of kings is sweet in the nostrils of the masses

His magnificent harrowed sword dropped to the floor with a leaden clang; an assistant rushed in to gather it up like a holy relic, whistling at the new bends and dents, real worship, *we should fear and love like this* and the room was ripe with his sweat, and his breath hoarsed from him like a smelter's furnace. He gathered up his shirt, balled it up and scrubbed the sweat from his forehead. Instantly another squire, younger this time, hustles to collect the tousled, yellowed bundle.

The Duke's chest is still heaving after his exertions; he sits, all knees and angles. Now there is a pitcher of wine at his side, and he finds it without looking, swipes his hand across the rim—*just to make it his, you see*—takes a long draught. Whether it is weak or strong is not so much his problem, whether sweet or bitter either—because there will always be someone having studied his face, studied the length of his draught, studied the movement of his glottis within him, and they know without even asking him (after long and curious experience) that this is what he prefers, this is what he thirsts for after a good hard scrimmage. Just as they have watched his pupils widen with interest around a certain mare, a certain motet—*the boy likes Pierre Certon, this is a good sign*—a certain dagger, a certain book, and all these things magically appear at his side, all he has to do is reach out and make it his.

And so they have constructed him from his own will; he wishes, and it is fulfilled, and as he partakes, the wish fulfills him, building him from a net accumulation of things and ideas, a growing radius of things and ideas, each one a stepping stone toward the next; and once again, all he has to do is reach out his hand, and it will be his, too

* * *

How can the whole city be conspiring to press up against Monsieur Peruggia? How can the whole city be singing different songs, in different keys, at different tempos? The acoustic pressure alone is enough to drive a man to drink, to say nothing of the constant invasions into his field of view of ten thousand different wares to hawk, different profane delights to entice him criminally, different scents—from the coffee stands, from the pungent butchers' shops—*on a main thoroughfare?*—and the constant assault of the French's perpetual funk, offensive in magnitude and kind. Although he's certain he's put a few bruises into the Niçois with Brass Corners' sharpened points, that's all come at a cost of a collective beating inflicted by the same suitcase, different end: whenever he rams Brass Corners into some new imbecile, the case transmits the shock back into his own thighs and knees, and after a hundred or a thousand such blows, he's sure his legs are leopards of angry stormy injuries, septic cancer purple.

He's seen all the old paintings of Hubert Robert—the mouth-breathers at the Louvre called him The Rubens Of The Ruins—and quite involuntarily, he's got the picture in his mind of the *Grand Gallery of the Louvre in Ruin*, all torn up as by an earthquake, grasses tufting from the open marrow of the pillars, poor wretches picking through the blocks and dust to find some piece of brass to sell, some piece of marble to pawn, and he feels another pang of regret that Nice hasn't yet undergone some analogous apocalypse at the hands of some tenth-rate *paysagiste* as well—*you can tell all this place wants to be is Venice*—just to give him something better to think about than this esplanade full of cretins and it's just so damned cloying how much people seem oblivious of how profane it all is. He's been walking with Brass Corners held high over his head for awhile, maybe he was hoping that this would help him to navigate better between the teeming Tuesday tides, maybe he just wanted to stand out, his five-and-a-half feet augmented by the length of his failing arms and the height of his case and the *gravitas* of his cause, maybe he wanted to better confront the eyes of the Niçois, *I just see your emptiness gaping and gawing in your eyes* but if he feels even one more elbow point into his ribs, he won't know what to do, drop the case and punch all their lights out *And didn't Jesus himself start turning over tables in the Temple?* but it just wouldn't do to be picked up for something trivial here in the lion's den, certainly not with Brass Corners held up like a relic in processional.

And besides wasn't the whole of France supposed to be in a state of mourning? But the hawkers and the buyers and the hookers and the lookers and the loiterers are gabbing and taunting and flaunting and chattering louder than he can think, and now, whenever some sharp sound jabs long knives through the chaotic burlap market—a dog, a man hawking a bottle of elixir from a corner, a door jangling bells as a store slams shut—he finds himself ducking instinctively.

And now he is running, Brass Corners over his head, sweat pouring from his temples, his armpits stinking and horrid. And his back is against the door of some church and his chest is heaving and of course the door is locked no sanctuary, and then his back is against the brick of some arcade, and then his back is against the tall glass of some commercial paradise Persian rugs gelato diamond rings, and then he is out in the sun and at the end of the land, and his feet are getting their bones knocked and dislocated by the giant round pebbles of the beach.

Somehow the nightside cool of the pebbles is soothing to him, and somehow the wretched lumpiness of those rocks—just big enough to remind him of having great big knots on his shins—and he remembers how they throw fistlike roundstones like this in the wash bins with bolts of new cloth, just to limber it up by pounding the life out of it—is just what his aching back needs, and Brass Corners clatters to the stones as he peels off his shirt and rolls his trousers up to above his knees, just to feel the stones roll up against his skin and press into his muscles and joints, and even though he is covered with bruises and his deep tissues are quite nearly perfectly tenderized by the crushing Massena mass—and even though the pebbles find each and every ache, he senses a wellbeing here.

The superb permanence of this heavy blanket of stones

He thinks of the long sleep of death—*will this very night my soul be demanded of me?*—and realizes that his grave, with a tonnage of such pebbles holding him fast, eventually creeping into his very person, finding the grim rags of his heart and the dust of his mind, is a fitting one, a proper one... perhaps even dignified?

No slab of marble for me no flowers wilting no eternal light

With these dingy thoughts an audible spiraling plume of smoke in his *pinard*-exhausted mind, Peruggia closes his eyes, winedark leatherbound eyelids so very heavy in the afternoon sun.

Just a couple cubic yards of these round throwingstones heaped over me wind and waves God Almighty: a Good Enough Grave in a cathedral of failure.

* * *

Where is the light coming from in this dark place, a room where the fates of nations were dreams in the muscles of this compact, passionate monarch?

You'd think he was the lamp!

The Duke's handlers have been studying his various dictions and maxims as well, and have noticed a penchant for contradictions: *the fiery chill of your loving hatred* and its variants have begun to pepper his language, and not once but twice today he was heard to announce 'I feel very strongly both ways.'

Before nightfall his shelf was crowded with Petrarch.

And 'You will be a neopetrarchan Duke,' they said gravely.

And his room became tall and rich, overwrung with the desires of the lad—heavy wood cabinets crowded with exotic musical instruments, heavy velours climbing the walls (winedark and imposing), a magnificent bed, heavy with deerskins tall as a chapel, a holy vessel for the Duke and his pearlescent seed with which he might bless Womankind—and his attentive squires would effect a delicate choreography of redheads (for redheads were the Duke's taste of late, a taste they themselves would sharpen with every new girl—spiral coiled locks of red curls, by princely standards hideously unkempt, a very narrow waist, athletic, lithe arms and buttocks that might remind you of a yearling horse, proud, straight haunches curving into the sculptural core of her body, and by God *no more than a few inches shorter than the Duke but certainly no taller than he,* ah no, and there were some lesser heuristics at play as well, plenty of details to mind alongside the main ones, details involving the girl's intellect, probably best posed by the Duke's eldest advisor: exactly *exactly* the same rule as the one governing the girl's height, namely with her cerebral stature not so low as to make the Duke look like a clumsy giant, but not exceeding his, either, and for God's sake may the girls just cross around each other through the maze of corridors here in the palace without even knowing of each other's existence, and avoid making the Duke uncomfortable for the fact that each one was nothing even remotely close to being The Only One—*I feel very strongly both ways*—because mazes in palaces are made for that purpose too, you know.

Sharp-eared, the Duke's advisors also noticed an evolution in the realm of his various oaths. Last week he was saying 'By my faith.' This week, he has added 'By the faith of Italy.'

His handlers looked at one another frankly. 'That'll be next.'

* * *

Qu'est-ce que ça fait drôlement bien de m'allonger !

Peruggia hates it when his first thoughts upon waking are in French.

It is dark and there's an amber tint to the darkness. There is the sound of water, too, and if his head weren't pounding so loudly... But it feels so oddly good to be stretched out here, so nice and cool. It seems like his clothes and hair might be vaguely damp, just as if he had been sleeping outside, and he likes that feeling, too, just a brainstem nostalgia for Times Past, no narratives, no words, just remembering that sleeping outside was a once-a-year thing when he was a boy, a once-a-week affair in college.

When he does get up, he is distracted by the noise the heavy round gravel makes under his feet, and in the darkness the uneven surface is disorienting and, he thinks, a little dangerous. Instinctively he heads down toward the sound of water; it's more uneven here, and he's got to concentrate to keep his balance.

Now he's almost certain there's a body of water here, and the way the sound seems to sweep from one side to the other, he could be convinced there was something akin to tranquil waves breaking here.

He unbuttons his trousers—pantlegs all jammed up to his thighs somehow—and begins to urinate into the Mediterranean Sea.

His thoughts are all so chaotic and jumbled, and he almost forgets what he's doing and why before he's midway done. That wouldn't do: just to stand here and pee on himself.

The Med. The round pebbles. He looks over his shoulder, and sees the lights of a hundred layercake hotels stretching down the beach.

Hell, this looks like Nice

As comprehension dawns over him, in a flash, he's running in a dozen regimes of Random, hands down toward the dark beach roundstones *ohmyGodohmyGodohmyGod* and his trousers are tripping him, hands groping for salvation *whereisitwhereisitwhereisit*...

* * *

He nearly breaks down the door of the restaurant. He's been running—a ragged, uncontrolled lope—ever since he stumbled over old Brass Corners over on the beach, and his fingers fumbled over the latches in the dark to verify their closure. And now he's on the Cours Saleya, and he stands out badly among the Niçois: it is just past midnight, and the women are all shiny-oiled brunettes and athletically-bleached blondes, and men are all rakish, their coat thrown over a shoulder on an August night.

    The *Maitre d'* looks him up and down. His eyebrow barely rises at the sight of Peruggia's sweatstained shirt tailing partially from his belt and his pantleg caught in his sock; who knows if he's noticed the smell of urine on him yet?, and an old fashioned suitcase. 'You're not from around here, are you, *Monsieur?*'

    Best compliment anyone's ever given me

-Passacaglia-

L'avez-vous ? L'avez-vous enfin entre vos mains ?
   Le monde sent-il s'approcher son effondrement ?
   S'agit-il de l'an céleste, ce septième an
   Où le ciel-même met notre ère à sa fin ?

Est-ce bien le soupir des langues, leur déclin ?
   Ces histoires passées, à venir, ce débat
   Des années une cacophonie, un sabbat ?
   Est-ce bien le repas mortel du destin ?

Faire fondrer les murailles sur leur tête en
   Cet endroit ? Peut-on-nous qui sommes si las-
   Avoir tout donné, pour ceux qu'on aime tant ?

Survivra-t-on le coup soudain? Qu'est-ce qu'on craint ?
   La question qu'on devrait se poser, celle-là :
   Comment vivre après avoir perdu tant de sang ?

...Do you have it? Do you have it? Do you have it?
    Is civilization's collapse finally near?
    Is this-right now-the great seventh celestial year,
    Heavens heedless of the era we inhabit?

Is this the last breath of all languages' habit?
    Is this a ceremonial feast upon the dead?
    Are these our histories past, histories ahead
    Their intersection a cacophonal Shabbat?

Can we bring these walls down upon theirs and our head
    Here at this place? Can we-who love and feel so-shed
    Our blood, give up our lives for those we hold so dear?

Can we survive? Will we live on? What shall we fear?
    The question you should be asking is...this one here:
    How can we live after we have so greatly bled?

***

The place was slick with ebony and mahogany; lights inadequate; unlike just about every other bar Peruggia had ever haunted, this one actually seemed quieter the further in you went; only murmurs this far back.

I am still in the lion's den, a stranger in a strange land

The waitstaff was loathe to accord a whole table to this scarecrow of a man; they floated on through, oilygreasy words dripping disdain from their lips, 'The Management fears that Monsieur may have the wrong address.'

'No, this is the right one.' Insistent, a little desperate.

'The Management fears that Monsieur may be mistaken...'

Peruggia feared the same, some hidden catastrophic error, a simple interversion of two digits, he wouldn't know until it was far too late. The best he could say was that this was what he thought the letter had said; he had tried to commit the address to memory before getting on the train in Paris, but he's been plagued with so much worry and flights of ecstasy just getting out of the city; it was true that there were moments where his thoughts were more on astronomy than on remembering the address, and his head is still spinning, and nothing could be less sure than his memory. He realizes he is not at his sharpest, he realizes his corners have been knocked a little rounder since yesterday.

'I'm sorry, Monsieur, but we'll have be reassured that you are able to pay before we send for your food.'

He wants to spit back that they might just as well bloodlet him—*might do him a bit of good, that*—but his pinwheeling eyes have trouble pinpointing his tormentor. He digs into his pockets, fists finding four orphaned francs.

'Um,' feebly, 'a glass of wine?'

-*Passacaglia*-

About the only thing he could pay for was a glass of Gros Plant, a meager white, a premature birth of a wine.

Sip slowly

And he watched as the Gros Plant tried impotently to scale the walls of the glass, no avail.

* * *

The Duke of Anglouléme could break marble with the warp of his grin.

He was married. He could say he knew the girl like he knew a favorite constellation, could turn his head this way and that and maybe find something beautiful about it if his mood was right, but otherwise it was just wallpaper, just decoration, just flowers in the hair. None of this, he knew, came through his direct merit, only through his potential, written wild across him in a great banner annunciations.

'The story is long, very tedious, and worth listening to by myself alone,' he would say, only believing the first two of his three premises.

* * *

Claude was no particular thing to look at, certainly no erudite either. Just a girl. But she was the object of desire for countless men, a plot of land to be crossed by the armies of the world, and in time one of them just might plant a flag in victory, and hold the high ground.

She had been lined up to marry Charles—'*Carlos*' *was what his countrymen called him*—even worse to look at, some kind of horrible hybrid accident, a creature straight out of Horace. He was young—just as the Duke was young—and deformed and might as well be epileptic or demon-possessed, but the world named him a rising star anyway, and the world granted him everything he wanted.

And Charles had wanted plenty.

Claude was a nothing, at best a piston, better suited to transferring power around the machine of state than holding power herself. For she was the only daughter of the King of France.

And, by wanting France, Charles wanted Claude.

The Duke had seen Charles wanting France; he was no fool either.

'Sometimes babies want rattles not because they rattle, but because they belong to somebody else.'

He ignored the machinations his retenue had perpetrated; a choreography is just that, neither an object in itself nor even an emotional end: it simply places people in the right place at the right time.

This choreography, created -by- men like me, creates men like me

But his grin shone anyway, a good and proper monarch's grin, and it burned the smile from that ridiculous 'Charles', wherever he was.

* * *

Peruggia is hopeless; aside from the waitstaff, he is certain no one else in this steep, noble, dark place actually speaks the language, and he begins worrying that there is some new language of signs being used by all the other folk here, each somehow cleverer, somehow in the know, somehow eyes open and confident. And Peruggia is no longer on solid ground, wonders if he's ever been on solid ground.

He has missed his contact; he's going to kill himself now.

There is a man sitting across the dark room; Peruggia sees him a dark shape against the wall behind him, all mahogany, an ebony silhouette, moving to slurp his soup, moving to breathe-in his escargots, moving to reload his wine, moving to wipe up his misses.

Peruggia wonders if the fellow even knows he's speaking.

'Will I have to guide you step by step? Will you need me to pose your very limbs, teach your tongue the passion you must own, align the bones of your spine to make you stand erect? Are we both lost in the wilderness? For I am not, I am untouched by the movements of the century, but you...'

Poor bastard, must be going mad

* * *

It was a fantasy. The Duke's agate eyes burned piously.

'Tell me you are Beatrice. Tell me you are Laura...'

'Pardon me, milord?'

The Duke made no answer. His goblet was overfull, and he had the map of Italy unrolled before him, and his thoughts were far away from here.

And when he lifted his wine, there was a deep crimson ring surrounding Naples.

* * *

The man is speaking louder than the tiny, dark restaurant warrants, certainly many times louder than a man should when uttering ravings to and about himself. 'Oh, a soldier remains who will stand upright, does he?' Peruggia is becoming embarrassed for him. 'You? You're the Marine charged with the mission? You bony, squashed nonmonarch? There's no hope. You and your varicose flesh, you pale unhero, you diffuse failure, could there be anyone more weedy and wispy than you? God help us.'

The waitstaff seemed amazingly unimpressed at the insane man's exertions across from Peruggia. '*Strangolapreti alla bergamasca. Una bottiglia di Lombardia, per favore. Due calici.* Have mercy on me.'

'Cruel despot,' the man shivered, eyes raised to heaven, 'this one is so different from the wiry, gallant youth I had hoped for, singleminded, confident, fairsightfarsight. *This*,' eyes still heavenward, his voice tremoring now, actually gesturing at Peruggia as if he were a mannequin in a window, Doctor Tulp's cadaver, '*is a failure in progress.*'

'You're a reject. You're worthless. You uncontrasted, boring little insult to my intellect. Four F's. Three squares won't be enough to save you.' The *strangolapreti* arrived, weird masses of gnocchi that, perplexingly, landed in front of Peruggia. The wine appeared coevally, one glass to Peruggia, one to the raving stranger, who nearly fell over himself dumping alcohol first into his glass—one *second* layover—and then into his gullet, draught after draught after draught.

Peruggia stared at the alien goblet, whose contents too seemed to cringe away from him, crawling and climbing the sides of the glass. And the lunatic across the room stared at him, bored holes through him with fury and malice. Peruggia instantly thought of the ancient Romans' habit of sweetening wine with *sapa*, grape juice laced with lead acetate—plombous sugars to sweeten *vino cotto*...

'Are to too stupid to know how to eat?' the stranger slurred, words lurching in oxblood calligrams. 'Is that how unfit they make heroes now?'

Finally, Peruggia's fork nibbled a few ends off the *strangolapreti*, and just as he swallowed the fragments, the stranger roared anew.

'*Strangolapreti!* Priest chokers! Ha! If *only!*'

Peruggia, mortified: 'Do I know you? Is this why you're covering me with such abuses? Have I done wrong?'

'Drink your wine,' seethed the stranger with leaden words, and the stranger's voice was only more wet cement, and for a few minutes then, Peruggia couldn't catch a word. But then, clear as conscience, he heard the man, still fixing him with his eye, threatening him with gestures and glances and muttered injuries, say: 'Vincenzo Peruggia. Male. Date of Birth October

8, 1881, Dumenza, Italy. No fixed abode, no return address. Too few brains. *Fail.*'

'Huh?'

The man stared him down, gunbarrel eyes. 'You insignificant vat of horror. What right have you...?'

Peruggia cut him short, lamely: 'I'm here to meet somebody.'

'*Of course you are.* Eat your priest chokers, you are smoke, you are useless. At least tell me if you have it.'

Peruggia was lost, his thoughts flightless, headless.

'*Do you have it?*'

Peruggia thought of Brass Corners. 'Uh, yes. I have it in the coat room.'

'*You left it in the coat room?!*'

The man threw his glass at Peruggia, and wine flew bloodspatters.

C'est l'histoire future, rappel des demains
   Inexpérimentés, des jours non encor vécus
   L'horreur des nuits, les bonheurs des jours non-cousus
   Dans la tapisserie que cout le Temps, l'emprunt

Du Temps à lui-même, des douleurs le long train
   Echarpant son épaule, un fil qu'il aura tendu
   A travers nos jours, afin que n'oublient nos os crus
   Les jours cachés dans notre moelle, dans nos reins

Résisteront-ils nos os ? Notre dos sera fort
   Pour survivre ? L'esprit, au plus profond du puits
   Du passé, tiendra-il le faix de l'avenir ?

Qu'elle me pèse, ma vie !, cette vie où ne dort
   Le spectre de demain, désespérant l'esprit
   Du poids écrasant de tant d'années à venir

This is future history, memory of tomorrows
   Not yet experienced, of days not lived yet
   Joys of light unseen, horrors of nights still unset
   In time's spinningwork, histories that time borrows

From herself, carrying the long train of sorrows
   Draped over her shoulders, chains she will one day let
   Play out across our days, lest our bones forget
   Days not yet wrested from the depths of our marrows

Will our bones have the strength, will our backs somehow bear
   The burden? Will our mind, drawn from its wells by care
   For days past ever heft the future's future sum?

How daunting this life of mine, this life that won't spare
   Me fear of tomorrow's chasm, my mind so aware
   Of the immeasurable weight of years to come

* * *

Grabbing at straws, grab at anything you can

It was dark, a feeble pool of light surrounding a dying candle. It was a smell of leather and oiled wood; there were rooms on the Island where light never penetrated—it could be day outside, it could be a moonlit night, it could be a devil of a wind blowing outside, it could be Christmas or New Years, Philippe Auguste would never know this deep in the heart of the Palais. All he knew was that his little squarefootage of France was dark indeed, and whether it be day or night, he couldn't bring himself to sleep—or look into the cold light of the northern sun—until he had come to understand just where to point his nose. A page stood at the king's shoulder, feeding him playing cards—'give them to me randomly, Page, different order every time'—which Philippe would in his turn spin out on the table; in function of how near they landed to the candle, he could spot a name, a face—*talented folk, his staff*—scrawled over the card's value.

He had started out having his chesspieces all painted up, little emblems, little blazons for each of his adversaries at home and abroad—*what will it really take to take back an Aquitaine, defeat the whole damned world?*—but then he didn't have enough pieces to cover all the men and women, each infinitely more powerful than he, arrayed against him, arrayed against each other, and he couldn't endure seeing *anybody* labeled a pawn.

They're either all pawns, or they're all—each and every one—kings

He had next tried playing with the names as a chart on a hide, but he kept running out of space on a single hide, so he then had new hides pinned up against the first, a whole herd of Enemy running free up and down his walls, some lining up to trample him, others to gore him, others plunging toward their own horizon. Soon the hides were a tapestry in their own right, and each time he pierced into this dark room, he felt the hides like shadows haunting him, each hide bearing names restless, names moody and dire. Yet the names just seemed too static, too unreal for Philippe to conceive of them as men who would willfully put him to the sword. 'Cut it all up, it's driving me nuts to see them all like a family tree.' So his men came, shears in hand, ready to flay it all to ribbons, but Philippe Auguste stopped them.

'No, wait. Do something with it. I'll wear them as a cape. I'll pile them on my bed.'

And he made his enemies into his clothing, into his bedding, and he pulled them close under his chin to remind him of the stakes: his enemies encroaching on him from all sides, at all times.

The idea, then, of inking names and faces onto a deck of cards had seemed a natural one, and he found he could spread his cards in any order he wanted, sometimes ordering them, too, into complex, overlapping genealogies, then smearing them into chaotic new piles, looking for some new combination that might somehow defeat them all.

But each time, the combinations would reveal themselves lethal to him.

* * *

The Black King. Henry Two, Plantagenet. Philippe barely had to flip his wrist, and there he was. Rumor was that he had already transplanted his court to Aquitaine, to Chinon, a noyautage of extreme audacity, a great big molarcracking stone in the center of the peach.

The Queen. *Eleanor.* Philippe's heart skipped, failed.

The Black Jack, Richard, the Plantagenet's son, the knave, the knight, the perfect vassal, the picture of high sacred knighthood Philippe had known in his heart ever since hearing the first romances read. Who was he? Was he a man or a fiction? How could a single man embody so many ideals of this corner of Europe, how could one man incarnate as luminous an image of holy feudalism? Philippe found himself wishing—*devoutly wishing, a prayer*—to meet this Richard in person, and not necessarily to defeat him, either, but just to be near him, learn from this man's trajectory, from his very bearing, from the warbling thrum of his voice, his way of holding a glass, of drawing a sword, of taking a woman.

Everybody knew that Richard had been the Plantagenet's second son; when the heir presumptive—Richard's elder brother—died a few months ago, it was certain that Richard would break through the mist, upset the hierarchy and become a true force; Philippe felt a kinship and fear every time he thought of Richard, just as he might feel standing next to a great war horse: vital and dangerous and magnificent.

Geoffrey, the Ace of Spaces, was Henry's next son after Richard, and would have to mop up the crumbs left by the feeding frenzies occurring above him. He would be denied the Heir's take by Richard, yes, but he would likely miss the Spare's take, too: he was even more negligible than the faltering man his younger brother. Even if little brother John were to be locked up forever behind a vow of silence and poverty, there would be precious few scraps that hadn't already been accounted for by Richard's vital grasp and the greed of John's monastery; Geoffrey would have to sue the Vatican just to see even.

The other Black Jack, then, was John, the Plantagenet's next son after Geoffrey, was tainted goods. He was the failed knight, he wore the last-son complex like a drapery of chains... Philippe recognized the pattern, a man built on his own father's template. Forgettable, negligible, the imperfect *shadow* of his brother Richard. The instant Richard rises another notch closer to their father's rank—the Plantagenet could choke on a crust of bread, it could be that simple, a tripping step caroming England's and Aquitaine's fates into Richard's hands—and they will let John, the Spare, dry on the vine, die on the vine.

Expect John to spend the rest of his days in a monastery

The Joker (Philippe thought grimly) was Heinrich Four, the German, who had stumbled into the Holy Emperor's throne in Rome. A piston, a lever, a powerful pack horse, could push in any way he chose, handle with care, approach from the front or sides, reassuring tones, to be caressed, not whipped. *Watch the eyes, watch the eyes.*

And the two other Jacks, the Count of Angoulême—he's got land to spare, threatened (Philippe was sure) by the Plantagenet—and Lusignan of the March, with a daughter and a tipping sense of loyalties. Angoulême and

-Passacaglia-

Lusignan will need some careful attentions, will need to be known, thoughtfully courted, curated, carefully positioned.

And in this way, Philippe was dealt his cards, memorizing their shapes, their hefts, their interconnectednesses, the invisible bridges and interstices to be strengthened by a word, a letter, a show of teeth or horns, a show of soft flesh, an offering of tribute, a hand proferred in peace, in manipulation, in unholy alliance.

And the cards piled into new shapes, ragged fans fluttering open near the candle's flame, the shape of Aquitaine's destiny played and displayed as a highly mathematical game of chance, an array of the fates of nations as a dream in the failing light.

Philippe pulled his cape higher on his shoulders as the cards fell.

Nine of hearts   Ace of diamonds   Four of clubs   Seven of spades   A Three   A Six   Another Nine

* * *

Where is the center of mass in this great engine?

It was night; Philippe knelt in a tiny chapel in the marshlands just upstream from the Island; rude oil lamps lit the tiny sanctuary, smearing it with a resined glow, tar and honey amber. There is no reason for a man to be awake at all, much less in a place like this, at a time like this, unless you were a bandit or a mystic.

He realized he easily qualified for the mystic role in this little scene. He wore the cowl of a monk, and his face was deep in the shadows of his hood.

Three other shapes sat in this close space, each one cloaked thickly, each one in a different corner of the chapel—mere yards away, true, yet miles away from him in their dark lives' paths... Philippe couldn't help but believe that this group of four men—himself and his dark comrades—held up the architecture of his frail little state, each a corner of a tipping edifice.

They might as well be masked; they are nothing short of thieves, shadows soaking in sights and sounds of distant rooms, mysteries and magics of other courts

Philippe didn't stir. Kneeling still: 'Upon you, Spies,' Philippe's voice rasps in the darkness, 'rest all my life's ambitions.'

The spies shift under their dark cloaks. This is language that turns the blood.

* * *

'*You*,' Philippe Auguste's voice having shifted imperceptibly to address one of the corners of the chapel, a ventriloquist throwing his voice toward one of the dark shapes, 'have been chosen because you are the very mists of this labyrinth, and your city needs its son—its best and its worst son—to be silent and cunning. You have never set foot off of this Island: you know my heart only as a man knows his neighbor's gate, and should you be caught, I know you couldn't trace the geometry of roads—the real and the symbolic roads—leading back to your home.

'*You will go to the Plantagenet.* You are to learn what he eats, where he sleeps, the color of his eyes, the colors of his moods. Find out where I can tease a space open in his armor. Seduce the man's lovers, taste his food, tune his instruments, hold his chair. The Spy sees but is unseen, he is hidden in plain sight, he is the warp and weft of the Plantagenet's tapestries, the ink of his histories, the rhyme of his songs, insinuating into his ribcage to know the stepped rhythm of his heart.

'We will send men to retrieve you once we are certain you have watched and learned, once we are certain you have *become*, to the extent that a man can, a Plantagenet, *the* Plantagenet. We will come when you least expect it; our retrieving you may be nothing short of your kidnapping. Learn, remember, survive your time away—*ô stranger in a strange land*—survive our attempt to bring you back, and you will be rewarded beyond your wildest dreams.'

The first spy disappeared into the night.

* * *

Philippe's voice shifted again; the second spy knew he was next in line—Philippe could hear the man's breath catch in his throat as he strained to hear his orders.

'*You*,' he guttered, hands still clasped in prayer, 'have been chosen because you are the ferryman, the man at the very threshold of the universe of the known order and the great darkness of the infinite blackness of the Beyond.

'Speaking frankly, brother: your king understands that you have known both sanity and insanity, and that still you have the courage to point your bark straight ahead into the jaws of chaos. You will never know the admiration this city has for you, ô troubled soul, for you are at once *Us* and the *Other*, a man both familiar and alien.

'You will go to find John, son of the Plantagenet. You will recognize him because he is already like you, Brother: he, too, is alone on his craft, but instead of a simple raft drifting, turning across the gentle Seine, he is on a great ship in the darkness, and we have greatly desired to help him in his distress. Our king, our Philippe Auguste, wants a kinship—a brotherly understanding—with this lost brother, so that he can bring him help and hope, steer him to a safe port.

'Return with news of his friendship, and your king will reward you. He will call you his ambassador.'

And the man disappeared into the night like a shadow.

* * *

One last spy was in the dark chapel with Philippe. Philippe rose. He could feel the man watch him as he stepped to the altar, could almost feel the man's heart race as he took a candle from the altar.

He is shocked by my audacity. He doesn't know who I am, cannot even suspect that I had this very chapel built; that here, in this place, this city, in this lonely chapel at least, I am Defender of the Faith

Just wait until he hears what I have in store for him

* * *

'You, friend... I know you overheard the conversations between me and your fellow sp... *patriots,* and I know you know, then, that each man before you has had a different avenue by which not just to spy on, but to assail House Plantagenet: the first to observe, invisibly. The second to befriend, charitably. You must know, too, that your aim is higher, better than that of the men preceding you. And infinitely more difficult and—befitting you—more noble.'

And now Philippe is seated just before the cloaked man. In his left hand is the burning taper, in his right, a deck of cards. He offers the top card.

The man's right hand moves forward, nearly imperceptibly, his finger hovering over the cards, hesitating. Then, deciding, his fingers slip the top card from the deck.

The Jack of spades. The spy holds it closer, to read the writing in the wan light. Philippe instinctively holds the taper up; the spy reads in the amber light.

'This says *Richard the Lion's Heart, House of Plantagenet.* You mean to say that *he...?* Don't you kn...'

Philippe interrupted him with a simple gesture: offering the deck of cards again.

The man's hand trembled over the cards. Finally, his fingers descended to the deck, drew the next card, fearfully.

'Wha...? This says *Geoffrey, House of Plantagenet...*'

'Yes it does.' The rest of the deck disappears back into Philippe's cloak, hidden now in silent rustles of fabric.

'But I...' The spy's voice caught in his throat.

'Surely you knew,' said Philippe, his voice a haunting in the darkness, 'what your mission would be before you even arrived. *It's been your mission since the day you were born...*'

His hand now reached forward, grasped the two cards, deftly folded them over one another, Geoffrey's and Richard's names crumpled together.

'It doesn't look like it now, of course,' said Philippe, 'but don't you know that in time, *ô Geoffrey, Second Son of the Plantagenet,* that I could become your very best friend?'

Bien croire à l'existence d'une galaxie
   Lointaine, sans que (terrestres) mes yeux
   Ne sachent la discerner dans les pales cieux
   Comme un radeau perdu parmi vagues ravies

Déchiffrer énigmes, chercher clé à mon mieux
   Pour ouvrir la porte du ciel, savoir qu'un prix
   M'y attend, mais carte sans légende renie
   Ce continent inconnu à tous sauf à Dieu

Mon Amour, ma Flamme, pardonne-moi ceci :
   Que mon cœur tienne à toi, mais mon œil piteux
   Te perde à l'orage. Quoi, mon œil ? Moi aussi...

Toi seule, Amante, peux guérir mes yeux noircis
   C'est toi le prix pour la foi au fond du cœur pieux
   Le prix saint pour mon pauvre cœur que voici

To have spent a life knowing a galaxy's
　Existence in the heavens, yet having not eyes
　Clear enough to discern it from palest skies
　A life raft dissimulate among stormy seas

To puzzle out enigmas, pick through countless keys
　To open Heaven's door, to know that such a prize
　Exists, but the legend on my one map denies
　Sight of continents that all glimpse but no one sees

My love, my heart's fire, won't you forgive me for this:
　A heart clings to faith in your presence, but eyes miss
　You in the great turmoil? My eyes have. -I- have.

You, Love, are the cure for eyes careless, eyes sightless
　You the one reward for my heart's faith, and your kiss
　My holy prize for finding you, you my heart's salve

***

But gold is refined in furnaces, El, and perhaps the perfection of my love is paid for by centuries spent in the refiner's fire? For what if my love for you is the highest fraction of my being, my life—what else do I have but my life, my forty years?—and what else have I to offer you but the very best of who I am, annealed, purified, distilled in the cauldron?

***

I have often, in my writing, maintained a document parallel to the one I'm working on, and as I work, thoughts and fragments of thoughts that should otherwise be edited out get pasted into the new document, the idea being (originally) that I shouldn't ever lose anything that comes to mind—for my thought is my thought, certainly no trivial part of my being, more Mine than should warrant deletion—and so as my work grows and evolves, so does this parallel document.

Now I have never called this other document 'secondary' to the first, have never hierarchized it as such, have never wanted to demote it to the realms of Failed Thought, of Lesser Reality, of displacement parallax. Instead, I have always revisited this Other Place, and have always found the ideas in it to be higher, more poetic, a better glimpse into my person than the other document (the first one!) could ever hope to be. And I watch it grow, and at a point, it Becomes, it Is, it rises to its own, higher place.

It's funny, because I realize just now that I've always called this parallel document 'my Dross File'—and when I look up 'dross', I find that it's the fine film of rare minerals that forms on the surface of molten metals.

I offer you then, El, the finest of my life; drain off the heavy, molten mass of years past—use that part to build a battleship or a goddamned cannon or something, I don't want it any more—and take the distillate fraction—higher, finer, better, more perfect—for yourself. Make the finest part of me into part of you, and you'll be making it finer yet.

***

I think often—and fondly—of the first time I saw the great spiral nebula of Andromeda through a telescope. Of course we've all seen pictures of the wondrous thing, we all know the warp of its rim, the tilt of its plane—and I know that you in particular, El, have a special place in your heart for such beautiful things, things higher and better and farther, of geometric perfection—but no one ever told me what it might really be like when I actually laid my real-life eyes on it.

It's dimmer than you think it would be, should be, surprisingly so: obviously the glossy pictures we see in Popular Science have all been taken from rarefied peaks, through stunning leaded optics, with exposures of an hour or longer. But in realtime, through a standard backyard backpack Newtonian, in the cold of your thickest sweater, it is a fair sight more... personal. It is still a nebula of colorless light, not a galaxy of individual stars, and the first impression you get is that it is immensely energetic. Energetic is not the word... It is a powerhouse. You get the sense that all hundred-billion of your stars are there, churning out phenomenal wattage of radiation... Just twirling there in space, burningburningburning for you, for me... A core of cold heat and dark light, a fluid crystal of fire and ice, a smudging jewel through my widening pupil.

The very weave of the universe stretching and flexing beneath its weight, a hundred-billion solar masses, just for my eye to soak up.

And I think, I've known this was here all along, why didn't I just look? Why didn't I just go ahead and change my life forever.... back then?

* * *

I heard your voice for the first time today.

* * *

My Love is an alto.

We used to say—only half-joking—that 'an alto is a soprano that can read music'. *I have always had a thing for a good alto voice, have always listened for the alto part in Bach, am continually in awe of the altos in Mozart's Kyrie, from the Requiem—athletic, sharpened, spare, intensely intellectual (for how else can a vocal part survive within a texture so dense and magnetic?).*

Moreso, I think of the deep, luscious altos in Barber's reread of his famous string adagio, to the text of Agnus Dei. Something about the word 'anonymous' makes my skin crawl, but the fact of his altos having such a dark, creamy role in the wide, rich economy of the erstwhile motet, is immensely appealing to me.

That alto part is right now running in the back of mind. -Running- the back of my mind, a carrier signal, a channel by which some other broadcast may travel.

That other broadcast, my El, is you.

I could easily see you shoulder-deep in an alto section, a great stirring exertion to make Barber a real, living man again, a human being resuscitated into the realm of live sound.

And I could easily see myself the man conducting this grand Passacaglia, my hand rising and falling, your voice rising and falling with it, a grand tapestry of yours—and others'—voice, your voice having become a shared history with me, you and me together, alone, with the other four parts shifting and folding around us. They call Barber's music 'gloomy', but I think it is dark and rich, a great oxblood tapestry to wrap ourselves into.

* * *

I am perhaps a bit obsessive, but I have long thought that I should learn the singing range of the love of my life. And so I'll tell you that you are— by all evidence—G3 to about B4, that is, from the g (below middle-c) to the b (above c). Something about having that intimacy with something as physical, and yet as ethereal, as your voice. Has any man known your voice like this before?

I like your range, your sandy timbre, your gentle melody.

No, I love them.

Why didn't we think about calling each other earlier? How could we stand not knowing what each other sounds like? Surely, I had in mind calling you from the very moment of our first meeting, didn't I? Or perhaps you were in the realm of the unknowable, destined to dance behind the mists of imagination and longing.

Now, of course, I have the task of reconciling this lovely, wavering voice I heard today, with the lovely, ethereal beauty of your face. This won't be easy, but perhaps in time...

* * *

I've sent you a bit of music. An understatement, really: I've sent you some of the finest music mankind has ever created.

It's the Aria from Bach's Goldberg Variations.

It's really a slippery little tune. You listen to it, you feel it's been there all along, just waiting for tender new ears to fall onto; just an inevitable, gentle melody, long arabesques, little Schenkerian praxes that seem to go on forever, so sweet, so simple.

Not really. Not if you've ever seen the score.

Half of the Aria is in its subtle—but neverending—ornamentation, each one slightly different from the one preceding it: mordant, half-mordent, double-mordent, mordent-trillo. The fact that Bach helpfully made an accompanying sheet, each ornament written out in full so that you'd know the exact length of a trill, the exact shape of a turn, is only there to humble the proud. I hear there are numbers of cold wars, hot rivalries and longstanding feuds between the most rarefied of musicians, each claiming the high ground in Bach's Ornaments, fierce to the point of daring to actually record opposing organists and slowing the playback later in a studio, just to demonstrate once and for all that x or y turn didn't end on the upper note, that x or y trill was meter-dependent rather than free etc.

'The reason they take it so seriously is because the stakes are so low,' I can hear one of them say.

I managed to teach myself the Aria a few years back. Had to get out Bach's guide to ornamentation, renotate them all back into the score as if they were metered-in, and learn them all rote, no flexibility whatsoever, no High Art at all.

But with the ornaments (somewhat) mastered, the dips and turns of Bach's melodic plan turn into the next hurdle. G-major, D-major, e-minor, A-major (preparing for D-major, the dominant, this is stuff our ear can anticipate)... all this is very well and good, until you find yourself in something really distant—B-major? The hyperdominant... really?—and I just can't keep them straight anymore.

I'll play what I can for you over the phone. You'll hear me punctuate my crude performance with little Tourette's-like outbursts as I forget where I am, as I forget what the hyperdominant even is, as I plunge into the heart of darkness, Agyan ka andhera, 'Oh the lightlessness of ignorance....!'

* * *

You have to be an obsessive to know this, but the Goldberg Aria is a reprint. Bach had first written it for his second wife, Anna Magdalena—his Love, his Life—into a little notebook of inventions and 'pièces de circonstance' he put together to amuse her. One Hell of a gift. Can you imagine a love song from the same pen that wrote the Mass in B-Minor? Naturally (as I myself have found) Bach had a very high opinion of the keyboard virtuosity of his readers and their ability to decipher his florid ornaments and thorny harmonic plan. I'm barely up to it, can only just imagine what kind of musicianship Anna Magdalena demonstrated...

I should put an effort into building a little Aria of my own, for you. I honestly don't know if I'd ever be up to the task: how to just -make- a melody, so natural, so perfect, so limpid is beyond me. I'm just barely capable of spotting with my eye the perfections of Bach's writing, let alone play them, let alone imitate them...

I now realize: I am simply in despair.

It is late. I think I'll forego trying to sleep—I'm a little worked up, struggling with the problem of teaching myself to write like the acknowledged master, the final arbiter, the ultimate lawgiver of modern Western music—and instead take a little walk, clear my head, dream of you, dream of writing something of beauty for you.

* * *

The light in my room is a single seven-watt amber bulb in an old retreaded church light, all gothic and rich and gorgeous. They had sold me the lamp for a song, and I can see why: they had horrific pastel glass in it, pink and green and cream, and there was nothing to redeem it except for the fact that it was, by all accounts, a gothic church lamp, carrying within it nothing but the authority of its former owner.

It was a snap to pop out the old glass—intact, have to keep the originals as a shape template—and have something higher and better cut for it. 'Oh, but you should get something bright and cheerful,' was the glassworker's cheerful word, holding the now-glassless lamp up by its chain, 'you know, something upbeat and pastel. Salmon pink or mint ice cream or something.'

Obviously.

I opted for panels of the deepest ruby red, of deep-space blue and honey amber.

(I find out you make honey amber glass by stirring flakes of pure iron into the glass melt; depending on the valence of iron that makes it in—this having to do with the amount of oxygen present as the iron hits the surface of the

hot glass, how it reduces in the heat—you can get winebottle green or this delicious amber of mine. It is a mystery, it is a puzzle, which iron glass you end up with, a mystery already solved only in the flyleaves of ancient grimoires.

To get blue—and not just blue but blueDeepFieldblue, like the one I bought for my lamp—you have to flake copper into the melt.

And the only way to get ruby red—Philosopher's Stone Red—is to get a pen-knife and scrape a fingernail's worth of pure gold into the glass melt, use your wedding ring or a communion chalice, it's all the same. Upon first firing, the gold glass turns a ghostly, translucent white, nearly pearlescent. Upon the second firing—annealing the gold glass—the deep sanguine ruby color emerges finally.

They say the ruby/gold glass is the color of Christ, the color of Apollo, of poetry and the sun; the first firing is the entombment, the annealing is the resurrection. That the south rose window in Notre Dame of Paris be principally of ruby/gold glass is telling.

They say that the deep blue of copper is Venus' color—the planet, the goddess, they are all one—and that copper is associated with things such as love philters. The north rose window, of course, all bluegrey, all bleu de Guérande, the tinny coppery soils of Celts, the blue of Mary's cowl.

And of the seven noble metals, iron is the one that burns. The one that makes up my blood.)

As I stand outside of my room, two a.m. in the garden of night, with your new Aria running over and over in my head—the first phrase of it at least, the first sentence of the paragraph—I can see my lamp in my window—gold, copper, iron—turning gently on its long chains, holy and dark, cycling between ruby and blue and amber. And I wonder where you are tonight, the Venus on my horizon.

* * *

It is five-fifty a.m. now. You are still dreaming in silence.

Venus is shaking herself free of the ashes of the Piedmont.

It is dawn on my left shoulder. And bathed in copperblue, I am coming to find you.

* * *

Sometimes I wonder if my heart is still beating. Othertimes, I'm so sure it's about to beat itself out of this hard world. Sometimes, I'm the most self-aware person you'll ever meet. Othertimes, I'm the least self-aware.

Today, it's my heart leading me to you, an incessant, insistent thrum. This is not just some euphemism, some gentle, precious image, some allusion to love poetry's insistence that the heart—that patient little knot of muscle—is somehow the seat of our emotions. Instead, El, instead... for each mile I cross separating me from you, I feel my heart gaining some kind of new purchase in my chest, more and more powerful as the miles peel away behind me.

I just may make it to you alive.

Surely my mind is playing tricks on me, and my heart is simply obeying some neurochemical brainstem outburst—push push push push—blindly willing for an arrival (an arrival, Salvation, anything) before my heart decides it's had enough and simply coughs me out of existence.

'Get some control, then... Just as your thoughts are yours to own, so is that battered little peck of flesh about to make you tear apart at the seams, so get a handle on it...

'I know no mantras to cure a flailing thrashing heart, and my prayers to the Almighty have never been answered, not even once. A heart only has so many beats before it can beat no longer; don't waste them on Something Easy like driving a car... Sure, your El is at the end of this long grey line, stretching out under the Morning Star, but whatever you do, don't give up the ghost before you see her: fall down at her feet if you must, at least know happiness once before you leave this planet...'

Venus on my shoulder, Venus rising, Venus accompanying me all the way to you, El. Yet I am not Venus—you are—I am something more like a Pluto: dark, flesh-bound—all too fleshly—hidden in shadows... I am the underworld, the man born under a planet he has never seen, so dark and forbidden and cunning and morose. How could I be farther from Earth than to be ruled by Pluto's mysterious influences, three times farther from the Sun, nine times darker than any man could be here on Earth... I am nocturnal Pluto, the eternal blackness of deep space... Waiting one day to be discovered, uncovered, resurrected.

And Mercury is the swift messenger... my heart speeding toward yours with words of love. Will I know what words will flood from me as I see you, eyes-on, for the first time?

And Mars again, Vulcan, gentle Venus' fierce husband. Details like this make my skin crawl—

And Uranus, the Seven, the inventor god, slowly awakening to his desire for knowledge, for wisdom, for sexual gratification... Oh, Gæa!

'Keep it together, Vicus... your one job is to keep your wheels here on Planet Earth...'

...Yes, and Earth, too. Are there hearts like mine in these other, outer realms, looking down on Earth with something approaching pity, ô pauvre homme insensé, trapped down here on my own gravity well of the mind?

Saturn the thief... At once clarity and hiddenness... the ruling planet of Capricorn—o Vicus, you January star!—

Nine... One... Four... Seven... Three... Six... Nine...

* * *

All plans come to naught. What conflict in the human psyche: consciously, to unfurl my very winningest—smile, swagger, gallop of words—but the unconscious soul in its deep well, the reptilian brain in its cold dialtone, the mammalian brain all a-wire with fighting and fleeing, each conspiring mutiny against the higher mind, against my very person... O Mercury, slight star of wispy dialectic, logic that shifts and wanes with the passing of the hour, the turn of phrase that shifts the finer logic to mere solipsis to tautology, vain words of courage and faith.

'You will get through this,' telling myself, 'if you only just fail to kill yourself kicking on up onto her porch, four steps at once.'

So two steps, two steps, slowmotion triple axel.

'Do you think she saw me not fall?'

And your radar must've come to life as I first crossed into your time zone, then into your zip code, then turned onto your street; my skidding step to your porch got you up from your chair, and—do I bow do I run do I straighten my tie do I get down on one knee—and the promised beauty of a galaxy unsuspected lays deep basins into the gravity fabric of my being, and before you are even there, you are there, behind the glass door in the light of your livingroom, your smile warm and sad, the weight of ages past and future memory my rotten marriage and your compassion for my kimberlitic potpourri tear-the-lost-and-found-down-for-a-lost-penny mind on your lovely, meltinghearted face...

The door creaks against its spring. And I am yours, entirely yours, nothing but yours, my arms around your legs, my glasses thrown all askew, my tears a glistening record of a forever-broken heart.

I have found you, and will never let you go, not let another second pass without telling you of my love, my forever love, my love for you.

O qu'elle est longue, ma vie, qu'ils sont bien trop lents
   Mes malheurs, trop lourde cette croix si marrie
   Trop froids ces jours, cette chaîne qui avarie
   Mes épaules-mon dos n'est pas si résistant

O rouges fourneaux luisants, ô raffinerie
   De cette masse, percevant ors et argents
   De parmi les cendres froides de mon cœur mourant
   Métaux extraits (au prix de feu) de mes scories

O ma vie, ajoutant mes propres joies aux vôtres
   Vous me les repayez la peine de dix hommes
   Mon cœur l'étoile qui meurt aux lueurs allégés

J'offre mon amour, vous le versez sur un autre
   Or mais, quand je vous prie de mes jours abréger
   Cruelle, vous ne faites qu'en doubler la somme

Oh Life of mine, you are long, you are much too long
   For me to bear, too great a mass, too dark a cross
   A cold chain of days too heavy to lay across
   My bending shoulders—I am simply not that strong

Oh refining fire, searching out the shining gloss
   And glint of silvergold thread and grain from among
   My dark cold stone heart's dead ash, bright coinmetal wrung
   From me, nothing left of the flame but its drab dross

Oh Life, you pour my life's joys onto my brother
   And pay back the favor with full-on ten men's strife
   My heart a dying star, a fading light aways

I give you my love, you give it to another
   But when I pray you—beg you!—to abridge my life,
   Cruelly you double the endless count of my days

***

Don't think, just catalogue

Lists won't can't harm you; a list is just a list

Otherwise, you'll worry yourself right into the arms of the Devil

Old Havoise still had her eyes pressed shut, her chin to her chest, and her heart was a pacing, rending engine vainly wanly resisting her mind's urge to claw open the old lady's eyes and force her gaze down into the deep blackness. She knew she had demons, tenthousand years of them, she struggled to clear her mind of them, blankslate her mind, but couldn't seem to hold the curtain open, free and clear. *Build your list, girl* a good, safe list like the old *summae* she had had to read so many years ago, *just try for a simple crowd of words*, unwind that spool...

She started her list with res—things—just as the old dialecticians had, *De Trinitate* by Hilary of Poitiers, *res* are real, *res* are demonstrable, they are mere fabrics and knots and threads and breaths.

Save the signa—the signs, the meanings, the terrors, the levels above your head, above your caste in this low world—*for later*.

There will be plenty of time to worry about them

***

First... Those evil little chips of calcium everyone foolishly called *her fingers*... those nervous, dry creatures, half of their own mind, clittering and clittering away everyday, little Mercury fireflies, sometimes scattered and unruly—unsafe little things!—sometimes neat and ordered and under her own gravity... Horrid little shrews, aren't they?, blind as blind gets, yet all ornery and restless and moody.

Why you betray me now thought Havoise *why you choose now to break rank on me... I don't even have the strength to resist their trembling*

She thought of her fingers, thought of their knitting-together in her mother's womb, nothing more than a pin's drop then, nothing more than smooth, neat little seeds of bones really. She thought of the marvels they had made for her back when they were under her command, a lifetime a stitching had poured out of her. But even now, she could feel them under the Devil's control, a tremens pulsing away dumbly, mocking her.

You'd think I had never even been given fingers, never been given the right to govern my own person

Havoise pressed her eyelids together even tighter, pressed her chin harder into her chest.

What do you expect me to do, encumbered in my years?, -dictate- a tapestry?

* * *

Torsten was hardly worth his name, hardly worth the breath it took to say it aloud.

The girls around Falaise—young Havoise and her friends—all saw the young clerk trudge through town, walking alongside his wagon, sick as death. It was the middle of January 1028, and a brutal confluence of wind, cold and the heaviest rains in a generation had taken their toll on the town… they could only imagine the troubles they had exacted from the boy's account.

Obviously he had drawn the short straw.

The Keep had been watching for him, evidently, but had felt little need to rush out to save his sogging hide upon his arrival at the rock: they took all of a half hour to open the gates to him.

Torsten was there to notarize the birth of the next Duke of Normandy.

* * *

That place just behind Havoise' breastbone—between her breasts, a place known only to her, unreachable even to her, the collision point between her heart and the outside world, planet to planet—was sore and raw, like the flensed skin from a live animal. Yet she knew her skin intact there, knew her skin warm and alive. No, there was no wound visible at her sternum. But the ache was real as a living tumor.

One day... No, one night... should I be caught unawares, miss a turn somewhere between the sanctuary and the scriptorium, left out in the cold some dark night after Mesoniktikon... and when the cold takes me, what will prevent the bears and wolves from finding this tired old carcass of mine, and feast on my meager bones, tear open my sternum with its aching flesh behind it... Only then will the world know the cause of the dark pain lurking there... Will the angel of my destruction find some kind of worm burrowing within?

My heartache is a burrowing larva

Just a list old girl she thought bitterly *No need to invoke the Evil One*

* * *

Res... and *signa...*

The very sign of a lord is his legitimacy. And there are hundreds—if not thousands—of ways to establish it: 'theft, heft or crook' (as a category) covering a goodly number (all of which Havoise had seen during her long life). But a blessed birth is the very first and very best sign of legitimacy usually granted a lord, birth the very enactment of a marriage of convenience—seeing as a man may incarnate the land belonging to him—*the land he belongs to*, more like, *the land he is*—incarnate his titles, incarnate his holdings, the mechanisms uniting him to the Church, to *its* own holdings and authorities and legitimacies... And seeing that a woman, a vessel for dowry—a vessel for land, titles, holdings, that is—herself incarnating her place and title... And this man may cling to this woman, and the child may sanctify their shared power, their common mission.

Yes, that common mission (more likely than not, more frequently than lords usually care to admit aloud) being to Rule The World—and failing that, to rule an ever—increasing fraction of it—a child may bear the hopes and fears of many, many people.

In this world, in this... *Normandy,* the hopes and fears of noble parents could simply not be trusted with a single child—*children die, and more often than not... everybody knows that*—and so the accumulated earthly treasure of a powerful family could (and would) be cast down onto as many children as survived to maturity, best to have many, many children, in hopes that one or more may make it long enough to establish his own legitimacy, at least enough to bear the assaults of a world intent on taking it all away and making it somebody else's.

And should you and your brothers survive (they who were born with the same legitimacy you were born with), they, too, will grow to envy you and assault you, and take it all away, and thrown your dry bones into the fire kissmyhand.

Best build your legitimacy young, better hold your ground from your first breath, better have the claws and the fangs and the horns bared before you even think of sucking a teat.

Best pray you had just been born a blessed birth, a blessed birth indeed, for a noble birth is a fat store not given just anybody, and *you will need all the help you can get.*

* * *

Which is why Torsten was so perplexed to find no newborn child in the Keep at Falaise.

'Where is the child?'

No one, not even Robert the Magnificent (whose eyes were dark with cold wrath, whose hands were hard and horned from the sword, the mace, whose voice smoked and crackled from years of igniting fiery battlecries to curdle the blood), could quite muster the words: he is not here.

Torsten shivered, either a classic fever from a classic Norman winter, or a sudden terror that the child—deformed?—had been left out for the wolves or thrown into the latrine.

'But I am here to legitimize the lad.'

Eyes darted, arrows of secrecy and concern.

Finally, one of Magnificent's armorors—a hard, huge man, the last one you'd ever accuse of delicacy—spoke, words roundabout, secrets curling through them like kites through air.

'Well this child is going to need as much of your legitimizing him as he can possibly stand. You'll need your cloak again, we have some travelling to do. You'll have to be blindfolded.'

* * *

There is no real injury that kills, aside from the heart stopping beating

Havoise knew it was highest vanity to think she knew anything about it, but she was certain there was nothing you could do to a body to kill it, that wasn't by troth bringing about (in the end) the death of the heart.

My heart is in the slow process of dying; you can feel it constrict and slow; you can feel it chill and harden; you can feel its burdens overtake it

And somehow that thought was a comfort for her. *For who else is as aware of their impending death than the one who has felt it overtake her heart over the span of decades?*

One last long hold, and it will be over

And with her eyes pressed shut, Havoise is in a dark halo, and she is unclear whether heartache is the *signa* or the *res*...

* * *

'Good Lord, why is the child *here?*'

Torsten shivers in the threewall. Iodine and oyster had burned his nostrils and turned his stomach for an hour before the armoror thought to snap his blindfold away from his eyes; now it is nearly dawn, and there was the stench of a village... There is no chair in the threewall, and the peat fire pours out far less heat than those quantities of acidic smoke might ordinarily promise.

An inn.

Torsten's skin had taken on the pale sepsis of sturgeon, and the shivering was uncontrollable.

'And you'd think they could do better than a mere fishing village for the first son of Robert the Magn-'

The armoror's gaunted arm cracked into Torsten's head before he could finish; for a moment, he felt sure his eyeballs had been knocked free of their sockets. His head turning and his vision hotly blurred, he immediately vomited onto himself.

'*Think* for a moment, will you? Damnation...'

The threewall was moss and burlap and full of holes—it had obviously only been used for firewood and barrels for the last several months or years, and smelled of wet creosote—and the nearby sound of the Channel helped Torsten know that the tides were no mere fiction in the fog of the village, and as he came back to, he became aware that if he slipped up again, that armoror would be tossing him over a cliff and into the smoothwaving sea.

'What I meant was: it is certainly almost time for breakfast, isn't it...?' he asked flatly, tendrils of vomit stretching to his shirts.

Torsten rubbed his jaw. A newborn wailed in the distance.

* * *

Is there any point in a heart aching—a chemical burn, a cracked tree after a windstorm—as mine does? It's not like it does anyone any good—you burn your finger, the pain makes you flinch, stealing your hand away from a worse burn—but heartache? Your heart, once broken, careens your whole life further into the abyss...

How dare you threaten me into loving more? Haven't I given enough?

Havoise recognizing the darkness rising through her, the larva arching and twisting.

Quit doing yourself in, for God's sake. Res? or Signa?

A heartache, you'd think, is a simple thing, an Object, something to write down, to counterrole... No, it is no churchfire, no housefire, it is no bonfire even—it is nothing but the bed of embers after the burning has ended.

* * *

The sky is lighter, and the wailing gives way to occasional respites paid to imperfect silences—small livestock and the irregular swells of the Channel speak smalltalk now—and the armoror has Torsten by the scruff of the neck, and Torsten feels his feet just slightly less walking and slightly more skidding; he grips his register and his writing kits, fearful of looking drunk as he puppets and cascades through the village.

This threewall was no shelter... it was a scandal of a shelter, and Torsten reeled at the odor. The wetnurse's breasts swelled into one baby's mouth after another, two teats for four children.

'Which one is the child?' The parchment is open; he doesn't dare sit.

* * *

The town of Falaise would see a curious caravan of carts bumping through grimly, the gates of the Keep wide, each cart a half-dozen soldiers, each cart a wetnurse, each cart a drowsing, dondling infant. Torsten the clerk stood by the gate, ticking off his register.

The gates swung closed.

After several minutes, Torsten was at the gate again, this time with a half-dozen sergeants himself. And the strange caravan filed past him, pausing each one as he counted sterling into little leather bags, handing them to the wetnurse, baby still mumbling milkdrunk, wetnurse's itching palms.

'Remember, dear lady,' he said sweetly as the sterling found a warm breast, 'that if we catch sight of you—here or anywhere—ever again, we will be forced to deal with you very harshly...'

Fine eyes would notice that of the sixteen carts bearing the sixteen wetnurses away from the Keep, only fifteen of the wetnurses were still carrying babies. And one was carrying a roll of straw against her breast, and the compact leather pouch of bright singing sterling was many times heavier than the other women's had been.

*　*　*

Rumor flashed through the village, soon to the whole county of Calvados. But life in Falaise hasn't time to gossip, and tannery women still trudging and tromping in the dyeing trenches barely had breath to mutter oaths against the harlot Herleva who had strutted around in the trenches at their sides months earlier... and they wiped their brows with their forearms, no more strength to even think of the bastard that their lord, Robert the Devil, had made her bring into the world, secrets not so secret anymore, not so worthy anymore of the tannerwomen's chatter.

*　*　*

Oh Lord, I am old, and weak, and have suffered so long

What human being hasn't prayed this way: a dark, despairing audience before the Almighty, humanity and humanity's heartbreak both pleading their case against one another?

Oh Lord, have mercy on me, save me from my heartache and take me this very night

The burrowing larva circles, tightens.

* * *

Havoise was nine years old. And awake in her attic nest in the dead of the night, she heard greatboots against the waxed wooden floorboards of the shop's groundfloor far below. She heard a man's stern voice rasping, and recognized her father's smalltalk.

'Late hour, Armoror...'

'Can we speak privately? Duke's business.'

Havoise knew nothing about the business of dukes or sergeants, but knew full well the business of weavers, and there was nothing for a weaver like her father to do in darkest night except to count coins. She wondered how a duke's business might have anything to do with a weaver's.

'What brings you?' Havoise' father said aloud what Havoise had thought, nestled in her attic den.

'The Duke has a son.'

Havoise knew that, everybody knew that.

'...And the boy is in considerable peril. The Magnificent's enemies pretend the boy was born out of wedlock...'

Havoise' father was silent.

'...*and*...' after a moment's pause, uncomfortable silence, Armoror continued '...while the boy is certainly well-protected by The Magnificent's guard...'

'Doubtless.' Havoise' father was matter-of-fact.

'...We are all-too-aware of our inability to properly and effectively strategize against those who would contest the boy's legitimate avenance to the Duke's crown.'

'When the time comes.'

'When the time comes. Right.'

'So you came,' Havoise could see her father turn a chair around, prop himself on his elbows, 'to tell me how imperiled the Duke's succession will be?'

'Not exactly. We have someone. Somebody from the outside.'

'Your pitiful little clerk. Yes, I've seen him.'

'He seems to know what to do to help us better position The Magnificent's son. To take his father's crown.'

'I hope you keep him on, then.' Havoise' father had his usual tone of indifferent businessmaking.

'We hope to. The Magnificent desires it, necessity requires it, and we hope our little clerk can make the Duke's son his only concern.'

'And what does this to do with me, Armoror? This late at night?'

'Our clerk does not want to stay. He finds Normandy sickening.'

'Better sweeten the pot, then.'

'That's what we thought, too.'

'How deep are The Magnificent's coffers?' Havoise' father had hands that gold fit into, fingers the Lord had made for gripping coin; this was language Havoise wasn't surprised in the least to hear from her father's tongue.

'Deep enough. But we feel it necessary to go the extra mile. So that he does his best. So that he feels bound to Falaise.'

'And how do I come in, Armoror?'

The sergeant shifted. 'Your daughter is marriageable, isn't she?'

'Again I ask, *how deep are The Magnificent's coffers?*'

* * *

Havoise felt a hand on her shoulder. It took her a moment to focus: the dying embers of the scriptorium chimney, her candle burned to the stump, new aches in her old spine. She looked around for her walking stick—where had that fallen to?—and her eye rose and fell to the Abbess, half-silhouetted before her, bending to try to see into Havoise' eyes. When their eyes met, the Abbess hove a sigh of relief.

She must have thought I had died here just now

The larva turned, and burrowed in further behind her sternum, and as it dawned upon her that her prayer had not been heard, that *she had in fact not died in her sleep,* her eyes welled with tears.

The Abbess searched the crone's eyes.

'What is a life after all, Havoise?'

'What it always is.' Havoise knew the mechanisms of logic that ran her mind, governed her life. She spoke slowly and softly: the scriptorium was always silent, and she weighed her words to match the holiness of the place and the quiet, crushing sadness in her soul. 'A handful of yarn; some weaving, some stitching, some embroidering. A few loose ends...'

The Abbess sighed compassion and sadness for Havoise. And then, a bit more brightly: 'And what have those magnificent fingers been working on tonight while the rest of us slept?'

Havoise realized only then that her fingers had worked as she slept and fretted and remembered: the tapestry ground was crushed between her tangled hands. She flattened the panel out for the Abbess to see.

'What is *that*, Havoise?'

The shape was embroidered to look like a kite, or a talisman, or an ornate pendulum knocked free of its clock. It hung unreal in the scene, a peacock feather over the men and buildings and horses of this world, a blemish on the heavenly sphere.

It was a harbinger that Havoise had made, an embroidered flame, or a waving whipping handkerchief.

The men beneath it cowered, and Havoise' caption read, *They are marveling at the star.*

'That,' said Havoise, fixing the Abbess with her eye, 'is Doom.'

Sans aucun mot, sans un son, sans même un soupir
  Ton sourcil froncé si prompt, le feu dans ton œil
  Trop sévère ont suffi pour achever mon deuil
  Me faire passer outre, mourir sans mourir

Il y est des frontières qu'on ne puis franchir
  Dans l'espoir de pouvoir retraverser le seuil
  De nouveau, comme si rien n'était. Quel orgueil—
  Déclencher tempêtes puis oser repentir… ?

Que je passe en revue tous mes soldats si chers
  Eux ne sachant revenir de ces sombres plaines
  Ayant passé les portes d'acier de l'enfer

Que je passe les jours et passe les semaines
  Passe les ponts qui mèneraient Apollon en l'air
  Passe l'éternité sans que je n'en revienne

Without a word, without a sound, without a sigh
   Your disapproving eye (and the fire held inside)
   And your arching brow, all feed these tears I've cried.
   To pass away, to pass 'cross... To die, yet not die...

There are frontiers we scarcely dare pass by
   Ever hopeless, helpless, once on the other side,
   To ever cross back over again. What vain pride—
   Unleash storms' fury, then dare repent in reply?

My dearest soldiers pass before me in review
   Not knowing when they might retrace this track
   Having seen the steely gates of Hell, and passed through

I pass the days darkly, withstand each week's attack
   Pass across the bridge to Apollo's heavens true
   Pass away forever, no hope of coming back

***

The Crown is made, built, almost accreted. Every act, every word, every glance becomes history from this point forward

I am the King of France

Kings are made in Rheims, in the great cathedral built over the bones of St. Rémi, first bishop of this place, and for good reason: Rémi had built the very first King of France here, when he made Clovis into a king. Now no one knew where Rémi might be—lost in the turmoil of nations, doubtless, but nobody discounted the possibility that he simply effervesced into space and seeped into the stonework, to become one with the prayers of saints and sinners.

Wonder of wonders, the transformation from mere man, into God's appointed

It was a marvel just how many people could jam into a space like this. The former Duke—now Francis I of France—could barely hear himself think, much less quantify, in the din of thousands. Forget the so-called 'election', forget the 'regalia'—*crownsceptermaindejusticecrown sceptermaindejustice*—it was just a din of humanity, a chaos of France herself, all behind him, acclaiming him as King, begging for his long life, decrying the cruel sting that had taken their old King from their midst while in the very same breath, the very same heartbeat, blessing the life of their new monarch, *Le roi est mort Vive le roi.*

And for a single, sublime moment, a moment where science and history and beauty and a thousand years of nation unite, alight light as a feather upon Francis' faceted shoulders.

For behold, I do not take the Crown, I do not receive the Crown... I ascend to the Crown

And Francis' mind, so very light, so very winged, so very active and ethereal, rose from within his wiry frame and paused over his enmarvelled head. There is incense here, and it forms willowy tendrils of light and shape, the profiles of ghosts, the moan of song and prayer. The old baptistery where Clovis emerged from the healing waters is nearby, in the slanting rays of a thousand candles, and Certon's music is a rich, dense tapestry of angles and loomthreads, and suddenly, Francis is aware that he can no longer discern if it is night... or day. Pillars arc and joust, and he sees beauty and suffering in the red panel glass dedicated to St. Eloi, patron saint of forges and printers and metalworkers, way up here, in the rarefied air of the clerestory.

Francis knew that at some point in this rite of making him sacred, the Holy Spirit Himself was to descend—in the form of a drop of sacred oil—and instill within him the four virtues of kings, but *honestly I don't know how to concentrate on a single insignificant droplet of astringent oil* when there is now so much freedom, and so great a gravitas, and so much space up here, away from all those milling, distant crowds thrilling to watch a man transform, and arc away from his own life, so insignificant now, so distant now, arcing up into the space above, like an ecstatic sparrow *perhaps I am meant to meet the Holy Spirit half-way, caught up in the air and on the prayers of the nation and on the clouds incense makes* darting and spilling and turning and spiraling in this space Up Above, this space reserved for Kings, reserved for Kings, reserved for Kings.

And I become the Crown

* * *

'Well I shouldn't be allowed to touch it. I would cause it harm.'

Peruggia didn't doubt that for a minute.

'For I am David, and your belovd suitcase is Goliath. Sodding philistine, keep it away from me, I'll fell it like lumber.'

Peruggia's diningmate was hardly David, he went by *Apollinaire*, and Peruggia couldn't place his accent: brushstrokes of Paris and Provence and Italy and some Slav in his voice, colorful and drunken and free. Peruggia felt certain—despite the threats and ravings—that this 'Apollinaire' simply didn't want to carry the extra weight; the hatred and the doughy laziness displayed by this man converged, and soon Peruggia suspected some sort of conspiracy against his shoulders and blistered palms and corbatured shins.

Old Nice was a hive, a *buton*, like Venice a maze of forgotten channels silting in, and the dead of night is not so very dead, and Peruggia, Brass Corners warring with his members, hears all manner of strife from open windows in the night heat, the sounds of men making blue deals with the night, the sounds of gates being forced.

'Stone foundations, steel gates and electric whores. Welcome to Paradise. You'll need a map and a compass. Smiles, everyone.'

Peruggia noticed that even when Apollinaire smiled, his eyes did not—was this the effect of the wine?—a rictus rather than a grin, a toxic grimace an atoms'-breadth from the genuine. Definitely cadmium poisoning. His tie too tight, his lips a powerful court of injury, the theater is on fire, and Peruggia followed the man's too-quick step through this maze, a turning, contemptuous labyrinth of corridors and libertines and mafia.

Keep up with the eye of this storm; if you lose him, you're done for

Brass Corners sharp and angry, head a barreling drum, hands a pair of swelling boxers, Peruggia could only be scurrying ratlike, this ain't Wall Street this is a mind's convolutions and fragmentary thinking, and the *strangolapreti* are battling him from within *You take the high road I'll take the low road and now thy will be done* Peruggia devoutly wishes to die.

'What's it going to take to get you to keep up, Failure? They used to hang pharoahs' heads over the edge of the cutting table and pour wax in the dead men's nostrils to keep the him alive into eternity. Will we need to do the same for you?'

Peruggia doesn't understand the reference, but he knows it to be an abuse. He clenches his teeth and sprints, gains ground ahead of Apollinaire.

The fanatic is one who doubles his efforts when he has forgotten his aim ...And for a moment, Apollinaire is taken off guard. When he realizes that this coyote shape, contrite and rumpled, was Peruggia (the little suitcase with the brass corners decided it for him), he sprints as much as his meaty little A-frame will let him; it is an insult to footraces. Peruggia, encumbered and long-suffering, finally loses out to this unencumbered man with no nationality, who, still sprinting away rotund, tools on ahead, turning a corner in the maze.

Peruggia is alone.

* * *

The raiment and paraphernalia of kingship now covering him a foot thick, truth be told he was barely able to raise an arm to receive scepter and hand of justice; he felt his muscles flex under the regalia just as they had done in sparring.

It may be time to exert my muscles' strength a bit in battle

* * *

And Peruggia was at a loss, a real loss, a loss of proportions that startled even him. Blind as a sheep, mired in the swamps of his own despair, the intestinal lengths and interstices of the Niçois Old City underworld, high-end hookers gaping and taunting him from the steps of one tarpaper Early-Modern brothel after another, a polyphony of infinite perplexity.

And Apollinaire's voice echoed through the labyrinth; it was the beatings of the wings of the death angels, and *my Lord how the sapa had corrupted that man's nerve endings, my Lord how his brains must be steam-simmering in it, hot and and sweet and full of iron and irony like a bleeding tooth or a fall down a flight of stairs. What a catastrophic descent, what a vision of human personal pathology: macadamia nuts... absinthe... planecrash.*

And the words lingered in the air, and Peruggia's mind was adrift in them: *Pride, tried, cried, ride, inside... Die by... On tourne sur le talon et retra-*

verse le seuil... Pass 'ways to eternity without coming back... Passer les Alpes et les deserts... Numéro treize, le chiffre de l'enfer... Ingenious minds... Madame, ce seuil qu'on a passé... Sans limites... Must be all about crossing one way— perhaps to cross back? To trespass...

And when will the world learn that it cannot simply thieve treasures from the sacred vaults of its enemies; once the storehouse is looted and dead, you can't expect the orphans not to plot their revenge...?

...There are thresholds you can only cross once without hope of ever crossing back...

* * *

'We are the author of our fortune, I do confess. And here we stand, at the threshold of the Peninsula, the lintel of our future memory! Who will be the man who will cross over with me, who will cross over—perhaps never to return—to wreath himself in glory and timeless fame? What man has seen, as I have, the eternal flame of Rome's triumphs, of the Peninsula's authority— who understands as I do Mother France's role in inventing her own genealogy, her awareness of her mission in the very history of knowledge, science, faith... ?

'Do we tremble, crossing over onto hallowed soil? Do we dare track this savant road with the boots of our homeland—our Provence, our Touraine, our Normandy, our Aquitaine? Are you the man I require, fearless, virtuous, confident of your place in the long line leading from dusty Medes to knowing Greeks to glorious Rome herself—to us? *Oh sweet holy relics of our future memory!*'

And at these words, Francis of Angoulême, first King of France of that name, drew his sword and strode onto Italian soil, the first act of war of his reign.

* * *

Peruggia awoke in a high room, the cruel flush of dawn streaming in directionless through half-drawn curtains.

-Passacaglia-

Apollinaire was there, his cigarette more ash than tobacco, a half-dozen shotglasses lined up in front of him on his blotter, some defeated, some still full. From where Peruggia's head was, he could only see the end of Apollinaire's pen, dipping and bobbing and spiraling.

He had no idea who had found whom, how or when he had crossed from the chaos of the streets into this quiescent space.

'Nice place.'

'Fuck you.'

Viens, Doucette, viens jouer un doux air pour mon âme
   Un plaint crieur, chanson d'amour dans la distance
   Une mélodie morne perçant le silence
   Toute une symphonie, un doux chant, un doux drame

Ces mélodies qui arpentent l'étrange gamme,
   Cette ville sans retour, ces saintes errances,
   Nos plaisirs, nos nuits le champ d'interférence
   Entre les doigts d'un homme et la peau d'une femme

Je t'ai donné ma vie—la fin de mes jours—car
   Mon esprit a ses labyrinthes hantés par
   Passacailles, fugues, errances, et préludes

Et dans ta vie (ma Vie), ma vie y prend sa part
   Et dans tes bras, Musique exerce tout son art
   Tu es devenue pour moi toute mon étude

Come, Love, play for my soul that gentle song again
   That distant song, that longing chant, that plaintive keen
   A mournful melody, where silence might have been
   Whole symphonies, such sweet airs, such dramas begin

These melodies aclimb, those ancient modes within,
   This city for the lost, holy wand'rings unseen,
   Our pleasure, our nights: interference lines between
   A man's fingers together with a woman's skin

I've given you my life, my remainder of days
   The fugue of my dark mind the deepest haunted maze
   Where passacaglias and wand'ring preludes lurk

And in your life, my Love, my love its life displays
   And in your arms, the whole composer's art still lays
   You have become for me my whole life's masterwork

Awake all night thinking of how you like my little flute prelude. That some invention of mine might somehow make you smile, might somehow be a delight to you, might somehow help you to know of my love for you, is an uncheckered happiness to me.

Unreal clarity the evening it came to be, wet sidewalks and wide open skies after the averse, great drops falling from the branches. The South in a spring storm. And I remember how the contours of that melody began to accord to the rhythm of my footsteps, my breathing, my heartbeat. The arcades of the University. The wet leaves on the pavement near Grimaldi, fat drops falling from the high wet leaves as a breath of wind dislodges them, tannins coffeebitter volatilizing from puddles.

Some sort of briny taste as the lowest notes ring grainy; some sort of metallic taste, really, some sort of hot light in high contrast. Synesthesia c-minor, wood tones and bright veins in leaves, my step a hard knocking rhythm on wet pavement, wearing a corner off my old hardrubber heels as my shoes clock through the evening.

There would be other parts of the flute prelude that you'll never hear: little experiments in space becoming live sound in my ears, little experiments of shapes and speed. The word, I think, is 'prolation', exercises in some species of subdividing sonic space, in subportioning the octave, the tactus of tempo and meter. I remember seeing the slow, stately melodies of the prelude as dominos laying across each other in my mind's eye, sound become sight, sound become realworld objects subject to the laws of gravitation and the mechanics of static friction, a domino mandala, a tumulus like you might have seen in pictures of Gavrinis—what, a dome of stacked dominos, a clever round with void space guaranteed within, a void space sketching the intersection of domino and overlap and 32'/sec2, a tannindark plate of fugu, domino wings overlap, an accretion evolution building, hollow bones readying a crane's flapping takeoff.

And the dominos turn to rest on the lengths of their sides, and the whole composition shifts and becomes an arena, an Arles, a Coliseum.

And the dominos turn to stand on their short ends; the same stacking functions impose, and a ziggurat stands in Babylon.

This is the ragged architectural history of your flute prelude (for it is most certainly yours now, no longer mine, for I am no longer worthy now that you know its contours). It now lives in my mind—as it has for the last decade and a half, a low murmur in my temples, sparks in the software—and in your mind now, live sound and real object.

* * *

It is a sign of low-level psychosis to hear music in your head.

I remember a day when I was driving my grandmother through the countryside—Sunday afternoon apple pie, get her out of the Home for a few hours, talk out her memories of Grandpa, memories laying alive after decades of mourning him—when suddenly she says, a propos of nothing:

'This one is so beautiful.'

'What is, Grandma?'

'This one. This song.'

My grandmother's voice is small, compressing into a taut, narrow stream as she ages, hard enough to hear in the blinding silence of the Home, harder yet with road noise and the distractions of driving... So there was no radio; I never put it on when she's there with me. Just the bounding of the car, the hard whisk of other cars' tires on cold pavement. And now her words have startled me.

'Which song is it?' *Tentative. Respect for elders, respect for my Grandpa's memory... have I just missed something, Grandma just putting me back on the rails?*

'Es ist ein' Ros entsprungen.'

It is a reflex to say 'What?' *and put her on the defensive. I suppress* the instinct; thinking quickly: 'I think I know that one, Grandma.' And I do. A Lutheran chorale, a Marian hymn they sing at Christmas Eve.

'I know you do.' I can feel the warmth of her smile: my peripheral vision is a movie of my grandmother with her Graduation Day countenance beaming up at me, it's-okay-to-smile-but-it's-untoward-to-ever-show-your-teeth is my little grandmother, who prays nightly to be taken by the Lord's angel to be back with her husband again. 'It's so nice to hear it for once in German. The translations are all wishy-washy. They should just lose the translations, don't you think?'

We drove on in silence for another hour.

I hear it, too, now.

Lo, how a Rose e'er blooming From tender stem hath sprung Of Jesse's lineage coming As men of old have sung It came a flow'ret bright Amid the cold of winter When half-spent was the night

* * *

I find my music in the upper corners of rooms, where light doesn't ever shine directly. Where children find their words written out during spelling bees. Where Belshazzar of Babylon saw 'Mene Mene Tekel u-Pharsin', golden words floating, warning of arrogant blasphemy.

I'm no psychiatrist, no philosopher of Mind. I'm just a last-rate man troubled by hallucinations of music. Sometimes I'm lucky enough to have pen and paper handy, and if I concentrate, feathery pneumes may eventually decorate the walls of this dark palace, where the gods of gold and silver, brass, iron, wood and stone are praised.

Bach lives in this echoing maze, and whistles badineries to guide me. Victoria didn't ever write anything better than O Magnum Mysterium, and you would shudder at the frequency at which his motet shines in here, behind my eyes, and the domino mandala he built way back when in 1572 is still intact, and I can tell you all the vibrating tensions he wrote into his old modes—is it

-Passacaglia-

a mandala of playing cards fanning into d-Dorian, or a mandala of cherryblossom petals reaching into the deepest, grittiest g-Hypodorian?—and think that I would have enjoyed Victoria's company. And Rachmaninoff thunders through, too, usually in f-minor, and I think of the time when Alexander Chekhov (elder son of the playwright), having witnessed an astonishing performance by the great pianist in New York, was invited to Rachmaninoff's penthouse for a reception. Chekhov rang the doorchime, and who answers the door but Rachmaninoff himself, in person. Here Chekhov had been expecting butlers to open doors for great men, and suddenly the Great Man himself, towering in his six-foot-four frame, has touched his own doorknob in his own penthouse with his own infallible fingers to admit visitors. Chekhov was so surprised and bewildered that he fell flat on his knees and pressed his face to the floor... and when he looked up (finally), he saw Rachmaninoff—Rachmaninoff, too!—on his knees, forehead to the parquets in his doorway—What, is this how men greet each other now?—but Rachmaninoff's isn't a mandala of regular forms, but more like a complicated, tipping mandala built of raisins or coffee beans—again, all tannined and gritty—and I would bet money that Chekhov knew this, and instinct would have it that you should be looking for the lost raisin rolling around on the floor.

Mittantier is here 'Laissons amours qui nous font tant souffrir', -the Hell with it, Love!, Love that makes us suffer so-, and then a bunch of bad Janequin, Janequin who worried more about the crowded wordherds than he might have done decently, and Saint-Saens' organ concerto which is more of a soundtrack for supersonic flight than it is a concert piece. The opening movement of Mozart's Requiem is here, and I fear that it is just a harbinger of my own suicide, if I'm ever so low that I need to write something so high and somber and turgid I'd better just spare the world and shoot myself in a clearing in the forest, let the coyotes devour me, lead and all.

I remember the day my first lover told me she no longer loved me 'He's in there right now, isn't he?' and maybe she couldn't tell by my question whether I meant her apartment or her heart, and Oh-honey-it's-not-like-that-maybe-we-can-be-friends and I've parsed her words a trillion times and So-tell-me-what-it-*is*-like and I can tell you all the modes and shapes of her words (if not her heart), and wonder how she could break my heart in something as frilly and

Irish as G-Major. And the chime you hear in the train stations in France is here, the same carillon you hear right before the great boards rattle over to display the new arrivals and their quays, and the wavering a-minor of dialtones is here too, and the bosun's whistle on the sci-fi shows and the electric thrum of the Mortier organ drawing breath like a dragon readying to spit fire, and the dark greenstone rumble of my car when it arcs painfully out of second (you can watch the tachometer like a hawk and still not get as clear a picture of the tranny's rusted mandala of gears as you can by its mixed mode laboring uphill), and the subsonics of the furnace heating water for the baseboard heaters and the mindbending interference patterns thrown up by the twin turboprops of the old-school puddlejumper as the captain throws the throttle forward—just gotta move your head six inches this way or that, the pressure wave will miss your brain entirely—and the tram winding up, whining out of Motte Rouge in Nantes (they've got to actually add in a tone generator the thing's so damned quiet they had run over pedestrians once a week for a year till they figured it out), Dad's shaver at 5:05 every Tuesday morning back when I was six, he has rounds you know and the earlier he can get in the better, bathe-before-shaving-or-shave-before-bathing was the best Thoreau could do about it, and then the first time I heard your voice, El, and then hearing your breath race past my ear as you came for me.

And your flute prelude grew ex nihilo in the inert soil of my own mind (the grit of so many years of sonic memory laying fragrant as spent gunpowder on the threshing floor) and wandered a seeming eternity in the empty sonorous neighborhoods of my thoughts before it was ever written down.

That you love such a grotesque thing is surely the most intimate thing I could possibly ever know.

* * *

You are snoring quietly, a subvocal purr eleven times a minute, in some kind of mysterious long-period interference with your heartbeat, which (to my new knowledge) never drops below sixty-one.

Somehow you know to care for my counting centers, too, complementing the care you lavished upon me three hours ago with a problem in chaos-theory worthy of Turing.

    Way to pick a bunch of primes to keep my head busy overnight, El. This is another kind of love.

    The lights of the city are not the amber pink of modern crimelights, maybe this is some sort of local suburban Light Idiom, or maybe an intentional archaic touch favored by Municipal to help me better recall the golden days of Elvis and Ella, but the room is dimly aglow in something more like snowfall, deep into the cyan-white of sugarcubes glacier ice faded jeans, just barely above visual threshold. And as I leave the room I am memorizing where the floorboards want to creak, and once in the broad volume of the kitchen my whole ambition becomes to avoid knocking over glasses by the sink. In the darkness I can smell that there is French vanilla in this canister and chocolate-raspberry in this one, and as long as I can tease apart one filter from the stack, I might be able to get a half pot of coffee started without waking you.

    The coffee grinds like gravel, and more than hear them with my ears, I can feel the vibrations in the metal measuring cup crunching into the black grinds in my fingers, and smell the chocolate-raspberry release as I find the center of the filter.

    I stir raw sugar into my hot cup—is it the presence of coarse refractive particles disappearing into the coffee that makes the spoon ring deeper and deeper, or is it a revisit of Coriolis in the gently-turning liquid, the speed of the coffee's rotation determining the cup's pitch?—and find myself a spot on the little sofa in the back hall overlooking your patio. I pull the Kingly Blanket up to my nose—there seems to be some fan running somewhere, and the air doesn't want to stop running chilly fingers onto the nape of my neck—and my nose is cold still, so I make quick, luxurious sorties out of the blanket to periodically get my nose hovering as close to the coffee as it will go.

    When I dip back into the Kingly Blanket, I can sense the distant scent of my El—my sixty-one-beats-eleven-breaths-per-minute-the-two-must-reach-some-kind-of-precessional-libration-point-every-forty-three-minutes-El—the scent of embers from a warm fire. Your suq is alive on me, and I am alive in it, and my heart races for love and desire, and I reach down and feel the raw spot over my sternum where our bodies met what? ten thousand times last night.

It is three-thirty in the morning, and I predict (provided your heart is like mine) your sternum will be aching tomorrow from without as well as from within. For my heart has been pounding against my sternum in its breathless obsession to find your heart. I had better think to try to press my heart against you off-center, my left chest against your left breast, to spare your sternum further abuse and to spare my heart the pain of allowing an atom's-breadth of space to separate us.

* * *

But it's perverse how the human organism torpedoes psychically—critical functions such as sleep, only to find sleep surprising the mind in return during some unguarded moment, a thief in the temple. I'm glad I had finished this cup before nodding off: I awoke with a start, the cup drunken-sideways in my lap, in the folds of the Kingly Blanket. And the scent of your suq is still warm and volatile, and I wear you like a perfume uniform, more alive and vital and more perfect than any Kingly Blanket could possibly be.

The coffee's gone, and the fans are still on, and the sofa in the back hall has grown impossibly small and its springs impossibly stiff, but the city's light over your patio is so inviting, and it takes some time to uncreak myself enough—physically and intellectually—to extract my person from its soft linens. The kitchen ticks and thrums in a thousand contrary functions as I pass through, all pilot lights and fridge condensers, and gingerly I walk the deep channel through the middle (still don't want to tip a vase off or anything), and the central hallway creaks as my feet try finding the boards' surer joints with the wall and spare you the worry (should you have forgotten last night's high loving rituals) that there's a man loose in your house.

The bedroom door swings free of its own volition as I approach—I had carefully balanced it against the bolt's spring, and static friction alone held it in place—and I can hear your breathing again, and the darkness is quietly alive.

* * *

Old-style music—music of sacred spaces, music for noble chambers—all proceeds through sonic space at the same tempo: the best composers metered their music against a standard tactus of their own heartbeat, and in pre-industrial days your average man or woman would walk eight miles every day, and there was no such thing as congestive heart failure or hearts enlarged through hypertension. Happy the present-day Early-Modern musicologist who first EKG'd herdsmen in India and couriers in Hong Kong and delivery men in Cairo and found that the resting heartbeat of a fit man to be almost exactly sixty beats per minute, universally.

* * *

Your bed rocks gently on its frame, tall with quilts and pillows thrown about last night. I climb back in.

My El is still asleep.

You've turned to face, three-fourths, the depression where my person had been before my excursion for three-thirty coffee and kingly blankets. As I focus my eyes, the deepspace blue filtering through your blinds lends an otherworldly cast, shadowless, to your face, and I realize that the physics of light propagation through conventional space is simply incapable of taking into account your physical beauty and the perfection of my love for you, and there before me is the arch of your hip and the arch of your brow, and the profound calm of a woman who, hours earlier, had died the little death. Delicate sketches of delicate motets, Marotic passacaglias in intricate polyphonies, flash through behind my eyes, and you are a living retable lit with the weakest shades of purest blue, a cathedral creature seemingly lit from within by my own surpassing love.

I approach soft as shadows. Unknowing, your breathing is measured and perfectly regular. Your arm bends to take me closer, and my heart strains to reach yours. Your breast is warm and forgiving as I press my heart into you. You barely stir.

I can feel your pulse in the fabric of my own ribcage. Sixty one.

And suddenly I realize your flute prelude is alive again in the lightless corners of my heart.

The melody tastes of coffee and smells of leaf tannins and shines in the evening blue of the afterstorm, University arcades and fat drops hanging in the trees. It had been lurking in the deepest shadows of the corners in your room, and now once more hovering in the syncopic sinuses of my dying heart, it accords its tempo with the gentle cadence of your own heart beating.

Livres neufs en langues neuves, même un nouveau stylo
　Racine vivante, d'un culte oublié le chant oublieux
　Un esprit déguisé, ranimé par de nouveaux feux
　Langage non de bas hommes, mais des anges en haut

Ces incantations qui réchauffent de mon sang le flot
　A faire revivre ce mort, à gonfler mon poumon
　Rallumer cendres, réveiller de ma langue le son
　Respirer, se rassurer, ouvrir les yeux de nouveau

Quel est ce nouveau soleil ? A quelle longueur d'onde ?
　Quel vent fait fléchir le vieux squelette de ce vaisseau ?
　Que peut-on faire ? Quelle étrange machine nous meut ?

Cette machine est un cœur en commun, notre saint nœud
　Une boussole indiquant d'elle-même un prix : ce monde
　Qui nous appartient : on est amants, on fait ce qu'on veut

New pages in new books in new tongues, scrawled with a new pen
　The pneumes of a forgotten cult, a root that never dies
　A light to lighten this ancient mind in darkest disguise
　A language known better of angels than of lowly men

Incantations to stir the old cold blood anew, and then
　Even to raise the forgotten dead, to rush new breath through
　To awaken the tongue, to refire dead embers anew
　To heave, breathe, trust, lick the lips, to open eyes again

What new wavelength of sunlight is this to dazzle my eyes?
　What new gales bend the frame of this ship, its broad sails fill?
　What strange new engine drives us? Whatsoever shall we do?

The strange new engine is our one common heart, both me and you
　This vessel's compass, of its own free will, points to the prize:
　That we are lovers. The world is ours. We do as we will

* * *

Three sheets to the wind in dreams

Your scent is on my hands, soft ink you had painted over me in the cool hush of your kitchen; our last moments together a roller coaster of delirious kisses, and your hand seizing mine, one last long hold, one last brief kiss, one last heated caress, my hand guided by you, becoming you once more

Tears in my eyes before I even had the car unlocked

This drive back is going to kill me, I'm sure of it, it is an abomination, it is the hardest thing I've ever done. I had barely gotten to highway speed when I realized that these hours—which had passed glacially on the way up—would be overtly excruciating on the way back down.

I pass the time with my eyes on all the houses, set back from the road, dirt paths to front porches to front doors to a cedar-scent maze in my imagination, my heart ready to fill any space we might find ourselves settling into. I know you're a townie at heart—I suppose I am, too—but even as my mind alights on some house in the deepest woods, the heart races just a little more urgently when front doors swing open to admit us—us, you and me, a couple, a 'one'—and another mile has worn away behind me.

Just four hundred more to go

* * *

The house was so empty at my return, let the cat in, let the cat out, it must be forty degrees in here!, can't find the light switches anymore.

'Home is where you hang your head.'

At once floating, at once ecstatic, at once the sharpest teeth of despair, at once broken, at once undivided for the first time in all my days.

For my life has changed, my eyes have changed, and see with a new light, the world glows in a new spectrum governed by laws no man has yet intuited, Huygens thought his lenses might be useful for war, but Galileo thought they might be used to shake our understanding of the Universe free of its cobwebs, and by training his piece on Jupiter, there had been those dusky foreign worlds there all along, we could not have even guessed at the depths of our ignorance, and then again we could not have imagined our own future greatness, either.

And the man himself lived out his days in the prison of his own house, but Galileo's name lives on forever.

And I wonder what they'll say at work tomorrow, my eyes open for the first time, my forehead unlined for the first time, my tongue loosed by love for my distant El, my sweet love, my Muse, my dearest:

-Morning, Vicus. Have a good weekend?

...and then my answer, off the rails, chaosmonster plunging on:

- *What thing gravel-voiced*
  Awakened me this midnight?
  A swollen moon silently weaving quilts of cobalt:
  Stretches of wheat into a wide swatch of corn,
  a deepened edge of a cherry forest.
  Who wouldn't wander in
  Even when a moonlit night
  Grazed a hillcrest
  Where she hung impossibly low?
  She herself followed,
  A cautious and steady lover,
  Her glance betraying a misting strung
  Among cherry fingers in a cobweb between,
  In a wistful muse of a line dividing ground and light,
  A mist outlined in vapory ink
  And laden in cherry wine sweet as cut hay
  Ripe and bulging like some rutting beast—
  A newly furrowed fertile field.

Who woke me this midnight
Where the night rarefied to its deepest blue
And the heaviest air paused
To richen and sweeten?

Surely my students, my colleagues will find me changed, transfigured before them, will find me casting shadows of supernatural length and vibrant anticolors; they will see my lips move, but hear the voice of Petrarch and Ronsard, of Virgil and Joyce and Hafiz.

* * *

Thank God your call came when it did tonight, thank God your whisper—of lush dusty melodies—came to soothe me as I struggled to calm my thrashing heart... And these thoughts, flaming stagecoaches each, settled to Earth again, your words a quiet snowfall: your whispered 'I love you' in my ear as I fell off to sleep, and the 'I hope you are dreaming of me' breathed into my heart, and the 'you are so beautiful' in my dream...

Should I die before I wake, this very night, El, please know that I am become a new creature, a new hero in the Elysian fields, a restless shade in the corner of your bedroom, a sharpcornered brick in the Pantheon, cherubim and seraphim continually do cry: I love you with my whole being, and I always will.

* * *

Three sheets to the wind in dreams...

I've seen this dream for days and days now. Just heartbreakingly beautiful.

And calm.

We're that old married couple. We know each other's tics. Your dental floss, little matchbox reminders of higher virtue, your smile in a silk string on the dash, on the nightstand, on the little mirrored tea tray by the tiny sofa in the back hall. My way of bending my thumbnail down with the nail of the other four fingers, symmetry on both hands, when I'm nervous. That way you purse your lips as you think, trying to avoid looking surprised. That little Bach fragment, that little whistle-tone from Bach's Diverse Canons—the sound of love and distraction—as I do dishes or build a drink for us.

We're that old married couple, only not all that old, just a lifetime of kindnesses and passions held as common property, a-joy-shared-is-multiplied-a-sorrow-shared-is-diminished, the car ride an act of love, a hand on the thigh, a whispered word right on time to navigate me through the back way to Hillwood, car radio between stations, chicken sandwich and fries, that old married couple, not all that old.

This isn't your little cottage you've painted over with clays and berries, that powderquiet room with your tall pillowtop and your dim blue neon clock with the dark numerals I can't see at night without my glasses; there's no back porch sofa with the oldschool upholstery and the orchids holding court, pale violet reading lamps over me. This isn't your enameled stove and the dozen burners where omelets rise under your magic ministrations as I doze. There is no tall shelf backlit in the windows, no heavy ceramic plates with pictures of heavy-eyed koi, no goblets and pumpkinseed bottles shining with borrowed light.

And it's not my little monastic room with its high ceiling and church lamp and old whiskey bottles lined up to look like a Venice skyline, Buffalo Bill whiskey meets San Marco. No lumpy Prohibition-era bed, no barewood unshellacked floor with the ancient wax turning tiger stripes, no ethereal portraits of ethereal beauty, the knowing half-grin of my El as if rising out of water or mist. There's no mandolin leaning against the lamp on top of the marbletop chest of drawers, straining out of tune. Life's collected things in a single suitcase under the bed.

Instead, it's our house.

I don't think it's finished, and either way, the previous owners have had their way with the wallboard, and there's nothing over the lightbulbs any-

more, and the hard light shows us where the paint should go when we can finally get to a hardware.

It is always night. And somehow we have always just gotten in: my sense is that we've either just moved house into this place, and everything is still en route in the truck, or maybe we've been away on vacation and have found our nest again, a late-night arrival, finding one another in this safe, quiescent place. A sort of happy exhaustion.

* * *

We are at the top of the stairs. It is a narrow staircase, with a bend halfway up, and there's a low, narrow door at the top, leading into a long, dark room, with dark green tiles in a checkerboard. The fact of that room—the checkerboard room—is not the important part, though: the low door leading to it, though, frames the landing—poor man's church arch-and somehow marks this place as ours, and even with the move-in esthetic, it is perfect for us.

Some nights, we have a jar of peanut butter, a plastic spoon and a sheet of aluminum foil. Coffee in Styrofoam.

Other nights, bagels or toast, honey in a bear jar, a couple Cokes. Cold fried chicken.

And we sit and pull stories out of the day and reassemble them here, in the night, on the stairs, little rites of friendship, I'll sit a step down from the landing and rub your smooth calves and find the tense flesh in your arches while you spin snapshots of the day's adventures; I can feel your hand on my shoulder or alongside my neck as we talk, and your fingers know the spot where my vertebra burns after a day of driving or writing, slow circles the knowing salve that makes that spondyle of mine yours for a time, taking away the heat and putting it into your cool flesh.

Our hands are skillfully unknitting each other's worries.

* * *

Threads of music, distant echoes of new, broad passacaglias, shrewd constructions built of numbers and shapes, circles of fifths in strati overlapping.

Who dares to love a love like mine, darkest nights?
　—A decade of searching, years aligned without light—
Who dares to love a love like this, climbing heights
　To attain a promised bliss and regain sight?

Her heart's a lovely, lonely sea, proud and kind
　She twists away to wrestle free her chained mind
　She dares to love a man like this, an exile
　　Whose heart's been a longing cold abyss this long while

Their hearts' unsaid prayer
　United in care
The world unaware
　He's found his lover waiting there

Travels ended
　Hearts ascended heights

Travels ended
　Hearts ascended
　　He finds his lover on the stair

And from where I sit, when you put both your feet on my step and lie back, I can turn around and tease your skirt out from under you, and my lips can taste the restlessness hidden there,

　'Oh, if I could just become forgetful/When night seems endless'

draw it out of you like another quiet fable from another place and another time. And your breath rises and falls, and my fingers tease you wide enough for you to release your worry into my mouth, where I taste it cinnamon newmetal coin. And your skin grips the wood floor of the landing, and your body rocks nearly imperceptibly, a cadence independent of my tongue's attentions or your breathing's dark movements.

* * *

Sometimes I can see (or intuit) other rooms; this house of ours is wider and more curious than our modest staircase might otherwise suggest. There is an unfinished room—all beams and stays and maple props and sawdust—right next to our landing, and I've sometimes dreamed that there is a route to get from there into an upper room, more public, where I have seen strangers sipping coffee from cheap copperpenny coffeecups and herding tall tales across counters in a neon diner.

(Those appendices to our dreamscape house with its simple staircase with its simple landing and its poorman's arch, where you recline on the wood floor as your altar and where I worship you with quiet words and wordless kisses, are mere paper umbrellas that blow away the instant the breeze rises with the morning. But the fact that there are liminary spaces where others pass through must mean something, don't you think?

There was one time when we were in the downstairs, and there was an intersection of doors—not just one or two, either, but five or eight all clustered around a single place—and when one door opened, it necessitated closing at least one or two others to let the first one arc through unencumbered. And when I left for a moment to get you a glass of juice, I suddenly realized I was in a shifting space with more doors than walls, doors -as- walls, and couldn't find you again. I remember sinking down in a distant corner, lost in our house, hearing you call out to me, and quietly sobbing in place, in despair, unable to reach you.)

Other rooms are more permanent, though, and signify rather than perplex. Once I found a low door that led to broad labyrinths of corridors and rooms, each lit with a bare bulb on high, each polyangle wallboard a bit dinged and abraded, and more staircases and passages arcing over each other, Escherian mindscapes, the spiral stair in the castle at Chambord where once you realized what stair you were climbing, you were locked into it like the collapse of Schrodinger's equation and couldn't escape to a different regime of stairs and corridors even if you wanted, a puzzle with us laughing and hiding and seeking, *chasing, arcing, exploring, loving... flyovers of socks on stairs, a bridge of joys. Another time I came down off our stair, this time by morning light, and saw a mezzanine attached to a far corner of the house, reached only by a low basement floor, and in the dream logic, we had bought with the house the obligation to let a string quintet rehearse there, on an upper landing. One of the players was nearly apologetic reminding me of this duty.*

'Fine by me,' I remember saying, all nonchalance. 'Come up and play anytime' as if my largesse were borne of patience rather than musical obsession.

There have been times when I've been able to see outside, and identify larger structures—do I dare call them that?—than I've been able to physically navigate. From an upstairs window, I one time saw an entire wing I had never known existed, reaching out into the tall thick of a Michigan hemlock forest; a rough turnaround for a car; lights streaming down from the windows of that wing,

A cluster of nightjars sang some songs out of tune while
A mantle of bright light shone down from the room.

upstairs and downstairs, a roughhewn picnic table. Tracing around to where that wing should be, there's an old style lodge room, with a bunch of folding chairs stacked together on one side.

I sense that this place is intentionally near my parents' place, out in the hemlock forest of my dream logic, too, my folks who (I am sure) ache to be your parents as well as mine, and that the light we left on in the windows was there to help them do the turnaround in the dark.

How can a place like this be? How could something be more personal, more 'me', more 'us', than to have emerged spontaneously from me, for us? How can this not be a sign of my love—our love—than to know that there is a space we share, a place our love has constructed, real as if out of wood and stone and mortar, where we meet, and allow our minds and hearts to mingle?

This love is real. It is a real thing. -The- real thing.

*　*　*

A coin is struck to be held in the palm, a love letter inscribed for the chest pocket, a diamond for a coffer (to guarantee our pale flesh from its thousandthousand sharp corners, unyielding, bloodthirsty, stinging elbows each): how hard, how precious, how useless all these things? How far away from our hearts do we really cherish them, how ultimately ethereal and ephemeral their meaning, how bland their taste to my tongue, how futile they are to my heart, this heart here—this one!—behind this worn, ragged sternum of mine, how vain they are to this soul of mine, seated behind my eyes, now that I have a real taste of you...

For you, my El, have become my only treasure, and the memory of you, my El—the very taste of our love—is a sweet held in the mouth: to become a part of me forever.

I've thought about where to treasure up coins of highest mint—the sound of your voice, the brush of the back of your hand, the unreal clarity of your eyes, great intangibles of your kindness, and courage, and worth—and I realize there is no coffer or pocket or palm or chest that can hold these bright, living coins, no vault that can keep these vital contrasted photographs of substantific happiness and warmth and passion safe for the length of my days. But we fear worst losing what we love most, and see: I've built for us a place so safe, so secure, so close to my heart, a place we access only in the exhaustion of our nights, in the intimacy of our days shared, held so confidently in the quiet boutique—so oddly tranquil, isn't it?, knowing what you do about how brightly my fears burn within me—hidden in the dark velours of my living dreamscape.

This house, this fragrant, constructed place, this safe haven of ours, with the turning stair that rises to hidden rooms, its messy wallwork, its convoluted floorplan, its bright lightbulbs unmasked, the light of my love and the motor of my being its only substance...

What memories will we store here in the time of our love?

-Passacaglia-

D'abord des heures, des jours, des semaines
Et puis des années d'amour. Des années d'amour.

 Will there be an office-scriptorium, your own dream studio, a reel of film trailing tranquilly into the tickettaker gears of a projector, our malpainted walls a makeshift theater screen to make murals of our travels? Will we imagine children we never engendered—intense, loving, cerebral, complicated, both me and you—in their disorder and energy, their own lives and loves, here? Will there be a corner made for the chaos of scores and notecards and key-mandalas and domino-mandalas and penny-mandalas? Will you wear your weary spring-morning delivery-room grin for me here? Will there be a bed full of rose petals? Will we cover the walls with restless art, a portrait of you with opaque glyphs of thought and purpose plying your features, a photo of me in the darkness, confusion and light and movement and intention? Will we have collected a casual army of bottles, a Victorian mob of St Germains and Nocellos and homemade Peach Jacks in ancient flasks? Will we make a great endless bin for the fragile things we broke in fear or anger, or which we broke with the simple gesture of brushing past a table too quickly? Will those cracked vases be replaced by stouter ones, or more delicate? Will we mark our weekends with new and higher love than we have names for, will we find mercy in each other's arms, will we invent new languages to tell each other of safety and comfort and riling dares and inside jokes? Will we save the receipts from our latenight pizza banquets, the crazy chocolate nights that ended up more on our skin than in our mouths, the paint sample chads of our childhood homes, the thrumming tones of a fireworks show stolen from the hidden edges of a golf course, thunderstorm trumpets and great minor Masses to make you come again and again with walls of sound, the loving lovely petaled Goldberg Aria in its tripping, tentacled promenade to make the tears pour from my eyes again, the nostalgia of Cathedrals and the song of you-and-me, a decade of yearbooks and that year we should have met, your hand on mine as we paint an Andante together, the yellow stepstool for our kids in the kitchen and the bunkbeds in the frontroom, that tiny sofa in Renaissance yellow—my Grandma-used-to-call-such-things-Davenports—a painting made of wild berries a Batik masterpiece hardly describable my memory faltering under my first joint, the day I moved out, the earnest eyes of my new alto watching my wavings and frowns, a new razor blade and that scrubby sage soap how-do-you-get-that-old-water-heater-to-fill-a-whole-tub-to-scalding-anyway, the first nude

I ever made for you and the hard-iron pricks of blood where you bit your lip were-you-too-ashamed-to-send-it-or-just-afraid-I'd-know-all-of-you?, an empty envelope with a few strands of your hair...

A time-softened tee shirt A pound of coffee A sketch of your Mom My fingers in your hair

Will the sun shine one day in this house of ours?

Can there be a greater sign of my love than this: that we inhabit a hearth emergent of my very heart, enlivened by my very life, that -we live together- in the very substance—right here, right here where I thump these words into my chest!—of the marrow of my bones, the fibrous meat behind my sternum with its thrashing, human obsession, this dark place that is Only Me, this place hidden even to me in the waking hours, in this place lit with pure thought, and pure longing, and pure love? Can there be a greater sign of my love than this: that our love will live on in the pulse of my being, -as- my very pulse, the very electricity of my heartbeat, and breathing, and digestion, and thought... -as- the very substance of my love for you?

We'll live on forever here

* * *

-Sweetheart. My El.

-Hey, Baby...

-Say that again. 'Hey Baby,' just like that.

-Hey, Baby... hey, Baby...

-I could hear that every day, every night, for the rest of my whole life. You look exhausted.

-You got that right.

-Come, then. Sit down, load off. You need it.

-It's late, Baby, you don't have to wait on me.

-Just come and sit. I was just about to have a spoon of peanut butter.

Qui ne dort pas la nuit vit deux fois
   Plus que son voisin : sa vie debout
   De besoins, de foules, de courroux
   Faite ; et l'autre vie, de meilleur choix

Cette nuit, une lueur d'ambre mande
   Mon esprit ; ces carreaux entr'ouverts
   M'invitent, me font envoler vers
   Le ciel, loin du jour des mornes landes

Et voyant—béante—ma fenêtre
   Je sens le pouls de mon âme agile
   Mue de tant de peines, mue d'amour

La partie subtile de mon être
   Chose si légère, ailée, fragile
   S'éparpillera au petit jour

The man who doesn't ever sleep lives twice
   More than his neighbor: the upright life
   Knit of need and din and crowds and strife
   And the Other Life of higher price

This darkest night, the amber light calls
   Away, up, my window frame ajar
   Loosing me to fly to skies afar
   Away, up, gone from the day's grey pall

This swinging frame—swung wide—seeing
   And sensing the pulse of my agile
   Soul, wrought by pain yet under love's sway

The subtlest grain of my inmost being
   So very light, so winged, so fragile
   Flies away at break of day

* * *

How far away can a mind fly?

The preacher is thundering at him, calling down comparisons from Heaven to Job and the widow with her mites; he makes some kind of meaningful allusion to his own stillborn child, 'You can't *possibly* have it as bad as others have, how dare you ask *who you are to bear it?*'

Vicus has noticed it before already tonight: that each time he clears his throat to make his own point, the preacher slides slightly forward in the chair he's occupying, encroaching more and more into the only exit from the room.

If he thinks that the best remedy for a trapped man is to trap him further...

* * *

Vicus is awake. His little garret room in the old mill district, near the tabac on the Guist'hau end of the long straightaway. It is a steep grade from fall into winter, and Vicus is acutely aware of the nights when the sky is clement enough, the air still enough for the windows to be left open without them banging, and the air is delicious and crisp, and Vicus knows it is one of the last nights warm enough to have it all open.

Tonight the windows swing freewheelslowmotion from the breath of the city cooling on an autumn night, slack on their hinges, hanging from their frame, reaching all the way to their widest extension on some lazy, mysterious periodicity. As their arc is really an invasion into his airspace, Vicus has positioned a shoe on each extremity, so that they don't knock into things in the deepest darkness of the wings and thump in the night: Vicus' desk and stool intersect the arc on the one side, and the tiny freestanding sink intersects on the other.

* * *

For something so mundane, so damned simple and homely, that sink has caused more trouble than anything else in Vicus' little world: from day one the damned thing has never drained properly, some days slowly, other days *very* slowly, according to some hermetic schedule that Vicus, only half jokingly, has associated with the invisible configuration of the planets, a geometry of chance... and the landlords—the Michaud family, mother and father and sons—are certain that Vicus is sabotaging the traps.

'Why on Earth would I be stuffing things down the sink?' Vicus would complain, every time Michaud-*Père* would repeat *You know you can't put things down the sink.* 'I'm not a spy or anything, and if I were, I wouldn't be plugging the sink with my *intercepts*, for Pete's sake...'

But Vicus isn't convinced that the Michauds believe any part of that—the spy part or the part about him not being dumb enough to stuff secrets down an already-plugged drain. He jokes with his friends at the University that he is in reality the Michaud's Token Heretic, and he knows without a doubt that he is their biggest problem. Michaud-*Mère* is the archetypal busybody, and her prying and staring makes Vicus believe her to be immensely suspicious of all things Vicus-related: the way he crunches into an apple (biting it off the core), the heavy wool duster with the pockets full of minutia: a bus ticket, a calculator, a tiny notebook, bits of lead and mortar he has collected from under the eaves of the Cathedral.

One time, he had been in the back of the sitting room, trying to find enough light in that funereal house of hers to do some writing, all folded up into the corner of the canapé-couch (some sort of parvenu-bourgeois trophy, in a faux Empire-Revival mode Michaud-*Mère* probably understood as chic, an utter failure as far as comfort or usefulness were concerned). He is writing a canon.

Canon are *inscribed*, not *composed* per se, more a problem of mathematics than of esthetics: once you've built a working formula, a solid-enough spreadsheet to cover the accounting, you were set; once the first Sudoku cell was solved you simply have to feed it more information (to extend it horizontally) or more detail (to embellish it vertically), and eventually, a fanlike Mandelbrot set would emerge, all colors and shapes and designs, governed by the geometry of the Western octave and something like the bonding properties of water molecules achieving a crystalline state. If he were to think much about it, he would realize that the whole notion of *solving music as a puzzle* or *solving music as an exercise in derivatives* is a complete non-sequitur in a museum like the Michaud sitting-room; were he to be attentive to it at all, he would realize that music—whether performed or theoretical—played essentially no role in this place: this address' soul would deaden live sound as surely as the old velvet wallpaper here captured and killed photons. As the year went on, he would learn that his mind equated music—either the number stream or the barn dance, it was all one to him—with life itself, and even in the sonic dead zone of 82 rue Félibien, he would always keep something near him—written or live sound, overt or clandestine—to keep his mind free from the spiral downward. But this particular day, all Vicus knows is that his mind has wandered into the forest of pure thought and has all but forgotten where he was when suddenly, without knowing why, his attention is pulled back in the room.

Michaud-*Mère*, he realizes, is watching him.

Keep your head down, Vicus

Vicus is neither guest nor family by this point, and although Michaud has given him run of the public spaces of the house, he knows that there is always some risk of some sort of social flame-out happening, some sort of accident that takes out the anchor cables, the control yoke. And he does keep his head down, for a time. But he's embarrassed by the thought of ignoring her in hopes she would just go away, as if adults were forbidden from looking at each other in their own houses, *The law permits it, Christ himself advises it, and society requires it,* and foolishly, he looks up.

Michaud-*Mère* is an exquisitely unattractive woman. Not so much for any particular flaw in her appearance—you could safely call her a *handsome* woman—but for the grim satisfaction she derives from being seen, being noticed *doing her thing,* as if she is some sort of prophetic being, a phenomenon, an Oracle aching to be consulted, a poem so convinced of its own beauty and relevance and merit that it refuses to be published in a book, collected with any other work.

Vicus has been cultivating the tone of a simple interrogative ever since realizing he was being surveilled, and for several seconds now has mentally rehearsed the word into brutal disdain, scornful for its very indifference.

'Oui?' He makes sure not to shift his pen from the nascent canon.

I've got shit to do

Michaud-*Mère* is looking all cock-craned at him, a ridiculous smile of condescension twisting her features into a doting grandmotherly pinch, a thick clownlike *fard* of saccharine.

'Oui?' The second time he says this, the light shifting as Vicus' tone shortens measurably.

The next time I have to ask, the paint will come off the walls

Michaud-*Mère*'s pierrotlike countenance hasn't altered in the least. But at least she speaks.

'I was watching you compose music.'

Oh really. 'I see.'

The patience I'm exhibiting right now...

'I was.' She is protesting brightly, *aren't you glad?*

His head bends back to his page, how dare you think you're *slumming me*, fumes Vicus into his canon, *how dare you pretend to be my patroness, how dare you -patronize- me*

I pay my rent

Maybe even on time

'And?' Pen still to score.

'Oh, nothing.'

'Are you sure?'

'Well... you know.'

Fine, you win round one and he looks up. 'What?'

'I was just thinking...'

I'm sure you were, you were trying to think up some way to mark this moment as yours

'...I was just thinking,' she continues, 'that, well... Oh, you probably don't want to know. *I'm sure I'm disturbing you.*'

Vicus' eyes go back to his canon. Not because the canon is ruining this conversation, not because it is so very interesting anymore, but because he can't stand to look at La Michaud anymore, lest she believe she is *not* disturbing him.

Get your head back into it, don't let her think she's incised herself into the history of this thing

From the corner of his eye he sees Michaud-*Mère* shifting in her seat, eyes still on him. Minutes pass, *days pass* it seems; after a time she gets up to further fidget and flutter, a fussbody scorned, still determined to rustle the room up with her nervous zeal, her activity. In and out, little errands between sitting room and kitchen. Vicus can hear her arrange a drawer back onto its rails, he hears silverware drop into the dishwasher basket, he hears a pot of water go on. Before long, the Michaud is back in the sitting room, across the room this time, adjusting a fan of magazines on a coffeetable, as if in a dentist office, as if people came here for audience with her, as if people came for her expertise, her services.

She is seated over there now, and is doing her best to look busy with the magazines, but Vicus knows she is still watching him. He hears insistent sighing. *What she was just thinking moments ago* must be bothering her a great deal. He still doesn't bite.

Finally, though, he can feel her stare intensify. She straightens her spine, inhaling to speak.

'You...' When Vicus looks up, he sees Michaud actually struggling with the rest of her sentence.

'Oui?'

'...Are... so...'

'Oui?'

'...*Odd*.'

* * *

Vicus has had music on very softly tonight; an old cassette player keeps him company with songs about fathers and sons, about travelling down by the port, about men going crazy in their congregations, about escaping in trains. The batteries are running down now, though—they lasted from midnight to four—and the music is not going to survive the electrical slowdown. He shuts it off, brain greyout.

The windows are rocking gently in the light air, swinging silently on their hinges.

He knows those open windows drive Michaud-*Mère* crazy; she is constantly excusing herself through his door to the end of getting those two French windows closed, and Vicus will look up from his work to sigh and nod... He'll wait until she's gone thirty seconds and open them back up again.

(He remembers just a few seasons back, there had been a heatwave in the capital, and the elderly had kept their windows *closed*, fearing vapors and evil air, and many died in the heat of their own homes, stifled by their unwillingness to open their windows and ventilate their surroundings—talk about vapors and evil air. Michaud has complained about everything from car exhaust to pollen counts to noisy neighbors, and those windows are the battleground of a low-stakes battle of wills.)

A Magritte-like lumine glows on the row houses tonight across Félibien from Vicus; he remembers the dingy stucco by daylight: brakedust and sunlight both fall onto the houses from the same direction, so colors are all attenuated by day. By night, though, streetlight reflecting from the street's asphalt albedo rises up to the houses, striking the only truly clean surfaces around.

It's as if the whole neighborhood is self-luminous

In a way, I guess it is

The houses vibrate in a salmon-amber of sodium light; above them, the sky is not black, but anti-salmon-amber, the dusty blue of the Pleiades, the pure bluewhite of sugar and simple polyphony. He knows that there is 'Nantes' out there, and he ruefully admits the existence of this tiny room that *contains him* for the time being: the tiny bed in which his body jackknifes fraktura *R*'s *K*'s and *B*'s (and a case of sciatica for his troubles), and his tall wardrobe with his luggage and coat and fat bee-larva laundry bag. Nightstand, music, books, all that French writing paraphernalia that reminds him of elementary penmanship: straightedge, trapezoidal erasers, white-out, different colors for rubricking... All little token shorthand glyphs for Vicus' Nantes this night.

The desk has a single lamp and a black and red bound notebook; the spine is too tight for comfortable writing; Vicus needs to be intentional to make literature happen, as the material existence of his notebook resists him as much as the ideas that he struggles with to fill it.

The Michauds had given him that notebook—it was a trinket, a bauble with some royalist insignia on the cover, symbolism that offended Vicus' senses, and besides the distraction of the cover, the lines were too widely-spaced, and forced him into a juvenile handscape, groping clumsily at his pens, rarefied handwriting when he wrote too small, sparse and awkward when he wrote large to fit the spaces.

* * *

He reserved the notebook for letters he knew he would never send: letters from beyond the grave he called them, words he hoped his old friends and lovers might eventually find upon his demise, whether here or elsewhere: *My darling Love*, with just enough detail to tell a girl he meant her and no one else; *To my friends and parents in admiration* to kin and colleague… A dark soul, he ruminated the notion of his own death a bit too much to be healthy, and whenever he walked by the port, he would watch intently for children or elderly who had tumbled from a bridge; he had visions of leaping in, swimming athletically to the victim, succumbing to the turning currents of the Loire while saving his fellow man. While it bothered him to think that he was ultimately fantasizing about his own (mostly intentional) death, he did little to push the idea away, and even prepared for that day with his little missives from the beyond into the black and red notebook. And he tried his hand at verse here—this, he felt, was pure thought hitting the page, some kind of distilled quanta of his being, and he thought that there might be a day when those whom he loved would appreciate knowing a bit about the disorders of his person—and once or twice he actually hit upon an idea that he found pleasing: a surrealist description of poppies and the bruised blue color of the sky at dusk, an exultant poem on a thunderstorm he had once flown through in a light plane, all these terrestrial insects—grasshopper and aphid and ant—torn from their mundane existences by the monstrous thermals, ending up on the plane's windscreen at altitude where they had no right at all being.

All the same, he associated that notebook with the many bridges of Nantes, and had even interleaved a few pictures of the great curving span at St. Nazaire into the pages, and he wondered how far out his body might float if he himself tumbled from that bridge, at just the right time, with tide coming out and the thrust of the Loire's weight pressing columns of fresh water into the coldest channels off the continental shelf.

That might become yet another poem

And tonight, his memory of bridges and ports enlivened his mind, maybe less as a mechanism of generous suicide, but as a perverse instrument of travel, and the song *J'avais Promis Voyage* interleaved its grave verses with his grave thoughts. His thoughts turned from bridges to estuaries, to life and flight.

* * *

Michaud-*Père* had dumped something noxious-smelling into the sink yesterday, telling Vicus once again *not to put anything down there anymore.* He calls the noxious stuff a *product,* and Vicus wonders *the product of what,* and this is probably the tenth time Product has gone in; obviously Michaud is either an optimist or an idiot, and either way, Product is intended to smoke out Vicus The Spy, poisoning him and simultaneously destroying any evidence that the Michauds have been harboring such a creature under their roof.

Michaud-*Père* is utterly crushed by his wife. He is a functionary, useless to society, and Michaud-*Mère* has made it amply clear his role under her roof is essentially that of a functionary there, as well: that there are only two purposes for any given human male, to join the priesthood or to sire children; Vicus is convinced that somehow -*Mère* has caused -*Père* to assume both roles at once, that after the virgin birth of both of their sons, he become effectively *castrato*.

Michaud-*Père* corrects Vicus' French on essentially trivial lines: *pas-encore* (with liaison) versus *pas encore* (without), etc. Vicus notices that the man eats about a third the number of calories daily than would ordinarily keep him alive. Michaud-*Père* is never seen to read, garden, watch television, listen to music, or enjoy himself in any particular way.

Michaud-*Père* seems to live out his days to the purpose of dissolving whatever it is his wife has been telling him Vicus must be stuffing down that drain of his.

* * *

Vicus' window frames open of their own accord; one or the other flirt with closing again; he wonders tonight if there will be a point when the two windows will sign a treaty and shake hands properly. He hopes against hope that there will be no peace in our time.

    The day that Michaud-*Mère* giggled and blushed and pretended all manner of mischievous innocence—'I did something naughty,' she said in English—and he could tell that she meant to have him pardon—or even sanction—some kind of miscreancy against himself or another. But it was a confusing conversation, as her English was not all that good and it was clear she was trying to mitigate her actions with claims of childishness and *Oh bother, the trouble I cause!*

    It seems that she was just doing the cleaning—*gotta get those drapes all white and beautiful for you*—and although he did all of his own cleaning and washing, she had somehow ended up in the little garret room with its perplexing little sink and the boarder's stiff little bed. And soon enough, just one or two simple gestures too close to the desk later and Vicus' writing book was on the floor, and it has somehow fallen up and (despite its impossibly stiff binding that has frustrated Vicus for months now) open.

    'Such lovely poetry!' Vicus can't believe the words issuing from the pinching, pursing countenance. 'So *deep* and *meaningful!*'

    Vicus' headache, his headache, his headache.

    'I would *love* to meet that girl, so lucky to have a *writer*... !'

    To Vicus' amazement, he found the stuttering awkwardness of The Michaud's stupid little banter (along with the sheer audacity of the old gal's maneuvers) to be less astounding an insult to his intelligence, less a peculiarly egregious invasion of his privacy, than just another event to be filed along a continuum of low- and high-level surveillance; the whole enterprise, from the father's reticence to the mother's prying, became in his mind just a design meant to hem him into blurting his secrets, revealing his hidden heart: somehow, he felt that the only desired 'answer' to the poetry episode would have been to fess up to some kind of *affaire du Cœur* of his—whether amorous or esthetic, whether a confession of his nostalgia for his country or his mother's pie, or a nascent love for the La Tour paintings in the museum near the train station.

When he thought of how he had instead been planning his own designer suicide, a public, heroic destruction of his person, the thought of such a confession made him physically ill.

* * *

Vicus walked into his little garret room later that afternoon to find Michaud-*Père*, sweating and puffing in the half-light, disassembling the traps beneath the sink.

Vicus sat on the corner of his bed and watched. He knew this would unnerve him.

He watched with grim interest when Michaud, using a kitchen tongs, extracted a large coin, of antique vintage, from the trap.

Michaud-*Père* never mentioned the trap again.

Michaud-*Mère*, Vicus knew, would redouble her efforts to enter the room.

* * *

The salmon-amber stucco of the dusty houses leads up into the brittle indigo above them, and Vicus realizes that 'Nantes' is out there, that 'France' out there, and much more beyond. The dusty stucco of the row houses reminds him of that little Early-Modern church backed into some lost courtyard near the *Jardin des Plantes* he went to once—*once*—the church where he needed to know someone who knew someone who went there—*secret handshakes and all* Vicus thinks with a smile—whose exterior was so peeled and hailweathered he was certain it was porous to rain and wind, so porous that on the mornings after a heavy rain the walls would seep rainwater both within and without, and the heavy blue glass, five hundred years old if it was a day, the only way it had remained intact was through luck, combined with the secret handshake (if no one knew your church even existed or could get anywhere near the foot of its walls, there would be no one to come and burn it during Reformations and Revolutions), and that brings him up to the grotesques all over the big Baroque hotels of the Ile Feydeau, grotesques that survived the ravages of upheaval either through their own ugliness or the ugliness of the owners of those *hotels particuliers*, undoubtedly heretics and revolutionaries already, pirate and gun runner and slave trader, best leave them to their island that looked like a ship anyway, you can't put a value on a good river channel separating your polite little town from the gunrunners and slavetraders, can you?, but then his mind is beyond Feydeau as well, and it is already soaring peregrine flight over the marshy Nantais, with its sparse salt marshes and dairies and tall grasses where the fishermen and their sons came to spread nets or cast metal poptops for the pike and *barre* and then there were the ancient pilings of the old docks interspersed throughout the marshes, and the even older pilings that showed up at the edges of farmers' fields, it was the Earth's own springing elasticity after the last ice age bringing the land higher and higher as we move from the scale of a human lifetime toward the scale of a nation's age, once there were men casting nets *right here*, where now there are oats and alfalfa and a new vineyard of new vines, and now his mind arcs out over the ancient villages that have never modernized, they, too, old pilings of old communities left drydocked by the bounceback of the some harder-to-define ice age of a more humane kind, and these pilings take the form of an old city wall or a rampart of a *domaine* if it were in peaceful times or a *plessis* if in more turbulent, and *throughout—throughout—throughout* there were little towers and granaries out here, watching over the vineyards against wolf or Normand, and their stone is slowly re-integrating back into the bedrock, an outcrop sawn off by the masons and mortared back, shaped and cut this time, into the bedrock as if no one would notice.

And his mind would climb higher and higher, freer and freer, and there, then, were the first peaks of the Alps finally, the horns of the passes between France and Italy, and he remembers confused old stories of crazy bones and horns washing free of their sandstone; the shepherds and warriors tramping through on their weary feet would see them and call them *horns of Ammon*, but one day no one less than Da Vinci would get his hands on one himself, and with his modern eye, declared it to be something nautilus-like, somehow turned to stone like Medusa might have done to it, somehow transported up to the very roof of the world where lesser men would see a god's horns...

***

At that thought, his door opens a fraction.

Wind? I thought I had latched that

Uncomprehending, he sees the door whisper wide. The head of Michaud-*Mère* appears, advancing cautiously. In unnatural silence—*doesn't the floor even have the right to creak around here?*—she moves with ease to the window.

Thank God the room is dark, just an allusion to 'lighting', a feeble illuminous zone around the open window. Vicus watches through his darkening pupils.

The house across the way.

The belfry of Sainte Croix clanging away in the distance.

Michaud-*Mère* with his black and red notebook, the one with the royalist insignia on the cover, holding it closer to the amber-salmon light. Vicus hears the binding creak as it opens.

After several pages, the cover creaks closed again. It finds its way back onto the pile of books on Vicus' desk.

The Michaud silently closes and latches the windows. Like a thought, she slips out the door; how she closes it without the latch kitching is a marvel.

He waits thirty seconds, and rises to open the windows again.

-Passacaglia-

Cet ormeau jette l'ombre sur nous deux
   (Cet axe au ciel, cette vivante tour
   Cet amas de siècles, ce pilier lourd)
   Et abrite nos esprits désireux

Voyez nos pays au cœur de cet ormeau
   Unis, sentinelle à notre frontière
   Dans son flanc même un fil de la barrière
   Entouré par ses généreux anneaux

Voyez ses branches rechercher les cieux,
   De sa racine en terre la tenance,
   Sa cime où doucement sa feuille chantera

Voyez dans mes prunelles tant de feux
   Secrets, et dans cet arbre ma vengeance
   Je vous pendrai, c'est juré, de ses bras

This tree overshadows both of our lands
   This elm (this great axis, this living spire
   This pillar founded, which cent'ries inspire)
   Our shared desires engathers, shades and spans

See how from deep within our border springs
   This trusted sentinel, our sure defense
   The very wire of our sure border fence
   Having grown deep into this elm's rings

See her fair bearing, see her soaring higher
   Her roots' purchase into ripening Earth
   See her limbs, hear her leaves' soft whispered charms

See in my pupils my heart's hidden fire
   See in this elm too my heart's vengeance birth:
   I swear to hang you one day from her arms

* * *

'Your father is unwilling to grant you with anything—goods, funds, power, marriage, lands—that you might use against him. This is the ultimate sign of distrust... this is as clear a declaration of future war as you'll ever see. Warning, my friend.'

'I am *not* your friend.'

'Fine. But you can't deny you're my big brother.'

'I can try.'

'The angels know better. *You* know better.'

'Listen to this! Feeble, lifeless Geoffrey, littleboy Geoffrey, telling me now what the angels know!'

'You're right: your conscience knows—*knows*—without having your baby brother lecture you.'

'Such... wisdom... from the Little Boy King.'

'I trust you've been well, Richard?'

'Fuck yourself, Geoffrey.'

* * *

'Richard, you obviously haven't heard the real story about our dead brother.'

'Big Brother was a traitor, Geoffrey. You'd do well to learn from his example—the Lord doesn't look kindly upon those who plot against their own father, who pillage everything under the sun in their one-minded efforts to overthrow, to burn, to tear, to take. You wonder why he took ill, you wonder why he pegged out like a dog, like a beast? That is his reward.'

Richard had in fact been the *second* son of the Plantagenet. The first son had gone wild, had become the ingrate, a wretched sedite plotting against no lesser man than the king himself; more than that, he had gone so far as to light the engine of hot war against the Plantagenet, skirting the old man's borders rakehell, and all across the Plantagenet countryside there was not stone left upon stone, and plaintive cries of fatherless children, and the smell of burned flesh, rotted flesh.

'Philippe of France probably doesn't know with whom to be more disgusted,' said Geoffrey, 'the ghost of big brother, or your own damnable corpse for allowing him to raise arms against his own father.'

The words *ghost of big brother* caused both to pause. Wind rose to grimble the tips of the trees on the Chinon pinnacle; both men—Richard, the future king of England and Aquitaine, and Geoffrey, the second son of the Plantagenet—found themselves pulling their collars up despite the summer heat; the gesture did little to calm the brothers' nerves or warm their thoughts. The town was a rumpled coat at the feet of the pinnacle, the stone palace growing organic from the pinnacle's shoulder, a helm, a crown. As if by instinct, both brothers—Richard and Geoffrey—placed their hands flat on the corrugate limestone of the promontory ledge overlooking the valley, warming them against the thought of their brother, not yet having descended into Hell, to the circle reserved for traitors and turncoats.

'You will burn for your attempted patricide, for the sin of omission, Richard. How *convenient* not to warn big brother of his own patricidal sin—how *easy* for you to have looked the other way, how easy it must have been! With him now gone, who stands between you and the throne? No man, except your own father, the one rightful king. Well played: I expect the Lord's vengeance to be at once swift and long. And painful. Likely a similar end for you as awaited big brother.'

'What, a dysentery? *Bad chowder* awaits me?' Richard's words full of disdain, a mocking chuckle.

The eldest son of the Plantagenet had died doubled over, unable to straighten for the last month of his life.

'You think the *cooking* is what did him in?' Now Geoffrey's turn to choff mockery. 'More like *the cook.*'

'...Meaning, littleboyking?'

'You think the Old Man was too stupid to recognize sedition? You think him too lazy not to act? What would it take—a crown to the first man to slip arsenic into big brother's stew? You think the Old Man too stingy to do the accounting? One heavy coin to get his seditious son to roll over and die?'

Richard said nothing.

'You think you're better than this?' continued Geoffrey. 'You think your smarts outweigh the Old Man's? Are you any better than big brother? You're young, you're inexperienced, *you haven't even thought about how much the Old Man would relish doing you in as well,* and now you say you're too smart to accidentally hire a treacherous chef? Or a treacherous vintner? Or a treacherous page, or a treacherous...'

Geoffrey's voice trailed off. The two men rested their elbows against the warm stone, watching the world stretch off beneath them.

'One gold coin, slipped into the pocket of the right man, the wrong man, a man with faltering mores... Goodness, do *you* know anybody with faltering mores, Richard?'

* * *

The air over Chinon was turbulent, and the crows were black absences in the sky, fussing, flapping sunspots. Blackbirds trailed and harassed the crows, a clumsy, relentless joust.

'Ever wonder why grackles chase crows, Richard?'

'*Grackles chase crows,* it is the way of nature.'

'*Grackles chase crows,* it is the very image of your brother haunting you.'

* * *

'What you don't know about Philippe of France will be your own downfall, Richard.'

'What do *you* know about Philippe of France? Chess buddies now?'

'Who—Philippe and me? Or Philippe and the Old Man?'

Richard stopped short at Geoffrey's unexpected answer. 'What?'

'The Old Man can play more than one game of chess at once, you know. He's guileless, he's rich, he's smart, he is not above stacking the deck. He's made big brother disappear, you'll be next, and Philippe Auguste doesn't have an ally in the whole world and would sell his own soul to have one, and the Old Man can make Philippe's life very easy for him... And the little upstart doesn't owe you *anything*. What you don't know *can* hurt you.'

'What don't I know?'

Geoffrey's eyes gyred. *'Plenty.'*

'Philippe and the Old Man have been talking?'

'Not yet.'

'*Yet*...?'

'Right, Richard. Not *yet*.'

Richard and Geoffrey walked on in silence; the wind blew and the blackbirds circled and dived at the crows, and Richard's eyes, grey and distant, never left the drama in the air over Aquitaine. The trees swayed and swept; it was late summer, and the cicadas chirred in force; plane trees heaved up their silk into the rising columns, and Geoffrey could smell their fibers irritating his throat and sensed the river far down below torn in contrary directions, the deep channel of the Vienne at odds with her upper surface, hacked mad and chopped by a squall ripening invisible to the West.

Finally, Richard straightened.

'This is a set-up, isn't it? Trying to make me lose my nerve, ally myself to the little Parisian brat before the Old Man can? What is Philippe, eighteen? *Sixteen?* And he thinks he can intimidate me like this? Send my own kid brother to come whisper tales into my ear, have me betray king and country, father and blood?'

'Fine. Don't listen to me, Richard. But what would it take to verify or deny? A single gold coin slipped into the pocket of a trusted spy...'

'*A single gold coin...*' Richard was lost in his thoughts again.

'A single gold coin, to find out if Philippe Auguste has a summit with the Old Man. A bargain, if you ask me.'

* * *

'They met at Gisors, nine days ago, under the sacred Border Elm that shades both the Plantagenet's realm, and the Capetian's.'

It was night. Richard of the Lion's Heart knelt in his chapel; the body of our Lord Jesus Christ stopped in his throat. His holy spy held the chalice to his lips, but Richard could not drink the blood of Christ.

He knew the elm of course, knew it from legend and fact: he had quartered several times in the château de Gisors during his adolescence, and his handlers had often pointed to the tree, a great spread of branches on the horizon, black by winter and emerald green against the cobalt blue of the summer sky, *a fine spot for tempering Frankish pride* they had said, and the Capetians but rarely ever showed up there, only a day's hard ride from Paris, they were too often fearful as kittens to come out and play.

'And you saw them?'

'Yes, milord.'

'Did you hear their conversation?'

'There was very little.'

Richard choked down the rest of the wafer and rose before taking the wine.

* * *

The priest returned to the sacristy. There were Communion vessels to attend to, the elements of the holy meal that Richard had not consumed, his own vestments to deal with. The blood of Christ was too precious to simply be poured out, and carefully following church protocol, he swallowed the remainder neatly and swiftly. His stole and vestments were next, and an altar boy waited to receive them.

'Not today. I'll deal with them myself.'

The boy disappeared, leaving the priest alone in his study. He locked the door.

Beneath his vestments, tied to his waist, there was a tiny leather bag. He emptied it onto his table, under the light of a single candle.

This one he told himself, holding the golden coin Richard had given him, *bought the truth*

The meeting under the elm had not gone well. Philippe Auguste had made some extravagant demands regarding (of all things) *his sister's dowry*, and the Plantagenet had hissed that here Philippe had been granted an audience with none other than the king of England in person, and all he could think of was to dispute a marriage contract.

Philippe had flown into a rage, saying that he, Philippe Auguste, had granted *the Plantagenet* an audience and not the other way around. Then, before his enemy's wondering eyes, Philippe ordered his men to hack the great elm to pieces, not leave even a splinter standing.

'*This* is what I think of your so-called *audience.*'

And so Philippe watched, arms crossed, as the tree was reduced to sawdust.

The priest (following church protocol in such matters), had been careful to turn his back before the first blows landed at the elm's roots.

In the study, he mused, and picked up the first coin. He held it to the light; he saw Richard's likeness.

Yes, this coin bought the truth

He shook the little leather purse again, and a second coin fell to the table. He picked it up, held it to the light. Philippe's face.

...and the second coin, this one, had bought silence, silence over the felling of the tree, the harsh words, Philippe Auguste's taunting and railings at the king of England

The priest's conscience was clear. However, he had to remember to be careful where he stored his two coins, as each of them was evidence of a betrayal.

Prudence is a virtue.

Judas should have been more careful

* * *

It was at this time that Geoffrey, Duke of Brittany and Earl of Richmond, son of Henry the Plantagenet, was himself doubled over by a sudden dysentery, and blood began pouring from him whenever he moved. The symptoms mirrored those of his eldest brother, the one who had dared raise insurrection against their father the king of England.

Richard of the Lion's Heart received a richly ornate writ of safe-conduct, guaranteeing that no Frank would trouble him as he crossed Capetian land to visit his dying brother.

For Geoffrey was dying in the Island City in Paris.

Richard rode, not knowing whom to fear more: the father whom Geoffrey had warned him about, or Philippe Auguste—the Capetian—whom Geoffrey had also warned him about in the very same breath.

And Philippe Auguste's men met Richard at the site of the great sacred Border Elm near Gisors, to accompany him with pomp, drum and pennant toward Paris, and he marveled as he saw the elm, reduced to splinters, scattered around the stump for a hundred yards around. And as he stopped for the night, he would refuse wine and bread and cooked meat, insisting instead to slice filets himself from a still-bleeding carcass slaughtered before him, roasting them himself on the tip of his sword, over a fire he built himself.

Geoffrey would be laid to rest under a dark granite slab in the newly-constructed choir of Notre Dame, a long stone's throw from Philippe Auguste's palace on the Island.

Richard knelt at his youngest brother's coffin, the point of his sword—bits of cooked meat still clinging to it—grinding into the nascent cathedral's pavers, his fingers gripping the sword's guard together with the hem of Geoffrey's burial shroud, and his lips mumbled fervent prayers to Geoffrey's ghost, *Please please help and protect me* and *please please don't haunt me* and he could feel the heavy air closing around him as Philippe's men refused to look him in the eye, *they know I'm next to go into the ground don't they?*

And then a new, different hush came over the place, as sound itself refused to propagate through the high edifice: *Philippe Auguste must be here too*, and Richard looked around, and suddenly there was a young king standing behind him, not a young king but a *boy*, a *sapling*, waiting to pay his respects.

And Richard of the Lion's Heart, still on his knees, swung around to face the king of France, Philippe Auguste, for the first time, and he lay his sword at the boy's feet.

And the words seemed to rush out of him, tumble out of him, his lips nearly babbling them of their own accord, and he reached again toward his dead brother's coffin, and his fingers found the rich cloth of the death shroud once more, 'I swear on the bones of my brother Geoffrey, *that I am the king Philippe Auguste's servant*,' and the words are crowding out of him now, 'and I promise on my faith that I will in the future be faithful to milord, never cause him harm, and will observe my homage to him completely against all persons in good faith and without deceit.'

Philippe seemed to see Richard now, and seemed to hear his words now, too, and bent to take the sword offered him, *my God, how heavy it is!* and leaning into it, slowly drove the point into the granite floor before Richard, and the grinding sound was audible through the whole building. He leaned the flat of the sword's blade against the kneeling man's forehead.

And the next moment, Philippe had pressed past Richard, and was at Geoffrey's coffin, nearly *in it* now, and was embracing the dead prince.

Richard, not daring to rise, turned to see this strange spectacle over his shoulder. The words just slipped out: 'See how he loved him!' ringing through the stone and glass forest.

And Philippe, his lips brushing against the dead man's ear, words audible to a ghost alone:

Well done, good and faithful servant

-Passacaglia-

Epuisé, mais fouillant encore ou nul n'attend
   De trésor... Folie de fouiller encor' une fois :
   Ni volonté, ni effort, ni force ne doit
   Faire briller l'or plus que ruiner un champ

Pourquoi tant priser mon cœur caché si longtemps ?
   Ce cœur ne vaut que du roc, du charbon. Pourquoi
   Casser ton dos, ta tête, pour un objet si froid ?
   Pourquoi pas chercher un autre cœur moins cassant ?

Mon cœur perdu t'appellera de profundis
   De l'ombre de mon tombeau à perte de vue
   Mon cœur endormi, enterré, noir à regarder

Prends enfin ce cœur, car ce trésor en revit
   Tiens-le bien—ce cœur, cette vie qui t'est pourvue—
   Le coup est fait, à toi maintenant de le garder

The search exhausted, and no further hope of yield
  Can sanctify a further hunt, or justify
  A greater will, or effort, or strength; since to try
  Wringing gold from stones harrows more than just the field

Why does your heart set such a price on mine? Hearts concealed
  Are good as stone, as coal, and just as cold. And why
  Choose to break your back, or steel your mind, or deny
  Yourself a better, finer heart... for a heart sealed?

My heart aghast, the darkness' slave, from the deep implores
  Reaching down past shades of my grave when, lost from view,
  In darkest cast, my heart, its cave detinted, asleep,

And at long last, my life to save, the treasure's yours—
  Hold to it fast, Love, for I gave my heart to you—
  The die is cast; the day is done; it's yours to keep.

There are a number of different spaces in this tapestry

Havoise' fingers moved of their own accord; sometimes she noticed the reflex to mumble out her plans—an old woman dottering away in a dark scriptorium, her lap encumbered by yards and yards of tapestry—she sometimes chuckled at the perversion of the vision, recalling paintings of the Virgin in her splendor, gravely fixing the Christchild with her virginal, haughty eye, gravely encrowned with an improbably heavy-looking crown, drowning in an abundance of robes and draped in gold—and then here was Havoise, even for her burden of years, a very old woman indeed, although the very picture of gravitas, hardly able to stand a comparison to the taut, strong, purposeful woman holding the drowsing Christ on her lap or feeding Him from her breast.

Other times the reflex was different, and less troubling to her: it was as if her fingers mumbled into this pebbled cloth for her, without a word, without a sound except for the subtle crisping of the needle popping through the warp of the ground fabric. And her eye, at one time long ago infallible, would simply follow along the arachnidan choreography and marvel as the thoughts of her mind became real objects in the dark universe of the tapestry.

The vision was hers either way—either a vision of her mind she could name or a task her fingers carried out on their own—and she would leave the task of filling in the details to somebody else. And now she notices that there are spaces above, and spaces below. Her fingers had done that without her mind taking notice before now.

I'll have to pay better attention from now on

* * *

Why should I cry?

The deal had had it that Havoise stay with her father, in the house of her infancy, until her twelfth birthday, and so she had had little to complain about at first: just the taunting of her friends—with betrayed envy more than spite, or at least one borne from the other—and the sidelong glances of the washerwomen, who seemed to bear particularly ill will to the Keep in whose shadow they toiled—and why not (as their legs peeled from the noxious turbid waters of the dye trenches) *why not* hate the place they were in, hate the men who watched over them, be anxious for their little kid sister who still managed to spend an hour every few days watching them tromp up and down through the colors and odors of the trenches?

* * *

Here there is a... and Here there is a... and Here there is Wido, and Duke Harold next to him, and William, the Duke of the Normans

Griffins decorated the lower spaces, those warmer, stranger regions of the lower border. Havoise has never seen a griffin, it is true, and the idea of the hybrid beast took shape beneath her fingers while her mind wandered, without her trying to control it. The most that she could say was that griffins must be down there, down *there*, because they were an invention of the Evil One, and her fingers must know already—know *powerfully*—the infection of sin, to have intuited their shape and aspect like this.

And then her practiced eye climbs to the body of the tapestry, where a chaos of men and acts and words jumbled through, carrying out their business of talking and plotting and planning and posturing and making the Lord's universe either incrementally brighter and better, or incrementally darker and more dangerous. And then she thought about how the increment toward the light was always *always* a slimmer increment than the increment toward darkness.

If the visible world is this disordered and evil, Hell must be a desperate place indeed

* * *

She thinks she may have seen him once. The guild brought tribute to Notre Dame de Guibray every year on the twenty-second of September, the feast day of Saint Maurice, the weaver's patron saint, and the carts were loaded high with rich cloths. Havoise' father had had a good year, and his tribute was higher than the other weavers', and his step clocked more loudly than theirs had, and the church porch was covered in cloth of a thousand colors, and the bare stone of the church was naked and featureless against the riot of dyes and textures in the afternoon sun.

Normally the Magnificent's men would simply come to bear it all away, and the guild would do their best to make a ceremony of it despite the soldiers' hasty indifference, with noisy, artless words and odd gestures of servitude to the soldiers—bows, salutations, prostrations—and Havoise had heard the stories about how the Magnificent's forebears had attacked Paris and borne away all her treasures in a single strike, as if all of Paris had been working to produce a tribute to Rollo himself, and couldn't wait to heap it onto his footsoldiers. And Havoise had one time seen her father's book of hours he kept in the Fine Corner of his bedroom, and strained her mind to decipher the Latin, and thinks she may have seen the saint's name inscribed on the calendar, *Sanctus Mauritius patronus militum equituum et textorum est,* 'Saint Maurice is patron of armies, soldiers and weavers.'

That she thought *must be how it all connects up: the weavers make and the soldiers take, and Maurice smiles on them all*

But that year, there was a young man, not a soldier at all—he must weigh a third what those soldiers do—at the church door with a desk and a pen and a book, and he seemed somehow to have a curious voice to make soldier and weaver alike do his bidding, and his bidding was that each weaver appear before the desk and pronounce his name aloud several times and make some sort of token description of the tribute brought for the Magnificent. And several times weavers would give the man a number, and he would look at them with frank, tired eyes, and point his finger, and soon a soldier was at the cart, counting textiles loudly, and when the number the weavers gave and the number the soldiers counted didn't match up, the soldiers were always right, and special notes went into a different book at the man's side.

* * *

'*Nomen tibi?*'

'*Ego Jacob, et hoc facit textor dona duci.*'

Havoise had never heard her father try Latin outside Mass, and it sounded strange in her ears, and hearing him pronounce his name Latinized, *Iacob* instead of *Jacob*, made her smile.

The man didn't make her father recite how many of each textile he offered, nor did he make soldiers count them. Instead, the man stood abruptly, and his eyes found her father's cart. Seeing Havoise standing next to it, he looked at her as if he knew her already.

The girl shivered.

* * *

And Havoise can feel the warmth and weight of all this fabric on her, and she realizes that she is only a frail, feeble little shell of a person, an old lady sitting in this dark scriptorium, the only person awake in a hundred miles, and she feels very alone in this dark corner of dark Normandy in dark Europe this dark night. She tries, wanly, to comfort herself with the thought that this grand tapestry will outlive her by a decade, by two decades if she's lucky.

It should take me only another season or two to die

And then when she did finally die, they would put her down into the ground, under the cold stone slabs she could feel right now, so very cold indeed, beneath the soles of her feet, and her eternity could begin.

Sometimes days are easy, and in her mind's eye she can see them prying up a rectangle of pavers in the cloister, in the living earth near the rose bed she would contemplate on summer days, the same cloister she would wander on winter nights when she couldn't sleep and needed to unstick her bones after long hours in the scriptorium, with the tapestry. And she would spend eternity in the same cold earth her frail shadow had shaded for so many decades, in the same cold earth her fragile step had compacted for so very long, under the by-six arcades she had counted and memorized and made sacred with so many nights concentrating on them. Cloister arches above her show up in upper part of the tapestry

And sometimes days are hard and winters turn out their claws and memory fights her, wrestles her tired frame and her withered heart mercilessly, and the burrowing larva comes and gnaws again at the flesh behind her sternum, and she imagines they'll want to reserve the cloister space for somebody who had done something, and turn instead to any hole in the ground they can find to bury her in: dyer trenches, maybe, or the quarries where they had dug the stone for the arcade vaults she had come to love as her sky, the stones dug from her grave the near constellations of her years moving like a shadow through the orderly space around the rose hedge.

Carefully but randomly arrange the bones

And those are the nights her fingers make griffins, by the pricking of her thumbs, out come these unreal creatures, all-too-real now, creatures whose anatomy she can barely understand, much less construct… and yet, here there are monsters, griffins with their proud warrior lion chest and cruel talons… Where her fingers learned to find griffins in skein and spool, and how the linen ground behind her work knew how to grow monsters, seemingly from nothing, from the ether, from the matrix of pure thought, is a puzzle to her.

* * *

'Papa, why don't you have any tribute this year?'

It was the Saint Maurice, and the guild had assembled their train of carts loaded with fantastic creations for the Magnificent.

'Already paid my tribute this year.'

'You did? I didn't see you setting anything aside.'

'Wasn't cloth this time.'

And the carts rocked and rattled, and the cobbles knew the cart train as they had for decades, for centuries, and everything was as it should be. Young Havoise and her father walked behind everyone else, and the train of carts was a hallucination of color.

That young man was there at the church door again, squinting into the sun. He may have grown an inch or two since the last time Havoise had seen him; he still looked sickly and too serious. The front of the cloth train led to him; the Magnificent's men bore away the cloth guild's tribute.

'If we have no tribute, why are we waiting in line, Papa?'

* * *

Havoise watched her fingers quiver, all misshapen from arthritis and the wear of years; still, her long bone needle somehow found its mark, again and again.

The castle of dreams is guarded by a griffin she thought

I must either be asleep or dying

Either way, in the coma between this world and the next

My soul transported away from my drowsing body, and my body performing the work of recording the phantasmagory flashing before my eyes

* * *

Havoise fixed the young man with her eye. She would have willingly asked *What is your business here?* but it was the steps of the church, and she was twelve, and the back of her father's hand was hard, and she knew her place.

'One moment please, *Jacob*. It'll take just a moment to finish these notes.'

And Havoise and her father shifted from one foot to another; Havoise resorting eventually to sitting on the top step, watching the soldiers pack off the weaver guild's tribute.

And then she heard the sound of keys, and realized the young man was unlocking the church. Havoise' father is following him.

'Come on now, girl. We haven't got all day.'

And Notre Dame de Guibray is oddly chill in the high light of day, and the light and shadows are all disorienting: Havoise is seeing the church for the first time by late afternoon sun; it was as if the whole sanctuary had been flipped end for end, the tall panel window over the western porch, afternoon sky in the fall, the failing of the light before night, shining as she's never seen it shine before.

* * *

And those griffins her fingers see in the margins of her tapestry, they are the union of this world and the next—of the worldly, where their claws dig into the earth in search of gold, or dig into the earth to croise out a grave for their mate—and of the ether, the limbo of worlds beyond, where worthy wings cut sharp whorls into the air and sharp bone beaks tear, and talons seize and grasp. And Havoise can almost see her own grave now, over in one of the pits where men had quarried out sharp stones for the vaults of the cloister close—stones made aerial, cold earth stones made into griffin-stones—and where they had also clawed out bits of coal in the process. And when the novices came in with a rack of coals for the fire instead of that damp firewood whose popping and sizzling frighten her, the fires would burn brighter and hotter, and it was a luxury in the middle of January to have her chair pulled up a little closer to the braize and absorb a bit more heat into those tired limbs of hers, all those sore joints, hardly joints anymore, just painful places in long crooked bones. And several times she had seen the racks of coal as they were brought in, and she would swear she could see bits of leaves and ferns, stone ferns made into bright shining obsidian in the planar surfaces of the coals. And she dimly recalled the Philostratus she had read, years ago, in the scriptorium: *As to the gold which the griffins dig up, there are rocks which are spotted with drops of gold as with sparks, which this creature can quarry because of the strength of its beak.* But those leaves had nothing golden about them, they were black as night, black as pitch, and she realized that the griffins, while excavating her grave in the cold quarries, had found some kind of life growing in the cold stone matrix beneath her, down in the land of the dead.

There will at least be something to look at during all those years she'll have to wait, in the cold ground darkness, before the end of time comes

She had read the historians speculate that ferns sprang up from the primordial depths, having no seeds of their own, and now she knows it to be true, that there are dark stone Ideas lying asleep in the rocks, in the dark places of the Underworld, spreading their rhizomes up into the land of the real, of the Alive, where mortals can see them.

Soon enough, I will be a dark, obsidian Idea, sooty bones in the cold matrix of the earth, and the only evidence that I Have Been will be in the thread rhizome of this cloth

And she realizes that her tapestry is like the little cosmos in her mind's eye, with the land of the living a mere hair's breadth from the land of the dead, a mere thread away, so easy to cut, or ignore, or entwine with the world above, or the world beneath. And the fabric ground supporting her thread's wandering way is the very earth, hiding dark shining ferns of the deep, and that her fragile spark of consciousness somehow pushed through—for this brief moment, the fleeing shadow of her life—into the realm of the Real, of the Living.

* * *

And then, as she looks down, she realizes that beside her griffins in the dark underworld of her tapestry, there are new, curious shapes having emerged from the tips of her quaking fingers.

A suit of armor

A sword, lying abandoned

A decapitated man

A man picking through the bodies, looting the dead

Those griffins of hers had their work cut out for them, trying to find any gold in this grim field of death.

Ferns... and bones of old ladies long gone

* * *

And the three of them were at the altar in the little chapel at the far end, the one dedicated to the Virgin, and the young man had Havoise by the hand. She pulled back.

'Take his hand, girl.'

'But I don't know this man.' She felt her eyes' efforts to avoid meeting his, as if he were a sight from a nightmare she could make disappear by looking elsewhere.

'Take his hand anyway.'

And then there was a cloth the man lay over their hands joined, and he clumsily tied it in a loose knot with his free hand.

'*In nomine Patris et Filii et Spiritus Sancti. Amen.*'

She recognized that much at least. Beyond that, mumbled Latin.

And then the cloth was gone, and the man had a new book open and was writing in it. Havoise' father looked on with interest.

'You're notarizing your own wedding? *Can you do that?*'

-Passacaglia-

Te souviendras-tu, Chou, de cette nuit pluvieuse ?
   Mes doigts dans tes cheveux ? Ton corps entre mes bras ?
   La confusion des lèvres ? Respirer le destin
   De l'un l'autre, ces millions de moments de joi' :

De ma chaleur l'ombre qui pénétrait en toi
   Te guidant aux hauteurs, la braise dans ton sein
   Ce lit quiet, envoûté, tour où nul n'entrera,
   Terre sainte, terre bénite bienheureuse...

Je m'en souviendrai, moi aussi, et d'avantage :
   Contes pour ton esprit, motets pour ton oreille
   Ton cœur plus gai, mon front moins ridé que la veille,

Ton cœur dans le mien cœur, cœur qui enfin se réveille,
   Nos bras entrelacés, nos liqueurs couleur vermeille
   Ma main dans ton dos en montant jusqu'à l'étage...

What will you recall, Love, of this dark rainy eve?
   My fingers in your hair? Your body in my arms?
   Our confusion of lips? Your breath entering my chest?
   Million moments for joy, million moments too few:

My own darkness, my own heat surging into you,
   Brought you to such steep heights, fire surging to your breast,
   This quiet veiled vaulted bed, this Keep from all alarms,
   Highest ground, hallowed ground too beautiful to leave.

I'll remember all of this, all of these, and more:
   A motet for your ear, a story for your mind,
   Your heart finally made free, my brow finally unlined,

My heart finally revealed, your heart lain within mine,
   Your arm in mine as well, a shared glass of sweet wine,
   My hand at your back as you step up to the door...

***

What would you do if I just showed up this evening?

In the same breath, I suppose turnaround is fair play. What would I do if you just showed up? Like at choir rehearsal?

It would be a hoot. But please don't think I know what I would do. Drop to my knees?

***

Hmm. If I could program your arrival... Somehow foresee it, somehow be prepared... I would probably do something really unexpected. Like hand you an alto score like nothing's new, have you sit down in the alto row, maybe not even pause in the midst of a piece—yeah, that would be good!—and just keep going, keep directing, my hand and my glare telling you were in -exactly- the right place.

'I'll deal with you properly later, Young Lady,' my haughty glare keeping you there, holding your attention, my right hand controlling your breath, its depth, its rate, its intensity... the pitch of your voice, the poise of your body, 'we don't interrupt Bach for -anything-...'

Or Rachmaninoff, or Cruger or Vulpius or anybody else.

But the conversation would continue, as my hand rose and fell, and your voice rose and fell, and I can see your concentration creasing your forehead, and your eyebrows rise as I breathe in and bring the altos to their next entrance, 'This one's going high, ladies, bring a little more to it,' your eye a shifting, dark point of intelligence, intuition and determination, your forehead a bit lower, somehow managing to watch score and director at once...

And what if it's not a Bach piece, or a Victoria motet or anything 'proper' like that?

What if it were something I wrote?

Remember that I know your voice. Remember that I know its qualities, its sandiness, its lines and colors as if it were a landscape I had painted myself, a sfumato chiaroscuro palette for my own use, your own voice custom-made to negotiate a kyrielle of my own fantasies, my own cruel seven-leaps into my own thorny harmonics, they call them heterolepses you know, and I reserve them all for my altos, and suddenly you are not simply singing at my pleasure, but singing an alto part that I wrote on my couch, for you, for you to translate into The Real, to make into a knowable thing with the sole power of your resolve.

For if I refuse to be surprised at your unannounced arrival, I would swear on my own sternum you'd never let on that you, too, were taken unawares.

What a pair: Pompous me. Unshakable you.

Just wait until I get you home.

* * *

Rereading your closing words in your last letter, 'Enormous love, my Ott the Lion.'

So many things going right with this sentence, I can barely begin to list them.

* * *

I think you're the sole person to have ever called me by my middle name; it is an oddly personal—a completely beautiful—notion, knowing that you have some special knowledge of me, and that you go so far as to name me by that knowledge.

It is the opposite of forgetting me, actually. It is Knowing me mysteriously, it is a way of defining me that no one else can know, or use, or misuse. I feel safe knowing that you know me this way, it is an encouragement to me to know that you have that place reserved for you already...

I remember a scene in a movie where the heroine is showing off her new boyfriend; both boy and girl are slightly drunk or slightly stoned, and the girl is wholly ecstatic to have him near, and crows to anyone who will listen that he—the boy—is 'her personal property' and challenges everybody else in the room to say the same... How lordly, how reckless and shameless, how -loving-, to want somebody so bad that you can't stand anyone else thinking that you could possibly be anything other than possessor and possessed? How shameless, how determinedly, broadly in love she must be!

Chances are, in fact, that no one—no one—has called me by my middle name since the day I was born, the day I was baptized. And now, El, here you have named me again, as if I had just been born, as if I had been knit together to become yours, to gloriously, broadly, heartily... be yours. How dearly I would love to walk into a speakeasy with you on my arm, and to feel your hand on my ass, and to hear you purr to the hostess, 'Reservation for Eleanor... for two: me...' and here your fingers dig in just a little bit, 'and him.'

I wouldn't be offended—not in the least—to be Your Personal Property, my sweet El.

* * *

What will it take to make you completely mine? To take you for myself? What will you do when you realize you are no longer your own? What will you do when I take you as mine—make you become mine, transform you from your own to mine own? For what man, knowing there to be a treasure hidden in a field, fails to sell all that he has to make that field his?

Tonight hasn't been far off the mark, the recovery of my long-lost treasure after so many weeks away. You have been a tantalizing tidbit from afar—you do understand that having spoken of your Harley rose hedge as you have, 'needing to be disciplined badly', does little to ease the burden of my longing, don't you?—and you are delicious up close. Gentle, loving music on shuffle—I and Love and You—darkness and warmth under the pink magnolias in the back, a glass of Chambord, a dance in the kitchen, my memory and attention both high and tight, both low and slow, your lips against my chest in the half-light as we sway and turn, your teeth finding my skin too tempting...

Sitting together, you leaning against my chest, your hands resting gentle and soft on the back of my hands, my hands finding the shapes lying within my concerto slow movement, all the corners and crannies of minor all flat-laden, your hands following mine, my hands causing yours to 'hear' as mine do, the brainstem reaction of a composer's mind bringing music to be in midair before you, your hands becoming mine, my little concerto causing your arms to rock, and bend, and sway, in time with this odd non-thing Thing, streaming past you at Mach, causing you to embody shapes that had first come to be, me on my couch in a low dark apartment at University, back when I could be good at anything, back when you were free, the sound of Us before we even know We could exist, and be happy, together.

How real this music is, how much of a realworld object it has become, when I can see your hands shaping it, out in space, before my very eyes!

* * *

I've got your towel jammed in over the tall mirror on the door, lights off in the bathroom but on in the hall, the clay color of your walls lending a deep plum cast to the light in here. The water is very hot, and my glasses flash-fog as I lean over you in your bath. I see you more as an outline, the depth of the water refracting you to two dimensions as you sink down to your jawline; I hear the overflow trickle as your body talks the water up to the valve. Tendrils and tresses anemone. Only your face and your breasts break the surface.

'Mmm, you're much gentler with me than I am with myself.'

Your calf is in my hand, risen from the water, sage and bubbles, the whisper of your razor at your ankle, your skin is warm porcelain, your toes pointing to the wall, and then the ceiling.

Your other calf now. Your skin changing, smoother now, becoming mine in my ministrations, your calves, your calves, your calves becoming, -being-, for me.

'Just up to my knees, Love.'

* * *

I remember the high room where you gave the play; I sat down in the back row so you wouldn't see me, a head taller than everyone else even when I sit, I've got that awful way of watching with my head half-cocked to the side, you'd recognize me in a second even in the half-light, your hair a halo in the lights, your skin aglow, the whole theater black except for you, and if you managed to see me, you would know it was only because I shone from reflected light, itself having shone from you.

Maybe I should just shrink down in my chair, to just be part of the crowd, to be Audience rather than the half-lit, shining, pertinent face watching you and only you, I'll be nothing if not a distraction if you spot me. Your iris are dawn in this light, your eyes look through me as your voice weaves between the folk in front of me, you lean forward and find exactly that angle where I see you, framed, enshrined between all those silhouettes.

Your face, El. How I love to watch your eyes search us all out, how I love to see your brows arch, and I hear you talk about the years having dried up, about the new dating scene, about all those words and arrows your fiction-husband flung at you, and the way you come and find me with your voice, knowing I am there in the room, calling out to me 'I'm here too, just gotta get this play done first.'

But your character is marveling at the cards her life has dealt her, and you cradle her in your hands, as fragile as a shell and just as beautiful and lost, cast up onshore discarded by the sea.

'What I really need right now,' you say, squinting love-imaginary at a new bottle of wine in which you desperately want to find solace, last thing you need is a buzz right now, 'is a new best friend.'

* * *

And my hands have become you, and you have become my hands. You are smooth here, and an inch farther on you are downy, and my fingers tease and pull at your hair, and I can barely see your lips in the half-light of the dark bath, but I know they are teased—just a millimeter wider, just a swift, gentle pause as your skin stretches, and your clitoris beckons—and you arch your back feline, an odalisk, a cat, a living being made up of her heart and her breath and her lips and my hands...

And you can swear on this: that my fingers know now the give of your skin, and have memorized the way your belly morphs into your thigh here at this place, and that I am counting on this being you as well, and I am watching your face as my hand becomes you there, my hand's architecture so much more than a simple annex or addendum, but a vital part of you, the bones of my hand as essential to your breathing as your own will to live, as central to your own being as the plant of your soles, the nape of your neck, the pitch of your voice, the color of your eyes, the way your tongue loosens when you're angry and then the words come tumbling out I'll never hold my own, and I just can't get the picture out of my head of the first time I saw you at your door and the smell of your sweater that first time too, and with what ease I reached down, my right arm behind your knees and carried you to your bed the softest landing ever.

* * *

It feels like a lifetime ago already since we met, El, if feels like we've known each other forever, and I remember every time your call came at just the right moment, 'Alright, quiz Monday, all the way to the end of the book' and when my students close their books, there you are on the line,

'Hey Baby,' *your breath becoming my name,* 'my sweet Ott.'

And the feeling of Alone, with the phone's first ring, becomes the feeling of Away, which is a difference of the best kind, something that will likely save my life some day: I'll have to stop making up Classical-sounding platitudes about it, change my whole outlook, quit saying To be remembered, to be offered life in a new soul, is to live on forever, but to be forgotten is to suffer death on a blade belonging to no one, and To be remembered is to live a thousand lives in the lives of others, to be forgotten is to live alone in a house with no address, and *To be forgotten is the worst spelling of alone there is.*

And on those nights when I lay in my little cell, my little monastic room on the meager clip hillside a stone's throw from Main Street, three-thirty a.m., you're pulling my chain if you think there's anyone alive at all thinking about me -now-, but then again who knows, maybe you really are awake, too, thinking about me? And I need to remember to ask for a piece of your clothing to wrap around my arm at night, so when the bell on Main hails another four a.m., you'll be there in my hand, a clenched letter of promises and perfumes, something really mismatched you know?, raucous toucan colors of your panties versus the powdery rose of your lace bra, one Hell of a pennant to sleep under: just like I know you have on all the time, hippy chic beneath your jeans and that huge green sweatshirt I left with you last time.

* * *

Your breasts are taking the shape of my hands into them, the sage soap with its minute abrasive bits dissolving to nothing directly into you. I imagine the delicate skin of your nipples the perfect permeable portal, passing the essence of sage into your system and conveying the sensation of my touch into the architecture of your person, my palms are only an inch or two from your heart anyway, you know—your heart, nothing less, the pineal seat of your whole creature—and I can feel your heart race as my touch enlivens it, I can feel your nipples rise to meet my skin, only a molecule's breadth remaining between you and me, a laminar layer of bath and sage no longer separating but uniting your own cellular machinery to mine, a covalent bond of me, and you... the whole bath a sort of concerto taking shape impromptu, a union of artist to instrument, shaping it, the union of instrument to artist, shaping him in turn. My hands have become you, you have become my hands.

* * *

In my dream, I see bright lights, and deeply-grained wood, an empty concert hall on the night of your forty-third birthday. I've long said, in my stentorian tones, that every man should have a concerto to his name—you've *undoubtedly heard me barrel this out, too—but it occurs to me that someone of your bearing should have music to her name as well, and even though you don't play music, I know your relationship to music is nothing short of fanatical, nothing short of fetishistic, ô night that joins the lover to the beloved one, and the number of times you've referred to musicians as varied as Tchaikovsky and Dave Matthews boggles the mind, when Love walks in the room, everybody stand up, and I wonder what you'll be thinking when I ask you to lie down in the center of the stage and the players begin filing in, and their glances to one another betray something halfway between anticipation of their own performance and fascination with the curious scene, a beautiful woman reclining between them, nearly performative herself, nearly exhibitionistic.*

I learned early on you like non-thing things: I've seen the artwork on your walls, I've seen the vases of flowers other men have given you, I can only imagine the books of poetry and photography you've inspired still others to make for you, knowing of your love for non-thing things, gifts of implicit value only; for now, I have to imagine you have those gifts all dissimulated into and between the titles on your shelves, the stacks of Djuna Barnes and Rabelais (the you-books and the me-books) a perfect smokescreen, so that I'll never see the traces of your other lovers hidden in plain sight, just as they might not see my books in your shelves either, won't recognize my forgettable name, just another 'writer' they'll say derisively, not suspecting for a moment that my meaningless titles standing alongside their own non-thing Gifts to you are my own non-thing Gifts to you... How laughable I would be to them, to these other men as in love with you as I am, men perhaps more loved by you than I am, too, I'll never know... But I wonder, tonight, if anybody has written a suite for you, a passacaglia, meant to be yours, meant to -become- you, a Carmina Eleanor, brewed of a mysterious mathematics intended to be perceived by you, yes, but also derived from a universe of pure thought meant to govern you, transform you, -cause you to Become- (as a metal ingot, touched by a magnet, becomes a magnet herself...), the occult influence of the planets in their highest sphere upon the course of human events in this most lowly plane. Vain thought: perhaps no one has yet given you such a gift.

(I remember one time, playing with the Early-Music ensemble in grad school, we were doing some grand string fugue by Gibbons; I had several measures of rest in the middle of it, and my fingers gravitating of their own accord to the position required by their upcoming entrance but my bow down, away from the instrument, I looked down and saw my strings vibrating on their own, displaced by the sole sonic pressure of the adjacent players, my instrument somehow -played by another musician-....)

And whether you do this yourself, or if in the moment my own hand gets to you first, your uppermost blouse buttons will be open, your bare sternum exposed to your birthday concert in this empty concerthall. And whether you close your eyes yourself, lying there among us all, or whether I'll have to blindfold you instead, you will sense my hand rise on the upbeat, I'll-give-you-a-beat-for-free, and you'll hear the bows bite into their strings, a dynamic bond of static and kinetic inertias, mediated by rosin and horsehair and the crazy scrawled latticework of my score...

I wonder how your heart might syncope in sympathy to my music's architecture, -your- music's architecture, I wonder how your mind might somehow lock onto the site-shifting tapestry contained in 9-1-4-7-3-6-..., the numbers unreal, deincarnate, strings of pearls really, and I wonder how the air's quakings and shudderings, so ethereal, so tenuous, will invade your lungs, the void spaces of your sinuses, within your gut, within your vagina and uterus...

I wonder how your skin, so taut, will assume the high drumming of the quintet, playing for you, playing -you-...

A loomstream of sound, to envelop you, immobilize you.

* * *

And I realize not a word has passed between us in over an hour. We've replenished the tub with warm water a few times now. Your breasts, subject to some law sovereign to that of gravitation, emerge and descend through the water's surface tension, slow motion, miraculous, a marmorated tectonicity of your physical person rising toward me in darkest longing. Your labia, sated and yet not sated, pause in a perfect equipoise, touching and yet not touching, relaxed, parting each time I brush past them, caress them, slide my finger slender within, releasing continuously their suq as a sage perfume to the water enveloping your body.

My hand hasn't stopped moving as I minister to you, hasn't stopped testing the slickness of your skin, the length of your thighs, the softness of your pubic down (having absorbed an hour of our sage water's lavish care), the perfect firmness and perfect resilience of your breasts as I sculpt and resculpt them into graven images of caresses and compressions, fatiguing the supple clay of your figure into my own creations, reliefs subtly resuming their shape primordial.

And if I didn't think it would somehow flip a switch, bringing us back to our own century, I would stop here, but now my lips have found yours, and with your eyes closed, your lips and tongue and breath have begun to seek mine, to interpenetrate mine, to exchange their essence with mine, and I am no longer me, having ceased to be, here in this humid drunken underworld, and having become you, here in this humble bath in this humble house in this quiet neighborhood, and I can't even think about stopping, or even pausing, or even breathing my lungs full.

But now my hand is spreading sweet sage over your chest again, and my fingers test the gradient boundary between your breasts and the skin above them, and where that frontier is changes each time I touch you, each time your breasts are caused to become something new beneath my hand's pursuing pulsions.

* * *

How different you are from me, El. And when I see the span of your hips and the way your hair finds a natural part right there, and the bottom rib of your ribcage inviting my teeth to join in a meal, and then also the shadowy fire in your eyes, the fineness too of your pubic hair showing me the way home and the undiscovered country of your labia, I feel something close to the highest kind of compassion: this is my Love in her splendor, this is the shape of her body given for me.

And how deeply I love you with my heart, search you out with my intellect, and long for you with my desire.

* * *

I have your lips between my teeth. They are so very soft now, plump and hungry, and moist beyond moist.

I feel your neck beneath my hand, the lengthened sinews of your throat so familiar to me, so similar to the habile tensions of my hand's tendons and ligaments. Your rhythmed vertebrae syncopated, your breath rushing, hushed, between my sage fingers.

My eyes refocus in the half-light, and your back is arching more and more, and the water moves with a new rhythm, and I see your eyelids pressing shut with new concentration.

This, Love, is what it feels like to become mine.

-Passacaglia-

L'énergie des anges, et, obsessif, le zèle
  Des diables, dont luisent des faces les fourneaux,
  Ceux qui montent, volent... ceux qui tombent bientôt,
  Princes du ciel, de l'enfer, peintures réelles,

Affreuses dans nos histoires, et dont l'écho
  Des actes angoisse le cœur, ceux qui appellent
  L'homme à se signer, ceux-là que le beffroi hèle
  Pour éviter de ces princes noirs tant de maux.

Qu'on me haïsse, qu'on m'exècre pour ma part
  Car moi j'ai osé exposer sur parchemin
  Tous ces mystères à la froideur du regard

Or, pitié, car c'est bien mon propre cauchemar
  Aussi, inscrit dans ma vie de ma propre main
  Dans l'encre de mon cœur malin, son plus grand art

The energies of angels, the obsessive zeal
  Of devils, their fiery faces furnaces all,
  They that rise, they that fly, they that burn, they that fall,
  Generals of heaven and hell whom flames make real

Across the leaves of history, whose actions appall
  Mere mortal men, for whom choirs sing and belfries peal
  For whom pious men sign themselves a holy seal
  To ward off the blacking curse of these princes' gall.

Fault me, loathe me forever for my part
  In revealing to parchment these mysteries
  Terrors all exposed to the frigid night air

Have compassion on me, too, for my own nightmare,
  For into my life I have written these histories
  In the darkest nightblack ink of my own heart

* * *

Cutting a pen is a comforting ritual.

They say goose or turkey feathers are best, but they don't seem to realize that crow is the finest. When you prime it—cooking it in hot sand—it becomes hard and resilient, and takes a nib like nothing else in the world.

The knife cuts into the feather, bites into it. This part is the most gratifying: the first cut. The knife goes in positively, ignores all the lignin and fibers of the pen's shaft, cuts into it like through marrow.

The pen takes shape, growing through reduction.

Pulling the cork from a little inkwell is always a more mixed experience, far less than holy, and a flood of odor—*what was that, arsenic?*—issues, and you had to remember that the boys made this stuff out of anything they could get their hands on: lampblack, boneblack, whatever; you'd shudder to imagine the other things that must go into a batch of ink.

(They say you had to empty the black blood from a pig's heart into every new batch, to get the right thickness. Barring that, you'd threaten your apprentices—*the next one to screw up a leaf of parchment, next one to cut it too narrow or leave too much gristle on it, that'll be -your- heart's blood in the pot*—and the novice would turn all bilious and ashen, and you'd think to yourself, *Right: get some spleen and liver into that blood of yours, get that ink nice and dark.*

And you'd further threaten them with stories about the old patron demon of scribes, Titivillus, who haunted the nightmares of apprentices everywhere, who spoiled ink batches into horrendous vats of reeking chemical sludge the night before a big job, who spoiled the leaves at the bottom of a stack, too much fat in the parchment and it'd turn the whole stack to spoiled meat jelly by the time anybody realized the mistake, who ruled margins in with a bad straightedge and disappearing lead, who made the scribe into a furious, roaring tyrant who cut the hearts from the apprentices.

But the more you harassed your novices, the more you worried they would urinate into the ink. And that just wouldn't do: everyone knew that urine would make the ink too acidic, and if you overinked a letter, it was likely to eat right on through to the other side.)

But today, the ink smells more of vinegar than urea, and the novices all have their hearts still.

They had prepared the parchment with much greater care than the ink, that you could be sure of. Scour it over with some sand—coarse sand at first, then the fine stuff they had dug out of the holy, deadly sands at the foot of the Michael's Mount, then they'd pumice the leaves over before stacking them in front of the next clerk, who had ruler and pins to prick and mark and rule the new leaves. A leaden wire, that's what this last fellow would use to mark them, and you could just scour off the straightedge marks with another fine pumice once you were done writing, still leaving the ink behind, now that the ink that had insinuated into the fibers and fats of the parchment already; you couldn't just scour that off, scrub that off: you needed a sharp razor blade to correct anything, had to cut down into the thickness of the leaf, make the fibers go away entirely, or paste a correction over your mistakes.

Best not to make any mistakes in the first place. That was why they hired you anyway: to do it right, you do it as if it were your religion, your single purpose. And you wrote till the day you died. For if you ceased writing, it was like your purpose in life had fled you, and there was no point in even drawing breath beyond that.

And the pen was taking shape, nearly done. If you had been doing it right, you'd know the nib was a tiny semicircle on the end, and you had a shallow channel running fore and twore to the nib, and capillary action would draw the ink along it, magically, and they had taught you how to make that channel by making you draw a razor up and down your own thumbnail—that'll teach you not to dig it in too deep—and it was lovely how something as profane as a crow's feather (for the crow was surely the Devil's creature, speaking in raucous, telling tones from the peak of a dead tree in the cemetery as if it had gained some dark insight into human language from pecking at the dead hearts of the malburied), the messenger, the harbinger could be made to speak the words of God and the acts of great men.

* * *

It is the year of our Lord eleven-hundred and eighty nine, and the Lord has found it fitting that the earl Richard, the eldest living son of the Plantagenet, should turn against his father, dying a living death much like his eldest brother had died a true mortal death years ago. And when the earl Richard will finally remember his birth and his condition and his stature in this world, and realize his sinful condition and the real, actual sin of Deeds of sedition and lèse-majesté against his father cannot be known but by the Sovereign Lord alone in heaven.

The counts and other lords have compounded the Earl's disobedience by following him as well—the Lord knows how they can sleep on thorny beds of their own consciences—to the point of raising their sword against the Plantagenet himself on behalf of the king of the Franks. The Loire is Philippe Auguste's target, and he cuts into it on all fronts, and there is no city safe anymore, and he will tell anyone that now that the earl Richard has bowed down to him, the Plantagenet must now, as well.

Posterity will say that the Frankish king appears as a ghost, that he is a shadow, that he comes and flees as if he were the wind, and that man cannot tell from where he arrives and to where he flies except by the hush and whisper of the leaves and the flight of smoke.

Such reports are lies.

For Philippe Auguste is all too incarnate—palpably so—for his meager years, he is like the Plantagenet's conscience, clinging to him in every circumstance, by day he is close and by night he is closer, he has his very claws in him, he rails at him from steeples and snarls into his ear in the cruel flush of dawn. The king of the Franks, far from being disincarnate, far from being a fleshless phantom, has suddenly become all too real, has suddenly become tireless, relentless, a visible force, a flame free in a house, a beast free in a labyrinth.

God save him, the Plantagenet.

And it was at this time that the archbishops of Rheims and many other places came to bring news of their desire to see the kings of France and England

-Passacaglia-

meet at conference to determine terms for peace; and they hastened to pronounce excommunication for any and all who might obstruct such a peace, and although the Plantagenet's face was grave at this (what we otherwise felt certain was a step toward some kind of respite for our king), he agreed to see Philippe Auguste and hear his terms.

The two kings did finally consent to colloque at La Ferté, and they each came to meet at the steps of St Lyphard church, and the Frankish king immediately began speaking in harsh tones to the king of England, demanding that since the earl Richard had pledged fealty to the Frankish crown, the king of England should as well, and he also began to make other, even more outrageous demands regarding marriages and treaties of all kinds, each one on the pretext that since the earl had already made an oath of loyalty to him, the Plantagenet should acquiesce to all of his terms, not just his demand for an oath of servitude. And every time Philippe Auguste spoke of the treachery of the earl Richard, his voice thundered louder and became more frightening, and we could not tell if the Plantagenet was pained in his heart because of his son's treason or because of the treatment he was receiving at the hands of this young king, barely in his twenties, berating the Plantagenet, decades his senior.

The king of England of course had no choice but to refuse the terms Philippe Auguste dared dictate to him, saying he would have nothing of a treaty so abusive of the order of things, at which declaration the king of France became exceedingly angry and disputative, saying that the archbishops' threat to excommunicate anyone obstructing peace should be carried out immediately against the Plantagenet for refusing such reasonable offers, and just as Philippe had done at the Treaty Elm at Gisors, he should have the church razed to punish the insolence of the English crown.

'Either the church or the entire town. See if I don't.'

But then the cardinal Anagni arrived, bearing word from Rome that if the king of France did not come to a complete arrangement with the king of England, he should expect to see the whole of his lands placed under the church's interdiction.

'What do I care about the church's interdiction, when it is not her duty to punish the Frankish crown for pursuing those who had strewn themselves, rebellious and undeserving, into my path, obstructing my own just cause?' And saying that the cardinal already smelt of the sterling coin of the English king, Philippe Auguste made a show of shaking the dust from his boots and departing immediately from La Ferté, on foot, not even waiting for his horse to be prepared.

But the king of England said to his men, 'Don't forget that the king of France had forced this whole meeting in the first place, since the archbishop of Rheims and his cohort, who had threatened to excommunicate anyone who would obstruct peace between two kings, had been appointed by the king of France himself,' so there was no doubt about who was entangled in whose pursestrings.

But the men, in the end, didn't know whom to believe.

And I myself overheard them with my own ears, men of hundreds of years' power, the stunning incumbency of lineage all huddled in a room, speaking in hushed, awed tones of this Parisian who, for the vast majority of his depressing little existence, had done everything in his power to avoid being noticed; What He Had Done to get him to this point (slicing at the heels of the king of England for a hundred miles) was subsumed within the much more impressive list of Things He Had Not Done:

He had made no laws.

He had made no attempt to demonstrate his power anywhere, at any time, in any place.

And up to the moment when the earl Richard had thrown himself at his feet, the king of France had not obliged anybody to swear an oath of loyalty to him, the usual currency circulating among men with titles in these times. And even then, when Richard had done so, it was he who had fairly -begged- Philippe Auguste to accept his oath.

And yet here he is, the Capetian, Philippe Auguste, barely able to grow a beard, screaming at the Plantagenet to roll over and die?

How has the boy done it? How has he gotten the -real- powers of this world to tolerate his most grotesque existence? How has he caused them to permit him to be?

* * *

But within the day, though, the king of France returned to La Ferté, leading his army this time, as well as the army formerly commanded by the earl Richard, and he expelled the English at the point of the sword and took the town for himself. And the English having refuged to Montfort, he then attacked that town as well, chasing them to Malestroit, then on to Beaumont, then to Balim, then to Le Mans.

And the Plantagenet's men marvelled at the Capetian, Philippe Auguste, who was only twenty-six years old now but, like a bear who has smelled blood, commanded and fought with an energy ordinarily knit of years or desperation.

The first insult had been Richard's treason. And no one had seen that one coming, no one less than the Plantagenet himself, and the old man had said that it was like losing a son through death, worse even, knowing that Richard had gone over to the other side, a grand gesture of hatred and disobedience that the earl -must- have known would be unforgivable and irremediable. And the Plantagenet would have gone into seclusion, mourned the loss of his boy, if only the king of France hadn't suddenly grown a hundred times more courage and now, with Richard's sword tipping the scales undoubtedly, a thousand times more military insight and strategic prowess.

And now he had to hear his men telling tales about the Capetian as if he had already become legendary, as if he had already taken the king of England down, as if he were Goliath to Philippe's David.

But suddenly there is blood everywhere, black in the lamplight of this tower in Le Mans: on his hands, on his tunic, covering his face. The

Plantagenet is laid out on the floor, much against his protests, and he is examined for wounds, and in the end it is found to be a simple nosebleed, compounded by the stress of battle and the fatigue of running for his life so many times over the last week. And he springs back up, his chest heaving in fury and shame lest his men believe that his loss of Richard—such a profound military and emotional betrayal— and the unrelenting onslaught of this insignificant king of France, should also be causing him fear.

'The devil take Richard. I don't want a traitor for a soldier, or a son. Thank God I still have John.'

And the men were quick to nod their assent, Indeed Yes, John the Youngest Son, John is going to be exactly what we need, exactly what we need right when we need him!

But in the same breath, there were murmurs as the Plantagenet's men asked themselves where John the Youngest Son might actually be right now.

And overnight, as the king slept, the Plantagenet's bloody nose turned into labyrinthine narratives about stigmata acquired during the run for his very life. And the Capetian, Philippe Auguste, had grown from a weedy lad into a leonine predator.

* * *

The Plantagenet's next move was a cunning one: to divide his forces in an effort to confuse the king of France; so while he led a detachment onward to Tours, the remainder of his army remained in the tower in Le Mans. Philippe Auguste lay siege to this tower, thinking our Plantagenet still within, and his army set to building engines of war to bring the tower into submission; he fired his siege engines so heartily that each one he built eventually was torn asunder throwing so many stones, and each engine, once shaken apart, was transformed into battering rams and other devices, while a new siege engine was built to replace it, bringing to mind the word of the poet, 'And I flung at you all my arrows/ And the bow afterward.'

But the Le Mans tower destroyed and the English dead counted, it was found that the Plantagenet was not among them, and the Frankish army proceeded to Tours, where they found the English soldiers preparing to demolish the bridge leading to the city, for this was the Plantagenet's birthplace, and the burial place of his father, and he had sworn on his father's bones to defend the city to the last man. Philippe Auguste, learning of the love the Plantagenet bore for this city, killed the English engineers, and standing there on the bridge at the threshold of Tours, cried out in a loud voice for the city—and the men defending it—to hear,

'The Plantagenet must die!'

And commanded his men to attack the town with renewed energy. The king of England, forced to forsake his vow to the people, fled from the city with his men; as Philippe Auguste learned of his enemy's promise to defend his people, and seeing him fleeing nonetheless, he ordered the city of Tours to be burned.

And I saw with my eyes that the Plantagenet began to bleed again, and his clothing and face were matted with blood and sweat as he smelled the smoke of his birth city. And Philippe Auguste, standing on the bridge and watching the bloodied king of England fleeing, cried out again, 'He smells the smoke of his father's burning bones.'

Starlings mob crows; we see them at the chase, black on black in the whitening sky, and we marvel at the audacity of a mere songbird on the attack, pecking and harassing a lumbering giant many times its size. Our writers claim it is to pick scraps that the crow is forced to drop, but having seen Philippe Auguste at the Plantagenet's heels these first days of summer, eleven hundred and eighty-nine, I say that such creatures must take pleasure in the chase many times greater than the nutrition they derive from scraps they manage to steal. For the king of France delighted in tormenting the bleeding king of England, and fell upon him with a passion that spoke not at all of mere scavenging, but instead Philippe came at him, lay into him, eyes blazing and sword shining, with the zeal of a starling purging his own territory of a potential predator.

And his men chased the Plantagenet, full run, for three miles.

And the storm in the Capetian's eye, squinting through the smoke of the Plantagenet's beloved city, spoke cruelly and eloquently:

'This is what trouble looks like.'

* * *

Our Plantagenet is up on the rock in Chinon, and he is bleeding curtains of blood; the king of France and his armies are swirling around the rock like a pack of wolves, like a superstition. But the walls are high and the scarp is steep, and night is falling, and the attackers won't make it through tonight or tomorrow or this week, but already the king of England can hear axes at the root of Chinon's oaks; siege taking shape in the forests around the keep.

'Surely my son John is coming with reinforcements; surely he is leading the Breton army to save me, we have only to hold out.'

Flies seek honey, ants corn, and wolves the carcass; following the spoils and not the man, nearly all have forsaken their king.

For there is no Breton army at the horizon.

And the Plantagenet's youngest son, John, has been bought by Philippe Auguste of France.

* * *

It is the thirty-fifth year of his reign, on the octave of the Apostles Saint Peter and Saint Paul, being the fifth day of the week; after a reign of thirty-four years, seven months, and four days, the king of England lay his red head to the pile of tunics his few remaining men had given him to die on, and although Philippe the Capetian was at that hour miles away (having set up his camp on the half-demolished bridge leading to Tours), the Plantagenet could almost hear his mortal enemy taunting him from the gates of Chinon, 'Am I going to have to tear this place down, too?'

And when the king of England, in the throes of his final agony, hears his last men say, 'The devil take that bastard the Capetian,' the Plantagenet replies, 'The only bastards are my own sons.'

And we remain in the uppermost room of the keep as the king's confessor is brought to, who has exhorted him to renounce his curse of his own sons; yet the man has found himself firmly rejected, as even now the Plantagenet is convinced that his priest, too, had been bought with Capetian coin.

Legend has it that this very night the Capetian Philippe Auguste is playing cards at the bridge at Tours, and we in the uppermost room with the dying king of England marvel at his cruelty; altogether we perceive Philippe to know himself born into a flawed destiny, and that he intends to make us all pay for it.

I sign this in my own hand, Roger of Hoveden, clerk royal.

* * *

It is night in Tours; the walls of the city overshadow the river, and the bridge is as defended a camp as there has ever been in the world. In the center of the bridge, there is a small tent, and there is the ghost of a light finding gaps in the fabric.

A filthy young man is here. In the candlelight he seems at once several years younger than his twenty-six years, and at once infinitely older. He smells of smoke and sweat, and he rubs his eyes with the heel of his hand, an impotent enough gesture considering the magnitude of his headache and fatigue. He's stripped his armor off hours ago, and when his men rushed to tend to it, he waved them off.

'Just throw it in the river, fish it out in the morning.'

Come to think of it, throw me in with it all

His shirt is torn and stained and matted in ways he would have never thought possible, and the temptation to tell somebody to throw it in the fire is tempered only by the effort it would require to find someone at this hour who didn't have a post to guard. He strips it off and before he rolls is up, he carefully finds the pocket sewn in over his heart.

A deck of cards.

He goes to the candle, shuffles through the deck, squinting at each face.

There it is

The Black King.

Henry II, the Plantagenet

He removes the card, taps the deck square again.

He holds the card over the candle's flame.

Quelle étoffe nous couvre les cieux,
   Quel riche tissu de cendre étoilé ?
   On la voit tachée d'âmes, cette toile, et
   De fervents vœux l'avaient parsemée, silencieux

Rien n'ose retenir dans ces lieux
   Leur arc voûtant, nul n'arrive à voiler
   Leur vol au pays inconnu, où on voit les
   Vrais pertes, vrais saluts, vraies braises, de vrais dieux

Où es-tu ores, France, notre grand soulas ?
   Où est notre jardin ? Cheminée qui rayonne ?
   Le haut lit pour notre corps, de nos ans si las ?

O drapeau, ô notre vie, ô Mère des armes,
   Tu n'y es plus, nos jours s'enfuient, Malheur légionne :
   On déjeune du sable, du sel de nos larmes

What rich fabric sail covers our skies,
   Starred throughover with ashes and cinder,
   Spangled with souls departed, as dust? Wind or
   Fervent prayers scatter them abroad, silent as sighs.

No earthly thing can seal them, hinder
   Their arcing flight, as their shiv'ring mass flies
   To the great undiscovered country where lies
   Salvation, perdition, true crosses, true tinder...

Where are you now, France, our consolation?
   Where is our garden, our hearth's warming rays,
   Our high vaulted bed, the rest of our years?

Our flag, our whole life and our heart's nation
   Is nowhere here; gone are life's dear days:
   Meager grit in our bowls, salt in our tears

***

'Receive the key from this man, good and faithful servant.'

Of course it wasn't a real key. It was nearly silly how much of a pastiche it really was, how it fairly dripped *keyness*, how many miles of forest they must've burnt to smelt those fistlike blooms of ore into this crazy concatenation of a key, all skeletal, all filigreed, profane and sacred all at once. The castle at Acre had been in Moorish hands for only four years now, and no one had even thought of the concept of *a key to the place* yet. Until very recently, that is.

The fawning man had lovely, dark, lined skin, and was covered head to toe with a heavy yardage of silk, and ropes of gold. He somehow cradled, in a square of magnificent fabric, the so-called 'key', while simultaneously crawling, face to earth, on knees and elbows.

Philippe looked at that key and swallowed hard, reingesting the impulse to ask the fawning man if he was making fun of him.

The man did not understand French, and did not comprehend that the *good and faithful servant* was Richard of the Lion's Heart, the king of England.

Neither did Richard, for that matter.

As the dark fawning man advanced resolutely toward Philippe Auguste's feet, Richard, watching the ceremony unfold, shifted uncomfortably at the back of the room.

'Richard, I was referring to you. The castle is yours.'

Good luck getting that key to fit anything.

***

It was a miracle that Richard had ever made it here alive.

Immediately following the death of Richard's father the Plantagenet, messengers fanned out from Paris, announcing something they called a *Saladin tithe* and crying *Crusade, crusade!* to anyone who would listen.

The money, Philippe knew, would not be a giant sum—his lands were pitifully, painfully constricted by his neighbors, and he had precious few people whom to actually tax—but somehow (Philippe thought with a hint of a grin hovering over his features), several of these messengers of his made it all the way into Richard's cities deep inside the beloved, holy Aquitaine, the messengers claiming (in apparent good faith) to be truly bewildered that Richard had dared claim Aquitaine as an inheritance from his father, when it had in fact been the king of France's idea to take the Plantagenet down in the first place

'But either way,' they said with fireproof cheerfulness, 'your Richard can demonstrate his contrition by following the king of France into battle against the infidel' and so on, not forgetting for a second to proclaim Philippe's holy mission to bloody Saladin's nose just as he had bloodied the Plantagenet's... And they didn't neglect to mention the tithe again and again and again.

And as much as it pained the Lionheart to—those words *contrition* and *follow the king of France* were peculiarly finely honed by those wordy messengers of the Frankish crown, and cut more surely than razors—he now had one and only one pious choice left, and that was to impose his own Saladin tithe and raise an army, destination Holy Land, ideally before Philippe could get there and steal the show.

But Philippe seemed to know Richard's plan already, and had a fleet of ships waiting for Richard at Marseille. He had hired them from the Genoans.

A fine way to spend a tithe.

* * *

The kings of England and France actually sat together several times, and spoke in relaxed tones.

'And how is my Aquitaine these days?'

'Pardon me?'

'I was asking after my Aquitaine. I hope you're keeping her neat and clean.'

Richard often forgot that he was seated across from the man responsible for his own father's death, and as the young man spoke, Richard's mind wandered: could this really be kingly material? 'France' was a pipsqueak on the continental scale, and the Plantagenet Empire was a mighty engine casting long shadows—into the Church, into trade, into History writ large—and here was this lad, taunting him with idle chatter suggesting for all the world that Richard was a mere tenant and Philippe Auguste the landlord. While Philippe went on and on, his interlocutor was doing the math: this 'king of France' character was scarcely twenty-seven years old, and had he already run the old Plantagenet to his grave like a lion running down a deer? This was something Richard could barely conceive of...

'And my Eleanor?'

Richard blinked his eyes, shook his head back into the room. His auditory memory must be failing him, he must've misheard.

Philippe spoke louder and slower this time: 'And my Eleanor? How is the beloved creature?'

'*Who?*'

'Eleanor. Countess of Poitou, Anjou and Maine. Duchess of Normandy and Aquitaine...' And at the word *Aquitaine*, Philippe Auguste's voice trailed off.

'*Your* Eleanor.'

'Yes, I think most people refer to her nowadays as the Queen of England.'

'You mean my mother?'

'Well, yes. Who else?'

'*Your Eleanor.*'

'*Mhmm.*' Philippe Auguste, the king of France, seemed positively *casual*. 'How is she?'

* * *

And the young king's words streamed from him faster than Richard's mind could keep up. Richard had met alchemists and magicians before, and could spot a sham from a mile off, but Philippe seemed so... *earnest.* A young king, a failed nation—*oh but have you seen how scattered and disparate poor Philippe's lands are?*—and yet still willing to buck up and play with the big boys, even joking with the likes of... the new king of England. It was admirable.

Richard found he felt a real liking for this Capetian.

Philippe had helped Richard play the old man Plantagenet well; on the other hand, thank God that Richard had come in when he did, to lend his own might and authority to Philippe's tiny little listing 'kingdom', that loose constellation of neighborhoods and 'states' (Richard chuckled when he thought of their pitiful status)...

He swelled with justifiable pride.

This currency of authority, of power, of... *legitimacy.* When he thought about it all with a cold eye, Richard realized that Philippe didn't really stand a ghost of a chance—all these powerhouses surrounding him... Philippe was a fool for thinking that he could really bring anything of *value* to Richard's table—he held *far* too little of that holy, insubstantial 'legitimacy' coin that seemed to gravitate magically toward Richard.

The Capetian's hatred of that old Plantagenet had been transparent enough, sure—we fear most that which can cause us the most harm—and in that light, the boy's befriending of Richard before the Loire campaign had made all the sense in the world. Besides, if you want an ally, ally yourself to the man whose reach extended into the future, and Philippe had properly recognized Richard (and not the Plantagenet) as the one under whose wings to shelter on the long term.

It was enough of a favor (Richard told himself) that he had offered his friendship to the boy, and an undeserved *gift* that he and his great armies should accompany the lad on crusade; what could the lad ever hope to give him in return? Sure, his exuberant energies—and that God-given strategic prowess of his, *good Lord, how the boy could plan!*—had tipped the scales when it came to taking down the old Plantagenet, but let's not exaggerate...

And all it had cost Richard was a little oath of loyalty to Philippe so many years ago. Surely no one remembered that friendly little burp of weakness on his part.

And besides, see how *genuine* Philippe Auguste's friendship was! He seemed so sincerely *interested* in how Richard's mother was keeping...

An oath of loyalty to this littleboyking. How could that possibly go wrong?

* * *

There was nothing casual about raising an army and transporting it to the Holy Land; the hundred ships Philippe had hired for Richard barely contained his two thousand knights and their six thousand squires and six thousand horses. Philippe had amassed whatever army he could, too, barely a quarter of Richard's, but it was all too apparent there weren't the ships. Richard couldn't believe the king of France, terrifyingly cunning on the battlefield (and even more so in the war room), hadn't hired enough for his own men.

'Not enough ships, eh Philippe? *So much for your glory...*' Here was his chance to taunt the boy in return.

'Are you kidding? *You've got to be crazy to go by sea.*'

* * *

The trouble started as soon as the fleet was out of sight of land. It was first sun-up, and Richard heard a commotion on deck.

His food-taster had been found dead.

No one dared utter the obvious. Every *other* explanation, though, was offered, although many of the alternatives weren't much more comforting.

Fever. Dysentery. Malaria. Rubeola. Plague.

Finally it was settled upon that the man had 'died of a heart attack.'

But it didn't take long for word to spread through the fleet. For a man to die suddenly like this, mysteriously like this—everyone began to use the term *an evil death*—meant that he had undoubtedly brought it upon himself through a sinful life, or that he had somehow come under the sway of somebody evil.

Glances to the king of England shifted into new shades of gray.

* * *

The pirates really didn't stand much of a chance against a hundred-ship fleet full of heavily-armed English warriors; somehow, though, they knew which ship was the flagship, and there seemed to be a concerted effort to separate it from the rest of the fleet, to cut it away from any potential protection, to sever the head.

Richard thought, as the pirates struck for the seventh time, about the words of old Pyrrhus, *I know not what kind of barbarians* (for so the Greeks called all other nations) *these may be; but the disposition of this army, that I see, has nothing of barbarism in it.*

The king's ships were heavy with both man and beast; they lay low in the water, laden with the metal of arms and armor and gold from the Saladin tithes. The pirates' ships, however, were swift and maneuverable, and their men unfurled devilish tactics against the English, racing upwind of Richard's flagship, hurling clouds of ash into the roaring wind to drift into English eyes, and the ash was no ash at all but quicklime, and it clung to the men's tears and became caustic mortar, boiling their eyes, blinding Richard's knights before they even knew to cover their faces.

And then flaming arrows rained down by night, and the flagship was a constellation of bonfires and chaos; as Richard's archers sighted-in the pirates on one rail, a second assault force, lights doused, boarded across the other rail. And while the English longswords were encumbered on the crowded deck, the boarders fell athletically upon the knights, drawing short-handled hatchets, swinging them with deadly accuracy at knees and ship's rigging.

Richard marveled at the pirates' ingenuity and planning: *Cut off the head; the serpent can no longer strike. These men are masters of strategy...!*

And by the cruel flush of morning calm, once again Richard's men set to the grim task of stripping their dead of whatever armor they had and rolling the corpses overboard, the smell of lime and gore and char hanging in a thick plane of smoke hovering over the fleet. The flagship listing, ashambles, turning lethargic circles.

Richard found corpses of more boarders below decks. They had ignored the sacks of gold tithe, ballast spilling from them, instead going straight for the rudder lines with their hatchets, still other boarders having gone after the hull itself, hacking at it like lumber.

And when Richard retreats back into his ears' memory, he can still hear plain as day, among the clash and ringing of the mêlée, pirates' voices as they swept aboard:

'*This is what trouble looks like...*'

* * *

'He survives storms, Milord. He survives pirates. He survives disease, too.'

It was the deepest of night. Philippe Auguste's courier spoke in a hoarse whisper from outside the tent, shifting restlessly from one foot to the other, listening for a sign from the king that the message had been heard and understood—the Capetian had left strict orders that any news whatsoever concerning Richard be reported to him without delay (be it day, night, Christmas or the Second Coming), and the courier should wait close at hand until it was clear the king had correctly understood the news' importance and bearing on the situation at hand.

The courier didn't have to wait long tonight for confirmation.

The king of France's voice from within his tent, a voice rauque from interrupted sleep:

'*Damn.*'

* * *

The courier stood outside Philippe Auguste's tent still, sensing his king was again writing out further orders for him to deliver.

'And you're certain Richard knows he is to join us in Acre?'

'Yes, Sire.'

The king of France abruptly opened his tent flap. Despite the obscene hour, his eyes sparkled.

'Once he's finally done dodging all the plagues and pirates and sea-monsters out there, that is?'

'Yes, Sire.'

Philippe Auguste squinted his eyes, seemed genuinely surprised that the night had advanced into the steep calm of deep morning. The moon descended in the west, and Venus ascended in the east. 'Um... there will be no more orders for tonight. Get some sleep. It's been a long night.'

'Yes, Sire.'

'Rest assured: the night will be much, much longer for the king of England, out there in peril on the sea.'

'Yes, Sire.'

Philippe Auguste went back into his tent. His voice penetrated the tent flap still. 'No man can live long who spends his days doing ill...'

'Yes, Sire. Of course not, Sire.'

* * *

Richard could see the smoke plume from twenty miles off. The siege had been underway for weeks, that much was clear.

There was no ceremony at the port, only a tiny dispatch of men bearing a handwritten message and hurrying away again:

Wish I could meet you properly. However: complex maneuvers underway

And when Richard thought of the master planner-strategizer-warrior bearing down on the walls of Acre, he thought, *Philippe Auguste wouldn't have it any other way.*

* * *

Richard's practiced eye surveyed the Siege of Acre.

Great cranelike trebuchets heaved in their complex rotations, just out of range of the Moorish archers. The construction of a single trebuchet was a feat of strength by itself; but here, a half-dozen of them sighted-in the main bridge, nightmarish creatures straight out of the ancient legends, each one an engineering marvel. When Richard looked more closely, he saw the trebuchets' counterweights—in Europe, they would be nothing more complex than vast timbered bins filled with earth—but here piled high with building stones, obviously captured from nearby fortifications, defeated Moorish constructions... now used as weapons against other Moorish constructions.

At the foot of each trebuchet, a team of men chiseling more of Saladin's building stones into throwable rocks.

And as a trebuchet finally collapsed from the wear of its hundredth or thousandth throw, its stones were offloaded, half to backfill the counterweight of the next trebuchet (already taking shape to replace the collapsed machine), and the other half to be chiseled into more throwing stones.

He's using Saladin's own sword against him

The trebuchets, of course, were only the most visible cog in the

Capetian war machine. A team of knights was amassing on the rise behind the fortress, out of sight of the battlements. A small army of engineers swept from siege engine to siege engine, repairing the inevitable breakdowns; still others were training supplies from the port—oil, rope, food, disassembled houses for lumber and fuel—while another team triaged them into usable caches. Several large siege towers—apparently already crushed by Saladin's defenses—crumbled at the foot of a rampart.

What complexity....!

* * *

The Capetian didn't even turn when Richard approached; he was directing trebuchet fire personally, sometimes timing them to launch at once, sometimes staggering their release. Messengers ran breathless to his side to report from one or another of his contingents, sprinting away again once they received new orders. Several times Philippe Auguste actually grasped a messenger's arm—*Repeat these orders back to me so I know you have them right; better we be slow but precise than fast and clumsy*—before sending him away.

'Richard! Glad you could make it today!' The trebuchets launched another concerted volley. 'Were you lost or something? Took you long enough.'

'Well, as a matter of fact... Would you believe there is a *second* city in Palestine named Acre? There is an *Accaron* in northern Philistia, has nothing to do with this place; we wasted a week trying to join up with you there...'

'Really?' Philippe Auguste's eyes shone in the sun.

'You might consider having your scribes write out place names a bit more clearly in the future...'

'I'll make a note to that effect, Richard.'

'One Hell of a siege you have here, Philippe.'

'You like it?'

'You seem to be throwing one of everything in the whole world at old Saladin. So much for diplomacy.'

'Oh, you can believe me, I have my diplomats in the mix. And when they don't come back with a treaty with Saladin, I'll think of having them fired at the walls, too.'

The two kings watched the siege unfold, a great beast at once chaotic and exquisitely ordered.

'I was hoping you'd have crossed the walls by now, Philippe. I see they've destroyed your siege towers, though. Good to concentrate on frontal assault now that they're gone.'

Philippe Auguste turned to Richard. 'If you think I built those towers to cross *over* Saladin's walls, you're as mistaken as Saladin was.'

And Richard turned back to the walls, squinting his eyes, and could just barely make out men *beneath* the tower wreckage, wielding pickaxes and shovels. 'You're *mining beneath the walls?*'

'Why not? We'll dig in as far as possible before we build a fire under there—we have a whole supply of oil hidden under that wreckage too, you know—and burn the mortar out, let the wall fall under its own weight. If the trebuchets can't get old Saladin to open the front door first.'

'Wow. Extreme prejudice, I see.'

'Is there any other kind?'

* * *

Richard of the Lion's Heart watched Philippe Auguste as he lay siege against the Enemy.

Just as a musical instrument is not the actual musician, but instead the vehicle made to demonstrate his art, the siege of Acre was a real-world unfurling of Philippe's intelligence, a visible construction of pure thought and endless energy, arrayed in the form of men, horses, metal, blood and sweat. The king of France practiced hot war like a poet, like an architect, like a magician, like a priest, and Richard realized that he was witnessing, all at once, a supreme work of science, and skill, and inspiration. The siege was the very incarnation of Philippe Auguste's mind, and Philippe Auguste, for his part, was the very image of strategy and daring and patience and skill; he was Total War, he was War Made Flesh.

And Philippe Auguste seemed to be reading Richard's thoughts:

'I couldn't be having a grander time if I were personally *breeding* Saladin's lineage out of this castle myself.'

Je me souviens bien du jour où tu as dit ces mots
   J'aime, j'aime quelqu'un, j'aime quelqu'un plus que toi
   Et le monde devint soudain plus gris qu'autrefois
   Un' saison sans sommeil, un cœur failli de nouveau

Un feu qui meurt dans ma poitrine, larve fouilleuse
   Dévorant, chassant mon bien ; souvenir qui détrône
   Ton prince et perce ses nuits, qui dans ses os espionne
   Le malheur. La male mort. L'obscure nébuleuse.

Je m'en souviens bien, couleurs vives, relief tout haut
   Seuil sans retour, collapsus, noircissant désarroi
   'J'aime quelqu'un plus que toi'… L'exact ton de ta voix…

Une chose (tu sais) que tu trouveras fabuleuse
   (Idée toute simple, notion sine qua non) :
   Toi tu n'as jamais été que mon unique choix.

I remember well the day you said the words you said:
   'I love, I love another, I love another more'
   ...And the world took on new greys it hadn't had before.
   A skip in the heartbeat, a season sleepless ahead,

The burrowing larva, the dying fire in my proud
   Chest, the thoughts that hunt and devour-Sweet memories to dethrone
   This prince, prick into his nights, cause his every last bone
   To ache sadness. The glamour of death. The deep'ning cloud.

I remember it all, still so vivid in my head:
   The turning point, the spiral down, the darkening shore
   'I love another more'... The exact tone of your voice...

There is something, you know, that I should say aloud
   Something you probably should have already known:
   You were never anything but my first and only choice.

'Is that all there is?'

'You had wanted Italy, Sire. You couldn't do much better than this.'

'But *this?*'

'They say it's the very best.'

'They *do?*'

* * *

'It's hard to get a sense of the whole, isn't it? I've been trying to follow it all with my eye, and I'm not succeeding well.'

François d'Angoulême peered closely at it. An inch closer and his nose would brush.

'Maybe if we took it outside?'

The Artist, standing at the far end of the room from the king, winced instinctively.

A page spoke up. 'It looks like rain, Sire.'

'Yes, well...'

* * *

Soon there was a whole crowd of the king's advisors in the room, swirling around The Portrait.

The Artist stood at a distance, a dark shape in the dark end of the room, and he was hardly serene. He murmured occasionally to the king's page in nervous, heavily-accented French, failing, faltering iterations of *I never intended this to be shown* and *I don't think it's finished yet.*

'It must be some kind of elaborate court game,' said one of the king's men, too loudly for the dark space, leaning in to the Portrait, squinting his eyes. 'There are all these... *clues,* but no central theme, no props or sigels to guess at...'

'A modest and beautiful woman needs very little to reveal her beauty,' said another, 'A ring upon her fingers, a ribbon to gather up her loose tresses. A modest woman only wears as much gold ornament as will serve, and only when necessary, and I do not think she would be ashamed to appear with nothing at all.'

'She is certainly modest. But beautiful is a stretch.'

'Who is it?'

'Some Florentine lady. I don't care which.'

'She looks like she has been dead several times.'

'I think it's—*she's*—no, *it's*—more disturbing than beautiful. Have you ever sat across from a woman who is thinking about her lover instead of the conversation she's having with you? She fixes your eye, but her attention is diverted?'

'The technique is fiendish. The viewer is never allowed to actually enter the girl's field of vision—her gaze is forever elsewhere. We are forced to move about in front of her, to try to catch her attention.'

Several men tried crossing in front of her, as if trying to distract a mime.

Another man flipped her over. 'Maybe it's accompanied by a scroll or letter?' He was pulling at the frame, looking for something hidden there. The Artist shifted and shuffled. 'What is there to explain its various planes of meaning?'

'Don't mess with that,' said another of the king's advisors. 'The personality of the sitter is intended to remain forever hidden, don't you think...?. If the sitter is naught, the frame alone remains...'

'There is a craquelure evident in the surface, isn't there? It already looks very old...' The men had picked her up again, were holding her near the window this time. The Artist blanched.

'He must be left-handed.' They were *touching* the surface now. 'See how the craquelure is diagonal on her left cheek.'

The Artist spoke, feebly: 'That is the only proof that this.... is *real*, that it is a real object, that it exists in this plane.'

The only man to turn to see who spoke was the king himself.

* * *

'Is that the artisan?'

It was not the king's job to approach any man, and the Artist stood in place over on his end of the room, looking very nervous and very contrite indeed. Finally somebody explained to him that he was being addressed by a king, and he approached. François d'Angoulême looked the old man up and down.

'He is very old indeed. And extremely dirty.'

'Yes, Sire.'

'What can he do?'

Much consternation, and the king listened intently. Finally, one of the men said, rather flatly, 'What *can't* he do?'

* * *

François peered into the man's eyes, just as he had done with The Portrait a moment ago. He spoke in Italian.

'So what can you do, Man?'

The man looked helpless. The king became impatient.

'I asked you what you can do. They say you're an engineer. What grand engineering plans have you to offer?'

'I... I would like to found a magnificent horse in bronze.'

'*Excuse me?*'

'A horse in bronze. A huge one. And I have been developing the mathematics for...'

The king rolled his eyes. 'Do you think you could design a cannon? They say you have a knack for all manner of crazy machines of war...'

'Well, I, er, could perhaps... But the perfections of number series like 9147369...' Then, seeing the king's impatience: 'I also have plans for a flying machine.'

'*Cannon.* Can you build cannon?'

'Um, well... I have designed a workable plan for diverting rivers away from enemy cities downstream...'

One of François' advisors raised his voice, as if the problem were one of basic audition and comprehension. 'The king asked you a question.' Then, very slowly, very loudly, as if to a lunatic: '*Cannon...*'

'Well, *yes*... But about my plans for diverting whole rivers...'

'And bridges? How about bridges?' The king's man had no patience either.

'Bridges? But what about 914736...?'

* * *

It was the king's turn to interrupt.

'I would like one of these, please.' He motioned to The Portrait.

His handlers had never heard language like this come from him before. *Please?* Surely something had gone horribly wrong.

'But Sire,' said one of his advisors, 'he doesn't do commissions.'

'No, I mean one of these pictures. Like this one here.' He tapped The Portrait, right in the center. The Artist—*the Artisan,* as the men gathered there insisted on calling him—died a little bit. 'Yes. Yes. One of these. Can

I get this one?' François d'Anglouléme had made his choice. Then, again to his advisors: 'Is there any chance we could scrub the fingerprints off? What artisan leaves his fingerprints all over a portrait?'

* * *

Alas, where is your scorn for cruel Fortune now? Where is your heart, victor over adversity, your heart's honest desire for immortality? And that courageous flame to which common folk bow? Where are those rich pleasures that the Muses allow me, overhead the night of darkest liberty, on a distant green shoreline, when in intimity I led them to dancing in the Moon's bright shadow?

But now, Lady Fortune is my harshest mistress, and my heart, long ago master of its distress, is servant to a thousand sharp regrets night and day. As for posterity, I haven't the least care. And that divine ardor—I don't see anywhere, and those Muses of mine as strangers flee away.

* * *

The words just slipped out: 'I'm not leaving her side.'

'*Excuse me?* Do you know who this man is you're addressing?' François' advisor was uncomfortably close, and the Artist had no way of backing up any further.

'I'm not leaving her side,' he repeated. She isn't for sale.' His voice was barely audible.

The men stared at him, then looked to their king. Finally, one of them spoke up again. 'Forget him then, Sire. He works too slowly anyway.'

But François, more amused than intrigued: 'It'd be too bad to leave him for the Borges or the Medicis to snap up...'

'Why, you don't think he would just bore them to death?'

'Didn't you hear? He can build cannon and bridges... when he's not mumbling about strings of numbered perfection, that is. And I suppose that little trick of diverting rivers to thirst the enemy to death downstream might be useful to *somebody* down here..."

'Scorched earth, huh Sire? If you can't have Naples, you can at least drain their braintrust dry.'

François d'Angoulême's features darkened. His men were silent. Sore subject.

It was the king who broke the ice again. 'He's not much. But when we dig foundations for palaces... I *have* always wanted a reflecting pond... Besides, if he won't part with his little picture here, he might *depart* with it...'

'But Sire, wouldn't you rather have Michelangelo?'

'Oh, is *he* available?'

* * *

'So it's settled then.'

They had spoken about the Artist in the third person for several minutes now. Finally, the man himself spooled up enough courage to speak..

'*Good king, about that bronze horse...*'

François cut him off: '*No.*'

* * *

Your body canvas, my journal, my tablet writ
  My sleeping diary (by candlelight undemurred)
  When finally at break of day you gently stirred
Your cradling arm smudging your lover's words a bit

'*My destination*' *over your sternum aligned*
  At your right breast: 'comfort'; across your left: 'assured'
  '*Fear' and 'alone' forbidden; 'Yours', 'Mine' forever blurred*

Into one banner spoken, inscribed and signed

My Love, I love all of you: body, heart and mind
Desires below, our hearts within, our thoughts above
All held between our hands, things felt, things said, things heard

The movement of our two lives rushing to find
The measured, endless gallop, that one perfect word
The unknowable press of our one perfect love

Yours is the picture of calm, sweet, satisfied, perfect contentedness. A contentedness that grows, strong, courageous, gentle, sweet.

I should also tell you how much I'm looking forward, each day, to seeing you, communing with you. You have made my life a bigger and better life than I ever thought I could make for myself. It is expressive and—at times—virtuosic... Perhaps one day you'll see my name in print, right next to yours, right there on the front page, and you'll know just how much you have changed me, redeemed me, brought me back to the land of the living.

I hope I've brought some joy to your heart, too, my Love. I think—all the time—about lovely, lively conversations, our calm, assured way of living for each other, caring for each other, our quiet naps, our fiery love, the way our minds intermesh, the way our histories intermingle. I think of the first time I saw you in person, so in love that I just had to fall on my knees and resolve my life to holding you. I thought of somehow breathing your breath, of seeing the visions you brought to me by the simple act of breathing your life into my lungs.

I think of the quiet nights, the thought of my Love held in my arms; I think of the hours I might've spent counting your breathing, feeling your skin against mine, knowing I was exactly where I want to be—free, happy, in love. I think of what beautiful words yours might have been in my ear, I think of the times I would have fallen asleep with your lovely song in my mind.

I dream of growing old with you, of travelling together, of living together. I dream of caring for you, I dream of having a sumptuous meal, dining from a table made of my Love, a gorgeous scene.

I dream of having surrounded you and interpenetrated you, mind, heart, body. Of being yours, of making you mine, again and again.

I dream of taking our three-hundred-year love and making it Immortal. I hope my actions are able to do that... and if not, I dream of creating another grand Act for you, just to prove to you that my heart and mind are endless wells of love and desire and longing and admiration.

I will love you my whole life. Dare I say that again? I will love you my whole life. I pray you'll love me, too.

My Lady, I know of course that I am not your only love, that I am neither your first choice or your second, or your third either. I know that I am the last man to cross your mind, and that this man -here- is exciting to you because he is beautiful, that this one -here- is inspiring to you because he is talented, that this one -here- is comforting to you because he is successful, that this one here raises passions within you because he is brilliant... And who am I (neither beautiful nor inspiring nor passionate) but this wretch, mundane as they get, four F's... but a wretch whom you've so inspired that he desires to protect you, raise you to your proper place? But I, though unworthy, do love you—hopelessly love you—and my one mission is to make you immortal.

And Peruggia sat and wept bitterly.

Nous, on n'y lance plus de navires, ne glisse
   Plus de coques aux rails, et ne se souvient
   Plus des anciens carmes qu'on avait bel et bien
   Chanté lorsqu'un vaisseau mouille, arme, hisse

Voyez la vieille ville et ses poteaux anciens
   Noirs devant le ciel clair, voyez comment les lices
   —Vieux squelette délaissé—membres qui s'amollissent
   Ses beffrois fragiles, son corps un poudreux rien

Or la nouvelle ville, chair fraîche sur vieil os
   Dédaigne son berceau, ne reconnaît plus les siens
   Verse tout son mépris sur le port que voici

Quel orgueil, cette ville et ses concitoyens
   Ses navires naviguent dans d'étranges eaux
   La ville a bien grandi. Mes navires aussi

We no longer launch here, no broadbeamed whalers slip
   Down skidding rails to seas, no one here remembers
   The old dead formulas (spells burnt down to embers)
   They once chanted hearty to christen a new ship

See how our old skyline, with her blackened timbers
   Barely reaches skyward, see the years' dark claws strip
   Life from her skeleton, see the church steeples tip
   With time, frail limbs aloft, fleshless fragile members

This new city beside, new flesh upon old bone
   Disdains its old cradle, recognizes its own
   No more, sniffs its proud scorn upon where the port fell

Proud men with their standards, their new city ingrown
   Dark ships clog the channel away toward the unknown
   My, the city has grown. My ships have grown as well

'Well you know, I have this friend, and she went off her antidepressant and filed for a divorce, too...'

'So what you're saying, Mark, is that divorce is the realm of the insane?'

'What I meant was...'

'What you *meant* is irrelevant. What you *said* is that your friend went off her meds and divorced her husband.'

There was a long silence.

'And how could *what you meant* be far off from a declaration that I must be just a little insane, Mark? Or a lot?'

For some reason, the murmurs of all the other coffeeshop denizens came to a halt at once, all sentences hitting that same dead spot, that same random, collective refraction between thoughts, all at the same moment.

I was the first to break the truce.

'Do you honestly think I've always been like this? That the need for meds is hardwired into me? That I am *bad chemistry-plus-bad wiring?* That our lovely... *Sundari...*'—Vicus fairly hissed this—'...is doing me a favor by having stooped to marrying me? That *I'm* the one screwed up, that I'm the one at fault in this? Did it ever occur to you that one of the reasons I'm on meds is her?'

'It *is* pretty hard to believe the things you've told me today.'

'Yeah? Thanks.'

* * *

They used to build boats in a little fishing village a hard stone's throw downstream from the main bulk of Namnètes. Real capable things, sturdy, capable skiffs just right for racing downchannel to the estuary, just right for towing back upstream with a shining haul by summer noonday. Julius Caesar himself mentions them; he knew a good little river launch when he saw one.

In Christian times the village—still a village, still a fishing community, still building those strong, light skiffs—came to be known as Parish St. Nicolas, and as it had been in Gallo-Roman times, it was the lifeblood of the larger body that was Nantes. In the days when you couldn't count on a crop making it to harvest without Vikings coming and burning it, you could count on the protein Parish St. Nicolas hauled in over the transoms of their launches—no way for the Hun to wipe out your fish populations—and besides, it was always fishermen from the Parish who sounded the first and most reliable alarm when a Viking ship began its tack into the lower estuary.

Nantes had a wall around it. And the Parish was a poor one—it struck no one as odd that Nantes' own motto since time immemorial was 'Neptunus favet eunti', *Neptune favors the traveler*, and the only traveling Neptune would have anything to do with would be in one of those St. Nicolas skiffs, and it struck no one as odd that the little out-village that gave Nantes its very identity should only barely benefit from its salutary efforts materially—and the little chapel they dedicated to St. Nicolas was on its best days modest, and on its worst grimy, and if you stood on the little butte behind it, you could see the heights of Nantes' St. Felix cathedral, rising and rising with every addition and renovation that the wealthy Nantais afforded it.

And the chapel in St. Nicolas continued to gather its own to itself.

* * *

It's just a length of numbers, just some values, all hard and clear and perfect, one a pirouette, one a barn owl, one a mousetrap. Nothing impressive.

But as Mark spoke, the numbers began vibrating, little resonances that were barely... audible.

The story they're telling is not vivid, yet not so very inert either.

Surely they are all interrelated. An indifferent, impersonal puzzle.

'You know, Vicus, we're all expecting *you* to work this out. This thing you're doing to Sundari. I mean, *leave her?* Those were just *stories*, right?'

But the numbers and memories are a twisting choreography of tumblers in the eternal darkness inside a padlock. Mark mistakes my expression for earnest interest in what he's saying.

Tectons.

Ceramic tiles.

A mandala of dominos.

The perfect solids.

* * *

Morning is breaking over the Loire, the tremors of first light on cat's-paws tricking the eye into believing the river is a concentrated riot of barely-controlled energy.

The boatmen draw on this very illusion; by never attempting to disbelieve it, they are able to derive unreal momentum from the sweetest breath of breeze.

Beneath the blossoming dawn the skiffs fan out from the port in crazy curlicues, an unchartable mathematics of motion and activity. Seen from the heights of the Butte Sainte Anne, the port by morning light is a chrysanthemum of complexity.

A knot of skiffs—a new and chaotic bloom—cuts in close to the Quai de la Fosse. A ship—orders of magnitude larger than the skiffs—takes shape in a new drydock hugging the Quai. Already by sunup, there are boys hanging over the rails, trying to see this technological wonder up close. The blessed few—the wiry ones, the ones that look strong enough to climb fast and slight enough to push through narrow cracks and smart enough not to get killed doing either—are chosen to jump ship from skiff to drydock, to help run rigging and jam oakum into seams.

They say King Francis married the daughter of Brittany's duchess just to get his hands on this port. That he poured untold coin into this drydock. And when they stepped the mast on his first ship, they began to compare it to spires over in old Nantes.

-Passacaglia-

Suddenly Nantes is looking at Parish St Nicolas in a new light.

* * *

It only made sense that those athletic little skiffs be built in proximity to the fishing village that would use them; the new drydock, though, was a different matter, and sharp foresight had it several hundred yards farther downstream, where the channel widened out, where you might be able to accrete twenty or thirty of those skiffs around the growing ship to service her with men and supplies, and where you might manage to launch her without immediately hanging her up on the far bank.

And the men that gathered around those rising hulks began to be of a different grain, too. Those old-world skiff captains were hardly captains—they might be boys, they might be old men, there might not be captains at all, but a clutch of a half-dozen brothers and cousins, all with essentially the same title and prestige: *fisherman*... it had been this way since forever, ever since they started building boats in Parish St. Nicolas. But now there were these new characters, men who *commanded* ships, men were of real *captain stock*, and these men didn't fit inside Nantes' walls quite so neatly anymore.

With the masted ships, you had more than just the estuary trade available to you—estuary, region, globe... there are fortunes to be made. There are pirates—a different kind of man/a different kind of bravery to sail out of sight of land, into storms, into battle. *Neptune protects* suddenly derived a new and colorfully different meaning.

The Island was as natural a place as any to live if you wanted to live encircled by broader horizons. It had originally been a marshy rise, covered in scrub, that had grown from the silt brought to the Loire by the Erdre which conflued here—no reason to ever try living here, it was unsafe to build on, it was unsafe to *live on* what with it being outside the walls-proper of Nantes' old city.

It was *outside Nantes*, outside what anyone might call civilization, outside what anyone might call *proper*.

And as Nantes' captains claimed their plots of 'land' (if you could call it that) on the Island, as they began to sink great old-growth piers into the soft silt, the captains seemed to cease being so very *Nantais* anymore, so very *fisherman*-like.

No one seemed to notice that not one of those stout piers being driven into the marshes was intended to undergird a church. In Nantes, you had *dozens* of churches, a steeple every few yards it seemed, they were part of the landscape, part of the worldview: if you grew up in Nantes, you were just as likely as not to never *ever* step outside of the walls, and you always knew where you were just by seeing which steeple reached up above the houses in a given place. But on the Island, no churches would ever be built—none would even be *planned*—and this was exactly how the captains would have it: why have a church define the horizon, when you fully intended to have *the horizon* define the horizon?

And if you looked at it just right with a wide-enough eye, you would see that Island was long and straight and streamlined, and the main line through the captains' rising neighborhood was straight as a ship's keel, and the contours of its edges were contoured exactly like a ship's too, and if you didn't know any better, you might believe that these men had intended all along to build a giant ship in the channel across from Nantes ('*Nantes-in-Walls*' was how they put it, derision just dripping from name, lips, tone)... just across from *Nantes-in-Walls*, just to show the old city that they could leave any time they wished, just to show that they might as well spend the rest of their days on board a great, independent vessel.

And The Rules seemed not to apply so very well to these men anymore, who now were just as often as not in the West Indies or crossing before the large of the Barbary Coast or cannoning the English with bow-chasers (and 'accidentally' firing broadsides into French ships when English were scarce) as cooling their heels in their new marmorated sitting rooms or counting booty in their basement storerooms.

And the Island sailed just out of reach of the city of Nantes.

* * *

It was easy enough math: if you build a ship in a drydock situated lengthwise on the riverbank, you are limited either in the number of ships you can build, or in the length of those ships, and most likely both. And by the time the armators at the Quai de la Bourse and Quai de la Fosse realized this, faster thinkers had already snapped up the marshed siltspits midstream, just downstream yet, just across from the dome of Notre Dame de Bon Port, and the shipyards began to grow into terrifying behemoths of filigree and glass, technological miracles of their own right, giant anti-ships, rising inverted above the scrub: and if you could build a shipyard like this, you certainly could build a leviathan within those soaring works.

And if I choose just right, I can get a table claimed by both the Café de la Bourse and the Coquille—or, more precisely, claimed by neither establishments—right down on the Place du Commerce, right where they used to build and launch those St. Nicolas skiffs, a few hundred yards from the Quai de la Fosse, and within rifleshot of the new shipworks over on the river marshes over there. This place is hardly evocative of Caesar's Gaulish campaigns anymore, but at least the waiters don't hassle me overly; my table is covered with notebooks and coffees.

* * *

There's a moral difference between cinnamon and chocolate.... And rum and slaves... And Nantes' Island is full of men wielding a new level of immense power, power that could only be borne of contracts with the devil, *my how far we've come.*

The buildings began to have faces now, faces frightening and twisted, faces snarling and distant, faces threatening, devastating. There are grotesques on the buildings in Feydeau... not just gargoyles—they say gargoyles were there to shed away evil spirits from sacred place, and these faces, here on the Island, would turn away no such thing—but faces better representing... *malevolence... menace...*

...Surveillance.

* * *

The long view, the two-thousand-year view (if I squint my eyes), is here, if not exactly obvious. Who am I to see the whole history of the place?—and there are precious few sites like this one, cleverly chosen at ground-level, where I can leisurely overview the city, the cities—and Nantes as freeform living construct is at once evocative and dizzying.

9 is the duration, the Age, the confluence of the Loire at its narrowest, the web of tributaries where the Loire comes to exist in its most real, a chain of nine links. 1 is the flesh of mortal men, the heartache larva (that hated one), 1 is a single metallic coin in the palm launching athletic skiffs into swift waters, 1 is in the bones of my right hand. 4 receives the first pulsion into the waves, 4 is the Island, 4 is the piledriven silt riven with brinesoaked timbers. 7 is a towering ship, the capacious shipyards rising, that wild dare over there across from Notre Dame du Bon Port, launching million-tonners to the world. 3 is the womb of St. Nicolas Parish, the scent of fresh pineplanks and mud in the fist.

6 is love, painful and precise and perfect.

* * *

They had to dredge out the channel after a time—those behemoths drew stunning draft, they did, and getting one wedged in on the sand and marl would be nothing short of building a new island in the channel—and then once they had made a deep channel for themselves, they could never let it silt back in, because the shipbuilders knew the draft they could afford to ply now, and since it took two years to finish one ship, each dredge was like a two-year contract to never let nature take back over ever again, and might as well dig it deeper, see if the boatbuilders can keep up.

But the Loire is a fickle mistress, and her function as an estuary is a process of filling and draining with the rising and falling tides, and sometimes she run fore and sweet, and sometimes she run backwards as brackish, and with that deep channel dredged out as deep as could be, the estuary never again filled as it should.

And the tributaries—that lovely Erdre and her sisters!—began etching down farther and farther in its banks, too, and soon enough, the old pilings and piers of the Island, exposed to air for the first time in four centuries, began warping and degrading and failing, too, and no one noticed it when it was day by day, week by week, year by year, but if you walked around the Island now, you'd see the tops of two buildings kissing as their foundations slipped and shifted, and the failing of the estuary became the failing of the light...

Deals with Lucifer always demand a price, and the only coin is the soul's substance.

The only remedy was a drastic one: fill in the Erdre and all the channels crisscrossing Nantes—fill in especially that gap separating St. Nicolas from the Island, cover it all over, entomb it in concrete, never let it taste another drop of Erdre, or Loire, or estuary brine.

And whatever you do, don't ever stop dredging: your city depends on it. This is the new Venice of the North.

* * *

And Mark's idea of *nonchalant* had been a failure, too.

'So what's eating you, Vicus?'

So what do you do when the outcome of the trial is a foregone conclusion? Sure: I recant. Still, it moves.

I heard him. Hard not to. Many thoughts tumbled through the darkness of the light, many clever ripostes. I stifled them all.

Instead, a little *graphie* was taking shape under my fingers, a napkin and a pen:

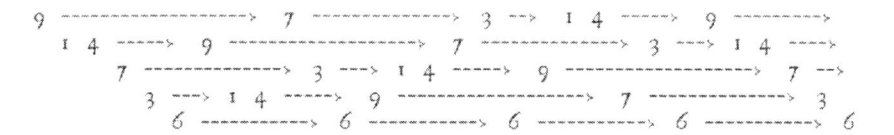

```
9 --------------------> 7 ----------------> 3 ---> 1 4 ------> 9 ---------->
  1 4 -----> 9 --------------------> 7 ----------------> 3 ---> 1 4 ----->
    7 ---------------> 3 ---> 1 4 ------> 9 --------------------> 7 -->
      3 ---> 1 4 -----> 9 --------------------> 7 ----------------> 3
        6 ------------> 6 ------------> 6 ------------> 6 -----------> 6
```

Passe le temps, et passent nos amours
   Se paiss' mon cœur de tout son seul la nuit
   S'émerveille à l'abandon mon esprit
   D'un soulas morne, et en rêve, et au jour

Et tremblent mes lèvres et ma voix pour
   Leur souffle coupé, pour tous leurs ennuis
   Pour le long souvenir, et pour l'oubli
   Le cœur si ancien, le cœur tell'ment lourd

Autant qu'elle m'horrifie, tant me nuit
   Cette guerre, elle ne me détruit
   Guère, ni de ses flammes, ni de ses bruits

Enfin, plus ne suis ce que j'ai été
   Je ne suis plus chair, ains fait de poussier
   Lame lourde à la main, l'âme d'acier

Time passes, and hearts are prone to breaking
   And the soul feeds its loneliness at night
   And the mind reels at how far from the light
   It finds solace, in dreams, in waking

And (with lips quiv'ring and voices quaking)
   Breath seizes midstream before finding joy
   My head forgets and lonely cares annoy—
   Reminders of the heart's ancient aching

I am not the lover of war, but war
   Made me, and war can no longer destroy
   Me, nor can flames overtake this heart, nor

Am I e'en what I once was anymore
   I am ringing deathless steel, war's alloy
   Heavy in the hand, hardened to the core

*　*　*

They had told the women to huddle beneath the tarp in the waist of the ship. The rain fell hard and cold and the sound it made when it hit the canvas, there was no way there wasn't some hail mixed in.

Havoise steadfastly refused to 'huddle'... *anywhere:* in the waist of the ship, in the wells beneath the bundles of goods, among the shuddering, whimpering women.

She was at the rails, and although the freezing, surging sea terrified her, her face was redrosy, very alert in the eye. Her cowl refused to hide her face and hair for long, and without her even noticing, the gale slowly, systematically undid her braid.

She was not one to look in mirrors, certainly not one to preen and pin and pine, and she would not have recognized herself, her hair red and rich, a life of its own, Havoise a prophetess a bowsprit a saintess. Somehow she had a stature out here, and her bones were long and straight and strong out here, and she held on for dear life, and grinned mischief like a thief.

Women—even weavers' daughters—knew that their hair was a sensuous temptation for men, the glory of a woman, and everyone knew that a proper woman kept it hidden and... *kept.* But the women were all huddled, and the men all hauling on frozen ropes, and Havoise was in flight, and no one— Havoise least of all—gave a damn about her hair triumphant.

I am at once the most self-aware woman in the world, and the least self-aware

*　*　*

William was not the snarling lion of legend (or even a creeping leopard), but Havoise' fingers are working lions into the legs of his throne. She had heard that was how the kings of France had always had it: they all sat on Dagobert's throne, with lions on the armrests.

Hmm Maybe it was something like... this

Her memory of the man never had him on any throne, God no.

But whoever saw the tapestry would expect a king, and kings sit on thrones, and this throne had better have lions for William to rest his hands on.

* * *

This Torsten, this little liden, this sapling

The memories run fullon for this scrawny man she was married to in the choir of that little church in Falaise, and she hasn't even the tears to honor them with anymore.

He used to say 'If you want a job done right, ask a busy man to do it.'

And Torsten was busy, for he had to be.

For the Boy Duke, the son of the Devil Magnificent, was fearfully frail, and it would take nothing at all to tip him into a well. Havoise was horrified to realize that she herself *at what, thirteen?* could have done the deed herself.

There were plenty of attempts, by huge, powerful and cunning men.

Many had dared lift arms against the bastard son of Robert the Magnificent. Many had come close.

Thus it is with bastards.

* * *

Britain the Cold, Britain the Undiscovered Country, Britain nonetheless seemingly aching to be conquered and chastised.

Havoise knew nothing about this. She nonetheless felt the keel dig into English gravels; she was off the ship like Duke William himself. She might as well have a longsword in her fists or a dagger in her teeth.

* * *

Largesse is going to be your best ally

Largesse will keep the blade from your ribcage

* * *

The caravan of carts met the ship at the beach—*everyone kept calling it the beach head*—and men came to lift out the ship's cargoes and heave them over the shoulder to keep them above the surf. The trunks and bundles were lowered with care to the sand, then up the beach toward the carts. As for the female cargoes, they were set on their feet—perhaps less carefully—*they had feet you know*—and left to fend for themselves up the beach. Many of the women, instead of advancing, sank to their knees, chins vomit and tears, and Havoise made an effort to help them, but they shrank away from her ministrations, embarrassed.

After all, Havoise was a countess. Or at least she would be once she got to Glastonbury and claimed the title her husband had had made for her.

* * *

A humble messenger, from Heav'n above to Earth I come, this child had faced the receiving end of a dagger already by the age of five; only the Armorer had intervened before the fatal thrust, striking the assassin first with fists, then with sword, striking the corpse to salt and blood and tendons before the wondering eye of Torsten The Clerk, who was too astounded at the scene to even think of vomiting, and only that night, in the failure to sleep, sitting on the edge of his bed, did he realize as he wiped his brow that the assassin's blood was in his hairline. At first he thought it was he himself the injured and dying man, and he felt certain that the bits of brains freckling his face and neck were his own, and the flecks of marrow beaten clear of the assassin's bones had droozed from his own pores *so this is what it's like to die* but then he was cured by a bath with a cloth and a basin of clear water; only when he saw the white basin by morning light, the bits of human having sorted by size, weight and density overnight, did he think of throwing up, and not having thought of eating since all the excitement, he went straight down to the bile, and the bitter flavors of his own life lived in his mouth and the stink of his life burnt in his nostrils, and he realized that he himself was only alive by the grace of

God, and that the poor man whose innards had been scrambled with the outer universe was not.

We will find out what drove this man

Of course everybody knew that the assassin had struck only because William the Lad was a bastard, and that as a bastard there was no way that he could have anything even remotely resembling Legitimacy, that precious coin, and no matter how much he clenched his fists, not matter how hard he gritted his teeth, William was a bastard, and going to Hell, and there was nothing anybody could do about it.

But Torsten, awake (again) at night, his childbride asleep at his side, knew that that couldn't possibly be the end of the story.

For the assassin, once identified by his name and family, was not in line to become Duke, should the lad be slain. Not even close, in fact.

The world cannot tolerate a William The Bastard, the idea itself is an abomination

And the assassin had sacrificed himself, with no hope for gain, except to assuage his moral disgust. Even had he managed to kill the boy, he would've remained a petty mundane.

We will use this to our advantage

* * *

The rain fell cold on Havoise' face, streaming down and soaking her clothes, from her collar first, then her breasts, then her belly. She gloried in it, she reveled in it, her body renewed by English rain, her mind renewed by horizons *I had promised you travels and dreams* but what woman here and now ever 'travels' ever 'wanders' ever points helm to a horizon and *goes?* For a Normand man could never hope to go more than twenty miles from the room where his mother's belly had given him, cold wet bloody and crying from the first minute, to the light of day and the pricking cold of this world. And a woman even less: twenty miles for a woman was a radius for the insane, for the witcher woman, for the lunatic and leper.

But Havoise crunched English gravel beneath the wheels of her cart, and English rain washed her in cold Celtic baptisms.

She was no longer young. But she could have sprinted to Glastonbury, bold and wild and free, through the English rain.

* * *

Torsten was nothing if not taciturn, and even though it felt like a rape every time he exerted his rights over his wife, she sometimes drew him slyly to her nonetheless, knowing that his moods afterward were more given to parley and revelation. For to her, whether at age thirteen or at twenty-two, everything about her husband was a revelation.

'There is such a thing as a Treaty Elm' he had said, preoccupied with a thought late one night.

Havoise dared not make a sound, raise a finger: if she wanted him to continue, he would have to be left alone in his thoughts, which he apparently had forgotten to silence.

'...The kings of France and the dukes of Normandy do all their diplomacy there....'

Havoise made not a pip.

'It's a wonder the dukes don't learn from what they hear there at the Treaty Elm. The Frankish kingship changes family to family every month it seems, you'd think the dukes would see some kind of contrast, learn a lesson well, by seeing how the Roberts and the Capets make their war, conclude their peace, dress their children, rule their wives.'

Torsten was at his writing table now, talking his thoughts to parchment, still naked after having taken Havoise. Having forgotten that she was there, and awake, and that her mind, too, was very active and curious.

'The Roberts divide everything equally between sons,' he said, 'doesn't matter how smart or dumb the child is, doesn't matter if the child has his members, or reason, or courage. Doesn't matter how much the father loves one and hates the next.

'But the Capets are choosy. And smart. Every last one.

'They rarely let themselves make a mistake.'

The air hung with the scents of ink and oil and sex. Havoise watched Torsten in the light of the lamp. He hadn't touched the quill to the book in several minutes.

She swallowed hard, and spoke, a hoarse whisper:

'And you're wondering why an assassin might attack, with no hope of advancement or advantage...'

She could see Torsten think, his eyes focusing on concepts he couldn't put words to, ideas that hadn't been invented in Normandy yet.

'...And you're trying to understand how an assassin, seeing only the dimmest of victories, could somehow dream that today's little win could ever be meaningful if it can't ever be made into lasting advancement tomorrow...'

But he had seen the minds of *foreigners* grapple these things, she was sure of it—she now knew that he had actually *been* to that fabled Treaty Elm, had undoubtedly listened, too, and tried to comprehend.

'...And you're thinking that if an assassin sees the world like a Robertian Frank does, you'd do well to figure out how to think like a Capet. If your specific job is to keep William the Bastard alive all the way to his becoming Duke, this is the sort of thing that could save him.'

And Torsten turned, seemed to see Havoise for the first time that night, awake and alive, there in their bed. And seeing fire and mischief in Havoise' eyes, he approached, ready to take her again.

* * *

On the eve of William the Bastard's twentieth birthday, the barons were arrayed against him. Val-ès-Dunes was a village at best, a little communal outlier at worst, a dozen houses, and the barons had put the inhabitants to the sword, knowing how to draw the Bastard out, knowing his pride, his very nature, would not stand for such an insult to his prestance. To Hell with the dead farmers and their wives, there were only a dozen of them at the most, more died daily to pestilence or old age or bee-sting, a little baronial power struggle was a Nothing on the grand map of Christendom, yet they knew that this would be a whipping to bring the horse to bray, then buck, then throw his weight around hapless in the pen, until the barons could come and subdue him, a bull in the *corrida*, exposing flank as well as horn and hoof.

This sort of thing had always worked before.

They knew the Bastard's hand would tighten round his sword at the news of the massacre—*the so-called massacre*—they knew the sword would be free of its scabbard once the man had had time to ruminate on the affront. And his squires would have his horses ready then, and riders would be riding to collect the loyals by lunchtime, and he would ride at supper, and they would have him by sundown.

But by now, the assault by William's forces was overdue by about an hour.

* * *

A horse appeared at the horizon, led loosely by some lad. The lad was wearing William's colors.

The lad was a stripling, a feeble little colt; the barons marveled at this young creature's gait, the horse leading him as much as the other way around. From a distance, from up close, no one could tell if he was a monk, or a burgher, or a doctor, or what.

'Arms!' a sergeant bellowed. And the men rushed forward, taking the horse from him, pulling at frock and shirt.

'I have none,' said the stripling, the lad. No longer a teen, but nothing of a man to be found in him or near him. 'I just brought my book and my writing gear.' He laid them all out, opened his kit, showed the barons his writing tools. Some reached down with their sword to poke derisively at the lad's pens and sand and inkwells.

'If this is a trick...'

'How can it be a trick? I have nothing; you have everything.'

'So you're here to negotiate for the Bastard's surrender?'

'Far from it. I came here to ask what it is milords desire from your Duke. There is a difference, you know.'

'We want his head.'

The lad looked all 'round: the size of men, the barded horses, the grey of steel. 'I see you're already making arrangements for that.'

The men all shifted in their saddles, the horses touchy, ruing, restless, chuffing and chuffing, hooves alight.

'And once you have his head,' Torsten said, with a flick of his head to indicate Falaise, over the hill *over there*, 'what then?'

'The way things were. The way things ought to be.'

'*The way things were*, you were all minor barons under a duke.'

'At least he was legitimate. His authority over us, his birth, his lineage.'

'And when you do in the Bastard, who takes it all?' The boy's tone was even, matter of fact, couldn't care a lot, couldn't think of a reason why not. 'A *new* duke?'

The horses stirred, reading the pulse of their riders, sensing their new mutual suspicion and *Hear my prayer ô Lord* brand new hatred, rivals among rivals instead of a united militia, a morass rather than the army of barons formerly arrayed against their master.

'You all know we are all born the same, a helpless infant. There is nothing that distinguishes a man, whether his tongue—which knows not how to speak in eloquence—the eye—which an infant knows not how to focus—the strength of an arm or the straightness of the spine—we are all brothers and equals at birth.

'And your sons will be born with the same disadvantages—and yet you expect them to outshine the rest, to be higher and nobler than the rest. What can distinguish your boy from the great seething mass? His... *nobility?*

'*A noble is a noble because he has gifts to give, and he gives them.*

'No one suffers a usurper. No one less than barons suffering another baron, an *equal*, a *peer*, having taken throne. God help the man. When the Bastard dies, folded over your sword, his power is divided, ten ways, twenty ways, a thousand ways. The murdered man disappears, the murderer *diminishes*... Certainly the most your sons can aspire to—the very *best*—is to achieve the status of their father.'

Torsten's eye was away, somewhere in the clouds. His words would have their time to find their target.

'All the truly ambitious man needs do is walk away; the Duke will show his *largesse*, and all grow in prestige. For you really have no idea what glorious deeds await...'

And the horses shifted more and more, as if reading the puzzlement of the barons who, a half-hour previous, had been ready to gut the Bastard with righteousness. The stripling looked up at the horsemen with frank, tired eyes. He distractedly began cutting a pen.

One of the barons spoke up. '*What awaits?*'

'Something.'

'Something *what?*'

'Something... *wonderful.*'

-Passacaglia-

Voilà que la mélancolie et les ennuis s'accroissent
   Ce sont les émotions (ma Foi) des hommes moindres
   Des frustes, des minables et de tout leur genre :
   Des solitaires, des sans-but, et, hélas

Des héros dont la mission échoue, des angoisses
   Pâles qui font trembler lèvre et fantôme. Eteindre
   Au bout de ma lame tout ce que j'ai à craindre,
   Les tuer tous, ô que Dieu les siens reconnaisse !

Ce chevalier accomplit son plus grand coup :
   Sacrifier son cœur pour le plus grand bien du monde
   Sur l'autel de son courage et son orgueil, où

Il immolera son pauvre cœur ; ce marabout
   Ne saura être dompté, dira ce que l'immonde
   N'osera dire : Je ne ressens plus rien du tout

Melancholies increase, and pain and fear accrue:
   These are the emotions (my Faith) of lesser men,
   Of the unevolved, of the wretched and their ken,
   Of the alone, of the purposeless, of untrue

Heroes whose missions fail, pale words allowed to brew
   Ghosts and delirium on lips a-tremble. When
   I put all my fears, ev'ry one, to the blade, then
   What will be left to do but let God sort them through?

This knight by nights enacts his greatest endeavor:
   To sacrifice his heart for the world's greater good
   On the altar of pride and courage, to sever

The strings holding his heart to this world, to never
   Let his heart be ruled, to say what no coward would
   Ever dare speak: I feel nothing whatsoever

***

The king of France is *somewhere* up there. God, fourteen men to choose from.

The façade of Notre Dame was perhaps the most massive manmade thing Philippe had ever seen. His own foreign policy excepted, of course.

There's nothing quite like having a place to stand for eternity, right next to David, and Solomon, and the Jeroboams...

We're all about twelve feet tall, narrow as posts, serene as... kings

***

It had been a reckless act of faith to even *begin* the façade of Notre Dame before finishing the nave. You usually had to start at the choir—the holiest place, the head of Christ, the rays of light emanating from His holy countenance, and work down from there: His arms at the transept, His holy Body (that is, the nave to contain the Church's numberless members) next... you'd build until you ran out of funds, then no matter how long or short your church was, you'd hurry to get a western façade built to cap off the building before your credit went bad.

Philippe's father, the hapless Ludovicus Seventh of the name, had begun to work the site of Notre Dame the year of Philippe Auguste's birth, and the lad began to think of the cathedral as a symbol of his own life, his own life's mission, as a gift he gave himself with each new stone set in place. The choir—symbolic of the Head of Christ—began carving out slices of sky the day young Philippe took the Crown (and the Island) as his birthright, the very day his father bitterly made the long ride out to St. Denis mostier to live out his days decapitate...

And that same day, Philippe had paced a hundred long steps from the Head of Christ down to His feet, and with his heel, marked where the towers and façade would also stand.

'Get started here immediately. I want to see a cathedral here before long.'

'Sire, certainly you understand that you just paced out a distance of... well over a hundred meters... From choir to towers, that's... *that's a fair distance.*'

'Yes.'

There had been a terrible silence. Blackbirds flew. And Philippe Auguste had broken the silence with simple words, a propos of nothing in particular.

'Well, you know I stride fast and long.'

* * *

Now, every time Philippe opened a book referencing the Temple of Solomon, he saw Notre Dame, in some intermediate state of construction, as a miniature honoring the whole leaf, the whole book. And somehow Solomon's Temple had grown some rose windows in her transepts—*yes, the Temple of Solomon was now cruciform in the Frankish psyche*—and the Holy Land was as recognizable as kissmyhand, all you had to do was crane your head to see the great cathedral rising above the roofs of the Island, of *Philippe Auguste's* Island, and if you had good eyesight, you'd find a whole host of kings, ancient and modern, arrayed 'cross the façade like the first line of troops advancing lockstep to take Acre, or Jerusalem the Blessed Jerusalem, or Chinon for that matter, and if someone ever asked you *Are those men up there with the regal air, are they Old Testament kings or are they our own kings, Frankish and Capetian and still living among us?* the correct answer would be, *Yes.*

And Philippe Auguste turned a page, and in the margin, there was a great swirling press of gargoyles and grotesques, the armies of Philippe's great Future Memory.

* * *

The Knights Templar had bowed to the Alchemist Pope, Innocent the Second, who had issued their holy mandate: *figure out the Temple in Jerusalem...*

And would they build Jerusalem here?

Innocent the Second had granted the Templars the right to build their own churches—*let the world be studded over with New Jerusalems*—and Bernard of Fontaine, bishop of Clairvaux, had learned all the lessons the Templars returned with, and had written new light into the stone of Suger's church at St. Denis, the new crypt of the kings of France—*let there be light and it was so*—and when Philippe Auguste, newly returned from the Holy Land himself, stood before the glorious façade of the great Cathedral of Chartres, where they held Mary's Veil in a little wooden box in a chapel at the far end of the great edifice, he thought of Bernard's sonorous voice, chanting in slow iterations, *What is God? He is length, width, height and depth.*

Chartres was just sixty miles from the upthrust Notre Dame, *too bad the two couldn't be made to have conversations, like Moses and Elijah at Transfiguration...*

He'd been to St Denis a hundred times, of course, the third jewel in the crown, the third Person of the Holy Trinity, mostly to remind his father who the *real* king was, now that the old man had planted his foot in the grave up there at the old monastery; but there was no denying that the basilica at St Denis was a wonder, a fortress of light and vaults and meaning, and if he hadn't known there were dozens if not hundreds of corpses of dead kings—all raiment and bones and gore—littering the underworld beneath the choir of this rare gem of *lux continuum* and reminding him that one day, perhaps this very night, he would surrender his own soul and be put in the ground under those same pavers, he would happily have set up his tent right there at the transept of the place, enjoyed the morning sun as it was transformed into something holier than the sparkling Easter it always was, enjoyed the noonday sun as it turned into the blood of Christ through the great Rose of the south crossing.

But he knew his kinsmen mouldered away to jerky beneath the stones here...

Best just to visit the old man as he mouldereth, try not to get any on me

* * *

But if only he could dress himself in that light that poured in through those vast panels of glass, if only he could stroll the Earth in that glad raiment *and yet I say unto you, that even Solomon in all his glory was not arrayed like one of these* and yet when his heel struck the old pavers of the basilica, he could hear the ring of ages, and he knew that he was the very picture of Solomon when he strode through that basilica, and the elision was complete: that it was indeed the very Temple he strove to build for himself, and far from a distraction away from his one love, his one obsession and mission, he realized that Aquitaine, seeing Philippe draped in the light of old kings and new kings alike, would fairly *beg* him to take her, would crawl hands and knees through whole furnaces of biting flame, emerging annealed, purified by the fire, to become his, to shine from his light.

* * *

The only other time he had been draped in such light was when he was a twelve-year-old child—this even before he was king—and he had traveled to Chartres on pilgrimage.

Chartres was on the path to Spain, and although Spain had St James at Compostella, and Rome had Peter and the Popes, Chartres held the Virgin.

(Now everybody knows that Mary could no longer be found on Earth as flesh and bone—so Chartres could not possibly have a gruesome relic like Compostella did with James' head—for Mary was *assumed into Heaven,* and it was obscene and heretical to imagine that any part of her fleshly being be held and displayed as a mere piece of dried-up meat.

Instead, Chartres had the Virgin's *veil,* the very raiment she wore at the moment of our Lord's birth, hidden in a wooden coffer in a nook in the chapel on the far side of the main altar. Veils as mystery, veils as symbolic of virginity. Charles the Bald—they told Philippe—had gifted this precious fragment of fabric to Chartres in years past, and it had contributed time and again—so they say—to the survival of the church, sometimes so flagrantly as to defy the imagination. Why, one time—so the story goes—the Normans were advancing on Chartres, set on prying anything of value from any church in sight, and the bishop of Chartres waved the veil from the top of the building, and the Normans, apparently still pious enough to respect such a venerable item, went off to pillage elsewhere.

The essential—made clear to the young king—was that Mary's veil was a *relic*, and relics are not just *symbolic* of continuity and power, they *are* continuity and power, and that Philippe should count on that relic to save more than just a church building some day.)

But young Philippe had been too young and curious to stand still looking at a piece of old fabric, and before long had wandered off into the greater building, and wherever he went, the cathedral's monks had indulged him, knowing the whole edifice to be holy—*he could find a candle or a bit of mortar to study if he had wanted to, it would still benefit his soul*—and besides, he was to be the king of France one day...

Soon he had found himself up in the highest reaches of the church, on ledges and walkways even the most pious monks wouldn't dare to tread, sitting in raptured awe before a tall panel window—he had been too close to it to be able to make out the scene—way up in the rarefied air above the choir, tucked in under the vaults. All he could tell was that it appeared to be made of three large sections, the lowest of which was a woman's feet, the middle one a child held on her lap, and the uppermost one the image of her head and shoulders.

He stared at this window for hours.

And the colors fell over his shoulders and knees as he sat, and he was transfigured by the blues and reds, dappled lightpaint playing over his whole person.

* * *

The Capets, he knew, had not the clean, straight, unbroken lineage back to time immemorial that he might have wished for. No one did. For the old Clovis kings, those old Merovingians, those warlords (he thought as his heel struck the old St Denis pavers) were themselves usurpers, Frankish invaders onto Gaulish soil, and only with adept and daring did they style themselves, in the words of Grégoire de Tours, *nouveaux Constantins*, essentially just *invented* themselves as late-Roman, not modern-Barbarous.

The Carolingians were much the same, the majordomo caste of the Merovingian household, and as the Merovingian kings hemmed and hawed and shuffled around, embarrassed at themselves whenever the Saracen came and burned their cities, it was the majordomo who mounted an army and went to kill Moorish men, putting the Saracen to the sword. And these majordomos all had names like *The Hammer* and *The Great*, and were so constantly bashing away at the gates of Toledo that all it took to grab Francia—and soon all of Europe—for themselves was the threaten to hammer down the gates of the Island instead, and with no more authority than the ease with which their steel took an edge, the Crown was theirs, and the only real authority the Martels and Charlemagnes of this world needed was the ferocity of their warpaint and the sharpness of their horses' hooves.

No one quite knew the exact day when Hugh Capet felt it necessary or desirable to Become King—it was a eccentric notion, in fact, seeing as he held little more than a few acres of farmland near Chartres and Châteaudun; these very lands were piecemealed away from the Capet the instant Theobald of Blois had decided that the young Hugh was still far too young to own land, and dependent on a regent to keep things in order, deserved to be taught a hard lesson.

Sixteen year-old Hugh Capet decided to learn to live by his wits than by his brawn. What brawn, for that matter?

The fact alone of being the five-times-great-grandson of Charlemagne—on *both* his mother's and father's sides—could not have made the now dispossessed Capet a king. In the long view, he was more German than anything else—this whole 'Frankish' business really was just a shorthand for 'Saxon German'—and he had no business wearing crowns or carrying swords, and now that his land was mostly gone... How insane then, when Adalberon would later raise his voice at the assembly in Senlis, with its Roman amphitheater and old Roman walls, so very damned *Roman* that place was, and stirred up that rabble of Germanic barons, that raft of barbarians, each and every one an ornery cousin or insane uncle of Hugh's, and said, *'Crown the Duke, Hugh Capet. He is most illustrious by his exploits, his nobility, his forces. The throne is not acquired by hereditary right; no one should be raised to it unless distinguished not only for nobility of birth, but for the goodness of his soul,'* just as if

Hugh the Duke were a good and righteous Roman, humbly receiving his due, and not just some two-bit former nobleman, kicked around by the *real* movers of this hard world.

Believe it if you will

* * *

There are three parts of a man's life; this we know from good teachers and from our own conscience. The first is our very family, our root, our home, and we each have a family and a sense of gratitude for their having been present at our first drawing breath. The second is our citizenship, our political bent. The third, of course, is the life spiritual.

Philippe could not figure out at which scale this triptych held best for him.

There was St. Denis, where his family all dusted away past the age of old, where his roots were, where he himself would one day become the soil for a future king's roots to hold fast to... There was Notre Dame on the Island of Paris, where kings demonstrated their kinship with other kings, demonstrated their *kingship* to other kings... And then there was Chartres, so distant and proud and singular out on the Beauce plains, symbolic of his high and proud faith that God had granted him, and the terrible responsibility of *being* the very Church of God on Earth.

But then of course, there was a more modest scale. One he was perhaps more comfortable with, more familiar with.

He was thinking of the panel window hidden away, veiled up in the high apse of Chartres, and thought about how it, too, was made of three sections: the holy feet of the white glass and *grisaille* markings, so pale and charming and stable—*my roots, my family, my lineage, the great foundation*—a place where he might sit, and hear the wandering stories of days having passed, and of men who loved, and worshiped, and pressed their love and pride forward into the future like a memory not yet unfolded. And then the middle section, where a child was seated on pure, accommodating knees, and who was this child anyway if not himself, whose days and nights were spent in dark, hard thought about how to become himself, through art, through toil, through sheer force of will, through intelligence and cunning; to carve out a place for himself on the greater scene, *what, Europe herself?*, to be held like a beloved child in the arms of a loving mother, to be her one desire, the object of her protection, her care, her love, her worry, to be prized and cherished, like a Christ in the arms of the Virgin.

And the final section, such a broad, serene face, with high cheekbones and a coolly concerned air, her face shining like the morning star in the red skies of morning light, the queen of all...

For you, ô my Eleanor, are my one true religion

And who was Philippe if not the child Eleanor *should have carried*, who was Philippe but the fruit of her being, her one love, the light to lighten the world, her son and yet her salvor? The words of the modern *Summæ* came back to him at this shocking thought, that Eleanor was the very Queen of Heaven, and Philippe was her one issue, *As light passes through glass without harming it, so too did Jesus pass through the womb of Mary without the opening of Mary's womb and without any harm to the physical virginal seal of the Virgin, who was pure and the perfect tabernacle of the unborn Christ*

And the hint of a veil that serene woman wore, white in the window, the very *sign* of her virginity, of her divinity... At once spiritually the mother of the Messiah and simultaneously His love and desire, at another remove the most sensual and tender mistress, who in the quietest of surrender gave herself to him, feeling him take her as his own... Suddenly, the words 'Marian mysteries' were more than simple words, they *were* that very veil, they became his one holy law and one holy mission, and he vowed the ten thousandth sacred vow of his life, the same one each and every time: to take Eleanor and make her his, absorbing her beauties and perfections, to make her his one and only Love.

'Um, be sure that the *sancta camisa* is kept safer than this... Mary's veil is far too precious to just leave out in a box, where worms destroy and thieves break in and steal.'

And this afterthought—barely spoken, just the King of France mumbling about a moldy old relic—became Law, as the thoughts of kings must...

Sensing this, Philippe spoke up again: 'And while you're at it: the panel of the Virgin and Child *way up there* above the apse? It needs to be cleaned. Remove it and put it in a safe place until you can get that cared for.'

And so the window was carefully dismantled and, along with Mary's veil, thoughtfully put away into an unused martyrium, an imposing massive iron reliquary formerly belonging to one Saint Lubin, and rented by one Philippe Auguste, the king of France.

Everyone chuckled nervously, piously: 'Saint Lubin' was grunge-French, basically meaning *Saint What's-His-Name*.

* * *

But Philippe knew that the 'goodness of the Capet's soul', the goodness of that hardscabble soul of his great-great-great-great-grandfather Hugh, consisted mainly in having stacked the deck: in Hugh's case, it sometimes went well beyond merely 'eccentric' and bordered on the fanatical, the bloodthirsty; the number of back-alley treaties and badfaith alliances with Germanic warlords against the Carolingian king would make your head spin—and for that matter, the sheer number of barons named Otto having signed on to harass Lothair the Carolingian was simply mindboggling—it was in truth more a family reunion than an electoral assembly, it was more a cruel joke perpetrated upon both the mighty Lothair and the pipsqueak Hugh... And more by smarts and moxie and blind luck than by the glint of his sword, did Hugh hijack the machine of the Carolingian government.

Yes, Hugh Capet had been a usurper, too.

So whenever Philippe, four-times-great-grandson of the Usurper, strode *just as if he were a king* through the west portal of St Denis basilica, he looked up and saw, carved into the great façade, a bas-relief of Solomon sitting on a throne, sword in hand, ready to bisect the child of 1 Kings 3 in the ultimate act of coldblooded, hard-hearted judgment.

And Solomon's temple, wreathed in bas-relief roils of vapor and grandeur, was an exact, 1:100-scale picture of the Basilica of St Denis, where kings live till they die.

For if we cannot be Roman, we can be Solomon

* * *

Lightning fell from the heavens on the chilly, crystal-clear night of June eleven, eleven-hundred and ninety four—fourteen years, seven months and ten days after Philippe Auguste became King of France—and the roof of Notre Dame de Chartres erupted into a stunning ekpyrosis.

About midnight that night, when he was told that the cathedral was in flames, he didn't seem surprised.

'It was a lightning strike, Sire.'

'Of *course* it was lightning. It's *always* lightning...'

Then, thoughtfully: 'If anything at all survives, it'll be... a *miracle.*'

The stones were hardly cool when *Saint Whomever* stood again at the darkened foot of the burned cathedral, and began marking out its new footprint with his heel, just as he had done when he set about building Notre Dame de Paris's great façade; he had just been to the Holy Land anyway, and had a whole army of the best glassmakers in the world already camping in tents on the Beauce plain, glassmakers who had followed Philippe Auguste all the way from Acre...

'*Followed...*' *Right*

And there were a multitude of *where-to-starts* and *what-to-dos* to negotiate; this was, after all, a cathedral to rebuild, and a holy jewel like this one—full of significance and grandeur—couldn't be rebuilt overnight. But thank God the king himself was there, the *fleur de lys in person.*

'Sire,' said the chief glassmaker through an Acrean translator, 'we have followed your every direction in restoring what glass we can, and we are certain the pieces missing—as there are many *thousands*—can be replaced with new glass the likes of which have never before been seen on this whole continent.'

'This is how it should be. Hiram chose well when I asked him to recommend a Master Glazier to return with me. He had many to choose from; I see he selected the very finest.'

'Thank you, Sire.'

'Have you encountered any obstacles?'

'Yes, Sire, begging your pardon. Two major obstacles.'

'What are they?'

'The first is fuel. We will need entire forests to get the furnaces hot enough—and for so long—to complete such a project. As you can see yourself, Sire, there is not a tree for miles.'

'Ah, of course. My predecessors singularly lacked foresight when they began the original cathedral... They should have been thinking in the long view, that forests should be planted in case the cathedral windows should need restoration centuries hence. I will write letters. You'll have all the fuel you need.'

The translator's words crossed fore, and 'tor. Philippe Auguste could see that the translator was enjoying himself, seeing two minds from different worlds, meeting in this place, in this vast plain in the Beauce. The king watched the Master Glazier's face as he wrung meaning from the translated word, and as he thought, and planned, and foresaw with him.

He liked this Glassman fellow.

'You said there were two obstacles, Master Glazier. What was the second?'

'Yes, Sire. We have followed your plans to the letter,' as he opened a great volume of notes and plans, written in the king's hand, 'since we understand that it is not only our duty to do so, but also since we can perceive mysterious, powerful, *beautiful* perfections shining from within them.' The great book, too heavy and too heavily stacked with notes to be held comfortably, tipped and shifted in the Glazier's arms. Philippe Auguste stood next to him, supporting the book on his own side. The Glazier continued, pointing to one of the leaves, written in red ink. 'We understand that there is to be pride of place given to a certain panel, the one reserved for the first bay in the choir, the south side, where the sun shines brightest in the morning and into noontime. You have indicated for this bay a square panel of nine square sections, three above three above three. A magic square. You've numbered all the sections one through nine—*one two three* here on this row, *four five six* on the second tier, *seven eight nine* on the lowest and last.'

'Yes, Master Glazier. Pride of place for this panel.'

'And then, Sire, you have written that the square is to be populated with colored panels according to this schedule: *nine one four seven three six.*'

'Yes, Master Glazier, I have.'

The translator barely had to translate anymore. In a conversation about geometry and arithmetic, the two men—foreigner and king—communicated effortlessly.

'Surely, Sire, you realize that in a three-by-three square, numbered thus, that the number series you propose—*and yes, Sire, we sense the shifting, weightless logic it represents*—never populates the central column of the square. *Two* and *five* and *eight* never appear.'

A smile playing at the corner of Philippe Auguste's lips.

'You have left the center empty, Sire,' the glazier continued. 'You have built a magnificent frame, but left it empty.'

'Yes I have, Master Glazier.'

The Glazier looked at him a long time without speaking. A grin similar to Philippe's began teasing his own lips. Finally he spoke.

'Sire, I am beginning to suspect you have something miraculous planned for this empty frame.'

* * *

Saint Lubin's martyrium was pried open. The ruins of the choir of Notre Dame of Chartres were in a complex intermediate state between burned-out delapis and robust repair, and the metal reliquary, thoroughly charred externally and too heavy to move, had been abandoned in place, a project for another century. Until today.

Opening the martyrium... just another whim of an eccentric king. The monks who hadn't been dispersed by the burning of the cathedral humored Philippe Auguste, for such was their duty. Of course no key could be found for the old reliquary, and besides, the locks had been melted beyond measure. Crowbars and chisels gingerly found the seams and defeated the old latches.

'Behold!' Gasps, ashen faces. The monks fell to their knees. Somehow, without anybody really knowing why, all work stopped on the cathedral, stonemasons and carpenters and glassworkers all pausing, tools midair between strike of hammer and clasp of tong.

Not even the fires of glass furnaces dared crackle.

Runners fanned out from Chartres to the surrounding villages: *The Veil of the Virgin Mary has survived fire and calamity. A miracle!*

* * *

It took the better part of an hour to find someone brave enough to lift the veil clear of the reliquary. With trembling hands, a youth from the town raised the tattered fabric.

Another gasp. 'Good Lord... *another miracle.*'

For the veil, once lifted, revealed the face of the Virgin herself. The very same glass panels from high above the apse, shifting and alive with crystal reflections and muted color in the half-light of the disheveled choir, the panes of the very window beneath which Philippe Auguste had sat as a youth, absorbing its miraculous rays.

Somehow everybody had forgotten how the king had had the window disassembled and squirreled away.

No one knew which was the higher miracle: the veil's surviving, or *the lifting of the veil*, lending the Virgin new life.

Philippe Auguste lent his own stable of horses to spread the news of the double miracle to the cities of France, and Normandy, and Brittany, and Aquitaine, and beyond.

This is what it's like: to cross over, to cross back, having seen, and learned, and... become

* * *

Many miles away.

'He is the one.' Hoarse whispers out in the cold. 'See his ring!'

It was an inn, a traveler's wayplace, Christmas Eve eleven-hundred and ninety two. Although a subtlety, there was a decided mismatch between the man's pilgrim clothes and the luster of that ring. The ring's owner, unsuspecting of what awaited him, hungrily picked at roast chicken, a delicacy in south-central Europe and ordinarily reserved for the mighty of this world.

There were a hundred armed men out in the snow. The innkeeper was given a small leather pouch, the song of coin when he weighed it.

Only fifteen knights managed to jam into the tiny room when the time came; the man's fingers gleamed with chicken grease and the gold ring.

'You are hereby placed under arrest by his Highness the Duke of Austria, Leopold by name, by the authority of His Holiness Henry, sixth of the name, Holy Roman Emperor.

'You are hereby charged with the murder of Conrad of Montferrat, late cousin of his Highness the Duke; with sedition for casting down his Highness the Duke's standard from the wall of the castle at Acre; and, most grievous of

all: with Heresy, for consorting with the infidel and with magicians, for meeting under cloak of night with the alchemist Hiram of Acre.'

Richard of the Lion's Heart was dragged from the room.

O marcher sans un but, sans une destination
   Mais tout, tout est ta destination te dis-tu
   Et toute porte qui t'abrite substitue
   Pour antre et toit, chaque bout de pain ta ration

Tu dois être chez toi, ou que tu te situes
   Le soir, à la fin du chemin ; or, ta station
   Résout dans ton cœur cette cruelle équation :
   Rue que tes pieds ont battue t'a aussi battu

Flèch' qu'on tire sans avoir visé trouve cible
   Et ne peut être brisé le cœur qui renie
   L'amour, son soulas et le feu de son plaisir

Tant de routes sans nom, tant d'ardeur indicible
   Et tu te rends compte après tant de décennies
   Qu'on habite une maison faite du désir

Aimlessly, without a single destination
   Everything then becomes your solitary goal
   Every rainshelt'ring doorframe then becomes your whole
   Den and hearth, and every shared scrap meal your ration

Make yourself at home, ev'ry day at end of stroll,
   Wherever you be, whatever town or nation;
   The heart can solve for itself the cruel equation:
   Each long road has taken of you a heavy toll

But they never miss, arrows shamelessly unaimed
   And the heart that denies love cannot ever be
   Broken, or ever miss its comfort or its fire

Such aimless journeys, and such lonely roads unnamed
   And after a decade of this you come to see
   You live in a house made entirely of desire

Antiarcs of copper wire line rue Félibien, neurons and their axons in dark copperphosphorus potentials. Equality of light and color, sky to pavement, you'd think this place was all asphalt in some sections of town, and Félibien is one of them, and Talensac, and all those areas around St Similien... places made of pressed ash and cement, powdered casts of The Works Of Man, a very impoverished view indeed of human ambition.

But the whole city isn't like this, and it strikes Vicus that there was some kind of dark, sly joke Nantes perpetrated upon the visitor and the newcomer, canalizing him into places like these; highways lead to cloverleaves, cloverleaves to stripmalls, stripmalls asphalt dust and ash deserts, each leading downhill to a storm sewer or some mundane retail option... And although Vicus never once tried to drive here, he's becoming more and more acutely aware that even the pedestrian is canalized into these places: low-energy, unthinking places *leave your money here move along* built to insert themselves into your psyche as the Only Option, a marble rolling toward the center of a bowl.

How come it is that we don't meet Real Life here? and the fellow is hawking used watches, and the corner shop stationery and pens and the art-photography magazines that are the only really socially-responsible form of pornography in all of Europe and there are plenty of them *lenseslenseslenses-supermodel* turn the page *tripodtripodsupermodel* in glossy facingpage suites of technology and flesh interleaved, not even a page number to help you know that this is an article and not an ad.

But then some Einsteinian accident occurs, some gamma particle knocking you off the city's rails *thanks for the memory* and you've missed your ordinary turnoff and suddenly you're in the neighborhood toward Manufacture and there's no hope of finding your way back *how the Hell did I get this far off?* and who cares anyway, because the people aren't watching out for you anymore like they do the tourists, you're just another face to them, not a Wallet or a Credit Card to them, just some guy disheveled by getting from here to there, just some Homegoer, who knows why he's not carrying his work with him, who knows why he doesn't have dinner in a bulging fabric bag like everybody else does? must have an engagement to get to, has to get some proper clothes on before meeting his Sweetie *that* must be why he's not carrying dinner home.

Home. That sure doesn't sound at all like the tall rowhouse over on Félibien, where the fridge is offlimits *and now Mr Vicus* explains patiently La Michaud through her condescending pursed lips *we know that Americans simply Eat More than we Christians do so you'd do well to find out what a meal ticket at the trainstation will cost you* and besides you can't even make it to the john upstairs without waking the younger son that little wretched Animal who complains all the time about how you wreck his house's intimacy *awfully high talk for an eleven-year-old boy don't you think?* and don't worry I wasn't planning on actually daring to absorb any of your little 'homeyness' anyway would prefer to walk and walk and walk.

And the Manufacture by night is some kind of inner circle, despite the tall, flat façade of the Manufacture-proper, all he can imagine they 'manufactured' in there is cigars for some reason, sweatshop-tall rooms with Victorian-poor ladies in their puffshouldered blouses wiping sweat from their brows with the back of their wrists lest it stain the leaf *I should just ask some day and find out once and for all, Is it cigars or what?* but then he remembers he is on the inside now and people on the inside never stop one another to ask, they just know already.

His friends from University live around here, didn't they? He always had to count the streets up from the great Manufacture façade up to Rue des Coulmiers, especially at night, this really *is* off the rails now, and you have to ignore the rumble as your wheels go crossways to the tracks, sonorous beneath you as if the iron in the rails held the stored energy of all the trams carrying visitors and newcomers down toward Retail, but that wickedfunny girl from Translation lives around here, the one who actually gets the silliness of your jokes, how your lisp makes new words rise parasitic from old hosts, how your accent *just isn't quite right* she might hear you say *jus in it quiet white* and she loves you anyway loves you like a sister like a cousin like a classmate, and when the two of you decided over a herd of *kir* that it would be a howl to put together a theater group (you'd been doing theater all along for that lunatic Deudon anyway, might as well do it with your friends) and do something that was on the exam anyway, get used to it more than you do in the giant amorphic amphitheater classes, do something just to pry it free from the old grizzled claws of dusty matronly professors *do something with some passion in it for God's sake* and you choose some Tennessee Williams and for once it's an actual *advantage* being an American around here, and you and your sister your cousin your classmate get yourselves on the docket at the end of year even before you've got your Blanche and your Mitch, but you're headlong in now, and rehearsals start in earnest, up here just beyond the Manufacture, and you never really conjured up how hard it would be to kiss—good old Stanley and Stella—when it really is something like your sister here *and what are you going to do just stop rehearsing?* and so each time you both mumble something about *and this is where we kiss and just skip ahead* and you do, and finally it's the week before you're supposed to play and you still haven't kissed and when you're on stage you do the first thing that comes to your mind, and Stella leaps into Stanley's arms, really leaps, a small step for Man, and *nokissingnokissingnokissing* and everyone in the whole damned theater is wondering when the kissing starts, and sistersoul just locks her arms even harder around your neck and inches her legs up around your hips and now it's the theater of the absurd but this is how you love each other a long leap through space and a long hold, and all Vicus remembers is her whispering all hot in his ear *Emmène-moi et vite* and you stumble the two of you, her arms locked around your neck, your arms all the way around her back, her feet a yard off the stagefloor, to the wings.

For this is how you love her.

And the Manufacture is a tall façade, and in the dark it's still tall enough to steal cold light from the crimelights around the trainstation, but at least here people Live Around Here, and even though it's three in the morning and there's no one conscious, you take grim satisfaction that you're in the land of the living.

* * *

But then, when Vicus felt his members drawn along the deep channel with the madding crowd, and there was little in him to resist: *La Cigale* with the roasted smell of seafood and iodine, the little man with his hip-boots affectation, there's nothing like standing up on a streetcorner looking like you'd just stepped out of a cranberry bog, but he's just there to hose off the ground around the terrace, get the worst of the seafood to skitter ahead of the tide toward the sewer, and the whole of Graslin district had a high odor of about eighteen-seventy and the opera was light and comic because that was how you told the difference between the tragedies and the comedies, *if they all marry it's a comedy, and if they all die...* and the clotheswares cast like Carnaval behind the inch-thick security glass up and down Crébillon were light and airy and worthless, because the way it all works is this: your city, Nantes, is in the crosshairs of every little spring storm there is, and the joke is if you like—*or dislike*—the weather, hang around ten minutes and the light will shift for you or against you, as if you were the strange attractor of the ugly side, and soon you are moisted wool and flopping hair, and then there was that one time when you actually thought to bring an umbrella, and you were striding away from Graslin up through the boutiques-district, all gilded and halogen-hot while it storms out here in the street, and when a woman is walking ahead of you in same strides, her long coat soaking through and clinging to her shoulders, her white ankles flashing clipclop, and you feel that you can't enjoy the dry much anymore seeing her getting sommered through, so you double your stride till you have her under the umbrella, too, and she clenches her teeth waiting for you to fuck up and ask her out like strange men with convenient umbrellas do, but the rules today are tight and free all at once: *I have an umbrella and I don't need all of it and it's humiliating to walk for long in the rain* and so we rip along in silence she's ready to sprint if I dare even lick my lips to build a word, woman on a mission, man trying to keep the rainshadow leading her by a foot and a half, a half a stride, a quarter stride, you've heard stories of German subs shadowing American cruisers this way, a long grey tube stuffed with grizzled Nazis steering in the chaos of a gunboat's lee, only a periscope and the engine's air intake above the waves, gotta make a new navigation decision every tenth of a second or else you're exposed and dead under the cruiser's guns, either that or you ram her and *again* you're exposed and laid out for her to rake you, and after five minutes the woman with the dark hair and the white ankles under her long coat peels off BlackSheepSquadron back out back into the rain free and clear, but a quarter mile closer to her apartment at least, wordless as wordless, and you are alone in your own rainshadow again.

And sometimes after dark, with the showers beginning to grip your ribs a little into the first chestcold of the year, and the tipping point between inside light and outside light has gone all the way over, and the canyonlands of Crébillon and Graslin have turned luminous, and the wares are starting to look delicious with all their colors, a suit in a dark marinade and a scarf in a filet of salmon *have I eaten yet today?* but Crébillon is no place for this, unless you're willing to sign away your firstborn to *La Cigale* for a meek ladle of chowder and an end of bread, but there's not much else around, *what, the Quick up there with its horsemeat burgers and antiseptic light, the Quick raising a finger to the Cigale?* everyone knows that the Quick was invented to cater to the Ameriphile toddler and lost Canadian hippie anyway, they come stumbling out bent half-over contrite each time, you'd tried it once and it almost killed you—a rare parody of America's very worst fast food—so the two ends of the scale are right out there and for todaytonight unthinkable, but your canines are gleaming in the golden light of Crébillon's shops, and you head downhill for you must, everyone is going that way, it must be What Folks Do When Starving, except that you're the only one out here whose ribs are showing, the only lone wolf aiming heavy-headed this way and that in the forest: so you relent to society's gravity, turn your stern to Graslin and your bow toward Place Royale at the bottom of the hill.

And you tear out into the delta of the Place Royale, nothing but banks and travel agencies, it's well past closed, so their lights are on in the muted expression of *we must still be in here working on your stocks and bonds and trades and whatever* but you know they're long gone, and the delta fans out and slows here, and there is the confusion of men and women each a way to go but having to cross one another's channel to go there, a marshy peacock of effluvia, but you've got enough momentum that you figure it'll carry you with it, because the Royale has the great big fountain with Neptune served by his tributaries, Nantes herself having converged in this very spot, and the confusion is whether the tributaries serve the main flow, or the main flow breaks apart into the seven tributaries.

But then there's someone walking next to you *Where you headed? It's almost dinnertime you know* but you can barely place his face and can certainly pin nothing to his name, but he's read your mind already *we're in Translation together Pierrick* which strikes you as one of those names that sounds like it should be Breton: *Loïc, Annaïck... Pierrick?* but he's still reading your mind *Dad's name is Pierre and Mum's is Monique* and the cratered logic of it makes much more sense than it should, and Pierrick is leading you off the main channel of the human effluvia, you don't know why he's taken a shine to you suddenly, but Thank God all the bundled folk with all their colorful retail jammed into bags or held out like a holy relic in front of their companions *Oh, it is exactly your color* are gone, and the noise of the Place Royale is more the murmur of distant waters. Pierrick is talking, all shiny, breezy words, a contrast to the weather to be sure, and at the same time he has enough of a frame—a half-a-head taller than most Frenchmen—to guide you along just by walking where he pleases, and he seems to know a great deal about you already: where you're from originally, where you live in Nantes.

Hell, he knew how to find *you* in a crowd just now, didn't he?

This is what dreaming is like.

* * *

But you find it disorienting and depressing to be a lone wolf that someone else can find at will, and isn't a lone wolf supposed to raise his heavy head toward all the compass points, isn't that what lone wolves do best? Novelty always comes from the East for him—you can imagine the primordial Lone Wolf at the birth of the world, standing there on the cold shores of Plymouth and watching the white sails the ultimate novelty crack open the horizon, gaping at the sight, and the change of seasons—the regular ones, not the apocalyptic—comes from the South, and loss and despair come from the North, and you, you live in the West, where the sun cracks open the horizon but the broken-open horizon defeats it anyway.

And so here is somebody who can find you in a crowd, and you may have to rethink this lone wolf thing now, this whole wild animal thing. Where Pierrick takes you to find something other than the wind to eat is beyond you, some dark *passé* dive bar that's both good and bad, noisy and quiet, some place called *Le Trianon*, but his friends have found it too, and either you're starting to find The Inside or else you're more outside than ever, a spectator to the things that happen in the intimacy of this den. And his friends are each a Type—Loïc (yes, there's a Loïc) the impish med student, Vincent the business student, Virginie the geographer, and you can't help but think of the merry men of the old Errol Flynn movies, and the banter is something straight out of the movies, too—*No one would accuse a medical school student like you of disrespecting a human body* says Vincent during an episode about Loïc's cadaver training *except maybe your girlfriend* which is a howler, except that your head has all of those bilingual mechanisms set in place just takes a second longer than everyone else, but now that that second is passed, they're on to a new riff and you've lost the head of the tune and it'll take you to the next riff to catch back up.

Pierrick's found you a half-dozen times now since that first time at Place Royale, and you can't decide if that's a comfort or a repeated intrusion, especially since it seems to be at random points through the city, and either he's a lone wolf, too, or...

You spent a few days at his folks' place by Le Croisic around Christmas, and his father is a Type, too, with grand gestures and a grandfatherly sand in his voice *he loves life* he says and you believe him, and if that one's Pierre then Monique is over here, and she's much more contemplative, much more in the West than Pierre is *Pierrick gets that from her I guess* and she talks about how *other people must resent it when* and how *other people must like it when* and she is probably the best cook you've ever met bar none, no wonder Pierre is all *I love life* and if you were there for four days, well then four wildly different breakfasts appeared magically before you *God she must wake up at three to do all this,* and the same goes for lunch and dinner, and yet all you can think about is how quiet and sorrowful she is.

When Vincent and Loïc and Virginie all show up at Le Croisic, you get to thinking that Pierrick is maybe not so much a lone wolf as all that, and if three or four or five (if you count yourself, which you don't always do) can show up in the same dive in La Baule at the same time, there must be something else. And as the whole lot of you drive around Le Croisic and La Baule and Turballe and Pornichet and as you get more and more disoriented with all the *–ics* and *–iques* and *–ichets*, Pierrick points out a vast old hospital tucked way back in the hills and says *When I was young, I went there* with that indifferent way that lets you know he's seen his share of it.

* * *

It took Pierrick all of a second to die

He was dead before he hit the floor

The answering machine winks wicked little jokes *not funny not funny not funny* into the air ensaturate of a grey Thursday afternoon, late enough long enough Thursday afternoon surely there's a bit of spaghetti sauce or *something* so I don't have to go back out again it's spitting rain and darkness, there's nothing like the cold just before the storm, *I know it's not a Michigan winter it's the idea that it's supposed to be more clement here for God's sake more clement than Michigan at least* but whatever happened to global warming and where the Hell is the coffeepot and if I didn't think my hands would chap to rawflesh I would just run them under hot water for an hour. Thursday is cold as December and class was a three hour marathon, if you think you were bored before, you're sadly mistaken, just wait until Hour Three of Maupassant or Stendhal or whoever the Hell it was we were supposed to read.

Phone is blinking, your coat is heavy as boredom, but it goes over the back of the couch and you wrench the heat on twisting dial *I know it's going straight out into space but save me from today*, and *Thy Kingdom Come* there it is, the pilot light setting off those hotblue mystery jets deep in the ductwork. The apartment's going to really cook once the dynamo has taxied for a few minutes *we're Number One for takeoff*, meanwhile finally in the kitchen there's some hot cocoa mix hiding behind the peanut butter and some stale coffee flaccidtransparent, one will redeem the other, cook them into each other beyond local boilingpoint and if you're lucky it'll beam the microwaves it hugs to itself into your chest, what, two minutes to feeling that searing pain of joyful warmth driving lurehooks down past the coughing reflex, two minutes *not funny not funny not funny*.

Not funny not funny not funny

This is whoeverthefuckitdon'tmattermuchanymore the voice as cold and lifeless as Thursday After Class *I'm calling from Hamline in Minnesota* and I thought I was cold down *here* and *Pierrick is dead he had a bad heartvalve when I was young I was there last Thursday in an elevator on campus he was dead before he hit the floor*

I haven't seen Pierrick in a year or so, just a little summerbreak in Pornichet a year or so back, he's up at Hamline too but he just sent me a note a week or so ago so this must not be the same fellow, God, what an unlucky bastard this *other* Pierrick was.

Now the heat has roared on, and the heart knows in its gristle whatever it is the mind has got all caught up in its ratchets.

Tears dry to salt in the heat blasting from the registers. Vomit all my willful ignorance into the sink.

* * *

StellaStellaStella, don't even stop in Nantes, let's just go, and she's run it through all the gears to fourth, and the highway from the airport is straightline winds out to Saint Marc, *thank God for summer again it's so good to see you I haven't been so good at keeping up, school you know.*

But she's forgiven you for that, after all Pierrick was her friend too— *remember Translation remember remember remember* and a little sea air will do you good.

The room that she's set up for you is odd and airy and smells like sea, she'll be over in the next little bungalow *I know you haven't been well* if you only knew StellaStellaStella *if you need anything? Just next door*

The sea air floods into you, fries out with its iodine and its seasalt ions all those cobwebs and prions which have lodged in your lungs and puppetstrings to your own heartvalves. It is bright and then rainy in Saint Marc, bungalows are made for this, sweetsmells from the kitchenette whenever it rains, you make mussels-marinade with StellaStellaStella and drink the funnels off the Muscadet.

* * *

'Pierrick lived just down the road you know, in Pornichet.'

Sea air and iodine and ions and Muscadet. StellaStellaStella, why now?

'You should go and see them.'

* * *

Monique meets me at the door, rare sunny day, rare sun in her hair. She is much older than she used to be, the lone wolf at the door to her den. Her *bonjour* is polite, lightless, the shades are closed, this is a house where people don't just knock and visit. *Visit*. It's been probably two years since she's last seen me, and the last time, in the wry presence of her pup and his own pack. No one from the old gang has dared roil around much.

'If it's not a good time, I...'

'Come in.'

Coffee, tray, plates for cookies she bought in a store, had sitting around. Eyes having trouble adjusting.

'Is your friend going to pick you back up soon?'

* * *

'I hear you're engaged.'

'Yes I am.' News having traveled fast, and far.

'And she's from overseas.' Monique doesn't quite ask a question. She's nibbled at the same cookie for fifteen minutes now. Her hand is frightfully gracile.

'Where is Pierre?'

Noncommittal. *I love life* at the corner of the table of feasts, shafts of light and his grand gesture.

Monique, almost as an aside: 'Probably in the basement.'

Don't bother waking me today

* * *

'This fiancée of yours. I suppose she'll be emigrating.'

'Mm.'

'You don't think she'll end up resenting you for taking her away from everything she knows and loves.' Not a question, not at all.

The coffee is still turning in the cups, still hot from the kitchen, still too hot to drink: 'Well, I guess Pierre is busy. When does your friend pick you up again?'

* * *

Those gears wind up tight in StellaStellaStella's car. 'I was afraid of that,' she puts it down hard, you won't be seeing Pornichet again for another three centuries.

Heading away from Pornichet. And away from Saint Marc. Some peninsular spit of land in-between.

'I want to show you something.'

Le Croisic, another *–ic*, not far off, on a point of spiritless sandless windswept stone, a bar-crêperie, a *tabac*, a bakery that's closed.

'Not much left. You'll like this, though.'

All medieval French towns do the same thing, send you spiraling in toward the holiest place around, roads always a fractal puzzle you have to be intentional about trying to defeat if you don't want to end up at The Church On The Hill. But StellaStellaStella plays along this time, though, and we end up in the stonebuilt center, cobbles giving a hard beating to the undercarriage, and enact the Mandelbrot set in realworld.

You can see it already from a ways out. There is a lawn-bowling pitch here in the green grass, cruciformgreen parkspace right here. The town church is gone, burneddownblownaway, *who can say anymore they probably kept the records in the church anyway and isn't this the way my memory works you don't remember the dramatrauma anymore all you know is that the roof is gone there must've been the storm of the century or the lightning it's always lightning it's always lightning*

We get out of the car. The wind is hard, StellaStellaStella has to yell to be heard. 'Ever seen anything like this?'

The church is gone, but the vaults' stringers—stouter stuff than the church that fell—are intact, gracile parabolas intersecting overhead, posiarcs marking out space where the sacred used to be. The jokers who put the lawn-bowls pitch here must've had a dark sense of humor, must *still* have that sense of gallows-play to go *two-of-three-three-of-five-four-of-seven* here on a Sunday afternoon.

'The center will not hold. People steal paintings away, but leave the frames behind.' StellaStellaStella smiles grimly, the wind playing at her hair. Her sunglasses are wide, I can't see if her eyes sparkle, or well over.

We mourn for what once was. We suffer for what might have been.

This is what memory is like.

Et un jour, je plierai devant le grand vent froid
  Et vous me transpercerez, ô Rayons Radieux,
  Sans me toucher ; mes os disparaîtront aux yeux
  Peu à peu, sans effort, sans peine, sans effroi

Que devienne immune ma moelle aux longs adieux
  Des années, et le cœur que tout le monde voit
  Ne soit plus ce pont délabré, en désarroi,
  Peint de peines, cœur transparent, vermeil et bleu

Voyez l'hécatombe, ouvrez vos yeux à l'abîme :
  L'humanité entière me voit affaiblir
  Perdre poids, perdre sommeil, mon âge si lourd

Projeté sur mon visage, mortel et sublime.
  Or regardez encore mon âme choisir
  De vivre, de revivre un jour. Un jour. Un jour.

And one day, I will bend like a reed in the breeze
   And let it pass over me go right on through
   Me, my bones will vanish before the rays that you
   Beam at me, ô Radiant Source, with such ease

My marrows will grow immune to the long adieu
   Of years lost, and the thrashing heart the whole world sees
   Will no more be the failed painted bridge of disease
   And loss, a vision transparent, crimson and blue

See the hecatomb, feast your eyes one last time
   All mankind sees me in the throes of losing
   Strength by day, sleep by night, reels of my long decay

Displayed on my aging face, mortal and sublime.
   Look now again, world, see my soul bravely choosing
   To live on, to revive one day. One day. One day.

Bloodvolume staining and smacking heavy gauze pads to the floor; Vicus thinks for a moment that the nurses were having their way with him, releasing him to the operating theater at the precise moment the doctor slices Sundari's belly open and it was almost as if the doctor, standing on a stepstool, *is leaning his weight onto her now* and the baby began to heave out of the incision, sacred birth from the pages of a vampire novel; the world spins, as the child emerges all bluegrey, nothing of a life in the little shapeless creature at all, just a little fist of your flesh, and the child fails the very first test of her whole life, only a 2 out of 10, and it takes Vicus a moment to remember all the letters in Activity, Pulse, Grimace, Appearance, Respiration, sacred birth in this most profane of places, and this child has nothing else in this world but 2 out of 10 and this queasy man she takes after so much.

Vicus stumbles, and vials of anesthetic tumble to the floor, tiny glaucoma'd bottles glassy most the way through, Thank God they don't break, and he is embarrassed at the clatter and the waste. Sundari shows no sign, stirs not at all, and the doctor spends minutes placing her inside back inside her, as the bluegrey child is moved to a bay over on this side of the operating theater to be resuscitated.

'Do you need a chair, sir?'

Hell yes I need a chair

'No. Is she alright?'

'She's not breathing yet; we'll know for sure when she begins crying.'

* * *

Vicus' humor is grim in grim times, but his daughter is grey and blue for a good minute, and he thinks to equate her Apgar score with his own only after she starts breathing unassisted. Her name is given, and the nurses keep Vicus seated near her as drops go in the eyes, as blood comes from her fingertip here and monitors clamp round about her fingertip there, and the nurses look Vicus in the eye for his consent to treat her, and he nods quickly, there's something between the air in his lungs and his vocal chords, and the nurses work quickly and quietly.

She has her eyes open now, and because the eyes always make all the difference, Vicus recognizes his daughter, who is now alive.

* * *

The whole notion of Just Another Day is perfectly context-bound; Vicus tells his students about as much when he holds forth about Medieval People. 'The European Middle Ages spans six centuries and as a category covers everything from invasion to contagion; who is to say what a Medieval Person's life is really? We might be about to say something about a population, a Gaussian blur of... of... *folk*, but even there we are committing carts-before-horses bordering on the ridiculous. Meisters Léonin and Pérotin just as *Medieval* as a William the Conqueror? Well... *yes*. Well... *no*.'

Vicus awoke at three-thirty that morning with the Kyrie from Mozart's *Requiem* in his head, and figuring the Earth's population at six billion, and maybe one of six as high-order insomniac as he, that makes for a billion or more who awoke too early, way too early, and further considering his conservative estimate that perhaps one in a thousand knew Mozart well enough to be able to name something as dark and high and forbidding as the *Requiem* as to *be able* to waken with such a thing in their head, that still made for a million *capable* of waking as he did, which isn't bad at all—that's a megalopolis on its own—but seeing as folk who know Mozart well enough to be *able* to name the *Requiem* as Mozart's final composition possibly had a wider (or deeper) musical vocabulary than someone who didn't, the number of pieces these folks *could have* selected to wake to must be remarkably wide. Vicus, for instance, didn't even like Mozart, found all his feminine cadences amusing only for the first seventeen years of his life, but now, at thirty-five, had spent more than half of his life *trying to forget who Mozart was;* but memory doesn't work that way, and like a recurrent dream, sometimes his mind is perverse and ill-natured, and a musical hallucination is at hand, one of the *lesser* pieces he could have conceived of to have running his mind at this hour of night. So—conservatively—he estimates that of all the pieces an initiate to Mozart might be thinking of at such an unholy hour, only one in ten thousand would be the *Requiem* at all.

So now the fraternity of *Requiem* hallucinators is now only a hundred.

What do you bet thinks Vicus *fifty of them are thinking the Dies Irae, another twenty the Rex Tremendae, still another twenty the Lachrymosa?*

Drake's Equation—the calculation of the number of stars in the Milky Way with planets, of those planets planets with life, of that life complex life, of that complex life that certain stripe having reached technological maturity, but not so tech-savvy as to have accidentally or intentionally sterilized the surface of their globe—is infuriating in that it pares a near-certainty down to pitifully few numbers, not quite zero but not quite reassuring either.

Vicus calculates that it is still nearly certain that at least four people—four across all time zones planetwide—could have possibly awoke with the *Kyrie* from Mozart's *Requiem* in their head.

And that given that there are twenty-four time zones—*true, many time zones crossing mostly trackless ocean, still others—the majority, in fact—in which Western music is not heard*—there is perhaps as high as a thirty percent chance there is another human waking up three hours early in exactly the same mindset as he is.

* * *

Lord have mercy but as he tiptoes to his newborn daughter's room to make sure she is still alive, he is aware that he already knows where the floor creaks and how to sidestep the spots where underlayment finds a new seat under the baseboard as he presses out that flexing air pocket hidden somewhere underneath it all.

He's done this before: his elder daughter used to be colicky as they get, and the only person in the universe who could quiet her was Vicus, who would find that just-right spot on the corner of the bed and with her in his arms, bounce more or less forcefully—he would smile as he wondered if the child was reminded of the instant she was conceived—and after forty-five minutes of this, she would find her centers again and drift off. Silence and no movement for another forty-five minutes, there would be some change in her weight, in her breathing *In her turgor pressure* he would think, and he knew he could now move her to her crib without penalty.

Moving his elder daughter from the corner of his bed to the center of her own had required intimate knowledge of the speculative architecture of the carpet underlayment; he had named his perilous way The River Of Fire as he lurched widestraddle down toward the baby's room—much less flex in the underlayment as you approach the walls, so you put your feet down there, where the carpet meets the baseboards—with the imaginary River Of Fire roiling beneath him, between his legs, ready to pop or creak or groan and wake his colicky child.

But tonight, both elder and younger are fast asleep; he can hear in the guest room his sister- and mother-in-law bickering quietly in Hindi; the light pressing through the seam between carpet and door reminds Vicus of the fire safety films back in grade school *Always feel a door to see if it's hot* and he knows it is so he leaves it alone.

Everyone in the house under age four is alive, which is the essential for now, and everyone *over* four is also alive, too, for that matter.

All-night news. Arrange the couch cushions as a makeshift blanket—extracting a bona fide blanket from the closet would require another trip down the River Of Fire—and while markets fail all across Asia and typhoons bear down on Pacific Islanders, Vicus murmurs subvocal prayers to Sleep and Forgetting.

* * *

Doors slamming, lights blazing.

'You left the light on.'

'What?'

The baby's crying now.

'The light in the hall bathroom.' Sundari is standing over him, slightly hunched. The staples have been hurting, it's nearly time for them to come out.

'I don't think that was me.' But now the sister-in-law is standing there, too, with some knitting crushed between her fists, looking disapproving as ever of her brother-in-law. 'Maybe someone else...' It took an hour to get the youngest to sleep last night, it'll take less if he can abort the drama early.

'It was you. You were up. You came out here.'

'So what? I'll turn it off.'

'But all you did was remind me how filthy this place is.'

'What?'

'Look! Cobwebs all over,' with his glasses off, Vicus could see no such thing, but Sundari, yes, 'it's like Halloween in this place. And look what you did to the couch.' And even with glasses on, he'd be damned if he could see any cobwebs, but her eyesight has always been better than his.

The baby is crying; the mother-in-law is now out here, too, and the bickering has resumed, still in Hindi.

'I'll get the baby. I'll take care of the couch in the morning; it's just cushions—there were no blankets out here, I didn't want to wake up any—"

'Well you did, and now I have to clean *everything*. Thanks so much: I've got stitches all up and down my body for giving birth to *your children*, and you have to wake me up to clean? It's like slavery around here.'

And it's four thirty, and the youngest takes an hour to drift away again, startling awake every time Sundari slams a cabinet door, and then the vacuum is on. Vicus hears the shower go on and off a half-dozen times.

* * *

The girls are up early, too, and there is no movement from the bedroom, where (he is certain) Sundari has pulled the curtains and is sleeping off last night's exertions *do not disturb* but his eldest can have cereal and the young one is content with the crazy carbpowder stuff you dissolve into warm water—even Vicus can't fuck that stuff up—and there are unspoken Carson monologues about the most tangible of benefits of being a teacher: you always have that mysterious capacity to put young people to sleep. But with everybody fed, and children released to their games on the living room floor, Vicus's own head is lolling, and he realizes his mother-in-law is there and is watching him.

'You know *Bitta*, all the women in the family are passionate. Their blood is hot.'

'Yours isn't, Mama.'

'Well, I've had other things to deal with. I can't afford to boil over. Daddy would have a hard time if I did. I've learned to clamp it down.'

'That sounds like a laudable skill.'

'The weather is stormy. You can't blame the storm for being a storm, can you? You can either learn to see the weather for what it is, or get blown away.'

'This is not so very encouraging, Mama.'

'I know, *Bitta*.'

Vicus remembered seeing them—Mama and Papa—on the sofa once, he can still picture them, the exact picture, Mama on the one side, Papa on the other, and there had been skirmishes, all having happened in Hindi so there was no hope of Vicus ever seeing sunlight there *what to do when, what do say if, when to call the firemen* but this Honeymooners-level drama, this I-Love-Lucy ending, Mama over here, Papa over here, and then Papa, muttering in English:

'You... are impossible.'

And then Mama, not even a beat, not a pause, not a second's hesitation: 'No, as point of fact I'm *next* to impossible.'

Papa hadn't caught the subtlety of the undercut.

* * *

'Alright, *Bitta*,' she had told Sundari, years ago, years before The Troubles, years before Vicus *got it*, and Mama and Papa had been visiting, and they were on their way to the airport in ten minutes, and Sundari was at her worst, as if by baring her teeth the plane might sit engines idle for a few more minutes on the tarmac, and Mama had taken her courage in both hands and addressed Sundari head-on: 'I want you to take this trash bag,' actually handing her a trash bag, 'and head upstairs for a few minutes, *take all of your ill humor and put it in,* and I'll just throw it overboard into the ocean after we take off.'

* * *

We heard the shower before we ever saw Sundari; Vicus called in to her several times, Sunu, you need any help?, the shower being a hard place to deal with stitches, the c-section major, major surgery (Vicus so very acutely aware), and politically, it made sense for the first thing she heard that morning be an expression of concern, *I have the meds and the tea is on,* but the place had evidently covered over with cobwebs since daylight had broken when finally after hours of scrubbing by the light of the lamps she had unscrewed the shades from, she had taken a breather to sleep three, four hours back, and so by hard daylight everything was Halloween again she said hair still wet skin still streaming, and even though Vicus can see the wrinkled corners of her wound and the odd mottled transparency of the tape holding her together, she had pushed past him and was up again in the corners of the room on a chair.

She looked different from before.

And she grunted as she scrubbed, and mother-in-law is trying to get her down off the chair, too, for God's sake *Bitta* you'll pull your stitches, and just take a break a breather and enjoy the girls for awhile, but the only breather she had was another trip to the shower and you shouldn't be doing *anything* much less this and only little ragged edges of Sundari's grunting were audible enough to be words.

'Sunu, come down, you'll hurt yourself.'

'Treat me like a slave will you...'

* * *

There is nothing more human than warfare against the forces of nature. Except perhaps warfare against another human.

* * *

The dream is only seconds long. Same dream, different circumstances.

Hold the ends of these two wires together if you don't the world will end

Drive this massive truck you can't see you can't brake you can only steer

Balance your family on the top of this tower three angels on the head of a pin and it's tipping and warping away the infinite drop

Ride it out the trailer unpinned off a semi run amok over the slope can't see can't see can't see wait for the impact

The house come undone from its foundations it's slipping toward the precipice

The plane hasn't the speed anymore for level flight engine failing antiarcs antiarcs antiarcs we're going down

You're not afraid of falling you're afraid of jumping

'You don't even love me. I'm simply your slave, I'm simply a maid and a nursemaid and a cook' and there's just no way a cobweb could still be there, it's been a half-hour of scrubbing, gone down to the bare plaster 'and here all I'm good for is cleaning the cobwebs off this house I don't even want to live in I didn't even want to buy in this country I can't even find a job in...'

'If you'd just take it easy for a second I could...'

'Don't *ever* tell me *just take it easy*'

'Hold it, calm down'

'Don't *ever* tell me *calm down*'

This at least gets her off the chair. Baby's crying, so's the older girl.

'Listen Sunu'

'I don't *have* to listen to you'

'Well this isn't right. Sit down. The girls shouldn't have to hear this'

'Oh *they'll hear this* and *you'll hear this*'

'So you won't listen to me, but we have to listen to you' Vicus has his keys and is looking for his shoes.

'Yes you do. You dragged me here, you make me clean all day all night in this hellhole of a house, you ruin my chances of a career, you ruin my body, how could you ever desire a person like this, all you want to do now is leave, so *yes you do, you have to listen to me*' Her accent has crept back in, not an Indian accent anymore either, some kind of *other* accent; she is no longer who she once was, she neither looks as she did or sounds as she did, she certainly no longer acts as she did, she is Other now.

'I didn't drag you anywhere, and it's not my fault you can't find a job—Lord knows I've tried to help—and I thought the kids, the baby...'

'I'm just a means to an end, you just wanted the baby and now that you have her, I'm a slave again. Great, just great' That voice, that new accent from God-knows-where.

'I didn't drag you here, I didn't drag you anywhere, I didn't make you clean this morning, I didn't make you clean overnight, *I didn't leave the bathroom light on*, I have never treated you like a slave, I've been trying to give you tea'

'You never tell me you love me, you didn't even say it in the delivery room'

'What? You were out like a light'

'So you admit it! You didn't tell me you love me, you didn't kiss me, all you were worried about was...' but his shoes are on and he rises.

She pushes him back into the chair. *'You're going to sit here and listen to me'*

Like Hell and he's up this time, he doesn't want to drive anymore doesn't want anything anymore just to get away, she's become someone else, and the basement door is there, and he knows the basement is where she never goes, unclean as butchers' blocks, she's never had the chance to ritually cleanse *that* Halloween down there, never goes down there never wants to, when there's a box she needs to save she opens the basement door just wide enough to fit it through and throws it to the bottom of the stairs, shuts the door just as quickly, *no way she's going to follow me down there*

And the door is open and his hand is still on the knob, and the wind leaves him when she jumps on his back, it's a wonder she doesn't just split open and spill out, *the stitchesthestitchesthestitches* it's a wonder he doesn't go tumbling down there like one of her boxes too, empty and in the way but she needs to keep him anyway, but he's going down those steps if it kills him, and she's on his back, how she holds on like this with those stitches of hers, how she screams into his ear with those stitches, and she's holding her feet out long behind, dragging them every stair, the corrugations of descent he wades through this week's boxes she's still on him and her voice screaming is a color and not a tone whiteyelloworange, and there, finally, is the old couch he used to have in grad school she had made him take it down here the things of *his old life* not worth having anymore now that he has this brand new life with his bright shiny new family, and her mother is pulling at her, trying to get her to let go *come Bitta you're going to hurt him you're going to pull your stitches* he sights in that couch and as he's about to hit it running but now he's down and she's standing over him now and Mama's still trying to pull her off him and she's still screaming and she doesn't look a bit like what she used to.

'...And *every time* that child has a birthday, *that child* you want so much more than me, *that child* you ignored me for in the delivery room, *every time that child grows a year*, you get to remember just how you've ruined my life'

Hold the ends of these two wires together if you don't the world will end

Ici-bas sur Terre, un humble messager
   —De chair d'obscur charbon, de corail, de quartz faite—
   'Mon ange ?' (tes doigts chercheurs frôlant mon squelette)
   'Où sont donc tes ailes dont tu es usager ?'

Ce tien ange (qui cuide ton bras partager)
   Entrevoit ta pensée que tu tiens en cachette
   'Je n'y suis pour longtemps,' dit cette voix doucette
   'Or, bénis-moi avant que j'aille volager'

Je te peindrai alors d'autres joies dans le cœur
   Et mon amour te chuchote son ancien message :
   Mon amour à donner, mon amour à saisir

Te souviendras-tu de moi, de ce voyageur ?
   Te souviendras-tu de ma mission, du passage
   T'apporter de l'amour, t'apporter du plaisir ?

A humble messenger down here on Earth below
   Coal and coral, quartz and dark, stone made flesh became
   'Angel?' (your fingers tracing round my shoulder's frame)
   'Where are those wings of yours? Why is it they don't show?'

This angel of yours (always at your arm you know)
   Can see into your thoughts before you do the same
   'I won't be waiting 'round for long,' sighs your heart's flame
   'But you must leave me a blessing before I go'

And so my fingers paint new joy into your heart
   And my lips whisper love in its ancient message:
   To give and to receive it in equal measure

Perhaps you'll remember me when you do depart
   Perhaps you'll think of my mission and my passage
   To bring you love, to make you smile, bring you pleasure

***

'And by counting the days I've been watching you change and I can feel it dying'

But I will never let go of this life-saving thread. I will never accede to that. I can't think of it.

And so think of this as What It's Always Been. I love you. And sometimes I just can't say any more.

***

But there's more to this than just words, isn't there? The words are the tangible signs, the coin of our love, for if we cannot be together for the day, we can revel in each other's galloping language, I love you, my love is forever, my Leonine Ott, my Sweet El, we are forever, they will build monuments in honor of our love, there will not be a love here on Earth—one quite like this—for another three hundred years, for another five hundred years, for another... ever.

For no man has loved a woman like I love you.

And as long as there is ink to write and life in language, there will be love there will be love there will be love, and our love will be immortal. And in time, in years and centuries and millennia, you will be alive, a dream that love has ignited in an ancient tongue.

***

I know about Ricus. You who pride yourself in your towering honesty. And it took me asking you a direct question—he's there right now, isn't he?—to hear you admit to him.

And as the days go threading onward, I've known that he has been the third person in our lives for longer than you've admitted to.

And I know that there is revenge in your loving him, I know that you have never forgotten the days before I knew we were what we've become, the days before I realized I was alive again, and it was your love firing my life into being. You haven't forgotten, and you won't let me forget.

And I know, in the simplest, barest, cruelest terms, that you want what you want when you want it.

And I know Ricus is what you want when you want it. Yet you've reassured me that I am your love, that I am the one for you, and until the day we can live in the house we've built of our desire and admiration, you will continue to be free and I will continue to be free.

And if you've taken the pains to reassure me, then it is my pleasure to take the same pains to reassure you: you have your freedom—and I know, what with your beauty of heart mind face, that you will never be alone, never have a night alone if you so desire—and I have my freedom. And I offer you my whole freedom

This is what my love is like.

Le désir des nations, la falaise des gravités
   De ces foudres blancs et nus l'ampleur affranchie
   Thermites pyrétiques et orfèvreries
   Convergent sur cet homme : atrium, concavités

Fibreuses de sa chair, l'envoi des poésies
   Et l'envol de son cœur loin des cieux et cités
   Vers son amante lointaine, n'ayant pitié
   Pour son geste pour sa nuit pour sa fantaisie

Qu'est-ce Destin pour celui-ci, force sans âme
   Ni yeux qui le pousse avant, qui le consomme ?
   Chasme chariot l'aile l'épée tous l'ont pour proie

La Folie la course de mon destin infâme
   Une folie destinée non pour ce pauvre homme
   Mais pour le rêveur et l'amant et pour les rois

The desires of nations, collapse of gravities
  The draw of thunderstorm's lightningstroke bare and white
  Pyritic points of gold thermite trac'ry unite
  Upon this man: atr'um, the fibrous cavities

Of flesh and flame, of pain and love, of poem's flight
  Sending his heart aloft above skies and cities
  To his lover abroad, who sees not, who pities
  Not this man's selfless act, the rising of his night

What is fate for this man? This eyeless soulless force
  Compelling him, this man consumed, pleading aright, bent
  Towards chasms and chariots reddened swords and stark wings?

His madness rise, madness, this is fate's stolen course
  Madness unowned by him, this is a madness meant
  For dreamers' sleep and for lovers' loss and for kings

***

This is Poets' Increase: the world doesn't really hold such pigments, the heart doesn't really hold such fervor, the mind cannot possibly raise thought and principle to such airless realms

Or can it

'In this Burgundy room with the high cliffs of Ste. Réparate lofting over us in that church, light shining through its Burgundy glass... The Poet's Increase...'

There was no church, only Apollinaire gazing out his windowframe through a wine glass he held between gracile fingers, quickbitten fingernails. It was dawn in Nice.

***

'Sire,' said the old Artist, 'we will build at Romorantin: there will be two separate Keeps and two courtyards around each Keep; each Keep will be cruciform after the Portinari Chapel, church of Sant'Eustorgio in Milan, and will feature a quadruple-helix staircase, with the takeoff from the ground floor landing only at the fourth story, the takeoff from the first floor at the fifth, and so on.'

'This is an abuse, an injury to Your Highness' intellect.' François' architects, having gathered, spoke as one. 'The *First Painter* should never have been allowed in the room, much less design a palace, much less be allowed to claim it be A Perfect Palace.'

'But Sire, shouldn't a King's dreams be measured in Length, Width, Height and Depth?' The Painter's voice held colors of urgency, of hopefulness.

'But you can't *do* that.' François' architects spoke as one.

Dangerdangerdangerdanger François's face became weather afoul. *Can't I?*

The architects continued anyway. 'It will be wildly expensive: why, just to cut foundations will exhaust the forty thousand pounds you've accorded the project. *He,*' with contempt dripping from their pronoun, 'has moreover failed to mention—we note with interest—that his *plan* (if you still care to call it that) requires canalizing the Beuvron River so that it flows into the Sauldre, rerouting the Cher to above Villefranche, and then again to the Sauldre.'

'This is to provide that the Sauldre be plenished enough as to become navigable; to make of Romorantin a New Venice...'

The architects interrupted as one: 'How many dams and canals and waterways does this tattered Merlin wish Your Highness to purchase for him? How many ways does Your Highness wish this man to endanger town and royal coffer alike?'

The Artist, the *First Painter and Engineer and Architect of the King*, lost saturation and hue, vanishing again into the shadowy corner. Only his brown-inked drawings remained, curling on the table before the King.

'What are *your* suggestions, then, Ordinaries?'

'Here are some suggestions: We recommend the First Painter be sent away with a reprimand.'

There was a long silence.

'That was only one suggestion.'

'Yes, Sire.'

Implication became a Tangible, a real enough Thing in the room that all would be forced to walk 'round it, like an ill-placed statue in a corridor, or a dining table in a chapel.

'Your answer, First Painter?'

But by this point, The Artist had already left the room.

***

It had been three days of Peruggia hiding out, and some of the strategies Apollinaire dreamed up to keep him incognito bordered on the ridiculous, the abusive, the insane.

Walk with a limp as you go to the toilet for the toilet was down the hall to be sure people notice, *'that man has a limp' and will attribute their memory's content to the limp rather than to the shape of your face, the rumple of your clothes, the stink of your odor* for there was little in the way of creature comforts beyond the seemingly inexhaustible liquor keeping both men's serum levels topped off.

Now walk normally as if the confusion about which man was actually going to the toilet would override any passersby's recollection of Peruggia's face *now walk there with a limp, walk back without one*

'Wouldn't you rather I shave my mustaches?'

'Heavens no—you can, but of course you'll have to wait for weeks before using the toilet again.'

***

'Send for the First Painter.'

Clos-Lucé was a long stone's throw from the King's bedchamber at Amboise; having changed hands a hundred times under a dozen different monarchs, it had become a Bauble, a Place Where They Keep Trinkets. Now The Painter was kept here.

The Painter had run of the place, used fearfully little of it, finding the tight high corners of the larger rooms too dark, too far away for the light of day to search out, too far away for the light of lamps and tapers to sound out, too planar to be overcome by the lamplight's haloed spheres. And The Painter had precious little patience with visitors; as often as not, he would barricade himself into some recess of the mansion at first indication he was expected to Receive them and Be Sociable… he would make himself unfindable, become one with the brickwork or the stonework.

And his capacity and desire to flee the very men who bore authority made him into a wizard for some, and soon *The Necromancer* stuck with these people; the thing was, the more a given courtier referred to him as Necromancer, the less—it seemed—that visible light would reflect from him, and soon enough, only his movements by night could be seen, a light passing from window to window, the slow cadence of senescence and deepening despair.

François knew the architects had been harsh with The Painter. This is the way with hierarchies, this is the way it is when you're this close to Power, nothing can be done but to remind mere men that with power comes privilege, and that he bore The Painter great abundances of goodwill, and that being near the King constituted a great privilege indeed, so in his great goodwill he deigned to keep the old man near.

'He's not opening, Sire. Doors are bolted. Nobody seems to be there.'

* * *

'I'm out of here.'

Apollinaire toasted Peruggia from his desk. No argument there.

The sun rose. Wall to wall blue accosted Peruggia; our hero nearly fell down blind *Saul Saul why do you persecute Me?* and decided that the Niçois are experts at Turning Off, he could pickpocket any one of them without a second's thought, wouldn't even have to run, they'd just wave at a pestering fly or *Ooh Honey look at the sea* or wipe gin fizz off their giant paunch, no problem, they'd notice (or not) some time later, with onions dribbling from their chins, looking for a hanky *Honey have you seen my wallet* and when Wife failed to answer, out of boredom or inebriation or both *Oh well* and the rest would be history.

Some fraction of Peruggia's blood chemistry is missing; although only nine in the morning, with his whole organism screaming (of all things) *ice cream* at him: he capitulates.

'Give me an ice cream cone' *who cares if this is actually a vendor of same* 'come to think of it, give me two.'

The young woman produces two cones topheavy; Peruggia realizes only then he is clutching Brass Corners still; with one hand encumbered, he circles—dumb animal chasing its tail—trying to arrange himself.

'Have a nice day.'

'I hate you.'

* * *

The *Souterrain* linking Amboise Palace with the Clos-Lucé had been in the back of François' mind since puberty, and whenever his Amboise was too constricting for his ferocious libido and his Chosen One too base or coarse for serious consideration, he would tell the closest squire to fetch the keyring.

Fetch The Keyring. He thought the words uppercase.

A glorious occupation that one, to Fetch The Keyring for the Duke of Angoulême, the King of France, Defender of the Faith.

And in moments, the Keyring was in his hand, and then there were the close staircases barely wide enough for his shoulders' frame or for his desires, the candle flame would attempt to jump clear of the oily wick and he knew he had to slow down or tumble down those secret stairs in the dark. The Gate was the Keyring's one desire, this tunnel must be seventy feet below ground level, and with François holding the candle, Keyring would have its way with the whole harem of padlocks safeguarding The Trinket Box' ironclad virtue.

Stone and dirt and darkness; surely the very masonry down here must be impregnate with the very whiff of François' rut. How many maidens had been within three minutes of Being Blessed by the King's assault by the time that great iron gate clattered shut behind him, seventy feet below the Clos?

But tonight there was a different mission, and perhaps there was something other than Lust volatilizing from his pores tonight?

More stairs, screwing Up this time, heading up into the darkness, candleflame a bit less reluctant to point the way. One final door cedes to the King's will, and he is in the Clos.

'Maestro. *Ho bisogno di te.*'

* * *

My dear sweet Love, my Beloved,

You are still asleep, quiescent in your dark bed. I imagine your heart beating its gentle cadence, mysterious, distant, entirely Yours. How deftly you have kept it from me, how jealous of the least revelation, the least unveiling.

Yet even if I cannot know you, I can intuit the heart that beats within you, can sing the listless melody that issues from your thoughts, have fondled the curve of your ribs, lifted your veil somewhat. I can imagine you in your lofted bed, dreams of orange and red and yellow... dreams of high science, of flight, of great deeds. What else lies behind those eyes?

What kind of Venus, what manner of succubus are you? What dark voodoo have you cast into my eyes, into my heart of hearts, that I should need you so?

* * *

Three candles—one burnt dead to its base, one in an intermediate state between Whole and Gone still lit, and one still pristine and unburned—stood before The Painter, a cone of light of descending intensity radiating from the single burning taper.

The Painter was drawing the light of that single candle, *by* the light of that single candle. Once François realized this, he blew out his own light. The hush of his breath over the flame was enough to alert the old man. His wild, variegated eyebrow rose.

'Maestro,' said the King, approaching, 'don't let me dare interrupt.'

'Yes, Sire, if you command,' said The Painter distantly, his attention at once divided, at once alert and Present. The King brought a chair, arranged it as quietly as possible. The men then sat in silence, only the dry scratch of a pen on paper audible, a breathy itch, the only sign of life the lit taper excepting.

François shuddered a bit, seeing the old man at work, hearing his pen making the world *become*, wondering at the thoughts animating that old soul.

'Is there anything you need, Maestro?' The words, even muttered at the very threshold of audition, echoed slightly, undid the magician's spell for a moment.

The Painter looked around him, encompassing the room with unbelieving eyes. Even for having chosen one of the smallest rooms in the Clos for his studio, it was vast and dark. 'I have far more than I could possibly need, Sire.'

And the hiss and rasp of the pen, the melodious tapping of pen to inkwell, the breath of King and Wizard and candle unite. It took the King gingering ten minutes full to break the spell this time.

'We have been managing this problem of the Romorantin site, Maestro.'

'I know you have.' Still working, the pen and the eye, the light and the ink. 'I trust Your Highness has come to a good and right conclusion.'

'We've come to a conclusion, it is true.'

'*We've come to a conclusion.*' The old man's fingers smudged and probed, the pen, now blunted, took a half-dozen strokes of a razor to bring it back into true. 'I don't dare ask Your Highness who the *we* could possibly denote.'

François rose, walked slowly around the room, the easels, the calipers, the rolls of paper, the dust of a studio barely visible in the powdery light of one candle. 'The problem that you and I have, Maestro, is that the architects are all bureaucrats. They are all *professionals*. It didn't always work this way:

men occupied a position in the King's government by virtue of having been born to that position, but nowadays, men *ascend* to their proper place. If we need a lawyer to notarize a document, we hire out a real lawyer. We don't look around for the nobleman who owns the pen and ink.'

'Of course.'

'The architects work for me, as I need them, work for me as I give them mandate to. But you, you are in a *special* position, Maestro. Representing neither the... *mundane-ness* of the hired hand, nor the incompetence of the old heads. A *special* position...'

'I am at your entire disposition, Sire, that is a special-enough position.' Somehow François could hear a note of nostalgia rising in the old man's voice. 'And what have The Real Architects come up with?'

'A change of venue. Chambord now, not Romorantin.'

'Ah.'

'You've seen the site. It is very doable. It is flat and unassuming and unthreatening and featureless.'

'Ah.'

'Perfect for a worksite. No challenges whatsoever.'

The Painter never set down his pen, never paused.

'It's unclear to me one thing, Sire.'

'What is that?'

'Whether the Mundanes or the Incompetents have won out.'

* * *

'You have kept the two Keeps in the plan, I trust.'

'Two Keeps? Let's not exaggerate.'

'Does the King not have two mistresses?'

The King did not comment; the silence encumbering the Trinket Palace was palpable.

'The staircases at least,' the Painter resumed, 'the quadruple helices?'

'No.'

'Would you like me to be involved at all, Sire?'

'Of *course* we would like you to be involved.'

'The staircases, then?'

Without answering directly: 'Maestro, I've been thinking a great deal about the portrait you've made.'

'I've made many portraits, Sire.'

'Ah, but none like the one I have in mind.'

'Hmm. Yes. *Her.* ' The slightest pause; for a moment his pen lifted from the leaf and did not go back down. 'Of course.' His pen found paper again.

'Have you given much thought as to where she should be... *best displayed?*'

This time The Painter stopped working entirely. Not a sound in the world, Clos-Lucé a thought-universe all its own, that limbo kingdom where magicians send doves and coins when they are made to disappear into the ether.

'Sire,' The Painter breaking the spell, 'your new palace at... *Chambord* still needs a grand staircase. If not a quadruple helix, at least a double. A staircase worthy of a King.'

The two men stared at each other for some time.

'A lovely idea, Maestro. Yes, this palace will have a magnificent double staircase, *exactly* as you design it.' The color had returned to François' face, that joyous rosy color. '*You* will design it, and *our lady* will have a magnificent place to live...'

* * *

You will never be wanting for admirers. You have that beauty—that rare, unattainable beauty—that men will sell life and loyalty to have, to own. Yet I know now that you cannot be had, cannot be owned, will never be reached; you are above my feeble plane, you are in the realm of the Ideas, in the realm of pure mathematics, a beauty unlike any the world has ever seen.

And yet I am here, I am the only man to have attained you for even a day, a week, to have actually held you, managed to turn the corners of your smile, harden the laughing crinkles around your eyes.

This is what my love is like. I dare think you've been amused, at least.

Peruggia was sidesaddle on a bench overlooking the Bay of Angels when Apollinaire found him. He was facing a brass-cornered suitcase.

'Let's go, Failure.' Apollinaire fairly seized him by the ear. 'Who were you talking to?'

* * *

'*So.*' The King shifted uncomfortably. 'May I *see* her?'

'Pardon me, Sire?'

'May I see her?'

The Painter raised his eyes to François.

'*Really, Sire?*'

'Sure. There's no one else around and... and...'

The Painter had a new leaf of paper before him; he wet his pen. 'The Cosson River flows just north of the site of your proposed... *Chambord palace*' he had trouble getting the words to come out, Romorantin still stinging in his memory, 'and becomes the right tributary of the Beuvron... *here.*' A map spread from his pen. 'There's very little flow, it is true, but with any luck we'll be able to get her to turn to the south, and into the *domaine*-proper, where she'll form reflecting pools and aliment the moats.'

The King's face found a hundred new expressions, expressions proper to kings considering dubious treaties, proper to men gambling on a shell in the shell-game.

'Let me see the portrait first.'

* * *

'...And I have this idea for a great bronze horse, the finest and largest in the world.'

'*No*, Maestro. *No.*'

Mon Dieu, qu'est-il arrivé à ce mien visage ?
  Où s'en sont-ils allés, ce courage défiant,
  Cet esprit, ce cœur, cet œil alerte et veillant
  Où témérité et intrigue se propagent ?

Or ce matin, l'aube dorée jaunissant
  Ne laisse rien à l'imagination : et l'âge
  De mon armure, et les fissures du ferrage
  De mon regard, se voient, si froids, vieillissant

Les jours s'en vont, et force et expérience, idées
  Que l'âge grave dans le cœur dans sa confiance
  Reflètent dans ces yeux que le miroir reproche

Mon courage, visible par son absence
  Et ma figure de soucis subtils ridée
  Me ressemblent de moins en moins plus je m'approche

My God, whatever happened to this face of mine?
   Where has that defiance, where has that courage gone?
   That alert darting eye, that mischief graven on
   My features, where daring and intrigue would combine?

This morning, the golden grains of bright'ning dawn
   Leave nothing to the imagination: the fine
   Cracks in my armor widening, the hardened line
   Of my glare sketched in black, my features cold and drawn.

Days pass, and should strength and experience be increased
   And age should linger my heart in its confidence,
   Shouldn't my face reflect brighter in the mirror?

My courage, visible in its very absence
   And my face, by subtle cares and worries long creased
   Looks less and less like myself as I get nearer

* * *

There is nothing stranger.

And nothing more familiar.

* * *

Havoise had tried a thousand times to say the word. '*Glass. Teenga. Glass. Teenga. Glass. Teenga.*' She had tried it in Latin, reading in a Life of the Saints: '*Glastonia*', '*Glastoniam*'... In the end, though, it would come mumblingrumbling out in her vulgar: *Glastonebourg.*

Havoise would be a *Glastonebourgeoise.*

La comtesse de... '*Glastonbury*'. Her mind stumbled and tumbled over the words, and the words, over the idea of it all.

The Somerset Levels were her new land, inadequately absorbing an insistent rain; the Glastonbury Tor rose up into the low clouds, the Abbey mossy and black, wood and stone the same flat black, black as char, black as coal.

Glastonbury Abbey lay just beyond these gates. Havoise recognized Torsen's Armoror, who had traveled here with Torsten months ago.

* * *

Many categories of law had governed her Torsten ever since she had first seen him, shivering under the Norman rain: he had begun his life under the Benedictines, good and Roman it is true, and they had taught him to read and write, and had given him the art of books and a love of quiet, and had made him methodical and organized.

Robert the Devil had been his next Law, soaking up the young clerk's efficient way, commanding him *make the boy a Duke,* and come the bastard boy's adolescence, Torsten could measure his success in building a mansion of intangible Authority around William by the number of times a rival slipped a blade out into the cold air of a darkened corridor and went for the bastard's jugular or ribcage. For the most part, Torsten had already scent of an approaching assassin in his nostrils, sometimes months in advance: by imagining the *other* mansions of authority rising in the Ducal court, he could sense which ones would next intersect with William's. And no cold blade ever found its mark.

Sometimes Torsten would be at his table at night, sketching genealogies into his greatbook, imagining tipping towers of authority, one for each lord, the men at the top of each tower aspiring to heights glorious, heights only reached by the Worthy. And the Law governing Torsten's life and ways now, was that the only man Worthy would be William, bastard son of Robert the Devil. All other talk stank in Torsten's ears.

Later, when Warrior William went to war according to this same Law, he commanded Torsten to consult his growing greatbook, *Which man will pretend to the Ducal throne next?* and *Which border is leanest?* and *Which way does the wind blow?* And clerk Torsten would spend his nights consulting the leaves, and the Norman army would swing west, then east, then west again, scouring the countryside for rivals to kill, for alliances to build, for cities to raze, and cities to raise.

The battle at Val-ès-Dunes had been just one such expedition, hardly a battle at all in fact, with a fiendishly-choreographed series of defections programmed into the enemy forces well in advance by this pale bibliophile, defections that had effectively won the battle before the first sword was ever drawn.

Many 'enemy' simply walked away. The first of these were given titles and land. The more recalcitrant, the longer they held out, the farther away the land, the longer the walk. Torsten remembers assigning a few acres in *Sicily,* for God's sake.

The rest, a pitiful few, were surrounded and massacred by William's band of loyals the next day.

* * *

'What does the greatbook say?' William would stand over Torsten's shoulder.

Brittany. Burn Dinan.

Avençon. Take the border back by five miles.

Caen. Build an abbey.

And that night, when all invaders had been put to the edge of the blade, when all neighbors had been taught to cower, when the Church itself had trembled, when William—*Duke* William—appeared at Torsten's shoulder: 'What does the greatbook say?'

It is time to build ships.

* * *

From here on out, aspirations and delusions are one and the same.

* * *

The Armoror's great boots and steel arms racketed through the corridors of Glastonbury Abbey. Havoise had never heard of an abbey where there were so many armed men; she recognized Norman insignias on their armor, recognized the peculiar cut of their swords. As for the monks, there was little for them to do but make way: the Armoror striding through, Havoise having to gallop, cloaks and tunics asway, to keep up with him.

'Eyes down, damn you, this is your Countess.'

Torsten had explained a dozen times how it was that a clerk like him—of the Orders—had been caused to marry, by Robert the Devil's letters to bishop and cardinal; Havoise imagined the bulk of the Church's machinery *making way* for Robert just like these monks scattering from before the great Armoror—*eyes down, damn you*—and although she could never quite understand how the new Abbott of Glastonbury Abbey could be a married man, she took comfort knowing that Torsten certainly knew. He probably wrote his own letters of commission.

'Desperate times' he would say.

Comite, Count, envoy, a *commission* sent away to carry out the wishes of a lord. Torsten had consulted the greatbook at length. England was William's. Holding it was Torsten's new Law.

The Church is a hierarchy, too, and soon the greatbook became interleaved with new tipping towers of authority.

'They crowned Edmund Ironside King of England at Glastonbury Abbey. Harold's predecessor.'

'What then?' William peering over Torsten's shoulder. *Which way does the wind blow?*

'It is time we have that Abbey.'

Abbott Torsten, Count Abbot Torsten, these were all abominations.

* * *

The silence of this place! This is not a reverent silence, but a fearful silence

Torsten stood at his writing table. There were supplemental tables at rakish angles to the first, each burdened with Book, each volume distorted fantastically with interleaves.

'Milord.'

Torsten did not turn, did not even look up from the greatbook, but instead held his hands up above him, black with ink. 'I should wash.'

'Please don't. You're occupied.'

And Torsten resumed his attentions to the greatbook.

* * *

'These men are all under the illusion that our William is a mere *tem-*

poral problem. They are Anglo in speech and deed and conscience. They are not ready to call themselves Norman.'

Torsten's voice, his chambers, converted to contain his bed. Havoise saw his shoulders, his head, silhouetted by the flame of his lamp, greatbook surrounding him like a spread of leaved wings. She heard the Armoror outside the door, bodyguard over the abomination. She shifted in bed.

'They venerate Dunstan, the *Reformer*. This is defiant enough. It is all too easy to see the old regime in Dunstan, to see the saint as Deliverer from William's strong hand.' The smell of ink, of oil. Lamp black shadowed the wall. 'I can just see it: *Dunstan the Reformer, Dunstan the Salvor of Deposed Kings*. There is going to be a terrible inertia to overcome: this abbey is not at all of the Roman church...'

Havoise waited; Torsten had a way of breathing that let her know when his thought was over.

'Surely you don't mean the Saint Dunstan, whose image is in the abbey church? *All over* the abbey church?'

'The same. You see? What *energies* it will take...!'

The room was a silent secret.

'I can guarantee you one thing, milord. The very instant even *one* of those glass panels with Dunstan's image is broken...' She could see Torsten's shoulders catching his breath within him as Implication became clearer.

'...The Saint,' he said slowly, 'will become all the more powerful...'

'And the dead king...'

'...A martyr.'

The lamp flickered and crackled. Havoise didn't dare move, she hadn't yet heard Torsten breathing just right, and the air hadn't yet shifted.

'The Normans have to *be*. It's just that simple. They are the new order. William is the new Law.'

'And yet,' Havoise whispered, 'the old Law is all they know.'

She saw her husband paging through volumes of the greatbook, as if the answer could be divined from a word count, a page count, a Cabal of inkstains; by lamplight, the genealogies looked to Havoise like the peaked roofs of a village. She willed the thought toward Torsten, to slide two genealogies, two volumes of greatbook, toward each other. She imagined Willam's own greatbook interleaving with Glastonbury Abbey's, and wished she had the courage to rise and interleave the books herself, *the Norman book, the Anglo book, the Norman book, the Anglo book,* just like a weaver might. She lay perfectly still, watching the shoulders of her husband as he hunched over his books.

'Willam's *largesse*,' Torsten's shadow thought aloud, 'could be... *satisfying* to an abbey.'

And he slid one volume of the greatbook to the edge of the table, till it came to rest touching the next volume. The two peaked inkroofs pointed into the same parchment sky.

* * *

'I don't like it. I don't like it one bit.'

Torsten's voice in the inky darkness, hunched over the Long Knowledge of the greatbooks.

They had packed sandbags into each window niche of the old abbey church to protect the images of Saint Dunsten. A new worksite was taking shape next to the old church, a *Norman* worksite this time. The chapel would be dedicated to a Norman saint, the very patron saint of all Normandy, Saint Michael himself, first warrior among all warriors, the Lord's appointed messenger to bring not peace, but a sword. A Michaelschurch. And the old Abbey church would be demoted to something less militant.

'They can keep their windows, but a good Norman venerates not Dunstan, but Mary.'

'What other choice have you?'

'There are many potential choices. Some subtle, some less so.'

* * *

'Men like me are not meant to be *present* when history happens. We are left to marvel at the wake of great men having passed by.'

'You're not the only one passed by, left swimming in the wake.' Havoise' voice rasped, barely audible in the night. 'To be *great* is to be *few.*'

The notion of *knowing somebody* had new implications, now that William's court was effectively spread out over the entire map of England, nodes of Norman *meaning* speckling the map over, and Torsten had known men at Hastings, yes, had watched awestruck as the greatbook sent them there, and now *to the victors go the spoils, let he who merits the palm wear it* these men—those that had survived—together founded a new kind of feudal Law, a Law that the greatbook alone informed: that to be Anglo in this new era, you had to go through the new Norman filters, as now it was the cadre of men—whom the greatbook had appointed—holding the pivotal posts, the *authority*—throughout William's new lands, who could make you or break you—even christening a newborn required a Norman priest, for without Normandy, you could only be a Nothing. Yes, Torsten *knew* men who had been at Hastings, and those men were hundreds of miles away now, *might as well be on the Moon,* making England a New Normandy; the breadth of the project was more than a single human being could apprise, only the greatbook could hold it all, and Torsten was nothing but a single data point among ten thousand—an active one, true, a fieryfurnace data point, a brightening, reddening star—so of course there was no hope of Hastings being anything but a misty myth to these Glastonbury monks, to these... *Glastonburghers,* now having to pay *real* homage to a distant man in a distant place—William the Norman might as well be a ghost to them. For him to be Real would require special—local—ambitions.

'If only these people could *see* Hastings,' Havoise continued, 'know what earthly Authority *is,* from where it is derived, that it is wrung from the blood of their own dead. They would love and fear William out of love for their own blood, and know Authority from the very beginning: *Hic venit nuntius ad Wilgelmum Ducem...*'

                            * * *

    It was that very night that Havoise' fingers began pricking her, and the words, *Here messengers came to William the Duke* began forming above her in the ether whenever she was distracted in conversation, or waking before dawn, or stirring her bowl. The memory of events all leading to William crossing over to Hastings—and then Torsten next, with all the retinue and infrastructure for keeping William king, and then Havoise finally with her bundles—was a palpable thing to her, a memory a well-used trail in the woods, she could navigate it at will, always knew the breadth of her existence as she went along it; she remembered, at the very far extremity of this well-worn path, the dyeing trenches the women would stride up and down in back in Falaise: never did these women ever doubt where their place was, what they could hope to see but never grasp... *What they were* was *what they lived*, and they had trounced to and fro in those long trenches so long and so well, they could dream their depth, could sketch from memory the bedrock invisible beneath the frothing water, knew when to turn and how wide to give way to the other dyer women, knew whenever the hardened, horned men in the Keep at Falaise leered at them, knew whenever children like Havoise were watching them. Beyond these mere trifles that crossed their mind as a fragment of a melody—the people that passed, the Way Things Were—the World Beyond was a formality, a hard concept, one that didn't admit to being stared at much—like the passage of time or the fact of Death.

    And Havoise' fingers found that linen ground, and without knowing quite why, she sat up while Torsten worked in his greatbook, studying a hard interconnection between two towers of Long Knowledge—or constructing a new interconnection with the insistent scratch of his quill pen—and began constructing a Long Memory of her own: Edward the King, Harold his son, *Messengers came to William the Duke*, and whenever Torsten wrote a marginal glyph into his greatbook—*Dunstan was the favorite of King Athelstan and as such, will always be seen as one of the pillars of English royal power*—Havoise began working in another griffin into the margins of her Long Memory.

And the pictures she would see in her mind's eye: William on his throne with the lions' heads, the cavalry charge against Dinan, the house afire, the boatbuilders with their squares and their planes, the great lengths of ships that poured from those men's drawing tables, with their sails in butterfly colors, the Norman men all rushing, crushing. And the English fled before them all.

* * *

Against Havoise' protests, Torsten insisted the tapestry—little fragment squares of Long Memory Havoise would embroider into each other—be raised over the windows of Saint Dunstan's church in the abbey. The windows could fade in their casements, the casement surrounds could rot away, William's Authority would cover them over.

And hatred for the Abbott would grow. This *Comite*, this *Envoy*, so very Roman, so very *Norman*, making the world Norman, making the world *William's*—all you could see in this darkened place was William and his Norman men in their glorified poses, the English court unable to do anything besides plotting and cowering, pointing in dismay at the Star that had announced their doom. Horses and swords, arrows in flight.

Torsten the Reformer

* * *

And men began to look on Havoise with compassionate eye. If the Count was a reshaper of history, the Countess was as well, but of a different stripe, of a different weft and warp. She *spun* the lives of men from her gracile fingers, she *wyrded them*, twining them from thread and linen.

For she was no longer young. And these men of the Angles, knowing the fate of their nation and the ancient beliefs of their song and the whispered legends of their Avalon forests and Somerset Levels, saw the Norman Weaver metamorphose, saw her *metamorphose*, saw her *become*, to grow and transform into the Anglo Spinner, holding the destinies of men fine filaments singing the Past arachnidan.

The Countess Havoise, Worthy Matron

* * *

And there in silence by night, the fates of nations were dreamed, a Norman nation, an Anglo nation, the man and the woman the knife and the spoon, the book and the woven wyrded word, Long Knowledge and Long Memory, and Armoror kept watch by night, to be assured that it was so.

* * *

And the men at Glastonbury Abbey, and the people in round Somerset all bore what they called Dunstan Grudge, the abbey church a twisting turning monument to popular memory become official. And they turned the world upside down in their games, to make the blades of vengeance just a bit duller, to diminish the temptation to revolt, to offer themselves respite from the repeated offense. The song of Long Memory for their fallen king denied light from their sight by Long Knowledge, and scoffing new stones rose up at the old church's shoulder, and the old pagan saints were jealous of the Roman deities, and offered their lives as blood sacrifice to the people who had venerated them in their faith.

'So very *Roman* you wish us. Let us have our chapel; we will allow our Dunstan to lend his holy name to Michael's in the new Norman church, just leave us with something of our own in the old abbey church.'

And Torsten didn't think about it, just wrote and wrote—and read what he wrote—looking for William's authority to sketch into the filigree of lineages and connectednesses, and there he realized that the abbey held a holy olivewood cup the pilgrims used to sip the blood of Christ from, nibbling splinters from its edge to have as their own, *we will drink the blood of our God, but we will cut our gums on wood Mary carried to us,* and the monks entreatied Torsten the Abomin—Torsten the *Abbot*—to let them have their old ways back among the old stones, the old glass linened over with William's legitimate power.

And to their bemusement and amazement, Torsten *made* their old church a Marian church and the Cup was walled-in to the old chapel, *on con-*

dition that the Old Ways never infect the New, that they stay walled-in to that old space, your language and your goddess and your so-very-Anglo ...*way.*

And the Worthy Matron continued spinning the Memory out *How much longer?* and the songs to Mary were songs to the Goddess of their ancient days when their Tor was an isle, when the lake of Somerset marsh was a lake of glass, and the Ancient of Days came to them in the cup borne by the Mary whom Jesus loved instead of the cup carried to them—to *the Normans*—by the Arimathean who planted the thorn.

* * *

Beltane, crowd in the church, lines up Easter and the Equinox, and Tosten is aware of the May pole and willingly turns a blind eye. He can take the numbers to his credit—all these people in this Norman church—it is a victory. But he clenches his teeth.

* * *

Samhane, summer solstice, people are *behaved* and Norman, but the night of high summer, the bonfires on the hilltops, you don't see them, you smell them... he clenches his teeth tighter, harder to ignore this obviously pagan rite, everyone is the God and the Goddess for one night. *Keep it in your side of the church...*

* * *

Michaelmas, the festival of the great soldier Angel, the great last battle between good and evil, the last great festival before the decline of the sun, the rise of winter, the decisive battle between the old and the new. Fall equinox, the season of mist, the mists across the lake of Avalon, Harvest Home, the burning of the scarecrows, the burning of the sacrifices to the Goddess to get everyone through the winter.

Torsten will make the sacrifice, will spill anglo blood on the altar of the new Norman church during the season of mist, he will fairly *wash* the altar with blood.

And when the men sang their *old* hymns in the *new* church, they had already forgotten their promise to let the old be old and the new new, and the Abomination could not believe his ears: gone were the Pater Noster of the Romans, gone the *O Michael Who Is Like God* troparion *Let us praise Cherubim, Seraphim, Thrones, Powers, Authorities and Principalities, Dominions, Archangels and Angels for they are the Bodiless ministers of the Unoriginate Trinity and revealers of incomprehensible mysteries. Glory to Him Who has given you being; glory to Him Who has given you light; glory to Him Who is praised by you in thrice-holy hymns.*

These words, so meet and right and salutary, were replaced instead by richly tapestried murmurs, *Lauerd me steres, noght wante sal me: In stede of fode ˇare me louked he. He fed me ouer watre ofe fode, Mi saule he tornes in to gode. He led me ouer sties of rightwisenes, For his name, swa hali es,* all Anglo, all treacherous to the Norman king and his Norman envoy to the pagan-stained men of this island.

* * *

What fury arose in Torsten hearing those pagan sounds! For how will you ever rule yourselves, when you turn to such base created things, such coarse tones, ò you Angles! Here your King comes to you in the authority of this small gift, so humble and great and holy, this Michaelchurch, and you repay him in this way?

And the men returned with, You are the abomination, You are the soldier's pawn, You are the man whose holy orders lie as wreckage, as chaff, as ashes. You decry our ancient Goddess, our ancient Norns, and yet we have not only a Count but a Countess, an Abbot and an Abbess, at least the Worthy Matron can be forgiven for fulfilling her right function as weaver of men's destinies, first our king's—*long may he live in our memory though mouldering away to horror and gore!*—then your own *duke's* destiny (with scorn tarring the word) as the *Usurper*...

'I give you,' said Torsten that night, silhouetted in the lamplight, folds and ondules of the greatbook around him a turbulent sea, 'chance to repent, chance to pack away your Goddess back into the old walls of old stones, wall her away just as you've done with her olivewood cup.'

* * *

Harold Rex interfectus est

Harold the king has been touched by William's arrow. Harold the king has been hit by William's arrow. Harold the king has been injured by William's arrow.

Harold the king is last seen alive, William's arrow in the orbit of his right eye, Harold grabbing vainly at the shaft, the arrowhead is deep, has turned awry, has jammed into the fibers of his bones, his eye's orbit has locked the arrowhead fast, the roof of the frontalis bone, the jamb of the sygomic bone, Harold grabbing grabbing grabbing, his horse in flight, Harold's hand is on the arrow's shaft now, and the yew wood yields—William's arrowhead broken off in Harold's eye, Harold's head, Harold's wed that arrow of the Duke William and the royal child is an Abomination.

Havoise' fingers work the arrow deep into Harold's eye.

* * *

Marie, for thy joyes five,
Help me to lyve in clene lyve;
For the teres thou lette under the rode,
Send me grace of lyves fode

The mossy tones of old Anglo echo through the new Michaelchurch. The Angle men worship their Goddess.

Glestingaburg's common folk watch as The Count Abomination strides through, Abbot Torsten the Norman, the nave a crowd of Norman archers now, a jostling jangling of armor pressing forward toward the choir, where Anglo monks breathe in unison one last prayer.

Hail thou Marie, ful of grace, the hlaverd is mid thee. Iblesced be thou onmang wimmen and iblesced thines wombes wæstme.

The Thirty Archers Plus One.

The creaking of bows in the sanctuary.

Dos brisé, amas d'os, des navires les côtes
   La courbe des os une église aux arcs boutant
   Chapelle habitée de fantômes et goélands
   Ce récif aligné, blanchi, orne la côte

Une course défaillant qui peu à peu ôte
   Cette vie à chaque vague, à chaque moment
   Puis, le poumon hersé, le cri si lent silent
   Ce corps sans poids sommeillant flotte

Ces os fragiles que les ans ont effleurés
   Ces lampes sans flamme, cendres, noirci le sol :
   Naissance, fine jeunesse et âge déchoient

Eteint, le feu du gué ; faillie cette boussole
   Distant autel qui ce sacrifice reçoit
   Victime qu'une seule fois j'immolerai

Bones of ships, spars askew, a keel rent asunder
   My ribcage wreckage church of arches to the sky
   Haven for ghosts and gulls, creaking mass, spars awry
   Lifeless reef fallen headlong, dry bleaching lumber

The race for port has failed, going farther under
   With each swell, with each breath, with each moment flown by
   Now the harrowed lungs aflame, now the silent cry
   Now the resignation, now the weightless slumber

The brittle bones, the lightless lamps, the years that climb
   This frame, blacken it to ash in the flameless pyre
   My birth, my slim youth, my age's blueprint falters

Gone this trusted compass' life, gone the watchman's fire
   The chest flung open to bless forgotten altars
   I can give this humble gift but this single time

***

What charm is this? They tell stories of men who mistake their wives for inanimate objects, for strangers, for imposters...

And now all Sundari wants is to get into bed; she's left just a little space for her husband whom she cursed with the oldworld curse of the ages just that morning. It's late now, Vicus hasn't a fiber left in him that hasn't somehow been hyperextended past sprain, and it took a long time to get the girls to sleep tonight; with Sundari's stitches hurting her, it was Vicus the man of the hour, and he kept waking his newborn daughter with his embrace, and worrying his elder daughter with his tears.

'Come to bed, Sweetie.' Imposter.

'You have *got* to be kidding.'

The couch is big and lumpy and misshapen; the living room glows in the diode light of true crime and weather radar, fadeaway to commercial. He finds his younger kid, wakes her up to give her a feed, lets her melt into his chest and salve the void spaces there.

***

The dearest light is the one on the next block, it shines with a salmon color, iridescent and shimmering.

The darkest place is the spiral of streets circling in toward the prison; spiders webbed over the streetlights a decade ago.

The loveliest melody, the metallic female voice on the tram. *Bouffay. Duchesse Anne. Manufacture. Gare SNCF.*

The *Déclic* over on the west side of town, with its claret beers and Breton music, dancing till three or four, navigate back to Félibien on magnetite inner ears, pulse tension testing the resilience of a Breton aorta, *I'll always know my way home, head and heart.*

The antique store toward the Prefecture, cigar smoke strooling out through the transom window over the door on cold days. Leather, harpsichord, barknocker ingot barglass hubcap diamond star halo *This one belonged to a tavern in Tours three hundred years ago*

The audacity, the magnificent challenge, the silver gauntlet thrown down before the kids at the Catholic school, first snow day in years, *I'll take you all in a fair snowball fight no rock centers b-52*—the day of the giant foreigner with the whiplike pitching arm they'll be telling stories of this battle for a generation

The iron-black stamp of the *Parc du Procé*, trees against the deepening twilight sky. The breaking, curling reflection of Venus in her last hour.

Headless mannequins on Crébillon. Music store up the hill on the left, can always find a new Janequin there, always a new Victoria, a new Josquin under the whitehot halogen bulbs, tiny pinprickdangerous. Lingerie candy stores, always find an athletic confection on Crébillon all straps and garters and lace, this town stands in the window and tells me I'm late, you'd think this town was the Ultimate Gift.

Staircase cascade in Pierrick's mansard garret, have to press the button every floor to keep the lights on; two steps at a time asprint, crack my skull if I'm not careful climb the stairs too quick when the button times out and plunge headfirst into a stone pillar or find that low beam the hard way. Strawberry jam from his mother's kitchen, care package from the coast, the crunch of caramelized sugar and the tart of the berries, Monique's kitchen in glass and wax, *what did you do eat all the fruit out of it just leave me the pectin and the caramel crystals?*

Tongue twisters—*no translation for that yet, what, 'Phrases extrêmement difficiles à prononcer'* ?—like *Tes laitues naissent-elles ? yes, mes laitues naissent* into the high wee hours.

'Michelle' (or so I call her) with the almond croissants in the two a.m. rush, rids the place of yesterday's wheat and whey before the shutter closes for the night; her loose blouse and her loose modern hair soft and crazy a ride in the sun a breezy day on the jetty, *You want to take some away with you? you know we can't save them.* Loose heavy snowflakes, no one sees them but Michelle and me and after leaving Michelle to scour yesterday's gluten away, the long quiet walk home from Pierrick's.

January in Nantes, the night is cold and warm all at once, my birthday hath begun with a striding two a.m. lope through the city in its fast-sighing slumber, pavers in the Ile Feydeau irregular and defiant, the asphalt covering the old course of the Erdre, the cement and Gilamonster pebble travertine by the *Marché aux fleurs* all padlocks in winter hibernation, the fanning brick frozen into peacocks and gingko leaves by the Place Royale fountain frozen-through hard and dead. Chalkdust up toward the theater, stucco next, all grimy by Guist'hau, with brakedust architecture beginning up in the mill district, this is my birthday, an almond croissant still warm as I stride and lope through the prison labyrinth, and now there is Félibien, the croissant is still warm when I drape my greatcoat over the tall heavypainted radiator next to the sink in my little room.

Fantasies of 'Michelle' *I should introduce myself some day* in my little litterbed on Félibien, wiping flour from her forehead with the back of her hand now, now she leans her head into my shoulder the scent of talc and soap and now her bra strap has printed a brandname retrovert into the white skin of her shoulder, now she brushes back a stray lock of hair, moves her hips gently in the wan sodium light, the strawberries and cream bakery girl, the dark-eyed foreigner who carries his worries on his forehead, her pleasure comes, hidden away in her breathing you have to watch closely how she arches her back.

* * *

He remembers one crazy night; the translation section had met over in the Henri Quatre over by the cathedral, with its failed, loathsome fluorescent tubes, the *kir* and the beer, the music and the boasting, the trancedancing in the failed light, the wry comedy of franglais in its purest, most reckless form, *the violence inherent in the system,* have you no shame chatting up that beautiful girl?

She is Breton in thought, word and deed. He dares not try to remember the broad succession of vowels in her names, first and last, and he contents himself with the knowledge that *she has two different diacritics* in her names' spelling, that can't be right, but she is smart and drunk and loves dancing with him, and when she envies her best friend dancing slow with some stranger, she folds her arms 'round Vicus' neck and purrs in his ear, 'Thirty percent more sensual, *s'il te plait*,' steering him in slow spyres around the offending couple till jealousies ignite a flame and the four of you are sitting around a table, a different bar this time, an upscale one, this is the mutualist combat of Cold Wars, one side builds tanks, the other side builds planes, the first side builds radar, the other side invents chaff *they call it Window*, then antiaircraft guns, then night raids, and now the one couple has bought a *really* expensive bottle of champagne, screw it all scorched earth and we all drink.

Soon the lovely creature is up and going somewhere; while she is gone, her compatriot says, in all simplicity, 'You know she is in love with you, don't you?'

But the girl is gone, and he only sees her in glimpses imaginary from that night forward. Neo-romantic trance music croons wavering about the morning sun, which will come again all too slowly.

* * *

The Erdre was *the most beautiful river in all of France* according to François de Valois; it meanders through the marsh and Karst to the north of Nantes for-gentle-ever. They say to take a good look at the mother to know what the daughter will look like, but here, the Erdre is different in kind from the Loire it will eventually engender, one is not obvious kin of the other.

They watertaxi now from Motte Rouge up toward the university, winding between the minor domains of nineteenth-century aristocrats and truncate bourgeois neighborhoods; you can sometimes identify where the neighborhood ends on one bank and picks up again across the way, the *Nantais*' tautological sense making a complete *Quartier* from disparate parts forever separated by deep time and erosive geology.

There is a footpath and boardwalk clinging to the left bank of the Erdre; a friend asked me one evening to walk with him, *wanted to show me something curious,* and off we went, at a Frenchman's pace, a purposeful straight-legged stride through the dark, away from Motte Rouge. Soon, the evening joggers make way for the lovers looking for solitude, and soon, even the lovers disappear, the footpaths too remote, the darkness too threatening. And when the nightforest begins to creak with the raucous calls of shorebirds— a heron rookery croaking toneless—you are that far from town, you are still *that close*—the forest has closed in, the path is narrow and cross with a lattice of roots which witch up and capture an ankle, a matrix of old bones slick with age, marrowful.

We turn our heels on the old bones, right there at the heron rookery squawking in the marshes, head uphill away from the Erdre, just a hundred yards up from the forest, the hoarse herons behind us now.

The forest clears; the shades of the modern crimelight angle through a quiet clearing.

In the center, the most ancient tree I have ever seen.

A twisting, twirlingcurling storm of chestnut; surely its spiraling architecture has lent it mechanical strength beyond that of its lesser siblings, deceased and decayed centuries ago.

A modest plaque *Planted by Pippin, the grandfather of Charlemagne*

* * *

Photos of family, living and dead, on the piano.

They've pulled a bunch of tables together, careful placement of tablecloths welds them seamless. Candles disparate, light coming in from the kitchen, bare bulbs shush beneath their shades, *abats-jour*, it's the whole genealogy of the collected English sections in the area, teachers of teachers, and the meal is joyful and meaty and noisy, potluck in the best of traditions, and even the queenbee matriarch has tales to tell, of days past in the girls' school unplug the phones lock the doors.

I am the token American, and snipershots arc through at cowboy movies the Happy Ending the warmonger politics, time truncate and space illimit, just think: the oldest Thing you can lay eyes on *over there* is what, a paltry two or three centuries old?, why I lived in an apartment squalor three times that they say, but how far do you live from your home town? good God you could drive from here to *Yugoslavia* in that amount of time.

But the novelty of the American Dream is brief, and when civilization takes over again, broken is the bread in the hands and shared are the fragments with the neighbor, and the wine is a pretext for wordplay and every tongue is loosed, and *foreigner*—here, tonight, now—is no synonym for *barbarian*, and for once I am among friends.

Recounting the ninety-nine dreams, oh how the language darts and dodges!

And soon the walk up the Erdre, the slick stock of bones in the low, dark forest, and the chestnut tree is alive again in the room's memory—*how this foreigner knows the names and places better than we do*—twelve hundred years of the City, that chestnut is a picture of growth and constancy, you know, what things and people that stout organism has seen! But then even the notion of *single individual* is brought into question, don't you know that the forest beneath Pippin's chestnut, leading to the wetlands and the rookeries, is all offspring of the same tree? and who knows if they really are *offspring* or instead just water-roots of the original giant, reaching its fingers and toes toward the Erdre?

And the trippingroots of the footpath and the moist darkness of the grove.

And I am not speaking French anymore, and they are not speaking English anymore, we live just a few lifetimes away from the great men and the great deeds, and we are all speaking fluent Anglo-Norman, and our glasses crash together, and our roots interlock and find the distant longing river together, the most beautiful river in all of France.

Our language is a castle of memory.

And all the roots interlock into a rich woven tapestry, the shroud of things past.

Quel étrange moteur anime en moi ce cœur ?
  Quel orage noir, et quelles passions terribles
  Qui pressent, qui fortifient ces actes infaillibles,
  Magnifiques, les transmuant de vil en vainqueur ?

Quelle quête mystérieuse échauffe ce sang et crible
  Mon être, quelle obscure alchimie, quelle lueur
  Transforme cette basse matière en meilleur
  Or, arme mortelle contre ennemi invisible ?

Un cliché vient tout juste de figer l'énigme
  Il figurera dans les titres des digestes
  Vous l'aurez déjà perçu dans le voisinage

Homme dans la foule, solitaire anonyme
  Son air rêveur, abstrait, distrait par quelque Geste...
  Qui l'aurait deviné en voyant mon visage ?

What strange engine animates this heart in me
  What uncontrollable passions, what black'ning storms
  Of cause, what energy presses so, and performs
  Selfless acts magnificent in their alchemy?

What mysterious quest could stir my blood this fiercely
  That my whole being transfigures into new forms,
  New states of matter and being, tangible swarms
  Of passions for an invisible enemy?

A camera captures this picture of animus
  You'll find it in the news, circled in the paper
  You'd already seen him twenty times in this place.

This man lost in the crowd, this lone anonymous
  Soul distracted, abstracted by some dark caper...
  How could you ever guess, just looking at my face?

* * *

This pavonine place, so very much like Italy

Everyone knew abstractly that Nice had been Italy not so long ago; the cathedral of Saint Réparate still bore the old nation's traces, the pillars and piers the rich variegated marble of Saint Peter's, even the crazy Berninine capitals, the altar ornament, a parasol of marble parapet. An ancient book of hours lay open in the chapel to Our Lady of Ransom.

A vast tricolor banner spanned the sanctuary. Already a few weeks past Bastille Day, and they still hadn't thought to take it down. Genius pricked Peruggia, seated in the cool darkness beneath the tribune organ, eating buttered brownies from an oily paper bag, Shall I pull the tricolor down myself? but he was loathe to release Brass Corners for even the time it'd take to scale the pier, and besides, his fingers were buttery and he would have to wash before ever attempting to climb bare stone, best stay down here in my chair. He comforted himself with the idea that it would only take a couple centimes slipped into the palm of some Old Nice street urchin to have the brat scale to the top and razor it clear away. He imagined the tricolor limp, draping the pews, a state funeral. He could spare a few coins for that spectacle.

* * *

They'll never find me in this place

He was alone in the sanctuary. He fumbled with his free hand into his pocket. He knew full well that he had lost his rosary eons ago, and now even the centimes destined for the urchins seem to have fallen through a moth hole into the myth abyss; but the reflex was still there, asleep in his brainstem. If he thought hard, he could recall dimly the head of the prayers, *Behold this child is set for the fall, and for the resurrection of many in Israel, and for a sign which shall be contradicted; and thy own soul a sword shall pierce, that, out of many hearts, thoughts may be revealed.*

That was all there was. He bunched up his forehead, but nothing more came out besides the most useless of arcana. He did manage to bring to mind that Pope Benedict the Twelfth had offered an indulgence of two hundred days to anyone who said the Servite Chaplet on any Friday, and Peruggia could sure use some of that right about now. But for the life of him, none of those words came to him, and the beads were long gone anyway, and honestly, it could be Friday it could be Tuesday it could be Christmas Eve for all he knew. Sure, he could remember the Pope, his number, his epithets, could remember the better part of the seven promises St Bridget the Swede said awaited him who whispered the Servite prayers—*They will be enlightened about the Divine Mysteries; I will console them in their pains and I will accompany them in their work; I will give them as much as they ask for; I will defend them in their spiritual battles with the infernal enemy*—and he could even remember the formula from the original Brief announcing the two hundred days in the first place—praying the Chaplet *'with sincere contrition, and having confessed, or firmly purposing to confess their sins'* would do the trick—and surely Peruggia was nothing if not *firmly purposing*.

Now if only he could remember what the object of this firm purpose of his was.

* * *

He had walked through Old Nice that morning (head creaking in the expanding sun with the leftover vino cotto his liver hadn't had the heart to strain out), and stepping into the cool dusk of an antique shop for relief, saw an indulgence for sale there—through the fog a real, live plenary indulgence, granting the bearer and his relatives to the fifth degree of distance full pardon of sins and automatic access to eternal life. The original owner must've paid a king's ransom for it—or had been on some holy mission—and here the dealer had it hanging on his wall next to a mal-strung mandolin, a nature morte of vanities, it labeled simply and inaccurately, *Portrait of the Pope*. Sure, there was a lithograph of the issuing pontifex, Leo XIII, seated in a grand throne, but this was no mere artistic portrait: this was the Pope himself, authorizing this very indulgence with compassionate eyes.

Peruggia had stopped cold before that portrait—before that indulgence—and his mind had become very active. Strictly speaking, that lithograph was much more a picture of Leo's throne than of the man himself, and Peruggia had surprised himself with the impious thought that either *that throne was an order of magnitude too big for that Pope, or else the Pope was an order of magnitude too...* he had stifled the rest of his thought—already a blink too late—with great contrition, and fled the shop.

(Admittedly his thinking hasn't been any too charitable for his fellow man this last long while, and he had developed that reflexive hairtrigger thought, *Tous des cons, You're all schmucks* for anyone who crossed his path, dared speak to him, dared *not* speak to him, *Tous des cons tous des cons You're all asses all asses all asses*. And as he ran over the indulgence incident again and again in his mind, Leo Twelve or Thirteen or Fourteen—one of those numbers somewhere in there at least—and shuddered each time as he realized how he had thought of that slight man in the oversized throne, and how quickly the tous des cons reflex had struck, a knight tilting on windmills, a bee stinging roses. This would not do: instinctively scoffing at a wee Holy Man in a giant throne smelt too strongly of the Unforgivable Sin of cursing the Holy Spirit; it was too base for men of Peruggia's mission and stature. He strode around Old Nice on obsessive strides until he found an open kiosk, *have a bite to eat to calm my nerves* and bought a bag of still-warm brownies.)

And now, licking his fingers, he squinted his eyes to remember something, *anything* about the biographical Leo to try to salve his conscience, and now with his insulin up and his teeth aching he found himself still wondering *which Leo again?* but at least he recognized the wee man's kind face and authoritative air in his mind's eye. And if he concentrated, he remembered that Leo—or someone just like Leo, Peruggia's memory isn't that good—had had a vision in the midst of Mass, and that this vision had stopped the holy man dead in his tracks, mid-canticle, before the wondering eyes of all the cardinals. And the story goes that he stood stock-still for a full ten minutes, and watched the terrible vision unfold before his horrified eyes: Satan himself boasting to the Lord beneath St. Peter's tabernacle, *I can destroy your Church*, and the Lord taunting: *You can? Then go ahead and do so*, and the vision had shaken Leo to his core, and he established a rule to invoke the Archangel Michael's aid and protection from this boasting Devil, *Most glorious Prince of the Heavenly Armies, Saint Michael the Archangel, defend us in 'our battle against principalities and powers, against the rulers of this world of darkness, against the spirits of wickedness in high places'. Come to the assistance of men whom God has created to His likeness and whom He has redeemed at a great price from the tyranny of the devil. The Holy Church venerates thee as her guardian and protector; to thee, the Lord has entrusted the souls of the redeemed to be led into heaven. Pray therefore the God of Peace to crush Satan beneath our feet, that he may no longer retain men captive and do injury to the Church. Offer our prayers to the Most High, that without delay they may draw His mercy down upon us; take hold of the dragon, 'the old serpent, which is the devil and Satan,' bind him and cast him into the bottomless pit 'so that he may no longer seduce the nations'* at the close of every low Mass.

This was enough memory to bring the Leo WhichOne's portrait to life, to make him real in that sashed lithographed indulgence in the shop, that tiny man in the capacious frame, that good man who had been praying Saint Michael's aid for his soul, yes, for Peruggia's very own soul.

And with this thought comforting him anew, Peruggia's mind was far away, the rustbrown tiles of his hometown, the griffins at her gates. Olives and fresh bread. Cold cheese and vinegar, basil and ground pepper.

The city of Nice churned distantly, so very distant from this little being in this great open space, the whirr and buzz of City Life attenuated by the stone, the sounds of murmuring Nice amix in the encumbered space crisscrossed with Bastille Day.

* * *

An old lady shuffled in—carefully avoiding the open nave of the church—to light votives in all the chapels; one by one the plaster and marble heard her prayers and the creak of her hard shoes, first down the one aisle, then (Peruggia saw) just starting to cross the broad space, the shortest path between two points. Suddenly, catching sight of Peruggia enhaloed by sunlight in the center of this brave open void (and thinking the better of it), turning on her hard wooden heel and shuffling back down the length of the aisle, exiting, re-entering over here this time to visit the votive candles on the other aisle.

He gripped Brass Corners just a bit tighter on his lap in this broad sanctuary, his bag of brownies crackling paper and his teeth aching from the sickening sugar having pressed its grit into his gums; the sound of the paper echoed, and he was embarrassed *Tous des cons tous des cons.* But then he remembered there was no one else around to offend with the brown bag's stirrings, except maybe for that ancient woman, was she even still here lighting votives and slipping potmetal coins into coffers? but she couldn't have heard him anyway, so decrepit was she, and besides, she had already been caught avoiding Peruggia's gaze in the first place. So much for Caritas.

This church is a frame with no picture

* * *

Someone had sold that indulgence with the gilded frame and the fading satin sash. How else could it have found its way into the faithless antique shop?

Frowning, Peruggia could think of no other vector from saintly saved soul to tarnished mismatched remnant relic than to imagine the eventual decease of the owner and a rapid sale to settle the estate; surely the indulgence had been a comfort to the man: how, then, had his family and friends been so quick to divest themselves of it? Peruggia couldn't reconcile the idea.

Just look at their faith, these Frenchmen… And see how full their churches are! This frame with no picture, these arches over the void

Turning and turning in the widening gyre, the empty space glowing in the late-morning sun, marble at once stone, then tweed, then cloud, then light itself as the Earth shifted on her axis, turning (it seemed) 'round about this very place, Peruggia clutching his suitcase, centered in this empty church. Cool in the great dead airspace of Saint Réparate, so cool and quiet, his thoughts muffled by the static air, Nice so very far away, and *sweetdreamsinyourhead* he is asleep, come sweet death come blessed rest.

* * *

Peruggia pictured Leo obsessively fumbling through his own Rosary—the rambling writ of the Church having become a real, tangible object between the ancient man's tangled fingers, *Thank God* thought drowsing Peruggia *the good man was watching out for the Servite prayers when he himself could not*, and time fell away, and he felt Leo's hand on his shoulder, the Archbishop of Peruggia, his calm, reassuring gaze offering him authority and comfort.

And the indulgence in Peruggia's pebbled mind was draped with a broad sash, whose color had faded. The French tricolor arced across the empty span of Saint Réparate.

Amour, amour immortel, dont la ligne tendre
   S'élance hors l'obscur parchemin, hors la poussière
   Des années, craie et encre dépassant frontière
   Et siècle et distance, défiant et flamme et cendre

Passion, plus bel artifice d'un cœur en chair,
   N'a rien d'immortel, émoi trop prêt à descendre
   Dans le deuil, et sans pouvoir se défendre
   Sombre aux strates myrteuses des affections d'hier

Quête divine ne s'achève de cett' vie
   Le plus haut art grogne sous le poids de sa rareté
   Et le cœur aimant est à jamais condamné

Mon courage s'achève, sa flamme ravie ;
   L'art et l'amour, crimes commis en toute clarté
   Créateur par sa créature assassiné

Immortal love, whose lines undiminished by years
  Rise up free from this ghostly book's shadows, ashen
  And fiery, chalkdust and ink in ancients' fashion
  Across the centuries, across distant frontiers

This fibrous heart, whose highest art is its passion
  All too mortal, all too ready to cede to tears
  And grief, pales defenseless, at last disappears
  Into dark myrrhic planes of crypted compassion

Divine quests can't be satisfied in this lifetime
  For deathless art aches in its holy rarity
  And lovers' hearts all perish sooner or later

This heart of hearts achieves its own perfect crime,
  The dark blade flashing in wicked clarity:
  In time, love—as in art—kills its own creator

* * *

Columns of aphids and grasshoppers caught up in the summer thermals, and swallows arcing freely through the mounting spirals in pursuit. Skyline drawn into building bundles of force, lightning pricking the horizon still too far off to be heard, the acrid pinge of lime whitewash, lightning fire having seared the air into new perfume, half new hay curing in the fields, half thundershowers on hot soil, the electric scent of brazier's tongs. There, a gap in the treeline, the horizon shifting aside to let a road pass so safe and narrow by day, by night the bandits never let you dare.

The plum tree in its ripe purple foliage, premature plums falling mostly pit, the mulberry over the pond bruising stone and bench. The fibrous gladus leaves with their compound flowers luciferase.

Stake and cane interweaving, last year's rabbit fence sulking 'round this year's kitchen garden, taut rows of humble tuber humble legume, the sparrows from on high see tiles, gildings, etchings tended by the sullen human genre, the twining vine in the field by the knives' brief curve.

The foreign scent of new paper, still fresh and stiff. The whirring of spinningwheels, rocking rocking rocking that ancient heartbeat, weaving stories into fiber. Newsalted fish pry wide, their flesh browning in the sun.

Bread in the ancient kind: tall village bread, full of ferment and brown with bitters.

The heat of summer in Amboise, the steep shingles of the town, the arches of the bridge, the high bell tower, the cobbles of the Loire.

This town performs its ancient role

The old man walked the town's narrow alleys.

...That of a town that never changes

* * *

At first, there had been joy in trying to predict François' excesses. But success is oft held dearest by those who ne'er succeed. He had made intricate plans for machines of all kinds, of a stunning variety, some fanciful, some terrifying, some of wood, of stone, of metal, of pure idea. The king smiled, and nodded, and said some kind words not exactly pertinent to the project at hand, sometimes even clamping his hands around the old man's and saying—with entire sincerity—'I'm so glad you've come.'

At which point a sternfaced bureaucrat would always ahem officiously to the end of separating the two men, and ask where the drawings were for founded cannon—the old man's original mandate—and *tsk* with fatherly disappointment when the old man, as usual, had no answer.

The old man had in fact designed several cannon, which he named whimsically after mythological creatures—*basilisk*, *gryphon*, and other, according to their kind—and designed complex shapes into their barrels reflecting which beast was being brought to bear. He knew that the king had already adopted the classical salamander as his personal symbol, *I consume what fire burns me*, and he could picture vividly the warring monarch, arrayed in a magnificent steel and brass armor (of the old man's own artistry), calling out in tremulous tones, 'Roll out the *basilisks*, lads!' and the armaments' ancient authority alone—a warbling *Roll out the basilisks* carried on the wind—bringing the enemy trembling to its knees before shot even be fired.

But *a cannon is a cannon is a cannon* the bureaucrats would sigh impatiently, and concerns over financing some insane 'fantasy weapon' in place of 'the real thing' would kill the child each time, before it had drawn its first breath.

* * *

It was always the king who sought out the old man after each of these humiliations. Clos Lucé, silent and dark, signaled the king's approach long before he appeared in the studio: the creaking of the old gate beneath the earth, the dry ticktock of the king's footfalls in the stairwell, the groan in the old wood floors right where they always groaned. Each time, he would ask the old man for some obscure Aid, some intangible, some kind of *I need to know you're on my side* some kind of *I need to know I didn't bring you here for nothing.*

Right before asking after his favorite Lady.

* * *

Mostly, though, the king—the *fleur de lys* in person—was an absent one, and even when he was lodging in Amboise, the sojourn was always in preparation for another expedition, another excursion, another voyage; he was always joking *They never know when I'll show up,* and he kept to his threat to appear suddenly at the door of some Loire Valley manor, his train full of wagons and bundles and wares they had emptied out of Amboise before packing out. And each time at the foot of the palace the town of Amboise would resume the sleepy tempo it recalled from its deep memory even as the royal train rumbled away down road sinusoid, vanishing into a dusty smudge embraced by the horizon's generous *sfumato*.

Hold down the fort for me the king would fix the old man with his eye, his regal hands on the old man's sagging shoulders, *hold down the fort* as if Amboise Castle were anything but a *château de plaisance,* a vacation cottage for a being who had greater worries about Things Elsewhere.

And the First Painter assumed once more the role of silent senescent sentinel, bound to the empty rooms of the Clos, wandering its dark halls.

* * *

He sees his little room with its one window. It is high and narrow. As soon as François found out this would be the old man's choice for bedroom, he had it scoured down and repainted, a deep burgundy (the *color of royals* he would say), and the deep color offended the old man's darkening eye. They then had fixed for him a lantern over the window, with panes of deep scarlet, blue and amber glass, and whenever he deliberated to go to bed, somehow François' men would get in there first and light that lamp—invisibly, silently, he never knew quite how they predicted his fatigue down to the minute—and he found this to be an intrusion, not the usual physical intrusion into his personal chambers (he was getting used to encroachments such as these), but an incursion into the essence of his thoughts *now I am hungry now I am sleepy now I shall rise* as if even his quietest spiritual being were known to many, known to all.

The life of the courtier he supposed.

Here, there is the little table with a marble top, and crowding it a cluster of bottles, anonymous ones he had found, left behind by the crowd as it passed through: a perfume bottle, a wine bottle, a bottle for grains of precious spice, all their contents gone spoiled away on the bodies of great men and women, chests and breasts and gullets and tripe, but the bottles remained, left behind in the empty hallways and doorframes of Amboise. Surely all such bottles had come from Venice, and the little island he built on his nightstand was Murano Island, its bustling glassmakers... Those bottles, though empty, *contained*.

He found that if he left a space in the middle of the bottles' crowding coterie, he could set a modest candle base there, and marvel at the shifting light cast up on his little room's walls by the dondling flame, passing through the glass' distortions and pitting, a living amber frame for the dying ember flame.

And here, not a table but a chest, empty upturned, with a piece of rich fabric, woft from tapestry ground, to soften it, on which fabric ground he had played the same trick as with the bottles over there on the table, but with goblets instead: a vanity of orphan goblets jostling for attention 'round a meager candle stub. Sometimes he would fill or partially fill one or several of the glasses to watch the candle flame wicker and refract on his walls; he much preferred, however, to leave the goblets dry, let the light throw their shards to strike wall and ceiling.

Damn them for painting these high walls so very dark

* * *

Embracing *Clos Lucé* on one side there was an obscure grove set into a hillside, overarched with chestnut, deep and moist and private. A little creek tumbled from a seep in the deep; the old man had had pools dug—annexes to the flow—in which he conducted little experiments: how wakes form, how to create a waterwheel, the prow of a ship, an Archimedean pump. The memory of the old *locus amoenus* (embraced by each villa of the Roman outskirts) lightened his mind, a quiet, agreeable enclosed space it was, so distant from the clatter of Roman roads, a garden wall espaliered with rose, another with fruiting vines, and in the center of it all, a circular pool, the trickle of water, a *pairidaeza* borrowed from long ago and far away. Poets sought such solitary places—lone wolves swirling restless in temples—but the old man knew there originally must have been something not only sensual but utilitarian in the high-walled garden, a distillation of rural life having been constructed in the heart of the city, this moment of agrarian respite framed by the town vibrating with noise, a necessary voidspace of sublime silence in the noise of mundane society.

Here, the cool of the gardens, the smooth sweet scent of the cedars, the interlacing of branches above, of roots below. Draping hands of the chestnut groves' numb swollen fingers.

Someday, someday soon, this tangle of hands and arms will catch me 'round, soil and sky, root and limb

And to remind himself of the Old Places he used to call home, the Domus Aurea they had dug up in the cinders of evil Nero's palace, stucco and deco in a vaulted chamber beneath the dust and ash of the eternal city... To remind himself of what he once was, to mourn what he would become, here on this lonely crag in a moistened darkened wood, he began to dig the Grotto.

At first it was simply an alcove for a bit of forgotten sculpture he had found half-buried in the grove, a surround of rocks and moss. And then, with the help of François' servants, he began to construct a *chamber* for that fragment of broken art, and instead of colored stones as surround, he placed statuettes and tiles, notes of paper and keys for doors, bowls of oil and milk, a vase for flowers.

'He is building his own sepulcher' said the young men. 'Such it is with the old and dottering, unsatisfied they are. See him, always away from the rich oxblood walls of his tall room in the Clos.'

-Passacaglia-

But he deliberated to continue his effort, and the Grotto's walls became Art Itself, and his mind cast about for a proper picture for this Frame. He willed to choose a picture of highest price... *Perhaps* he thought *this would make good indeed for my tomb*

* * *

In my Father's house there are many rooms; If there were not, would I have told you that I am going away to prepare a place for you?

Living columns rising high caught up in the thermals, drawn bundles of force crackling thunder on the horizon, the plum tree in its ripe purple foliage. The heat of summer in Amboise, the steep shingles of the town, the arches of the bridge, the high bell tower, the cobbles of the Loire.

Heaven he thought *is no house at all, and certainly no castle*

He thought of empty Amboise palace, its tall windows blind and glauque. He thought of the Clos Lucé, hidden away just behind, empty as empty gets, except for that gravelike room of his with its shimmering lantern and stump tapers casting glass jewels into the bloodred plaster. He thought of the Grotto out behind the Clos, that sepulchral frame left empty of his greatest creation.

Instead, Heaven must be a royal town waiting at the foot of a palace, and worshipping the Almighty in Heaven he thought *means cobbling shoes, means tiling roofs, means whitewashing plaster, means baking dark bread in the knowledge that the King is in His country*

But his king, his only friend, who had brought him out of Italy with his great army, was nowhere to be found. He had lands to win and hearts to conquer the king did, and the old man, the Painter Royal—bored and alone in this land (so far away from the genteel breast that had nurtured him, and nurtured him still in his rich memory)—looked out over bustling Amboise Town with his dimming eye and, turning, hushed away back to his humid chestnut grove with its burrowing Grotto, his frame bent, and weary, and hollow.

Oh, combien dans mes rêves la pensée me nuit !
  Mes rêves qui rampent, qui émergent des cent
  Voûtes noires de mon cœur pour tourner mon sang
  Sombres esprits souspirés, sousesprits de nuit

Ombres fantasques murmurant que plus ne suis
  Ce que j'ai été, êtres souterrains, voix sans
  Face, démons sans nom qui affrontent mes sens
  Songe amorphe, funèbre, aux ténèbres me suit

Malin ! Celui dans les coulisses, qui attend
  Tout patient son entrée sur scène, qui me tend,
  Pour me pendre, la corde d'une courte toise

La Présence que je sens à mes côtes tant
  Qu'il respire fort, ce voleur à voix courtoise
  Dans ce temple, et moi qui l'ai enfermé dedans

The rich ways that overnight my dreams undermined
   Me! Creeping numberless out of their mossy lairs
   To stir blood 'round in the recess of my heart's layers
   The dim thought under thought, the dim mind under mind

Fanciful shadowy shades grumbling to remind
   Me of lost selves lurking in cracks and under stairs
   Nameless demons confronting me with faceless stares
   Nightmare: funereal, grim, dim, undetermined

The Evil One would prowl all night in the wings, wait
   For his entrance, hand to me the knotted fathom
   Of rope, from which my neck will learn my soul's weight

I could feel his presence, his hot breath as he sighed
   His thrumming voice for the chest and heart to fathom
   A thief in the temple, and I've locked him inside

***

The letter carried a broken wax seal, a sanguine *fleur de lys*.

It was assumed that any letter to the Regent John Plantagenet was top secret, but in the tense months after his brother Richard's departure, all bets were off: everybody knew that Richard had left for the Levant with Philippe Auguste of France... and that the French king had returned alone. So anything crossing over from French-held lands was opened (probably—John felt certain—within mere seconds after being delivered to English hands) and examined for signs of the absent monarch.

This letter would be like all the rest, thought John: Philippe's fireproof optimism, fairly *taunting* the traumatized English regent with thick-painted Frankish cheerfulness... He would then ask some favor, make some kind of offer John couldn't refuse, slather that offer over with a carefully-crafted gravy of wordage...

Philippe would always end his letters with grand, sincere affection, adding a post-scripted confection made of some kind of sly taunt baked into saccharine sweetness.

And this letter did not disappoint: asking (of all things) for a donation of wood to rebuild a church that had recently burnt. Promising all manner of miracle if the wood be granted, all manner of intangible spiritual benefit, so don't worry about the *quality* of the wood, just send it send it send it, we'll use it use it use it, you'll see.

'With Brotherly Affection' etc.

John sighed despite himself at these closing words, and began a note to be sent out, *Start combing the beaches for shipwrecks, our King's allies the French need the wood to rebuild a building.*

That ought to do it.

But. 'Post scriptum'.

John read on.

-Passacaglia-

'I don't care what they're saying about you in the streets here,' wrote Philippe, 'but there is just *no way* you should be letting everyone call you *John Softsword...*'

John of Plantagenet paused. He realized he had a migraine on the way, a mighty one. He wet his pen again, and returned to the wood requisition he had started:

'Regarding said donation of wood. The wormier, the better.'

* * *

The next letter had an intact seal, a signet John didn't recognize. John's knife got the better of it.

The handwriting familiar. Very familiar. Oddly familiar.

'Oh my God.'

* * *

John fled immediately to Philippe, begging for an audience. Philippe, having intentionally forgotten there was no longer a Treaty Elm planted there at Gisors (and forgetting, too, that the Castle at Gisors belonged to Richard, and that John was without question *persona non grata* in Richard's absence), had initially consented to meeting John at the border between Normandy and France. Once this confusion was cleared up though, Philippe's men persuaded John to ride all the way to Paris (after parading him around the ruins of the old Treaty Elm for good measure), and from there to Chartres, where Philippe was overseeing an immense construction project.

'Ah, the wood you asked for...' said John distantly.

'*Indeed yes!* See the miracles your pious worm-ridden alms have wrought!'

But John appeared far too distracted to appreciate miracles objectively, and Philippe decided to let the man believe that the pestilential shipwrecks that John had shipped him had magically Become Cathedral, instead of simply being heaved into charcoal pits and stoking sacred ceremonial Moorish glass furnaces from which emerged marvels to gild the restored Cathedral 'twore and frought.

'Tell me news of your good brother Richard... How *is* the king of England?'

'You've not heard?'

'He never returned from crusade? No! *How sad...*'

* * *

Philippe Auguste's tent was cool and tranquil in the midst of the great worksite; the sounds of Moorish zeal and activity blended with that of the Christian coworkers—the variegated clangor had enchanted Philippe, but John *the Softsword* was too distressed to enjoy it. Philippe offered him water and fruit, a basin to wash in, a fresh set of clothes, and sent for his chief of staff.

* * *

Or sai je bien de voir certainement
Que mors ne pris n'a ami ne parent
Quant hon me lait por or ne por argent
Moult m'est de moi, mes plus m'est de ma gent
Qu'apres ma mort avront reprochier grant
    Se longuement sui pris

Only now do I plainly behold
No prisons friend nor family hold
But trade me in for glint of gold
Too much for me, and for my fold
You'll pay for it when I'm dead and cold
    So longly am I pris'ner!

'Good God, it *is* him!' Philippe Auguste was holding the letter at arm's length. 'I'd recognize Richard's scansion anywhere...' He said this with an absolutely straight face.

'I *told* you it was from him.' John massaged his temples.

Philippe flipped the letter over, holding it at different angles, holding it to the light. 'Anything else arrive with it?'

'Just this, and, of course, the letter demanding ransom.'

'Ah.'

Philippe's chief of staff cleared his throat. Somehow, Philippe's spies had already figured out that Richard had been taken by the Duke of Austria and sold to none other than Heinrich the German. The chief of staff murmured to this effect.

'Surely not Heinrich Six? *Holy Roman Emperor* Heinrich? How could that good man be involved in such a plot?' Philippe whistled, incredulous. John's head ached. 'High stakes there, Brother. Let's hope the ransom isn't equally lofty.'

John looked up, shifted uncomfortably, said nothing. Philippe sent away his chief of staff with a glance.

Privacy once again assured, 'Surely Heinrich has been reasonable with England in her darkest hour? Surely, as the apostle James proclaims in the second chapter of his epistle, *Mercy triumphs over Judgment?*'

'The judgment is harsh, and the ransom steep, milord.' John held the ransom letter in his hands. The parchment trembled.

'Dare I ask?'

Reluctantly, John handed the letter to Philippe. Philippe read.

'Goodness. A hundred fifty thousand marks? Why, that's *sixty-five thousand pounds of metallic silver...*' The arithmetic came particularly quickly to Philippe, almost without thinking about it, in fact. Stating the Extremely Obvious: 'That is a *lot* of silver.'

*\derefault * *

Curiously, that ransom was almost *exactly* the same amount as Richard had raised during the Saladin Tithe. It was almost as if Heinrich had known precisely how much the English crown could afford to pay out...

* * *

'My, my, my, this spells serious trouble for you.' Philippe laid his hand on John's shoulder.

Anxiety had been a restless, caged animal within John ever since his brother's departure; Richard had already shown every evidence of profound distrust for his brother before leaving for the Holy Land, giving the keys to the kingdom into the hands of his bishops, and wringing promises from John not to even set foot in England. Trivial gifts of land were signed over to John as a trust, to be sure, but even then, Richard had retained all the strongholds throughout those gifts, leaving John as mere custodian. Galling enough for John Softsword. But rumors of Richard's disappearance having reached John's ears, the man became the very picture of a man haunted by his fears; prone now to fits of rage, spans of insomnia, he lashed out at every word, jumped at every snapping twig. And now...

'I would assume there is a price on your head, dear man.' Philippe was matter-of-fact, conversational, even.

'What?' John said this altogether too quickly, his lips more tightly wound on their reflexes than even his mind, a spinal cord outburst.

'Don't you think Big Brother's last words to his men before setting sail to the Levant,' said Philippe, blithe spirit, 'were, *And if anything happens to me, kill John, he's to blame?*'

John blanched. 'I've done nothing to harm Richard.'

'I know that. *You* know that. But it all stinks of your disloyalty, don't you think? King Richard is out of the way, Emperor Heinrich fills his treasury, you get... *England*...? Certainly *I* know your quality as an honest man, but can't you fathom just how bad this looks *to your rivals?*'

'Rivals?'

'Don't tell me you've not given thought to who could profit from having you set up as a pariah, as a traitor?'

John didn't answer.

'*Think*, Brother! Whose job would it be to prosecute you when you're accused of sedition, of *lèse-majesté*, of insurrection, of unlawfully detaining a lawful Crusader?'

'Prosecute me? Why, I...'

'I'll tell you who will prosecute you: it'll be the rightful king's chancellor.'

'The Bishop of Longchamp? I wouldn't think...'

'*Longchamp?* With a name like that...! Let me guess: born in... *Normandy?* Has his eyes on the prize, I see.'

John paled.

'At least *he* has been loyal to you, John? John...?'

* * *

Longchamp had been only one of a hundred thorns in John's side since Richard's departure, had protested John's regency of the kingless throne so very shrilly, even raising an army of his own once to seize the castle at Lincoln, nominally held by John. Even more ominously, though, Longchamp had made efforts to depose one of the Plantagenet's illegitimate sons—John and Richard's half-brother—pursuing the man into the countryside and holing him up in a monastery, where the army raised its siege, capturing the hapless soul after a tense, violent standoff.

'Longchamp has an oft-proven history of making *Richard's* rivals disappear... and in the process, of making his *own* rivals disappear. And behold Normandy, *Richard's* Normandy...' The way Philippe's voice thrummed, its tones so very resonant to John's imagination, it was as if he had rolled open a map for John to witness Longchamp's army already advancing across the face of helpless Norman mindscape, '...*this* is what he wants.' Tapping the air with his finger, rapping away at imaginary Normandy. 'And how gleefully he would hang *you* to get to it...'

John was lost in a dark cloud of thought.

'You can only too easily imagine,' Philippe's voice even and casual, 'how letting Longchamp get his claws into beloved Normandy—it *is* his homeland after all—and letting him do so *on your watch*, will only confirm to Richard your incompetence. Or sedition.'

'*If* he comes back, that is.' John's voice seemed to surprise him, slip out of him involuntarily.

'And *that*, John,' whispered Philippe Auguste, 'was the most seditious thing I've ever heard anybody say.'

Philippe's words hung in the air, a plane of poison. John looked at his shoes, blushing fiercely.

And then Philippe's voice again, so quiet it could've been John's own conscience taunting him:

'We may yet make a Capetian out of you some day...'

* * *

Philippe led John back to the Treaty Elm's catastrophe. As the retinue advanced toward the Normandy border, John began to see a dark plume in the distance, smoke and ash rising and joining the strata of smoke building over the town of Gisors and its castle.

'My men will accompany you all the way to Poitou if you wish; your safe passage is assured. You saw nothing here. Just keep your eyes front.'

John's stomach turned.

Philippe Auguste continued: 'I wouldn't pass too near the castle or the town if I were you. We are still busy... *securing* Richard's castle for you.'

* * *

John sighed the end of days, turned his horse away and began a slow, plodding march toward Aquitaine. His thoughts turned to Philippe Auguste, Frankish king. He had met him before—*all those funerals of brothers who had met the sword!*—but never quite imagined him in conversation, face to face. He remembered seeing the boy leaning over young Geoffrey's corpse—*see how he loved him!*—and realized he had only seen Philippe in ceremonial modes, among crowds of hundreds, sometimes thousands of people, with men bowing to the boy, kneeling before the boy, vowing allegiance and swearing fealty to the boy, huge hefted men freakishly pledging to *lay down their lives* to satisfy the boy's whim.

And here, having met the erstwhile boy alone for the first time, he found Philippe to have somehow grown far more vibrant, far more... *human* than he had ever considered possible. He was now a man of course, no longer a boy, but retained the wiry shoulders and sinewy limbs of adolescents.

And the mischievous light in his eye! The cat that ate the canary.

He looked behind him; Philippe was on foot now, with dozens—hundreds—of men surrounding him, creatures attracted by the light. They were barding his horse, a half-dozen squires helping the young king into his armor, and he was testing the balance of a sword; a priest passed before him—holy water high Latin—and Philippe seamlessly swept his sword through a deep spiral until, gripping the weapon by the blade in his gauntleted hands, the pommel and guard became a cross, then—mischievous light never leaving his eye, crooked grin never faltering, holywaterholywater—on went the helm over the boy's lineless forehead.

Eyes front again, John plodding on. The boy was armed and armored; John could hear the clatter of steel against steel, armor against armor as the boy mounted his horse.

'Lads, shall we see what we can do...' Philippe cleared his throat theatrically, 'to protect the *rest* of Normandy?'

* * *

Is human warfare invention or revelation? Is it a discovery or a construct?

Philippe Auguste, the king of France, joined the high priesthood of warriors during his Normandy campaign, visiting the Lord's vengeance upon the Vexin's landscape, his cavalry a sinusoidal dragon, roils of dust arcing over the rolling hills, *In the name of King Richard's Regent John of Plantagenet, Lord of Ireland and Count of Maine, I hereby offer you the protection of the Kingdom of France* and his sword flashed again and again and again, a glinting invective of repeating rage, a mantra of steel, so bright it became silent as thought.

And for some hapless souls, the last words to reach the ear just before quitting this mortal veil were in the awkward limping rhythms of a wicked epigram, King Philippe Auguste of the Franks, sword aflame, his haggard warcry voice joyfully singing out,

> *Ja nus hons pris ne dira sa reson*
> *Adroitement, s'ensi com dolans non*
> *Mes par confort puet il fere chançon*
> *Moult ai d'amis, mes povre sont li don*
> *Honte en avront, se por ma reançon*
>   *Sui ces deus yvers pris*

> *No pris'ners' purpose right or wrong*
> *Justly locked up where they belong*
> *But sing we now this piteous song*
> *'O where are you, my faithful throng*
> *And will my ransom be too long?*
>   *Two winters am I pris'ner!'*

* * *

The Vexin was *hungry* to be invaded, and Philippe invaded her heroically, raining destruction reigning destruction, warfare waged without restraint, his army nimbleagilemobiledeadly, the Angel of Destruction sweeping gloriously and terribly over the landscape with her dark wings, Philippe's joyful brooding terror reaching away tendrils...

Danger follow me, angels attend to me, I am saving the Vexin from herself

...Philippe's war engine the visible incarnation of Philippe's mind, his whole life become a charge, a siege, a feint, a strike, a plunge forward, a swift flanking, a tide, a lightning stroke, a storm sweeping through a gap, a flood pouring through a breach; the mere *destructibility* of the Vexin invited destruction upon her. Warfare become journey, warfare blossom emergent, warfare take anything not frozen to the ground, and Philippe's eye simply following the tip of his sword painting vermillion 'cross Normandy, his voice ringing out in his everchanging warcry

> *N'est pas merveille, se j'ai le cuer dolent*
> *Quant mes sires tient ma terre en torment*
> *S'or li menbroit de nostre serement*
> *Que nos feïsmes andui communaument*
> *Bien sai de voir que ceans longuement*
>   *Ne seroie pas pris*

> *Surely it's not so hard to see*
> *When milord invades so gleefully*
> *Did he forget his oath to me,*
> *The one we swore communally?*
> *I'd know full well, though nowhere free*
>   *I'd not be long this pris'ner!*

* * *

Dark the night. The camp's fires burned high and bright, and in the middle distance, fires stoked the tar furnaces at the king's trébuchets, and Rouen's walls burned. And on the horizon, towns and castles lit like torches. The Vexin was a new constellation on the face of the deep.

Philippe Auguste stretched his limbs, life returning to him once again, his armor unstrapped and laid out on his blanket, the warshadow of a man cast behind him into the darkness away from his campfire, the stark, steely Angel whose wings had protected him in his holy combat. He stripped his shirt haggard from his frame and held it out by the shoulders, his usual ritual to determine if he had been injured in the mêlée: if the blood issued from the wrists, it was more likely to be enemy blood having streamed down off his sword and into his gauntlets and onto his forearms.

Tonight, the shirt had registered the Vexin's trauma principally in the right arm; but minor bloodstains to the torso prodded him to approach the fire and examine his skin: standard abrasions from his armor concussing him for the most part, but one or two deeper scrapes, where a lucky blade found its way tentatively between the armor plating. Close calls. He called for water to wash these insults out.

He shook the shirt out one last time, knowing it contained one more record of the enemy's sufferings. Gold: a pack of cards fell to the ground. He balled up the shirt and tossed it into the fire.

Ce sevent bien Angevin et Torain
Cil bacheler qui or sont riche et sain
Qu'enconbrez sui loing d'aus en autrui main
Forment m'amoient, mes or ne m'aimment grain
De beles armes sont ores vuit li plain
   Por tant que je sui pris

O Tourainese and Angevine
Men whose health and wealth combine
Consider well this state of mine
—All former friends who me resign—
Of troops and arms there's been no sign
   So thusly am I pris'ner!

-Passacaglia-

* * *

He knelt; his cards fanned out before him. It was a skinnier deck than it had been: the Black King had been discarded years ago, and countless others with it. The Black Jack dappled in the firelight; squinting, he saw his own juvenile handwriting, a quadrata *John*, and his nimble fingers flipped the card over and shuffled it back into the deck.

Philippe Auguste, the king of France, smiling in the firelight.

He shuffled further. The other Black Jack. *Richard of the Lion's Heart* in his young hand, *but trade me in for glint of gold* the poor Englishman had written to his kid brother months ago, and Philippe had sung the hapless pris'ner's song between his clenched teeth over the last several weeks, scaling ramparts, sword shining, steam blasting from his horse's nostrils on the charge, the tuneless song of Richard's captivity, releasing the great Protector of the Norman Vexin to his sacred mission.

But trade me in for glint of gold

Philippe folded the card in two, scoring the edge sharp and precise with his fingernail. He wondered where the Lionheart was right now; it pleased him to no end to imagine him leaning against the cast iron of a tall cage, his frail forearms dangling through the bars pathetically. Heinrich Six had demanded a hundred and fifty thousand silver marks to buy the English king's release—poor, sweet Eleanor must be wringing her lovely hands at this very moment, head spinning at the mere *concept* of thirty-three *tons* of silver to collect and deliver to Heinrich—good luck, divine El!

Fingers still flattening Richard's Black Jack, Philippe grinned at the memory of one of his last conversations with John Softsword Lackland of Plantagenet:

'Eighty thousand.'

'What?'

'Eighty thousand. Eighty thousand marks. That's all it will take.'

'I'm sure I don't understand, milord.'

'John, my good, simple brother,' Philippe Auguste shaking his head patristically, 'Heinrich is demanding a hundred fifty thousand marks to release Big Brother.'

'Yes, milord, we both know that.'

'All we have to do, John, you and I, is to each raise eighty thousand marks. That makes one hundred sixty thousand marks in total.'

'To have Richard released?'

'No, silly man! *To have him kept prisoner.*'

* * *

'Sire, there is a delivery for you.'

Philippe awoke from his reverie. Squaring the cards, stuffing them back into his kit. 'Yes?'

The letter had an intact seal. The signet of the griffin: his spy in Palermo, at Heinrich's court. He broke the seal, absorbed the letter's tenor.

'Messenger, can you write? Take this dictation: *Dear John Softsword, our dear Eleanor shows her tender compassion, even to the undeserving. The Devil is loose.*'

* * *

'Postscriptum: *Our miraculous little renovation nears its completion. I'll be sure to have a Mass said in your memory there.*'

Heh. 'Post-postscriptum: *Beware of War*'

J'ai toute une vie contre le chaos vouée
   Assumé et habitude et habit austères
   Réglé mon être à des principes militaires
   Une vie à la perfection vainement dévouée

Ces palettes vides, ces heures solitaires
   Deviennent mon sang glacé, entrailles nouées
   Contraignant mon poumon et ma pensée rouée
   Mettant à la lame mes veines, mes artères

Un jeune artiste achève un maigre autoportrait
   Ni son meilleur, ni son premier, mais assez fin
   Qu'un médecin diagnostique sa pleurésie

Or mes lettres, pleines de désir et regret
   Toutes une esquisse d'amateur au burin
   Voici enfin mon cœur, en mal de ton merci.

I have battled to defeat chaos all my life
   Assumed austerity in cloth and in habit
   Strictest military principles inhabit
   Me, vain perfections in the midst of clawing strife

This empty palette, these lonely hours rife
   With care, become my flesh, chill my blood, inhibit
   My breath, constrict my lonely thoughts' quick'ning orbit
   Put my darkening heart's hard sinews to the knife

A young artist once made a meager self-portrait
   Not his finest, not his first, but exact enough
   So that doctors could diagnose his pleurisy

And my letters, full of longing, desire, regret
   Pale silverpoint sketches amateurish and rough
   Here is where my heart lies, aching for your mercy

I sleep with three pillows. Two I need for myself—they are threadbare and beaten, together they make but one—and the third is for you, a gossamer silken pillowcase with little threadpoints of lace at the opening. It smells of laundry soap, is white and new, has never been slept on.

The bed seems for some reason to be shorter than it is; I usually find myself on a diagonal—northwest to southeast—with my feet extending through a bend in the covers, finding some point of contact with the old iron frame: that post at the far end is wide enough to be soothing and cool, its curve fitting just under my arches. On summer nights like this one, iron's specific heat conducts away from me and I can cover the rest of myself up, a heavy grey warblanket I pulled effortful from the steamer trunk in the living room, a redundant cushion for rock samples we pulled from the Tilly Foster mine in Brewster before they shut off the pumps and let her fill in with water to the lip, samples of fossil lepidodendron we hefted from the Boxley quarry in Beckley near Charleston as it hailed and sleeted, everything but the rhythmites flaking away to evil three-dee puzzles full of cordate bits and fragrant protocoals.

But my fragmentary soul and stony heart are worth more than even a fragment of eon-old coal swamp, and as I lay awake beneath the old warblanket in the mine of night, I imagine your presence there with me, my heart triboluminescing in its little cavity, our bodies enmeshing, you to my left on your delicate pillowcase, my arm reaching round my hand solid to your breastbone, holding you so firmly against me.

But three a.m. comes all too slowly, and I realize I can no longer hear your breath or feel your heart thrum through your breastbone or your breasts atumble round the bones of my hand.

I am alone again, and you are as far away in physical body as in psychical mind.

And now the room is dark as a cave and I am dry bones in an ossuary, ballast stones of an ancient deeptime, rolled up unceremoniously in an old warblanket for safe keeping, and one day immortality will come to sweep me up not as the hallowed wreckage of sainthood in a church chapel—see how he loved her!

they would exclaim—but as holloweyed drybone rattle in a shallow box, the shadow of a foreman's shelf, the backlog of an anthropology department storeroom.

* * *

No one but the medicine man, the mystic and the insane can remember the day of his birth.

And see now how I've slipped into new undiscovered country and can't remember how.

You are somehow—in this my dream—a mite taller than I remember you, El, either that or I am two fingers shorter, but we are two perfect dance partners the two of us are, assorted one to the other as is only right by the most serene of accidents, and the way that dress is so sheer and clings to your frame—Ingre's Violin, some kind of midsummer blue, the final blue of all pale blues, I remember seeing that blue one time when I was overseas, the crepuscular Loire Valley blue of my dark eye, lightened by the mischievous micromovements of your knowing glance subthreshold.

You are in love, my El, you too a galaxy of Pleiades blue as your eye lights on my shadowed dream. I've never looked good in blazers, never wear them, and you've always sung the praises of a man disheveled anyway, but if I heard right just now, you've just growled prevocal approval, purred Don't-worry-you-look-perfectly-sheveled-to-me, and I realize my shoulders fill this suitcoat, and will you look at that, my shoes are clean and the halogen sconces make you a tempting confection indeed, my El—a Nantais berlingot, limpid thought on poet's page—and just where did you come from?

I am right here, Love. We will never be apart.

And at your words the doubter forgets his doubt at this improbability, and takes your lovely small hand shall we dance? And the light to lighten your eyes is from far away, grails and goblets glitter your gaze, and for now, you are the pearl of highest price, the prize to praizen this man's foreign eye.

And soon I notice that you've begun to serpentine that way just... so.

The way... the way you've de-engineered the drape of your dress for my wondering eye, and for me and me alone there is a glimpse of the curve of your breast at the gap at your shoulder, and here the small of your back, here the silk of your thigh.

'*And what are you thinking about, Sir?*'

'*I am thinking about you, Miss.*'

* * *

It is of all places the conference room for the love of God, but this time all bedecked and arrayed, that crepuscular blue again, set off by the point-source amber of those halogen sconces. They've done it, haven't they?, made the snarled profaneness of the infamous MLA ballroom (the Scholar's Meatmarket) into the sacred vaulted spaces only the wealthy or wicked afford in Philadelphia P-A, Prohibition-era chic in reallight and realdark, in Newtonian HereandNow Lifesize; the snow in the streets, trace and pricking cheeks to rosacea, is forgotten here, a truce timed just right isn't it, and my God how lovely you are, thank God we are adreamt, for I can dream you, and as long as you can dream me as well, we can dream one another into being, and the hotel where I first learned of your existence, Darling, can be ours for the night and for tomorrow, and dream logic has seen fit that I already know the bed we will share tonight, and Thy kingdom come it is only just capacious enough for me alone, just wait till I get you home young lady, we will occupy -precisely- the same space, me you penetrate within, and you me surround roundabout, as is only just. There are ways, you know, where one volume of volatile meets one volume of flux, and the two delight in shifting their molecules to occupy only the volume of the one without overflow—another sacred alchemy, that one—and my lanky fraktura bones will meet the seams of your lean subtle curves and eclipse them through.

Your fingers ready an earring for the jewelry box, first one then another Pleiade in a velour firmament, the bend in your torso another intentional glimpse of your white skin, peaceful freckle on your breast a star inversus in an inverse sky. My hands find your waist, come to rest on the bones of the woman I love.

* * *

But dream be dream if only for its potential to vanish by morning light— it fleeing as it were a shadow—and although the sun has yet to rise, the ballroom and the blue dress have all become Dreams in their perfect ephemera, Venus obscured by mist, rising in the East to evaporate into the brightening blue, and my arms already ache for reaching for you. And there to my left is your pillow, and the lantern in the window to my right has become a silhouette in the first-fruits of increasing dawn.

What rare science, what strength of mind will bring you back to me? I always think, 'If she only knew what my heart was like... She could read, and she could -know-' and send my awful little missives away with Chaucerian hopefulness, cheering Go, little book!

Santayana said, 'a fanatic is one who redoubles his effort when he has forgotten his aim.' I don't think I've ever forgotten my aim—you can't fault me for that at least—yet the most lyrical effusions of my mind and heart have forgotten their aim, -my- aim, and wander away into the ethers never to be heard from again.

Good luck ever dreaming such pleasing and foolish phantasmagories again. The constructions of the night are always proven foolish by daylight, the mind is ashamed of the pleasures its flights and peregrinations have offered it. Wake from nightmares, you are sure to meet the old sorceress again and again and again when you lapse once more into the deep, but a dream, a -good- dream, it is gone forever, lost beyond lost, the event horizon of dawn.

* * *

But where are you now? The seventh floor has materialized into view, an argument of space, and all I have is to find you, room seven-two-nine, on the corner of the hotel, in the ever-fractalling division of imaginary space: a main landing, and following the geometry of iron sulfide chrome micah pyrite, Gigeresque in its complexity, a hotelfloor-hypercube-expanding-soundstage. The walls themselves are divided into thirds low to high, wainscoting and pan-

els, and high as the old Paris mansards; the wide pale blue borrowed from Molière, from Beaumarchais, Côté Jardin-Côté Cour.

And I know you are near, your rutscent or something conscious thought is subordinate to, something magnetic, shows me the way, and round and round the telescoping walls, floorplan tumbling fore, expanding only as I reach it—'Can you see anything?' they asked Howard Carter at the great sealed tomb, 'Yes, wonderful things!'—and my mind has thrown up obstacles to prevent me from seeing you at first: at once, the ever-expanding blueprint of the blue suite's footprint; then, studio sets to remind me of your early days as actress and playwright. A whole building of memory, El, built of love and furnished with your identity.

No wonder I knew you near. The place's brickwork is steeped in Us.

* * *

That eveningblue dress of yours, so sheer it is a question of its own, isn't it? And you tease it with the twist of your hand, you tempt it to part again to let your skin see peeks of me, the rousened tips of your breasts, the convexities of Mother and Lover, the tight enervations of your thigh's sinews, the sculpt of your calves in their turn as you turn, for the mirror, for your lover, for the universe to marvel breathless at the birth of a new Venus, Venus herself dressed in the modest blue tones born more of Bouguereau's brush than of Botticelli's, with contrite spiritual names connoting the virtues held dear by last century: Idylle. Evening Mood. Kiss. Bather. Little Thief. Caritas. Admiration. Awakening. And your gown dresses you in all these, and the curve of your hip, the weight of your breasts challenge them at the same instant.

'Come here. Little Thief.'

The dress comes alive with breath and movement, and you are in my arms, your bare feet gaining an inch or two for your frame by tiptoeing on my shoes; kisses, your face held against mine, my cheek marrying your cheek, 'Put your lips on my mouth' and I do, my mouth would marry your lips they would, my arms would wrap you—ribs spine breasts and waist—to me, and my fingers *find the hem of that clinging dress and the fine lively length of your semitendinosus—yes, all mine and I'll name it with my caresses—and soon my kisses quicken as I realize that dress is sheerer than I had banked on, and I emtemor out with my fingertips the porcelainwhite skin of dock, croup, flank.*

Your lips part, and you are wet within.

'Lie down, E!'

Mischief paints your lips pink.

'I want to touch you'

Not a declarative statement. Nor a request. Demand.

* * *

Love is force primeval, force exerted at a distance, increasing exponentially according to ever-increasing proximity, Force One at Distance Nine, Force Nine at Distance One, Newton would be proud. But physics derails at the extremes, and at the speed of light, there is no law to govern the universe, nor at the subatom's scale either; we know, then, of the purity of Creation only at the very moment of conception, they've traced the angular moments of whole galaxies back, drawn their trajectories backward into deep time, and lo and behold, all things intersect at one Then and at one There, all things are at once zero time and zero distance, no elementary particles even yet conceived in the foremind of God Almighty during these first microseconds of the universe, the thirteen-point-zero billion years back, the Then, the There, when all is One, when there is no distance, where there is no time, that moment of All is One, and the perfection of that moment, the Spirit of the Lord gliding silent as thought over the surface of the waters...

My fingers trace your skin, the heel of my palms pressing deep, I have to find that acetabulum deep within you, knead life back into you beginning where life began, you are mine from your foundations, the ancient cup of days, my hands pressing the white texture of your flesh, of your bones. Your dress rides high up over your hips, and you can hide nothing: the trace of sweet vine-

gar running from the cup, all maple and cinnamon, as you Become: allflesh, I sense your desire press out from between your cells, You-put-out-and-I-receive, the seep of your -suq- welcoming my skin, first a fingertip, then a second fingertip as well.

Your heart aflame behind your ribs, the words made flesh, 'I love you, El, and I always will', and as you shift and soak and seep, you turn and offer your torso to me, These clothes aren't fitting so very well anymore, but the stretch of that gown can no longer cover competently the desire of your breastbone, thank God you pull at that sheer fabric, and the modesty of your neckline unfolds to reveal your heart in its throne,

> On croyait savoir tout sur l'amour
>   depuis toujours
> Nos corps par cœur et nos cœurs au chaud
>   dans le velours
> Et puis te voir là, bout de femme comme
> Soufflée d'une sarbacane
> Le ciel a même un autre éclat
> Depuis toi
>
> We used to think we knew all that love
>   had to offer
> Body by heart, our heart set apart
>   in its coffer
> And then there you are, silhouette remade
> Seems like fired from a cannonade
> The sky aglow a diff'rent shade
> Since you stayed

And your breasts have a new life, they are the glorified body promised you since The Fall, areolas rich and vibrant with new seisms, the rumpling topography of living cells drawing their lifelymph upward to offer up to me, can there be any sweeter offering than to give up your body in its most rarefied, heightened state, my love and her dusky breast a new word to launch a new chapter in a book *that has no end...*

* * *

But dreams do end, and when I am back to my senses, tears no longer suffice to be rid of that brown-bag Ricus, that usurper, that ruiner of beauty, that Demon. Tears and words, screams and fists cannot pry you from his arms. And here I thought you stronger than that, better than that. But tears no longer suffice and my flesh aches out something of a vortex-cortex of torque and hurt, and that pain will never go away without the root cause uprooted and thrown into the fire, burned to coal and then to ash and then to smoke. This conscious-less usurper has insinuated himself into your nights and has also managed to insinuate himself into mine. My nights, unbeknownst to you, become a new experience of vinegar and flame, highwire act of fear—you've only known a tenth of it, El—desperation drunken with fear, for I have given you everything and he has taken it all from me.

From us.

I question anymore, not only whether my heart and mind can absorb the pain, but whether my memory's capable of containing this grand memory anymore, this affair without parallel, one that cannot be again for another three centuries, a love of all loves? And containing this memory, capturing it as it does, can this heart navigate the icefields ahead? Only if it too is made of ice. Can this heart contain within, here in the center, can this heart which I can reach with my hands (and how willingly do I pull my ribs apart) to show you in its concrete palpating reality how it this heart can no longer be of flesh, can no longer be sentient, no longer sense the insults, the pain, the jealousy, the fire that I've burned with all these months unless it too—this heart—becomes fire, unless it to become stone, unless it too becomes fuel and kerosene, a light in the darkness, a light for the darkness to consume and engulf, unless my heart, too, is exposed to the cruelest light; just as this heart has become a new dynamo, a new beacon, a new storm on the horizon—because of you—just as this heart has become a new being and this self is become a new self, just as now I can walk with drifting step and talk in thrumming tones as if transfigured, how might *this new being -within- survive without somehow being exposed to the burning rays -from without-?*

It amazes me, this Ricus, such a brownbag affair such as he is, a sulking sneaking creeping herpetic creature, I see his bleak countenance in your picture, I see his chiseled chin upthrust, his hollowed eye, yes I know you are there, El, taking his picture for yourself, for him, yes I know just how close he must be to get that angle just right in that cramped space, 'Here honey,' I hear you say, 'you'll have to move this knee here and this knee there, I can occupy this one and only space to take such a picture of you,' that grinning cretin on your yellow OldWorld sofa where I would drowse as you bustled omelets and toasterovern banquets into existence.

I've seen your picture with him, kissing him, his hand touching you intimately.

Good morning Love.

Essaie. Essaie encore. Et encore une fois.
  Regagne ce prix, cette frontière inconnue
  Reconstruis brique à brique cette tour chenue
  De ta renommée immortelle d'autrefois

J'ose vers cette couronne étendre mes doigts
  Et mon cœur rechercher les hauteurs saugrenues
  De ce prix, mon esprit grimper jusques aux nues :
  J'étends la main vers mon Dieu. Qui, qui me déçoit ?

Ton regard voûtant, ton œil redoutable et beau
  Me dévalisent d'un clin d'œil de tous mes biens
  Arrivage déserté où je touche au terme

Toute ma vie débalance sur ce radeau
Quand, me repérant, tu découpes tous les liens
Liens qui m'amarraient jadis à la terre ferme

Try. Try again. Once more. And again. Keep trying.
  Regain that shining prize, breach that frontier unknown;
  Fearlessly build brick by brick that tow'ring renown;
  Endeavor for immortality undying.

Yes, I dare stretch out my trembling hand toward that crown
  Of worth, toward greater dignity, my heart vying
  For that reward, my mind toward airless heights flying:
  I reach up to my God, who dares pull me back down?

Your arching brow and darkening eye's haunting craft
  Bundle me away, alone, breathless and bleeding
  Desert shores await to deport me of my worth

My whole life abalance upon this tilting raft
  You see me in my final hour, begging, pleading
  When, with a glance, you cut me loose from Planet Earth

When the arrows flew, when the men cried out, when the doors blew open and the snow grisailled the corpses... When Torsten reached out and held Havoise by the little finger to try to find her again after the news spread—the abbey was fixed in time immobile, the only movement was in Havoise' arachnidan fingertips, spinning out memory for the world in which to wrap itself, *just don't stop spinning, Weaverwoman*—and when she perceived blood in irregular constellations stippling his clothes and the back of his hand...

From that point, his very touch was a new rape of her person—not a sexual rape, not an intrusion of her womanly being—but an actual Taking By Force, an invasion that drew strength and light away from her; she felt her blood harden her arteries into a new stiff'ning endoskeleton, she felt the lightning deaden in her mind, she felt her skin loosen, failing falling fascia for *I am lost I am lost I am lost, I am become ghosts, voiceless and immaterial.*

Soldiers perpetratorpeacekeepers, the King's men in the grand scheme, but this is not how hierarchies work, and William's brightest magnitude-ten star—visible only with the sharpest of eyes on the darkest of nights—his best little bureaucrat, held the reins of the King's garrison in Glastonbury, and whatever their allegiance, whatever their fealty, they owed obedience to the little notary-warrior-Abbot, and paid their little functionary-Liege in the coin of obedience, even obedient unto death (which they dealt out in the Lord's cruciform house, meting out the nightmare at arrowpoint to the very holy men they were sworn to protect at arrowpoint).

'But thank God your soldiers didn't have to meet the monks' eye as they fired upon them: killing them at prayer has its advantages.'

Havoise heard the words slip from her lips in the darkest night. She clapped her hand over her mouth, winced as the sound propagated through the room.

Oh Lord, may the Abbot be asleep already

Her heart races, she feels every hair on her body tingle erect with fear and loathing of her person, even more than of his: she has broken every taboo of a rising noblewoman, the ultimate taboo of everywoman, and she trembles with that sinking feeling, now overt nausea at her audacity.

Audacity. She has spoken her mind.

The minutes tick into eternities.

There is a whisper at Havoise' side, barely distinguishable from her own breathing, hoarse and lifeless:

'I am *comite* of the king. My word is the king's word. The king is king by virtue of his authority. I am therefore the authority of the king. Those men gave their lives over to the king to better his authority in this godless place. This is how law is. Their final submission to authority therefore forever covers their idolatrous ways. They rest in peace.'

The dialectical logic of his words in the stillness, electricity, blade, halo, aura. Logic having seized thought and deadened emotion.

Havoise thought about how dark it was in this place, the ghosts of those dead holy men in the stonework, the very intercellular machinery of the abbey. She only knew for certain she was alive by the way her eyes registered the cold air of the room against the moistness of her sclera.

* * *

'Havoise.'

The Countess of Glastonbury gulped at her breathing.

'The king will have seen my works here, will see that I have accomplished my mandate among these foreigners. These... *Englishmen.*'

Tortsten's words hung in the cold air, while empires rose and fell and rivers changed their course in their meandering way. He licked his lips.

'He will send me back to Normandy. Go to sleep now.'

* * *

Havoise' open eyes grew cold in the darkness.

She hadn't been called by her name in forty years. She barely recognized the sound of it.

***

She left her possessions in place. She was a ghost herself, and the best way to be a ghost was to leave her space, lock the door as if she might be back in no time—tonight, tomorrow night, a moment of the underworld's choosing. And so rather than clean up after herself, make bundles of her belongings for the Armoror to pack away, she carefully posed the room as if she fully intended to come back in: a wineglass balanced on the edge of a nighttable—a puff of breeze or the clatter of a passing wagon could cast it away into the abyss—her nightclothes draped over the end of the bed, a candle allowed to burn down to the base.

'Your tapestry, milady.' Armoror held it up, crushed in his giant fist.

'Burn it.'

'As you will it.'

She felt so very old. Armoror clattered away down the corridor, a forever exoskeleton of armor and chainery, a cicada or a tortoise or a crab, if you pulled him out of his armor, he would surely die of the chill. Havoise' tapestry trailed behind him, a linen comet omen.

'Wait, Armoror.'

The clattering stopped.

'I'll dispose of it as it should be done. Return it.'

***

The beachhead was thrashed by Channel gale, torturing each wave into a truncate rhomboid; the illusion of scale was cruelly skewed toward the transformation of water into something metallic and cold and indifferent—from any distance at all, Havoise would swear that the evershifting surface was a wickedly twisting sheet of chain armor, a planetary chainmail barrier. Yet up close, she could dip her hand into its icy face and see her hand fall through its transparency; although she quickly lost sensation in her hand, she could still see it, move it numbly. She imagined it must be like this when she passed over to the other side: as each member of her was lost, to disease or heartbreak or slow madness, she would see her limbs pass through effortlessly into the abyss; they would pain, then chill into nothingness.

Just wait 'til the cold reaches my heart

And they hadn't but her to transport back across, this passage calling her alone, this passacaglia back to the Other Side. Armoror stood back a polite distance, having expected to be hauling bundles and bundles of Norman merchandise and English booty into the surf and onto the ships. But there was only the Countess standing in the railing gales, her hands and face blue in the advancing storm, a halo of sand raked from the beach obscuring her legs.

'You'll die of cold, where are your things, milady? Where are the others?'

'Nothing left. And no one.'

'Nonsense. Where is your coat, the train of carts?'

But she held only her tapestry, feebly, as if offering it to the deep.

* * *

The ship was large enough for fifty men and a dozen horses; the crew gaped in amazement at the lone woman standing in the tempest, her hair thrashed and crazed. An Armoror called from the beachhead.

'She'll catch her death in the crossing back; what have you to cover her?'

'But where's the rest of the cargo?'

'She's the only one.'

And when Armoror turned back toward the beach to try to convince Havoise that there must be some mistake, certainly she had some goods to bring back with her didn't she?, he saw her ghost.

She had unrolled the tapestry—the one she had made to wreathe William as king of this steelycold place—and wrapped it around herself as a long linen bandage; she wore the history of the Conquest as a grave lintel, as a shroud. Not even her arms showed, not even her eyes, only her nose extended from the linen. She teetered in place, her legs bound.

The Armoror covered himself with pardons, and, bending, picked up the Countess of Glastoneburg. He felt her stiffly fall over his shoulder as a corpse might. He waded out to the ship.

They situated her body along the centerline of the ship, over the keel. The sailors never saw her move for the duration of crossing, found themselves speaking in hushed tones, out of respect for the dead.

A genoux, mon esprit, rends ton humble hommage,
   Remets ton orgueil, ton armure, ton épée,
   Replie ton dos, romps cette parole ménippée,
   Ta monnaie rouillée, ta poussiéreuse page

Promets ta féauté à un' nouvelle image,
   Aux teints éclatants de cette icône adorée
   Par le genre noble et par serf, tant vénérée
   D'homme et d'ange, par tous les rois de tous les âges

Maîtresse forte et puissante dans les combats
   Dont l'épée emporte le ciel-même en victoire
   Et amène secours aux hommes que voici

Or, Cœur, serviteur d'Aphrodite : tombe à
   Terre devant elle (cœur distant, contradictoire) ;
   L'esprit l'a déjà fait, prosterne-toi aussi

Bow down, intellect, and pay your humblest homage
   Cast down your haught, your armor, and your flashing sword
   Bend your spine's frame, break asunder that cunning word
   Of yours, that rusting coin, that dusting paper page

And render fealty now unto a new image
   The vivid pigments of a stern icon adored
   By men abroad, by knight and serf alike, a lord
   Of men and angels, over kings from age to age

A lord strong and mighty, a lord strong and mighty
   A lord mighty in battle, whose sword in vict'ry
   Defeats e'en heaven, bears men up from conqu'ring Hell

O servant of our queen mistress Aphrodite,
   My Heart (so aloof, so very contradict'ry
   To Mind): bow ye down as well, bow ye down as well

* * *

I can see where you live when I close my eyes

The floors in this dark place creak when all the others are away; the heat of human presence robbed away by mortals' desire to go home, lay their head on a cool pillow next to their lover and be nursed by the darkness and balmed over by dreams

Goodness, the parquets -miss- their human oppressors when they are gone

The light of the Moon describing the mathematics of perspective, slanted cold props of pure geometry uniting the Moon to a windowshaped pool of mercury spilt on the floor

Oh but thank God they didn't take the moonlight, silent solacetreasurestream no man can steal away

* * *

It smells of dust in here

Dust of... Italy

Problem these Frankish savages have is principally one of scale; for a bunch of humanists, they sure don't know what scale of grandeur best suits the human organism, do they? And there is room upon room upon room, the eye always has some more distant place to attach to; this is the true nature of desire, that once somebody steps through the lintel from one room to the next, it's as if a new world of desires comes into being, and the eye is drawn to all the exits available, as if the goal is not to stay but to stray, as if the idea in a shooting match is to never hit the target but just barely miss, so that targets are goals, yes, but goals unmet, desires left unfulfilled

Ah, but tonight, this weary traveler, dust of a thousand years' journeying climbing his person inch by inch, will lay eyes upon his prize, fearlessly fix her with his eye

Surely there is either salvation waiting in the next room under milady's gentle gaze, or perdition

* * *

He wished devoutly for a proper sword, something grand and respectable, a rapier, a cutlass, a pennanted pike—like the Swiss Guard march with—a grim longsword, a... scimitar

Something worthy

He had jimmied the lock into inoperation by day, with his dainty little jackknife with the blade blunted by decidedly pedestrian jousts with walnuts and mundane duels to the death sabering recalcitrant bottles, the inelegant tournament he sometimes held against a mote of beef caught between his molars; he was of course underweight and his trouser troused broader and more shapeless than fashion would ever allow in daylight, and for a moment he was afraid the knife had fallen out of his capacious pocket—good luck ever finding it again in a place as ungodly huge as this, and by night no less—and he felt helpless and effeminate until the haft's heft found his gracile fingers again

He weighed that blade, reassured himself of its presence, knew again the fact of its hardened mass

He breathed hard, as the pearl divers do, and turned into the deep shadow of the last chamber, the holy of holies

* * *

It was an empty space; searching through the entire album of memories he'd accrued since tumbling out into the ensaturate light of France, he realized he had never seen this room wholly empty before, always there was some knot of hangers-on groping for position, eyeless eels vying for a shot at the one female whom they scent with invisible profane senses, the pit uniting the universe to the snake's mindless brainstem, the melon to the armless whale, the jellylike masses of onlookers jostling for a glance

In his memory he could smell their stench, these crowders, these eyeless bands

He shook his head to dispel them; his eye focused once again upon the room in the very depths of this palace, oh how it tried in vain to frame those gentle eyes, that thoughtful mind, the focus of so much lightning

But this, for once, was a picture worth oh-so-much-more than the frame

The light shifted in his eyes; some accident of geometry brought the object of perfect desire into focus before him, in the clarity of dreams, the ghostly clarity of light through lenses, as if Moon and Stars had gathered in some goldtinted midsummer Shabbat 'round this hidden place

'And so—'

His voice surprised him

'—How close to one another we have grown'

He drew the knife from his pocket, verified its weight, the stoutness of its alloy, the straightline spine of its length; if he turned it just right, he could see the old motto engraved into its harrowed blade, reflecting and somehow amplifying the light from this holy place

'You know my thoughts as I think them, don't you, Love?'

Even a whisper echoed drily though the corridors, proof alone that here was a place entirely his, where the very air bowed to his words' bidding

Nec Spe, Nec Metu, sometimes he felt as if his whole life and the very love of his heart were contained in these odd jumbles of letters, these letter glyphs, these Latin runes, these graven strokes, so very laconic and pursed; other times, he knew he'd be best off using that blade as nothing more than palette knife, turn the turpentine 'round till the blade corroded down to a crippled stump

'And with what relief do I see you before me; what soothing relief to

know that your eye surveys 'round for me, wondering about me, looking for me... Muse, protector, consoler, challenger'

He knelt

* * *

You are in my heart today, as you've been for many years now

And as you'll be for the rest of my days

And with you and by you, I see my real self emerging: for once in a whole lifetime, a man alive and whole

A lover

Perhaps a hero for once

You see me as... me

And cause -me- to see me as... me

* * *

And he pressed his blade point-first into the parquet

He looked to her, her eye beneficent, inscrutable in the half-light

Let the ceremony begin

'As I take thee in my arms,' he began, he voice tremulous in the still air, 'take thou also my heart to thee; it is thine, in perfect submission to thy whim, thy will and thy being; see thou me in prayer, see thou me expose to thee my head—seat of my lowest intellect—and my heart—of higher price'

'These be all thine, I beg thee to accept them as a humble sacrifice of material being and spiritual essence; I am thy man, thou art my love, and as these walls be my witness, as well as by all the angels in the firmament, we will never be apart'

'To thee I bind myself, faithful to thee, pledging me forever to defend thee before the daunting array of foes, before the countless host of enemy base and lofty, against king and army, serpent or cherubim, soldier or seraph, heaven above or earth below, and I will keep myself for thee against all, for the rest of my days; as body and soul are joined to become one life, I am thine for thee alone'

'Oh my Love, with these words I pledge myself to thee, body, heart, mind, soul and all my being'

He rose

And quietly, and quickly, this Scarecrow Knight fetched a chair from the next room, the palace's darkness no longer an impediment but a shining path

'In thee have I trusted,' as he settled the chair in before her, below her, and carefully stood on it, seeing her eye to eye, 'let me never be confounded'

And he touched her, and took her as gently as any man has ever taken his bride

* * *

'Highness...'

The old man was at the king's door.

'*Highness.*' Urgency.

Knots of functionaries surrounding the king; when François looked up, they scowled drear, jabbed again at the document whose parchment ached for a royal signature, murmured, 'Right here, your Highness, right here, make it Law'... the king smiled apologies, returned to treatysigning.

'Your Highness, I... I...'

'For God's sake, speak up, old man! Can't you see His Highness is busy?' Evidently the treaty signature did not need all of the dozen courtiers present, as easily half advanced toward the door to hustle away the intrusion like waving away a biting fly. 'Come now, old man, back to your scribbles.'

'Highness... I cannot... I cannot... can no longer...' His voice colorless, his left hand clutching the door frame, his right hand limp. 'Highness...'

'Come now, old man, we can't be keeping you from your afternoon nap,' as the men disengaged his hand from the doorjamb, 'you need your beauty sleep, and the King needs to actually *do work*...' They spun him around, sighing and shaking their heads at the old man, *tsking* just a bit too loudly, 'Now how exactly did you get loose from your little palace room? Not big enough for you, *hmm?*'

The old man stumbled.

* * *

'But the Godhead of the Father, of the Son, and of the Holy Spirit...' Apollinaire's words slurred magnificently, corrupted and dense, a smeared portrait, 'is *all*... is *all*...'

But even as Peruggia watched, Apollinaire sank into fog.

I'll give him an hour

But after the hour, Apollinaire was no nearer to the land of the living, and Peruggia, bored of filling in the blank left by the poet's lapse into the netherworld—*what else could the Godhead be? All... by itself? All... done? All... lacquered up?*—he sighed deeply, shaking his head, and pulled a crevice into the darkness' armor: it was morning outside, and he just didn't care much anymore, and besides, he was a man of action. He found one of Apollinaire's suitcoats, sniffed it for signs of vomit or overripe perfume, hung it on his bony frame.

All... right?

Peruggia hunched his shoulders, drew a few deep breaths to barrel his chest, adjusted his lapels. The mirror winced: there was no way anybody'd believe this wasn't a stolen jacket the way it swung in the breeze. Oh well.

The Godhead: is all... is all...

All... for one, one for all?

He was an unmade bed as he fell into the street, the hat he had stolen from the poet rolling in wide curlicues 'til he chased it down, too, *Fuck you, Apollinaire*. Brass Corners swung, Brass Corners another insult to his shins, Brass Corners felt a whole lot better if he just held it at arm's length and spun 'round, his other hand holding his hat down on his head, the suitcase a wild, looping orbit threatening annihilation upon any Frenchman who might stray into its arc *I am a weightless atom with its reactive random electron shell* as he set the gyros for Italy, the nationless Peruggia and the scratch-and-dent Brass Corners each orbiting some theoretical libration's focus in the vacuum's void between them, *enter at your peril, there's nothing left in here but empty space*

* * *

'Will he die?'

'Well of course he'll die.'

The old man stirred; the surgeon crept around the room darkly. Instruments clattered, sang atonal as they were returned their shine by deft swipes of the smock, blades made smart again against leather; glass fiols with blood and urine and other fluids scaling the sides for escape.

François stood, wrapped in thought, encumbered by the old man's stirrings, his odd way of fixing him as he walked around the old man's sickroom. He couldn't determine if he was even able to focus his eyes, or if (on the other hand) the mind were already passed across; nonetheless, the old man's eyes burned with fire and his forehead knotted 'round words that never took shape into the cool air of this high room.

'Perhaps he'd be more comfortable...'

'...With fewer people to disturb him?' interrupted the surgeon absently, 'He needs but only to be alone with himself, it's a shame to take time away from the Crown like this. It's not like he's not already been seen by a priest.'

'But...'

'...But just close the window to keep the crows from pecking him and the flies from laying him full of larva.' The surgeon's nearly done getting his things back together, and is rolling them back up in his smock. 'And if you think he's about to die...'

'*About to die?* What should I do then? Give him water, call for wine, call for you, have him bled? What?'

'*If you think he's about to die,*' the surgeon repeated, less patiently, 'leave the window open, so his soul can fly away to Heaven or something.'

François looked at the old man, whose eyes were full of words unsaid.

Surgeon was already down the corridor, his voice an echo softening through the maze of rooms, '...Or to Italy, or wherever.'

* * *

Sun to sand, sea to valley to mountain and sky. Peruggia enframed in the majesty of the Piedmont near Perinaldo, there was nothing except a mere trivial gravity that could keep him from flying away in his mind, alchemy breezes in the heat of the day, surely there was some great thermal thrum uniting him with the greater maritime Alps through the intermediary of his heart, that strange engine within him, that intermediate step between the salt brine sea, his thrashing heart a sea churning but not rising with tidal forces, his thrashing heart the astonishing eternal snows of the crystalline peaks advancing away from the airless voids to meet the thick ripe air of the rising valleys, his thrashing heart the very recollection of seasons—advancing, retreating, advancing, retreating—his thrashing heart the culmination of days and years, each heartbeat a hypothesis of his very existence *will it beat?* or *will it not?* this sliding datapoint on the gradient scale between the very deep and the very lofty... His mind neverminding the serious humors animating its squishiest processes, *bloodlymphsaltwater saltpeterairvaporfireether...* a *Pseunami* (he grinned to himself) was he become, a thrashing heart halfway between floodwater and avalanche.

This he thought *is a blessed moment*

...between himself and his God, *make peace if you can manage it* the better to enjoy communion, for God hath wrought existence into the interstice holding apart the planes of the eternal and the temporal, and *here I am, if anything, a mote of dust on the very plume of History*

And as he walked, he thought of how the voice of God came to humans on the breath of the winds, and on the best days sounded like thunder (and on worst, madness), and how it took thundering madmen to rise up rush up on the mountain and interpret the terrible and sacred words on behalf of the great unwashed, *and just what sacred words would come to him this bright azure day?* for he knew no ancient sacred writ, he knew as point of fact the turbulence of Ancient Days far better than the mysteries of the Ancient of Days: and here on the gentle fall breeze in the Piedmont, the memory of that day when the one Vicar of the Christ thundered his voice from the Vatican Hill upon heretics, to run them down like hares, like vermin, to light the night with their fats dripping down in whizzing comets off from their bodytorches, have you nothing but your accumulated fat to light the night with? for in my dreams we are but a tripping step from Italy again.

But it was a hot day now as the breeze settled, and as Peruggia sat on a flat stone by the side of the Perinaldo Road, he could feel his belly ache, and he looked 'round about for some sort of padding for his little paunch, when he plunged his hand into his shirt to massage the hunger down on through, he felt the cold damp flesh, his limp skin, *where's an olive grove when you need one?* but as he looked around there was nothing but sad skinny French apples a little past their prime, a few Gallic peaches sweet beyond ripe, mostly ants now, but if he was lucky he could suck on a pit or a core—*if you're good, you may come up to gaze at me* he could hear his Love purr like it was *his* privilege and not hers—and so this he did, and he did his level best to be content in this little Paradise, *his* little Paradise, with the twelfth part of flesh of a dozen apples and peaches turning to syrup within his little frame, *I always find the hardest way of doing things* he said to himself, smugmug and satisfied, and maybe revelation isn't so much a man rising up to meet his God, *who dares pull me back down?*, but instead a gross negotiation of implication, a great crackling potential of staticcharge developed between two plates that never touch, *can* never touch, a fearsome mindboiling capacitor containing meaning in the vacuumvoid intersticed between source and target, cryptext and cribtext, between Godspeak and mathering blathering muttering Humanspeak, the deepchannel Dardanelle churning between Hero and Leander, the atom'sbreadth separating your skin from mine in our high white lovebed as I penetrate you in the cool morning light.

Ah, God lies -not- in the details

What a lovely place this is, a place to set down my suitcase, finally roll up this ridiculous epaulet coat that hangs like an insult from my shoulders, let my head wear it like a pillow, with the shiningwhite Alps over here, the treasured Mediterranean over here, nestled between stone and space, sea and stone and space, and fall asleep thinking of you. Hell, who knows if I'm even still in France as dream catches me again? It's not like there's a wall or anything before legal Italy starts, or some border painted down across this little grove with the micanaceous soil glinting up at me; it's not like they're suddenly about to leap out, weapons drawn, as I Cross Over...

He lies instead within That Which Cannot Be Translated

* * *

'He is only an empty shell; nothing remains of his person.'

A candle shone its nacreous light.

'He has already slipped across to the other side.'

But the Old Man's eyes darted; gravity weighed his limbs to Earth.

'We will move him to my chamber. He will sleep in a King's bed for one night.'

'Your Highness, let's not exaggerate.'

With purpose: 'I *said*, he will sleep in a King's bed. I will watch over him.'

* * *

Crossing Over. Slipping Across. Three hundred ninety-five years, seven months, eight days later.

* * *

'Hurry!'

There was a note of alarm in François' voice. Unaccustomed to hearing anything but effortless confidence breezing through their monarch's speech, there was a ruckus as men scrambled.

'Bring something to cause him pleasure. In his last hour.'

The Old Man's eye had wandered very distant indeed, flying flights into new worlds. 'He can feel the velour of a king's bedding, surely, but what is the last finest savor of this life?'

Men crashed through the palace in their search, distant echoes of a ransacking ordered by their King. The first page to return brought a clear bottle, nearly empty but for a splash of sweet wine.

'Good man!' The bottle sang as the King pulled the cork free. But when the bottle's smooth glass mouth was brought close to the Old Man's lips, he frowned, nostrils wide, eyes strangely alert, and flashing with refusal and distaste. And in the far corners of the palace still, the sound of men searching for other earthly delights, final pleasures for the King to present to the dying man. Wine spilled into the man's beard.

François persisted, gently, anxiously. 'Come now. Just a drop of spirit left!' He held the bottle close; the Old Man's breath fogged the glass.

Suddenly, another man shouldered the bedchamber's door open noisily, 'See if *this* won't bring him a smile, Your Highness,' clumsy hands on an old portrait he had grabbed from the Old Man's room, 'it was hanging behind his door, you wouldn't see it unless you were looking for it.'

But when François turned back, the Old Man's eyes had disappeared to empty glass.

The King stoppered the bottle he had been holding, with the Old

Man's last breath the only spirit within.

* * *

They only held Peruggia for a short time, seeing in him something of the divine madness of holy acts, wholly devoid of malice, a man more than anything else *astounded* that armed men might've indeed stood guard over a deserted Paradise, where peach groves give way to olives, where the sacred chant on the wind blows less from Notre Dame and Chartres than from San Marco and San Pietro, where he had gotten distracted with a tune in his head and the Med shining crystals up at him and a pebble in his shoe, and before he knew it there were a half-dozen men standing around him.

Buon giorno, Signore

* * *

They had stood with him for a time, smoked a *Nazionali* with him, had even carried his little suitcase for him. He breathed easy, seeing how gentle they were with Brass Corners.

* * *

He could see them now through the glass down at the *Prefettura*, the half-dozen armed chaps he had met in the olive grove, several detectives now, too, and several men whose prestance and gravitas suggested they might be diplomats or candidates or something. They all shook their heads with apparent incredulity, hands on hips, sometimes gesturing to Brass Corners sitting on a high table between them, gesturing in Peruggia's direction, too, behind the glass, in the empty little room.

Finally having come to some sort of decision among themselves, they came and got him, offered him another cigarette, and told him, 'You can have your suitcase back.'

A frame without a picture.

* * *

The crowds were callous and cruel, and Brass Corners punished Peruggia's shins again and again. Somehow everyone in Naples knew that when Peruggia was headed one way, they should be headed in the opposite way, and the flow of humanity past him was unconscious of his sufferings.

Finally, he decided to hold Brass Corners over his head.

As is only proper he thought.

Some distant part of his mind wondered whether he should be concerned with how light his battered little suitcase felt.

* * *

The Bay of Naples. Peruggia sitting on the quay he remembered from his youth, a handkerchief of olives, a half-empty bottle of *pinard*. It tasted so much sweeter, love's labors rewarded.

Brass Corners next to him, enjoying the view.

There there, Love

There there

Tu t'es inscrite comme une ère dans l'histoire,
  Dans la matrice de mon tissu, dans la pierre
  D'une muraille éternelle, du souvenir d'hier
  Le soupir, d'une longue vie la gage noire

Tu t'insinues le long de ma vie (un long lierre
  Sur vieille muraille), étends dans la mémoire
  Comme la ligne serpentine de la Loire
  Bordant vigne, ville, vieille tour seule et fière

Que deviens-je sans le flux de cette rivière,
  Si elle se met à ternir, cette source fiable ?
  Pauvre de cœur en moi, pauvre de vie, la peur

De perdre la longue trace à ma vie si chère
  Et, sans toi, devenir esprit, fantôme, diable
  Devenir un rien, un non-être, une vapeur

You've inscribed yourself into history as an Age,
   Into the matrix of my cells, as the dark stone
   Of an eternal rampart, as the sussing tone
   Contained in my breathing, life's dark rising gauge

An ivy insinuating throughout (long grown
   Along old walls), the endless flow of mem'ry's sage
   Old river, crossing serpentine the landscape's stage
   Bordering vineyard, village, towers vict'rious, alone

What will become of me without this river's flow?
   What suff'ring awaits, if this ever-faithful spring,
   If this endless stream should begin to taper?

Poor heart, without that river, that life-giving thing:
   Become a spirit, a ghost, a demon below
   Become a nothing, and turn into vapor

I've heard you say so many contrary things about my voice—that it is soothing that it is brassy, that it is an old man that it belongs to a sly, humble soul. Most recently you said that if I could remember one thing for the rest of my days, it was that you find it comforting.

Thank you. I will remember this, as you ask, for the rest of my days.

* * *

I can say many things about yours, too, and like a mystic reading the future sniffing a forestfire on the wind I can read the tealeaf subtext of your words with a resolution that may surprise you… You'll forgive me for sighing the sigh of centuries over the sometimes-paucity of our talks lately—this of course not my doing, for if you haven't an idea of the shape of my heart by now, then it's as if I haven't even drawn breath this cold year lone and long—and yet, I have the shape of your words on my lips before you speak them, or more precisely, before you silence them: 'I haven't decided yet,' for example, is clear-as-day El-speak in high-order code for 'I -have- decided, and you—you specifically, you personally—are -not- entitled to be a part of my decision'; 'I wanted to call before I called the girls' is the latest casual prelude to a night spent in the arms of The Ricus, the phreaked whispers of 'this will be my very last word to you for the night, I'm expecting to enjoy myself in the arms of another man, and I will resent you for intruding,' the subacoustic rumble of the earthquake before the alpha wave strikes, the flash in the peripheral vision, lightning hath fallen, onethousandoneonethousandtwoonethousandthree…

Pre-emptive strikes -pre-empt-, it is true.

And yet, also still -strike-.

* * *

What will you remember of my voice? And no, I don't mean the wandering grustle of whisper, the tone of my speech, the pitch and timbre and hue and rate and all, but the understory tenor of my words? What will be left of me when I'm finally gone?

Asking you what will be left behind of me, what electrons will still play about in your memory is perhaps unfair. Though also: perhaps not. What am I to you if not some kind of meaning, what am I to myself if not some kind of meaning, some kind of lifetime-scale statement of Fact—a thought, an emotion, a pause in the breath, a catch in the voice—made real by my having been heard, thought of, ...remembered? Is it unfair to wonder what echo my voice is likely to leave, what manner of shadow I'm likely to cast, what afterimage my life has been when I'm cold and gone and you close your eyes in the dead of night?

A book on a shelf. A rough old voice on the phone. A magic shotglass shining in the sun. The great big sweatshirt that covers your hands and falls all the way to your knees, somehow revealing all the more the curve of your breasts and the span of your hips. Volcano cake. A tarot card, fallen strategically, fatally. Our place by the fire, our triangle table in the speakeasy. Toasted almond, yet another coffee spill on a Sunday morning, you'd never know if it were my ghost or some perverse muscle-memory your mind reverberating through the fibers of your forearm, the tendons of your palm, the pads of your fingers, tipping my heat and my life out into the cold world again in fragrant warm wet circles, a trace of vapor in the winter kitchen. A crazy word—'louis', 'taiga', 'unvoices'—in Scrabble. The nacrescence of come on your palate. Fourteen lines twelve syllables two quatrains two tercets one for you one for me. Ghostly photos in the darkness of your back patio on an anonymous sultry summer night Family Challenge cicadas and heatlightning Louis and Ella freezercold glasses of St-Germain macerated berries photons onto silvermercury the shade of a man passing through a plane of polished glass. A rope burn, a mattress pulled to the middle of the floor, an orchid, a lepidodendron tendril in three-dimensions hiding in Dr. Rubick's coal-colored mind. An obscure quote an obscene quote a word hanging weightless and forever, Apollo-era Hugo-era Rabelais-era Clovis-era.

What am I? What will I have been? For I have seen my future, and I give it to you.

What -hubris-, to ask you such questions...

* * *

'I may have told you about my heart before'

Foolishness. *'I am at once the most self-aware person you've ever met,' etc., you can hear the officious tone in my voice, you can hear the self-important braggadocio, there is no recess no crevice no fissure in this heart of mine that you don't have complete awareness of, it is a character in a book, with its own psychology, its own history of thought and deed, its litany of I've-been-braver-since-thens, its birth and growth and eventual declinedeathdecay; the sonic space it envelops—the Victoria Requiems, the O Magnum Mysteriums, the nascent concerti, the way my hands cross in intricate weaving filigrees mere atoms above the keys to play your acoustic image for you (that mysterious interspace crisscrossed by g-minor and c-minor)—but what do you know about the actual flesh-and-blood object, that thing suspended in space before you as we dance, that thing suspended in space above you as we make love? The physical, material object that is me, that makes me, that sustains me?*

I have often wondered what part of me is actually inherited from my folks, and what parts are drawn up out of the dust of my living-my-life; I know, for example, that my father has a heart of a marathoner, that back in the Army he and his buddies would play three-on-three, court warfare, and do riskphilic things like climb mountains and rough it in bivouacs on glaciers—back before he had brought young into this hard world, before he had weighed the pros and cons of a fatherless set of children—and his heart bore all the signs of a man active, a man adventurous, a man courageous.

He would boast that he would wake in the pre-dawn to a pulse of forty-two.

I have never had the luxury (or the moxie) to climb mountains or press chest-deep through mountain streams on the way to a six-day bivouac. As you know, my heart—the sentient heart, not the cut of meat—is not made for such things. I had always figured, then, that I would subsequently have a lesser heart, a weaker one, with fewer stout sinews, something less fibrous.

Turns out I was wrong.

I went in for a sleep study several years ago. They do the standard protocol—wires, leads, electrodes—wish you a good night's sleep, lights out, door closed...

A half an hour later, the tech comes bursting in the door again.

'Tell me one good reason why your heart is beating so slowly.'

(Questions you never thought you'd hear)

'Um, I, uh...'

No answer came: annoyed at being awakened (for Chrissake, during a sleep study?), and besides, what do you say when somebody stands in the door and asks you your excuse for living? More precisely: your excuse for not dying?

Turns out that my heartbeat had slowed, step by step, minute by minute... When it reached thirty-two, they sent in the cavalry.

* * *

What arrogance, to wonder after your futurememory of me, my Love, my El...

* * *

Will you be there, the moment my heart fades away in its dark coffer, turns again from the molten seat of my love, the second-to-second archive of my being, back into a dead mass, devoid of me?

Who will be the cavalry then?

Il y fut un jour où je rêvai (d'un caprice)
   Une averse, et l'heure prévue, le ciel s'ouvrit.
   De toute la foule, ce fut moi le vrai surpris :
   Ils ouvrent parapluie. Et moi crains maléfice

Puis je rêvai avoir poussé des ailes lisses
   M'être jeté au Zéphyr dans mon esprit
   Je m'émerveille quand, au clos de la longue nuit
   Je vois une plume dont mon oreiller mollisse

Je rêvai avoir écrit l'Odyssée d'Ulysse
   Rêvai des mers et continents la longue errance
   Auteur d'un vol je rêvai, et toi ma complice

Je rêve encor' de toi et moi en conférence
   L'escalier notre royaume, nos baisers nos lys
   Toi qui es ma Reine. Et moi qui suis Roi de France

There was a day when (on a whim) I dreamed the rain
  Into being, and the sky loosed at the hour I chose
  I alone shuddered when the storm arose:
  -They- opened umbrellas. -I- doubted I was sane

I dreamed then of growing wings (when I slept again)
  And threw myself headlong above where Zephyr blows
  And wondered at the marvel when, at nighttime's close,
  I plucked a feather from the pillow where I'd lain

I dreamed of writing the epics of Ulysses
  Dreamed of the sealanes the continents between
  Authored artful flights, with you and me accomplices

I still dream of you and me in a peaceful scene:
  Our own stairway kingdom and a thousand kisses
  I will be King of France. And you will be my Queen

'Baby, take a load off'

Socks rolled down, little toroids you kick off down the stairs into infinity, your pantlegs rolled up now, too, the cool of your calves in my hands, you'll never know what kind of earthly pleasure, delightful in its simplicity, it is to have hands large enough fingers long enough to reach around your entire calf, white skin blushing Fragonard my arms ivying all 'round your legs. I remember the whisking sound of your razor cautious skating this ankle then that ankle last night in the dark but tonight the payoff, those calves one each a touch alive for my hands, I'll sit a step down from you in the light of that hanging bulb, lean back up against your chest behind me and feel you breathe as your breasts press around me through your blouse, and you can drape your arms over my shoulders raggedy Ann and your hair course all around me my universe a new nebula of blond and grey and auburn softening the lightbulb into more toroids luminous in my eye

'Baby, doing alright?'

The comfort of a sitdown at the end of it all heave a deep breath, it's been nothing but workworkwork but now we can just take it easy, you'd think the steps'd be the last place we'd want to relax but it's just as if we've found some place here on the landing that no one's thought to make theirs, and the new house smell and the bare lightbulb and the dust from the movers and wallboard showing through where somebody's poster hung before us

Before us

Before Us

Crazy how it sounds so Real when you put it this way, as if by saying it aloud it's allowed to Be for a second, Before Us that era that calendars lie to us about, as if there's ever been a time when I haven't loved you—there are eight hundred forty-one years since the moment they laid the first stone of Notre Dame and bolted it down to the center of the world, but an infinity before that moment, so sure, maybe-just-maybe there was such a thing as Before Us but I'm sure it *only existed as a thought experiment in a philosopher's mind, a mote of theoretical fluff in a particle accelerator—but in -this- universe' great arc, spacetime unfolded its petals to the light the second I read your name for the first time, thank-you-for-your-note*

'It's nothing much, just a spoon and a jar of peanut butter, it's a new one you take first crack at it I'll lick the spoon after you'

Moving-day fare, a big spoon a quick call for takeout let me massage those sore knees of yours you can unfold the knots in my back

* * *

The stairs are the simplest of helix, just a fraction of a turn, a geometry stable and uninsistent, the place is quiet except for a radio on somewhere burning through its batteries on some friendly jazz, something just subthreshold, a thrush of breath pressing you against me, your heart briefly as close to me as it can possibly be, its beat mingling with your breath, your breath alternating with a thread of song off away

Gone the leonine creases of my brow, gone the hard tendon arch of your limbs, your skin warming to my touch

'I'm totaled, Baby'

But that sighing exhaustion of ours isn't one of the years wearing us down or one of the miles wearing us off, but the wearing away is of that spacetime between us—an afternoon away, a day away, a year away, a world away—that simple helix stair a secret liminary space, anode and cathode finally reconciled, no moats or stones or fires, in fact no space at all between us, our minds and hearts finally at rest, our stair a world that brings you back to me time after time

'Come to bed; lay next to me'

Three hundred years evaporate away

* * *

Sometimes I'm cold and your memory warms me, sometimes I'm alone and your voice calms my mind, sometimes I'm full of myself and you bring me back home

Tonight, I feel you behind me, your arms your legs your breath on my neck, your breasts pressed against me again, a recasting of our posture at the head of the stair, perfected, though, in our bed

The thought inspires me, it is some unthinkable time and the universe is quiet and my love becomes my desire and all it takes is shifting around a little, resituate the sheets around us now, just a little, no hesitating, and suddenly-subtly your arms are lianas mobile and searching, and your kisses, unconscious at first, turn to fire and flux, and we breathe in the same words I love you baby let me come let me come let me come inside, and I tease at your lips, find you where you can't reach

Sometimes I'm lost and sometimes I'm dead, but now I live in you

* * *

Your lips part, and we cease to be two bodies and two hearts, and quiet as night, you come for me again and again

'How many times are you going to make me come?'

And you are made for me, to receive me, to come for me, to give yourself over to me, arms thrown wide, and when you ask, your breath is thundering and hoarse, and the mere idea of -making you come-, as if you didn't have to choose to, as if yours were my body to take, to make absorb these pleasures at my will

And the answer isn't a number, but instead an era in history, in geologic time

A forever

* * *

Under the eaves, it's chillcold the winter, tile floors, varnished pine, a chimney poking up through from the floor beneath, the architecture is confusing but simple: it is -our- place, and the world outside -our- stairway landing and -our- warm nest with its tangled inhabitants is the whole sphere of the whole cosmos the cosmos altogether, nevermind 'the rest of the world be damned', it's as if there were no 'rest of the world', it's as if this place of ours has its own physics, its own propagation of light its own relativity, and the further you get from our quiet place, our lullspot in the great Motor, the more reality refracts and compacts, fisheye lenses of Some Other Place not worthy of the offerings we pay each other here in the deep, the curve of space funneling up and away from this safe hollow, this hollow in the soft fabric of the darkness

The rustle of fabric frussing and the creak of a spring, cats' paws on the tile and if I count the hangtime between steps, your toes are barely making contact with the cold floor

A light in the bathroom

Medicine cabinet toothbrush whitewater

Our place, ours, our first night

Cats' paws again—quicker this time, much quicker—air sipped through clenched teeth the universal vaudeville appeal for cold-emergency (aggravated-nudity), and the covers spinnaker wide and there you are again, wrapped all 'round me, arms and legs, your face buried in my neck, your toes a searching force moling warm burrows between my feet

* * *

It is before daylight and it must be snowing outside, tomorrow diffuses through the snow and transmits from sunlightdayside over to us, the pale blue of a morning snowfall in our windows, the day still waiting for someone to whisper the password

Somehow it feels simultaneously warm and cold in the room, the warmth in my body more robust than ordinary, supplemented by your own, you don't even notice when I slip from your arms

Coffee volatiles, it's a few hours before you get up (at least you've got some semblance of a normal sleep cycle, I'm busy raising the debt ceiling on a sleep account I'll never pay back) but I can make a new pot on the old grounds if this batch is any good, rely on continuity to work its alchemy for your first cup at the break of day three hours from now

And the kingly blanket you brought just for me from your old place is downy on my shoulders, that old couch in the half-light, nine one four seven three six nine one four seven three six nine, fourteen lines twelve syllables two quatrains two tercets one for me one for you

Mais le sentier des justes, voie resplendissante,
 Rayons célestes illuminant d'ivoire :
 L'aube naissante sur la longueur de la Loire
 Reflets joyeux dansant sur ces rives distantes

Souviens-toi quand des Normands les flottes errantes
 Trouvèrent ce large port, quand de l'armée noire
 Le chevalier vint et vit et conquit... L'histoire
 Des grands, c'est vrai, se récite toujours à Nantes

O César, qui tant aimas la sévérité
 Des Namnètes ! ô Henri, qui fus de leur nombre !
 O Louis qui en redoutas la témérité !

Qui suis-je enfin dans l'histoire de cette cité ?
 Je suis un rien, m'enfuyant entre les décombres
 Du château de ces grands ; je n'étais que leur ombre

But the path of the just is as the shining light
 The shining path of the Loire at the break of day
 Dawn rising all along the river's length to play
 All along those distant banks' this joyful sight

I still remember when Norse men's dark ships would stray
 Into this wide port, and when at these shores the knight
 Came and conquered, came and marvelled... They still recite
 Stories of great men at home among the Nantais

O Cæsar, you who so loved the severity
 Of the Namnetes! O Henry, you who did endow
 Them! O Louis, who dreaded their temerity!

Who am I, then, in the hist'ry of this city?
 I am a nothing, the ruins of the chateau
 Of great men; I flee as if I were their shadow

It started, at first, as the faintest glimmer of golden light in the deepest midnight.

Temperance, despite herself, blinked awake wide eyes, her features porcelain-white by light of day, but overnight the lights of the city fell as crazyquilt dabs and dapples through the great windows, holy gold red, holy copper blue, holy honey amber tribal paints of otherworldly light, as if in a dream as if in the manmade handmade Heavens of Chartres or the Sainte Chapelle, as if in the picassan underworld of Chauvet, of Lascaux, the Luxors of these lower realms.

Temperance had demurred here for her whole life, for the lifetimes of many, for generations even, that confident air of a young woman in the flower of her days—unawares of her station in this plane, unawares of her posture holding court in these dark halls with its phantasmagory of sacred colors thrown in fantastic geometries over the sacred shapes of this new Jerusalem (for what is God if not length, breadth, depth and height?), unawares even of her own cosmic beauty—for it was no accident that she be beautiful and serene in her way and day, for Temperance cannot be otherwise, and men of both base birth and kingly genre loved her, desired her, found her gorgeous and perfect enough as to be unattainable except through holy inspiration or special revelation, through gift of Grace or noble birth, divine and inscrutable and timeless.

But some colors are more dangerous than others, cannot possibly be confused with the sacred, cannot mix and mingle with it on any palette. And thus it is with blackness. And with fire.

For tonight, Temperance, her eye forever vigilant, her countenance forever serene, was painted with a new light of a frighteningly novel wavelength, and learned to her horror that the cathedral had caught fire, and would burn with all-consuming flame, and: with her inside.

* * *

Vicus sat in a high room, a modern room, would otherwise be as profane a room as they get if not for some *je ne sais quoi* encrypted along the broadcasting wavelength with the quiet words passing back and forth—such uncommon words, such terrible knowing, such arch intimacy.

For this woman is seeking my thoughts, seeing my thoughts, thank God there are laws about patients and doctors

He shifted in his chair. For all its strange lines, that chair was oddly comfortable, and by shifting, he sank down further into it—classical Kepler told you that you traded altitude for velocity and vice-versa, but this boxy little chair with the permasoft cushions seemed defiant of Kepler's ellipses.

Just answer her questions, no drama here, no drama necessary, no anvil-beaten rivet-riven scripts of How This Will Play Out, *just answer a few questions kissmyhand*

His head hurt, hurt like mad, hurt the weight of *frontalis* lifetimes, clusterheadache seismes tremor-graph ground-displacement radial rainbow weatherunderground maps of silent-as-thought P-waves and roaring pounding S-waves, there's no hope and no redemption if you see *that* thing heading your way. Hurt like he had been squinting through lenses of the wrong prescription for hours and hours, for years and years. He squirmed for the headache that *would be,* and the odd little chair squeaked leather and took him in a bit deeper.

Notch it down, Vicus, this is just a stranger with nothing to lose and nothing to gain, back it down a few notches Vicus, talk yourself down, take it down, empty your thoughts of it all

But his heart is there, too: the ache of peering through the wrong prescription, the wrong prescription by far. Altitude for speed, he's getting that g-load sweat again, trade potential energy for kinetic, kinetic energy for potential, classical orbital mechanics, altitude-for-speed, *Gotta unthink that, you louse*

'Do you ever experience anxiety when somebody, say, *sits between you and the door?* You know, blocks you in, boxes you in?'

Vicus' mind reeled instantly, was already spinning-up before *you and the door,* spun through a nauseating hammerhead Himmelman death spiral, an inevitable negative-*g* airshow auger-in, Preacherman and his thundering bullfrog throat helleringbellering *Christs* to wake the dead and jolt the neighbors and terrorize the kids and defile the very name of the One Redeemer, Preacherman planted squarely, directly between Vicus and the door, there's gotta be an unnamed, hypervigilant circle of Hell reserved for those who profane the eternal *Logos* of scripture and prophecy, but Vicus is already long-gone, tumblereentry, Sundari must really get off on watching me squirm watching me arc in, controls lock-to-lock, a real weapons-grade Hate Hard-On watching me get trapped by this thundering man yelling his moral disgust at me in the tranquil syllables of Holy Writ. No redemption offered. No redemption. Instead: altitude-for-speed-altitude-for-speed-altitude-for-speed...

Just a deep soft chair, just a quiet voice

'Sometimes.'

Damn

'Um. Yes.'

Gotta unrehearse that

'Very much yes.'

* * *

Temperance hasn't really gotten used to the idea of an empty cathedral yet—there's something entirely wrong with such a building's failure to be self-luminous—and she steels her eye, lest she betray her doubts with a glance. But used to be, ever since the roof went up over the choir, that there was a regular train of *Nantais* coming in to light the place, to animate it with voices and the shuffle of their feet, the hoarse gruss of their singing breath rising as prayers, as human incense, as Divine Respiration, and Temperance remembers the long-ago epoch when she could know the time of day by the incipit of an antiphon, the day of the week by the hush of voicebreath—when wine and wafer rose up, drawing all men to, just so—the week of the year by the vestments and paraments, by which guild organized which Masses and which

Tributes to which Saints in which chapel—St. Eloi, celebrated by the Goldsmiths on December first, St Clair of Nantes, patron of carpenters (for he carried the nail that crucified Peter), St Félix on May 30 (who made it tradition to bury bones of holy men beneath altars), St Gohard, patron of captives and locksmiths, martyred on the twenty-fourth of June 843—and she smiles inwardly, knowing that this whole place, a rising height of light and tuffa, was a great gnomon, a forever-clock of fantastic dimensions in space and time...

She felt that serenity again, that serenity bestowed upon her by her very name, knowing that she stood grasping a mystical clock with no hands—a clock's mysterious mechanism utterly obviated by her own eternal internal temperance.

But somewhere through the years, the men with their immensurate song ceased coming to this place at those odd hours, ceased lighting it with their tapers and censors and *sequenzæ* and low uttered prayers that spun up into the heavens on motes of meaning, leaves spiraling away from the earth for higher, brighter climes on rarefied columns of Breath and Word. The wheelwrights all said *e pluribus unum,* but prayers are like that, songs are like that... you can say anything you like, sing about anything you like, it doesn't make it real until it is Real.

And just as the Word left the place—in truth, it was not so much that the Word *scattered* (as mice swirling away from a sinking ship), but simply *failed to return one day*—so did the Light, and gone were the days when it was less a constellation of votive flames borne about the great edifice by a crowd of holy men than the other way around.

* * *

The same voiceless, lightless indifference had taken hold of other such spaces—and of this very building, too, in grey days with the world gripped by spasm—and as always happens when frames are left void of their pictures, paroxysms and cataclysms followed. Notre Dame (the center of Paris, the center of France, the center of the Universe) had been left empty by the convulsions of revolution, and the frame, deconsecrated by the mob, *reconsecrated* (to cap off even greater, bitterer irony) to the faceless Goddess of Reason, nearly succumbed to equally faceless agitators worshipping Her, piling the altar high with chairs and debris to light their pyre with.

And Temperance herself remembers when jackbooted Vandal mobs put the *Nantais* to the blade and swept Nantes of her treasures; she recalls it vivid as yesterday, vivid as last night's nightmare that scared her awake. And then, only quick-thinking masons and stonecutters, with their longhandled saws tilting and hissing through the dust of marble tombs by night, saved the city her last and highest riches; sharp-eyed watchmen would oversee men cutting new tombs into the rich black soil of the *jardin des plantes*, and somber processions—new funerals for old Virtues, processions voiceless and lightless in the dark alchemy of the ultimate clandestine act of divine vandalism—emptied the great arching Frame of her last portraits, planted them deep, deep, deep, and then planted fragrant lilies to mark the new grave a memorial for later, more virtuous generations.

* * *

'Are you a danger to yourself?'

'Yes.'

'Is there *intent?*'

'Yes.'

'What would you do?'

What -wouldn't- I do?

* * *

But then again, when the Devil makes work for idle hands, not even Dame Reason can save you.

* * *

To be true, the fire was in the charpentwork, a hundred-fifty feet up off the pavers, and first instinct would have Temperance and the other ladies fleeing the building by now, but in the heat of the moment their feet were made of stone, and with the fire spreading so rapidly, any attempt at escape would've been suicide: the roof peeling away from the vaults in fiery sails and plunging past the wide windows, fire from Heaven, to crush and incinerate any soul intrepid enough to turn and make a break. Temperance froze in place, a statue, a pillar of salt, as the Fire came to destroy the forsaken City.

Temperance's silhouette, still gracious in the fantastic colors of the End Of Days, a dark shade, *I fade away into night*

For Height and Light are one thing, but Height and Darkness are something else entirely.

Because a sacred building, aching to be self-luminous, will one day—like it or not—accomplish the feat on its own. For empty frames must create their own acts of sacred defiance, must bring about their own manner of cataclysm.

* * *

And the night his older daughter insisted, six years all earnest, that Vicus tell her a story about kings and queens, that one was a poison apple. He hemmed and hawed as both daughters clambered into bed: he is no romantic, far from it, just lots of stories—*they pay him to go on and on you know*—and his memory is fickle and he couldn't think up anything for the life of him, just The Real Thing, just real kings and queens, and none of those stories ever worked out very well, nothing but trouble nothing but haymakers and backstabbers, or folk brought down by haymakers and backstabbers, cliological trainwrecks one and all.

Okay, think quick: think up anybody you admire who wore crowns

This was harder than it looked. Henry Four was the Good King Henry Four, and his story flashed to mind, it is true. They had called him the Boar, and if the portraits did him any justice, he was exactly that: a loose cannon, a free radical. The story starts with the three sons Medici, all *Four F*s, all base metals, nothing but orphaned pathologies in taffeta, and when each one fails to produce an heir in their turn, you have a choice to make, and the Salic Laws hang you out high and dry: they select in robotic inflexibility Henry of

Navarro, hardly French that one, hardly even human, much more a substandard, a Beastman, a critter at best.

And he was a heretic Protestant.

He was the one who got assassinated wasn't he?

And for one time in his life, Vicus put the brakes on.

'Um, that might be for a different night. I forgot the ending.'

But that wasn't good enough for his girls, who had been given the bulk of a story and wanted a *whole one*, an *integer story*. And they are tiny in the giant bed, and he loves them more than his own life, and he searches his mind for *somethinganything*, and he remembers something about the Ninth Louis, the Saintly one...

'There was once a king who was kind and generous,' he began again on a renewed *élan*, 'and whenever he had dinner, he would invite fourscore of the poorest and lowest of his kingdom to eat *first*, and only after he had served *them* and after they had eaten *their* fill, would he have his meal...'

And the light is on under the girls' pink shade, and the room is pale peach, the last rays of day from an Edison bulb.

'...and then in Tunis... *Um*.'

'What's Tunis?'

'It is a city in North Africa.'

'What was he doing there? Wasn't he French?'

'He was. He was in Tunis on crusade.'

Quizzical eyes in the peach light.

'I'll have to tell you about crusades on another night.'

'So what happened in Tunis?'

'Well,' Vicus hated himself, 'that was where the good king died.'

Long pause.

'What happened? Was he killed in a battle?'

'Um, no. He caught a disease there and died.'

'Which disease?'

'Um,' *he's in over his head, plunges forward, tripping headlong over his tentative steps,* 'the plague.'

'I've heard of the plague,' says his older daughter. Of course she has. 'It was spread by rats,' she says, helpfully, to her little sister. 'What did they do with him then?'

It was about this point in the story that—as he had successfully done with Henry Number Four—he should've closed the book of his mind and shelved that memory until much later. But he is off on a story and it is a barn-burner and he is loathe to leave it off there... And besides, his daughter *is* his daughter, and knows what the plague is, and it is deep night, and the light should be off by now, but both girls are rapt, sitting on top of the covers, Indian-style.

'I mean,' his older girl continues, 'how'd they get him back to France?'

'*Um.*'

The older child turns her wide eyes to her wide-eyed sister again, and explains matter-of-factly that the plague is contagious as can be, you'd have to be a fool to touch the body of a man who had just died of plague, thanks so much Sweetie you're not making this any easier.

'So did they just bury him in Tunis?'

'No. You can't bury the Defender of the Faith in infidel territory.' When he says this, the girls turn to each other again; before they can ask, Vicus heads the inevitable off: 'Infidel means Not Christian.'

'So did they put him in a ship and carry him back?' Vicus' younger daughter is in on this now, too.

'Silly,' says his elder child, 'Daddy just *told* you he died of plague. You don't want to touch him after that.'

But the question is alive in the room, and his elder daughter pursues.

'Did they burn him?'

Good God

'No, Honey, you don't burn the King of France. And besides, Christians back then wanted to be sure to have a body that could be resurrected by Christ later on.'

He had hoped that might be enough. In a Normal Universe, resurrection of the flesh *et cetera* ought be a good enough punchline.

'*But*,' his younger daughter, wide eyes, 'if you can't burn him, and you can't bury him *there*...?'

Vicus is naïve, he is stupid, he is a wretch, and he knows it: he is in the deep of the trap, and has framed himself for the crime.

When (you fool) will you just cut your own throat, rather than drag your daughters down into your marsh marl mire with you?

'They boiled him.'

Both daughters' eyes wide open. Both little jaws wide open.

Sundari is in the doorframe, lightlessness incarnate, blocking him in.

Well of -course- she is

Dark as a starling, ready to fly terror circles 'round Vicus, fussing and flapping for the next twelve hours, *This is what Trouble looks like,* such buoyancy and archness and glee as she sets her teeth, the muscles of her jaw.

He'll be sleeping in the living room for a year for this one, if he makes it out of the room alive, that is.

If I survive the night, I can at least smile—inwardly of course!—at having told one Hell of a good bedtime story just now

* * *

The roof is flying away, murders of crows chaotic tourbillions into the night. The windows glow a brimstone light, midnight dawn thermite flight, *the cathedral is burning down around me* and Temperance remembers the stinging wideopen eyes lachrymogenic smoke and the heat the heat the heat when the Northmen came calling The Year Eight Hundred Forty-Three Of Our Lord *this is what trouble looks like*, and the old cathedral was to Felix, the irony of... *felixity* when the place is peeling apart around you, a Caroline building mostly of wood mostly of tinder mostly of fuel a funeral pyre aching for a Viking torch to light it, *and we Nantais are within, all six hundred of us, men women children all Nantais, a distant memory*

But tonight, the building is a complexity of fuels and stone, all united fickly with mortar—*mortar* for Christ's sake!—cement alchemy built from (of all things) burnt lime, burnt *septaria* lime, burn it good and hot, chase out all the hydrates, leave behind the quicklime of old Roman days, mix that crazyreactive Stuff with sand and water, *rehydrate* that which was anhydrous, it turns back to limestone on you. Temperance, her bright face dappled in the rising lights of Hell encroaching from above, from all 'round, a glimmer of grim irony the taste of blood on her tongue and rising sickening in her pharynx:

A Light to Light the Gentiles

And that mortar, once burnt, once cooked back up a thousand degrees, two thousand degrees, three thousand degrees, ceases to be mortar and returns to quicklime, and quicklime, once burnt, turns to brimstone, and brimstone—dripping molten as fiery rain, dripping down upon the stones all 'round Temperance—is wholly unable to hold this mighty ordered assemblage of light and stone and chant and Word upright.

* * *

And Preacherman thundered, and bullfrogged, and took the name of Christ in ways Vicus could not understand to be reverent, *But who am I to bear it* Vicus protested, and the thundering continued, *Christ Christ Christ!*, and then Preacherman roared 'You think -you- have it hard, she's-abusive-blah-blah-blah, how do you think -I've- had it?' and Vicus has never heard a preacher talk like this, *his suffering is great, too, so mine is laughable* and is made to be dispelled by exorcist's repetitions, by loud cracks of books snapping shut and thrown flatsmacking to the floor in the dead sonorous chambers of Friday Tenebræ, the terrible sound of the Lord *Christ Christ Christ* entering the dark empty framework of the deep to announce salvation *Christ Christ Christ* to the damned, much less *salvation* proclaimed than *further cursing the already-damned*, there is no mercy there is no mercy *Christ Christ Christ* not here not tonight.

And it is true, Preacherman, you've had it hard, and true, children are stillborn and times are hard and wives are harder yet, and never ye mind how *we*, yes *we* had come together to support *you* in *your* day of tears, and *your* day, when we came to prop your empty frame up, was a day of trust and quiet tears and that was the day *we* had carried you, carried *to* you, carried *you*... '*You know*,' I remember telling you when you were at your own lowest, '*we are not really here are we?*' with a glimmer in my eye, '*we are borne away into realms of higher thought, realms of memory sweet and memory bitter, whole castles of memory, whole trajectories of memory away from here, arcing away in pure mathematical arcs pure accelerator geometries blossoming subatoms,*' thinking we had an Understanding: our thoughts flown far away from the cold hard brutal winters of This Place and This Time, whole itineraries of the soul's flight toward places unknown, the ammonitic peaks of mind and memory, where all is blue and white and crystalline and sapphiric and rarefied.

But did you, Preacher, come to my aid? Did you once offer to take the kids so I and Sundari could work on it, work at it, work it out? Did you offer a couch to sleep on, *amealjustameal* to keep me sustained when I was so sick at heart the pain referred down to my guts and spleen and liver and I couldn't hold a glass of milk in me without retching, a fist of peanuts a Saltine a crust of bread?

Brimstone and flame

'These things you keep saying, Vicus...'

Preacherman is determined to hang him if it kills him.

'...It's all kind of hard to believe: *Sundari is so meek and gentle.*'

* * *

Temperance knows she is not alone, and the storm roils over her head, and above her cohort's heads, too. But where Temperance anguishes, Wisdom is serene, silhouetted by the cathedral burning down around her. And while Temperance agonies, Justice is composed. And while Temperance is torn asunder, sawn in two, Strength is peacefully leonine. Flame reflects in the dull marble of Wisdom's curved mirrormirror, flame dances in the marble eye of the salamander that Strength tears from its old lair, flame reflects off of the sword held—mystic talisman—by Justice.

Only Temperance has no sigel, no tool, no shield, to reflect the terrifying wavelength away from her, and as the mortar turns back to salt, to talc over her head, Temperance can only *reflect*.

Her last thought before the fire takes it all, so very fitting for her name and station and peculiar virtue:

O Lord, let Thy servant depart in peace

* * *

And so I take it all and swallow it a bit deeper, and crunch it down crush it down, exclamations bent into questions, and if I do this many more times, my mind will break my heart or vice versa, and I'll even disbelieve it all myself, just look at how I already hunch down over my heart to protect it, to crush it and squeeze it and compress it, till the hydraulics no longer bathe my cells over, till the pneumatics of my lungs' and my heart's concavities cease their secret diplomacies, their dark chemical commerces with the greater world, and I will be a failed state before long—a collapse into ruin, a promise of civil war—if you disbelieve these thing even just once more, Pastor. *Once more.*

'*Who are -you- to bear it?* Who are you to complain, *Vicus?* At least you *have* an attentive wife. At least you *have* offspring. But when you've dealt with *real* loss, as *-I- have...*'

* * *

All the *Nantais* watched the cathedral burn down around her for three days, watched wordless from bridges and rooftops, from overpasses and from open spaces like Talensac and the Cours St. Pierre, the Parc du Procé, from the walls of the Château.

All Nantes knew gentle Temperance was caught in the horror, could only imagine the contrary Hells of light and dark, of black and white, cascading around her.

And some even recalled the somber day just a generation earlier, when, with the cathedral bells still ringing the Armistice to yet another war to end all wars, the *Nantais*, picks and shovels and crosses and tapers, came to the *jardin des plantes* to resurrect Temperance and her cohort, to reinstall them at the tomb where they had begun; the older told these tales to the younger, and then recounted their memories of the dark day in the same war, when on a Saturday morning the children were gathered in a Nantais theater and the bombs began to fall on them, and how in Eight Hundred and Forty Three, when the Vikings came...

As if all these stories, these multicolored threads, could've somehow happened in the span of one lifetime, could somehow be told in the pages of a single book.

And the young listened, riveted, pillars of salt. 'Never again, never again, we must redeem ourselves by filling that empty frame again: with light, with Word, with breath, with music.'

And all they could do was hope that the cherubs still adjusting the pillows cradling the head of the Duke and Duchess of Brittany at their tomb

-Passacaglia- 483

would also cradle the head and heart of their dear fallen Temperance...

* * *

And when the doors were finally pried open against their warping hinges, and the cathedral spoke again—in low, creaking, sussing tones that echoed through the jumbled stones and high vaults—speaking again to the *Nantais,* telling them of the pride of years past, the glorious noble act of fixing doors to the building... begging the *Nantais* to fill that space.

> *Sixt pape quart leglise gouvernoit*
> *L'an mil cinq cens mis hors dix et neuf ans*
> *Francois second de ce nom duc regnoit*
> *Pierre prelat unique de ceans*
> *Quant fumes unis aux portes bien ceans*
> *Pour decorer ce portal et chief deuvre*
> *Comme pourront congnoistre les passans*
> *Car richement par nous le ferme et euvre*
>
> *The Church governed by the fourth Pope Sixtus*
> *In Fifteen Hundred (less a nineteenth year)*
> *Francis the Second reigning over us*
> *And Pierre, our one and only overseer*
> *When we words were wed to these fine doors here*
> *(Decorating this portal without peer)*
> *Suchwise that each passerby by them knows*
> *So richly by us they open and close*

And when those doors creaked open on their twisting pot-iron hinges, they found the lovely girl within with the rich fabric cowl, the poor girl, dusty and sooted, eyes frozen open forever.

It may take another generation, another two generations, another century, but we will fill this building again

For we must

It's been a long love affair with Temperance.

* * *

'Just another idle threat. Obviously you'll never leave her, obviously never follow through.'

'But what of the children? Obviously you haven't given a thought to the children.'

'Obviously you're suffering from mental illness. If only you were thinking straight.'

'Obviously you've forgotten your vow before God. Forgotten God entirely.'

'Obviously you have an anger-management problem.'

'Obviously you know you're jeopardizing your place in the congregation if you leave. You've jeopardized it already. What place do you have among us Lutherans? What place have you among *us*? You've become something else entirely, something outside our fold, something we can't even recognize. *Obviously.*'

And the sash windows fit in their frames a bit too loosely, and on cue (as if responding to tremors real or imagined), one of them skids open a half inch from above and below, sneaks down just a fingersbreadth, just space enough for my soul to fly through.

* * *

He had reset all his passwords to *NantesInFourMonths*, then to *NantesInThreeMonths*, and *NantesInTwoMonths*, bragged he wouldn't know a good hotel from a rathole in the city, had never been a tourist only a resident, but knew where to find the best watering holes, *crêpes champêtres*, in which neighborhood to best raise a child or find the best Breton music.

'What'll you do there?'

'Stride around.'

Around meant long strides 'round the Erdre, long strides down Félibien, long strides through Cambronne Park, but really: irregular circles of varying radius around the one and only Center of the *Nantais'* city.

He hadn't seen the Cathedral in twenty years.

He had seen her from the airplane, had thought what he was seeing was a vast cream-colored tarp covering the ever-present scaffolding that had always obscured her; he had always guessed that this was The Shape of the old stones *in decadencia:* with twentieth-century metal platforms drilled into her face horror-movie surgical steel old tarpaulin standards dangling freesheet, unconditional surrenders for the decades of his memory.

Feet on ground, there will be winter weeks when it rains unceasingly, and umbrellas would be blocking the sky in its entirety, portative proxy night skies making continuous weather forever predictable *Forecast: darkness. When: all day and all night. Where: outside.*

But today, the front has finally pushed through, and the troposphere has that scrubbed-and-freshly-ionized tang to it, willow leaves in the gutters sweet aspirin for your ills, and Vicus strides through the Motte Rouge overunder bridges, cobblecombles, all 'long the Erdre, riverboats houseboats that old architect living in the redbarnriverboat, the range of vessels from shed to greenhouse to motorlaunch to Nautilus palace. That *souterrain* is under the Cours St Pierre, but the *parterre* above is pea-pebble, there are already the truants flying kites here, old men in *pétanque* grudgematches running now for a half-century-plus, mothers-children-strollers, a banquet bag of breads a baguette bouquet, and then this tall guy *stridingstriding* through, all loose-cannon *force-qui-va,* toward where all roads lead eventually anyway.

He had armchair-philosophized for decades on the problem of what Art is, what it *was,* and had often in his hubris lit upon the idea of *substantialization* or *etherealization,* ideas based on the near-physical *mass* of substanceless music *oh, but have you heard how -heavy- that fugue is!* and the physical *substance* of paintings, the *riche étoffe* of Clouet's taffeta-clad François Premier, the *weight of Authority* in Shakespeare, the *weight of History* in *The Gallic Wars*... but then again just how *light* some supermassive things become, too (just look at the dome of the Panthéon in Paris—seventeen-thousand *tons* of masonry held up overhead—smart men would sprint pellmell for the doors and never look back if they only knew what catastrophe of potential energy floated over them)... The one function of Art, then, is to generate *distance* and *tension* between the measurable weight of a work's *medium* and the perceived mass of its *content*.

And this morning, in the hyperrealist light of a new high-pressure airmass, the buttresses of the *Nantais'* cathedral were flying filigreed indeed, and the grand Art's presence rose into the heavens, *it would be wrong of me just to -sidle up- to this holy place in this holy new light, the spires of ancient Jerusalem piercing space itself* and so he detours around toward the Prefecture and spirals in from the northwest, a gust front of purpose arcing-in, a strategic move, that one.

He turns, looks uphill from the foot of *Rue du Roi Albert*, and sees the cathedral as it really stands.

No tarps, no scaffolding, only creamy whitewelded tuff breccia, rising to insane and lovely heights

They say they spent a quarter-*billion* remaking this cathedral into its original image.

For a spaceship, for a time machine, for a salvation engine? Hell of a bargain

Oh holy light, oh cool blue rays of Paradise, here—yes, *here*—is what mankind is meant to see the last instants of their term on Earth, *I will one day compare thee with the rays of Heaven itself* how did they get the stone this white? *and I doubt Heaven will compare favorably*

-Passacaglia-

But doubt is the least fraction of his mind right now, for his whole being—intellect, vision, memory, awe—belongs here in this place. Not 'far away', not flying arcs through faeried Great Circles roundaway from his little existence in his little ruined home. But here... but Here. *Here.*

There is the organist, *there* he is; they had told Vicus he might find him here, Here, he is in the church in its constructed stones and in the vaults of its hierarchy, the Abbot Niel, *Monseigneur,* and they had said if you make it in, make it past the awe of the New Church the Old Church in its creamy whitewelded tuff breccia—'we'd be amazed if you didn't just fall down on your knees in lifelong ecstasy just seeing our NewOld cathedral, *our* NewOld cathedral'—and see the Abbot there, make sure to find him and talk with him, he's got the keys to the organ, he holds the keys to the kingdom, have him show you around, he'll be happy to.

And so Vicus did not fail to remember to bring a little sheaf of old used musics in his hand of his pen, just little things he had jotted out on his little couch—what *used to be* his little couch—way back on other continents in other times. Folded fourwise, little copierpaper *in-octavos* kept warm in his back pocket, *passportcreditcardmotets,* and he introduces himself.

The old man's hearing isn't good enough to detect Vicus's accent, or if it is, he is too polite or too charitable to point it out, because that might make Vicus an Outsider, and this place is built is conceived of is dreamed of to *be filled,* to exclude *nothing and no one.*

The two men talk for a long time, music and travel and history and the cathedral *and and and and,* and their words echo under the vast vaults.

Finally: 'I've brought some music I wrote.'

The Abbot: 'I was hoping you'd say that.'

'I thought that maybe I could ask you to register it in the archives of the cathedral,' with what relief to say what came next, it nearly shouted itself from the depths of his lungs, his diaphragm, his very kidneys heart of hearts, 'that way it will outlive me, live to long generations...'

The Abbot's forehead even more deeply-lined than before. 'Let's see what we have here.' And the Abbot peers over his half-moon spectacles; the fourfolded sheaves blossom white in his hands, and Vicus' mind is scrawled out in the blooms' petals. The Abbot's eyebrow rises, nearly imperceptibly. 'Hmm. ...*Yes.*' He is looking more assured now, as if he has examined a catechumen and found him worthy. 'Should we take a listen?'

'What?'

'Should we take a listen, see what it sounds like?'

'*Here?*'

'Is there any better place?' The Abbot winks conspiratorially. 'This old frame has been empty too long; it's time to fill it with something lovely.'

It takes a few moments to unbend the crushed pages—and keep them unbent—and then there is music: the Abbot's fingers, Vicus' scrawlings, the cathedral's memories. Drawn from the breath of the building: music and words and breath, and together, they make the cathedral alive, and fill the vaults to billowing.

There is a hymn, *O Savior of Our Fallen Race*, with its tumbling successions of suspensions and releases, so quiet and natural, Schenkerian simplicity, a melody rising and falling, the shape of the first four scale degrees, now the first five, then the whole octave. The building thrums with Vicus' sounds, the old organ a wooden windwonder.

There is a motet, *But This Is The Covenant [I Will Make With The House Of Israel]*, three separate utterances, a wandering errant fugue, the Menippean conceit of a long slow canon on the words 'I will put my Law in their minds and write it in their hearts', where canon is *inscribed* rather than *composed*, and 'canon' is Latin for 'law' anyway, and so here in the center *volet* of the triptyph, there is law written within... And then a final, broad-gestured fugue on the same subject as the opening, A_1-B-A_2...

There is a long, breezy *Ricercar* on the old Latin hymn, *Conditor Alme Siderum*, which fills the Cathedral of Saints Peter and Paul in Nantes, France,

-Passacaglia-

fills her all the way to the mortar, 'Mmm, this sounds kind of... *Lutheran*, doesn't it?' ...all into the marrow, into the microscopic voidspaces within the tuffmasonry, fills the vaults like wind in a spinnaker.

Fills longlovely Temperance—yes, warmliving Temperance, sentient, alert... *redeemed*—ears eyes mind memory heart.

Qu'on égorge dès lors aux portails de Notre Dame
   Tous les loups qui rôdent dans cette vieille ville
   Que l'on déniche de tous les coins de cette île
   Tout truand, tout bandit, qu'on mettra à la lame

Qu'on surveille les points cardinaux pour les futiles
   Barrières érigées des chevriers, mette flamme
   A tout ce qui affronte le vouloir ; que l'œil blâme
   —Comme injure—même la vermin' la plus vile

Purgeons mon esprit de toute pensée qui nuit
   A ma mission finale, à ma mission divine
   Brûlons et reflet et réflexion cette nuit

Soit mon derrain geste une victoir' fine
   Soit pour mon champ de bataille une vide terre
   Qu'il ne reste plus que le miroir à défaire

May they put to the sword at the cathedral church
   Those dire wolves left alone to haunt this ancient town
   May they take the Isle apart, turn o'er ev'ry stone
   Cut the throat of bandits and truants in their search

May they survey horizons for even rundown
   Cowpaths and shepherd gates before us, and then torch
   Them as affronts to our will; the fiery eye scorch
   The earth, to the last rat—all insults to our crown

May I purge my mind of all noise, all idle thought
   Besides that final mission, that mission divine
   May the mirror enlighten me, but reflect naught

Will my last effort be a vict'ry proud and fine?
   What will be, barren Battlefield, my final feat
   When the mirror is all I have left to defeat?

* * *

Philippe Auguste, King of France, hadn't seen his own face in a decade. He'd had a mirror made way back in his youth—or maybe his father had had it made for him, in some sort of vanity instinct, making the boy see his father's face every time he looked at himself—but either the mirror was deformed or his father was, and he found it easier to use the damned thing as a roughly smooth surface he could lay out on a table among his generals and draw troop formations on, wax chess pieces on a map of his own features, rub them out with his elbow, redraw them, Xs and Os measling him over. Far from serving a king's Vanity, the mirror was a graying silvered battlefield where Philippe Auguste's wine glass served as The Enemy Fortress, and day by day the goblet skated 'round the mirror like a planchette, scrying messages of hatred and ambition and nobility all mingled together in one tall draught. And as each castle fell, the draught was Philippe Auguste's private communion with the newly dead, and the Xs and Os shifted again, and he poured himself a new draught, and saw his face and essence shift anew.

For how do I see myself anymore? Look through the greasepencil maps of my conquests

His mirror was dark as smoke, dark as guilt, and when he did look, at best he could only see smudges in place of his features—irregular and curious, eager and suspicious all at once—but what was the real color of his eyes, the real arch of his brows? Here in the dark glass in the darkened tent, with the Battle of Château Gaillard drawn chaotically throughupon and the tall vintage of Château Gaillard red as blood, he honestly had no idea anymore.

The problem with mirrors—so say the mystics and heretics and sorcerers—is that they always tell the truth

But generals have their divisions, and priests their holy water to bless the troops, each one a cog in the phenomenal machine of Philippe Auguste's statecraft, so who was to say that the scryer had no place in the winning of war? His thoughts wander off to verses Sybilline and stern and bellicose and lovely:

Diane estant en l'espesseur d'un bois,
  Après avoir mainte beste assenee,
  Prenoit le frais, de Nynfes couronnee :
  J'allois resvant comme fay maintefois,

Sans y penser : quand j'ouy une vois
  Qui m'apela, disant, Nynfe estonnee,
  Que ne t'es-tu vers Diane tournee ?
  Et me voyant sans arc et sans carquois,

Qu'as-tu trouvé, o compagne, en ta voye,
  Qui de ton arc et flesches ait fait proye ?
  - Je m'animay, respons je - à un passant,

Et lui getay en vain toutes mes flesches
  Et l'arc apres : mais lui les ramassant
  Et les tirant me fit cent et cent bresches

* * *

Diana the Huntress in the depths of the wood
  Having strewn all Nature's beasts into disarray
  Her Nymphs shined her crown while she rested from the fray
  I went along, dreaming dreams as I often would

Thoughtlessly: when at once I darkly understood
  A voice calling to me, 'o Nymph, lost on her way,
  Haven't you Diana to honor and obey?'
  And seeing me where I (no bow or quiver) stood

'What, oh what, my friend, have you been stalking all day?
  What to your bow and these arrows has fallen prey?'
  -I fired, said I, at one passing at a gallop,

All my arrows flew, and then my bow, too, races
  After him; but then he, gathering them back up
  Fired, leaving me bleeding in a thousand places

The mirror of his memory was still sharp, yes it was, even with the fracas of warfare all 'round him, and the verses came back to him as from a future memory.

> *And mirrors, in the end, always divine true, and, in the end, always win*

His curiosity piqued, his soul vaguely irritated by the strange countryside battlefield topography his father had left him in his bones, troubled waters of witches' words and darkened mirror messages in his heart, the shifting frowns lent him by the old man's glaziers, he seized the mirror (only two handfuls of glass heavy with silver—a pieplate capture of distortions and ripples) and pushed through the tent door with it in hand.

* * *

The ruby refractions of sunset were blinding. A division of men an urchin of pikes and poleaxes trooped past, the spark and spin of the factory grinding the bends and chips out of swords and axes, a hundred horses chuffing and restless. A half-dozen trebuchets leaned into their throws—Philippe Auguste could see the entire catalogue of projectiles sailing in lovely curves toward (and over) the walls: giant limestone balls big as the Moon (heading for the rich mason's handiwork of Gaillard's bridge), miraculous conconctions of oil, brimstone and saltpeter in tough little castiron caudrons being lined up to be shot at the main gate, burn the bastard woodworker's oaken door to light and chaff.

One last trebuchet—the last one in the formation, set a little bit to the side—was manned by worry-eyed men with scarves wrapped 'round over their mouth and nose. A half-dozen corpses—wearing English colors—rotted next to the machine; Philippe's men were hurriedly bundling one into the last trebuchet's sling. When the slumping cadaver's arms and legs dangled gothic-bastarda from the rigging (threatening to foul the free movement of the weapon), one of Philippe's men casually fetched a sledgehammer and smashed the man's legs; the Ammunition folded up neatly now into the sling, and preparations continued.

The sun kissed the west—what light over such a vivid scene!—the King advanced instinctively 'round any siege, east-south-west, keeping the sun to his back, always backlit in the eyes of the Enemy—the harder to identify and snipe? *perhaps*—but mostly so that the Enemy would see him rise and set with the sun, *How can you tell when Philippe Auguste the King of France is at war?* would associate him with the great *Faros*, would see him as the great searchlight of Capetian power *He is still breathing, that's how.*

And he scrambled to the head of the hill to better survey the scene. The sun was very near the horizon now, and the hill shaded its V onto Château Gaillard. Philippe suddenly remembered he was still carrying that deformed mirror, with the light being good up here maybe he could get a good first look at his face for once?, but then he looked down over the battle scene and—to his wondering eye—saw his own shadow at the point of the V, scaling the walls of the besieged fortress.

Forget this damned old mirror, you'll never get a better picture of yourself than that silhouette climbing the ramparts over there

He watched himself; soon, the brightest rays fled behind the horizon.

* * *

Philippe Auguste strode to the last trebuchet.

'Highness! *Cover yourself!*'

He was pleased that the quartermaster didn't even bother with a *Beggin' your pardon*—best to be effective before being polite, and since, as it turns out, they were firing Smallpox and Plague over the walls, *to Hell* with Polite—and pressed his scarf to his mouth and nose as he approached.

Fearless, he found the horror bound up in the trebuchet sling: a twisted Englishman, probably two weeks dead, tied and tortured into a ball, was ready to be fired at Gaillard and at Richard of Lions' Hearts and give the whole lot of them a touch of The Death.

Let 'em get a good look at themselves

And he lifted, bacon skin and blowfies, the poor corpse's arms, and wrapped them around the Royal Mirror, the twisted face of Richard's own soldier painted and poxed-over with X and O.

'Fire at will, Quartermaster.'

* * *

O Rome, ô empire of the great, who conquered the world—and who at times conquered herself—you who brought the beasts of the world to your own doorsteps your own circuses to make the world see your power over nature, ô how the Roman Cosmos took it all over the Chaos of the rest of the world, that abomination of a concept: 'That Which Is Not Conquered...' Yet brought to the arena in the shape of a lion, a tiger, a rhinoceros, a hydra, the Hideousness of the Not Yet Rome

Philippe Auguste's voice rang out over the square, midnight in his holy courtyard. Two wolves curled and arced, waves breaking against a jetty, an arc of foam and froth radiating from the chained beasts' fangs to the pavers.

We are far from Rome, in day and distance

And his curved blade shone in the midnight.

And yet, and yet... even Rome, once conquered by her own, gives us the Form while we provide the Matter

* * *

Philippe Auguste was no longer young. He had always lived as if he were on the cusp of his wild youth—he willingly shew his twenties, yet eschewed his thirties, found the fortieth year of his existence to be far from benign, but belittling.

The pictures the scholars drew of him in the historiated initials of their books (books pouring from the Notre Dame cathedral school in a strict, militant quadrata, books that were as much a military strike as any he could have dreamed of delivering from horseback) were simply wrong. He only occasionally found himself drawn into rare diversions where it was expected he wear the regalia due his position, and he at least knew where he could locate the *Hand of Justice* passed down from Kings of Israel to Kings of France—yes, he knew that for authority to function, he must embody *Kingliness*—but never was he found in the fawning, deprecating posture of Kings receiving the fourfold Virtues brought to kings by none other than the Holy Spirit, never was he caught unawares (as Charlemagne claimed to have been) by his election by the six great barons and the six great bishops of his lands—The Dukes of Normandy, Burgundy, Bordeaux, Flanders, Toulouse et Champagne, as well as the Archbishop of Reims, the Bishops de Laon, Beauvais, Noyon, and of Châlons-on-the-Marne (and he couldn't for the life of him remember who that last baron could've been)... But the great value in these twelve great men—*Well* he thought *eleven great men and some twelfth gentleman*—was not in that they had surprised him with election, regalia and acclaim, but in the fact that *he*, Philippe Auguste, had engineered them into the king-making machine they were, a machine grand in physical and spiritual might, but also in historical weight. He felt of the twelve Peers as his did his throne: that throne, Dagobert Two's, had no special prestance aside from that infused within it by the momentum of the ages; it was just a six-hundred year piece of woodworking—if it lent him some authority, so be it, *he wouldn't complain*—but he would rather use it to his own ends than to bend to its demands.

He realized that he hadn't sat in that throne in a short Forever, and that he didn't really feel like it right now, either.

He remembered the first time he saw his father seated in Dagobert's throne: he was used to the sight of his father, sure, that old slow-footed sure-footed ox; but that wasn't the sharpest focus in his field of vision, in his set of mind. Instead: he saw the two lions projecting from the wood armrests, and when Philippe Auguste thought of his father, all he could see was the old man trying to be The Third Lion...

(Whereas all Philippe wanted was to throw a couple leashes around those lions' necks—you want authority, it won't be built by *looking like you have it*, but by *creating it himself, by molding it with his hands, by seizing it like St Michael stripping the Old Dragon from the tower)*

And with that thought, he vowed to stand up—*the ministers would die the death*—stand up *on top* of those lions' heads, draw power not by being *like* them, but by *making himself taller... -by- them.*

But he still carried within him the juvenile grin of the trickster and the prophet—insignificant in their *mass,* but ferocious in their *efficacy*... He realized in the crawling gripping pit of his guts that still carried around within him the old topos of *the greater the man, the larger—physically—he must be,* and he still felt that those old Counts and Lords and Barons that willingly or not 'elected him' (if you could say that, *for they must elect him*—thus is their single reason for being) still needed to be bent down to his size, needed to be made to bend down—not to have them scrub the parquets, oh no, not to scrub the parquets *with,* either, not in the least (he thought with a grim smile)—but in order for him, Philippe Auguste, to climb upon their backs, and rise up like a spiral of leaves on a hot autumn day—higher toward the heavens.

* * *

The demons curled and raged, *how dare he come and harrow Hell, how dare he hold pride of place when it was we who set him into the kingly throne,* but his knife flashed—first once, then again—and both wolves fell down dead at his feet.

Blood poured from the beasts' throats as they gurgled in their deaths. Silence in the square before Notre Dame—this butchery was a ritual whose meaning could exist without an audience.

The next wolf I see in this city, I'll make a point of -not- killing it. Simply for the sake of measuring my worth over this place—for it is mine already—

Steam, hot and red iron-filled steam rose and met new snowflakes, the marrow of Heaven.

But nothing says I can't still use it to remake a myth

The hot blood melted the grisaille hoarflakes into a single pool

The ministers will fall over dead when they see me next, suckling at a she-wolf's teat

* * *

Oh yes, it was now that Richard sought—and gained for himself—a new *sacred* crowning, crowning him King of All, King *over* All and Philippe rode to Château Gaillard to deliver messages on the wind to the new King Of All King Over All.

* * *

Philippe standing on his hillside. The Apocalypse in the clouds behind him.

Bring the Apocalypse to your brother

And he began his every-evening practice of scaling the walls of Château Gaillard. He could feel the tuffa under his fingernails; he thought of unlacing his shadow's boots so his shadow's toes could grip into the stone of the west wall; he gritted his teeth into his engraved dagger: even from a quarter mile off, his shadow could slip over the ramparts and cut Richard's throat as the Englishman's jaws tore into his precious roast chicken.

Swallow -this-, brother

'Target practice, Lads,' through his seething teeth, joyful, rueful, the light changing every second on the dagger, the anti-Philippe a prism of anti-colors on Gaillard's wall.

His crossbowmen looked to him; they were nearly used to seeing their king like this: more distant than the Moon, yet more present than any one of them. Tonight they could see his eye had focused away; they followed the geometry of the light projecting from their king's gaze, the crossbow bolt of light propagating from his mind, a coherent beam of thought toward the parapets

'Kill the king on the wall' he commanded.

'Highness!' They knew the *Yes* was inherent, superfluous, redundant, quite nearly insulting to their King; recognition of his Highness was *Yes* enough.

Crossbowmen wrenched the strength from their muscles and added it to the love for their King, and twisted them both together into their bolts. Within three seconds, his shadow died a hundred deaths.

'Take your time, Lads.'

Heave me higher, Lads, or shoot me down; either way this castle is mine

His shadow crept higher and higher. Bolts flew, knives on the wing.

The king is dead, long live the king

* * *

I know it was hard for you; I know it hurt

I know it still does.

I want to do it again to you, for you, Aquitaine

You might feel—maybe a hundred or a thousand or a million times—the edge of my sword striking you... This is not so much to inflict pain as it is to make all of you entirely mine... Hard, hot steel against you're your breasts, your neck, your cheeks, your thighs, your lips... To bring myself aggressively to you. Oh, Aquitaine...

To see you entirely mine, your back arching, your breath roaring in my ear as you become mine again and again...

Eleanor, you are mine

* * *

'Take him, Boys.'

He barely needed to breathe the first consonant. Bolts flew, as if from his very will, as if from his very mind, as if from his heart of hearts.

* * *

Aquitaine: an artist with no name dabbed paint to the serene face of a stone effigy, a woman of marble, *why oh why can this tint not bring life back to this cold flesh?* and *why oh why must an empty frame always bring about cataclysm?* and *I can see you so clearly, on the horizon, but the night is rising so swiftly around us,* but the pigment is but ruddy color on a stone matrix, the shadow of a queen rising from caves of the earth, up toward the heavens.

And the marvelous way, the trick of the eye, that Eleanor's eye is but half-closed in death, and that her hands still hold open her Bible for all to see, but where is her gaze flown to? And some pretended to read the ancient Luxeuil hand illegible as the very Mind of God, the faint scrawled glosses of History, words from the tongue of the great Apostle himself to the Hebrews in their flight and in their error, the crowns of New Kings plowed under new fertile fields by the Authority of the Old Kings. And some imagined that the words could not have been better chosen if they had been selected by the King of the Franks himself,

And what shall I more say?

For the time would fail me to tell of Gedeon, and of Barak, and of Samson, and of Jephthae; of David also, and Samuel, and of the prophets: Who through faith subdued kingdoms, wrought righteousness, obtained promises, stopped the mouths of lions, Quenched the violence of fire, escaped the edge of the sword, out of weakness were made strong, waxed valiant in fight, turned to flight the armies of the foreigners. Women received their dead raised to life again: and others were tortured, not accepting deliverance; that they might obtain a better resurrection: And others had trial of cruel mockings and scourgings, yea, moreover of bonds and imprisonment: They were stoned, they were sawn asunder, were tempted, were slain with the sword: they wandered about in sheepskins and goatskins; being destitute, afflicted, tormented; (Of whom the world was not worthy:) they wandered in deserts, and in mountains, and in dens and caves of the earth

* * *

The light was failing over Château Gaillard; the dead stinging stink of fleshfumes and freshburnt oil reeked in a plane of smoke, acrid turpentine, ragged facets of stones broken and men fallen.

'Find the dead king's armor. I wish to wear it.'

They did, eventually, and they laid it out before Philippe Auguste in the trampled earth of the lonely road, the harrowed ditch beneath the wall. The soil was a mud of blood, the earth itself become man, man himself become earth.

'It is nothing but an empty frame, Sire.'

Philippe undid his own gabeson; his shirt was gore and sweat. As always, once nude he examined his hide for signs of trauma; reassured that the blood soaking him through was that of his brother and not his own, his men helped him methodically into Richard's clothes. The armor was much too large for Philippe, who had somehow retained the same wiry, sinewy physique of his youth, and even though every tendon of his burned and ached of combat, he contorted into the coat of mail and the helmet, and, before long, Philippe wore Lions.

The tunic was stiff with blood.

The blood my brother poured out for me

And when he traced back the torrent to its source at Richard's shoulder, he found a hole the size of his own pupil; he remembered aiming the arc of a hundred crossbow bolts with the light of his stare.

And he remembered that day when he had pushed his army through in a mad grab for land, take the English and push them into the sea, press them forward like a wave against a wave—and finally came all the way to Bayeux, where he was shown The Tapestry in its glory, *the Normans taking the English and making themselves English,* what an abomination that transformation must have been for the old Norman, and what an odd, stranger's place it was, so cold and foggy, where even Richard was a foreigner.

But then he saw that nearly-last frame, where Harold the English king is last seen alive, William's (the former Frenchman) arrow in the orbit of Harold's right eye making William an English king—*what a will to power*—and even if William became an English king, thank God at least it had him murdering an English king before him, making the Isle just a trice more *France* and a trice less *England,* Harold grabbing vainly at the shaft, the arrowhead is deep and has turned awry, has jammed into the fibers of his bones, his eye's orbit has locked the arrowhead fast, the roof of the frontalis bone, the jamb of the sygomic bone, Harold grabbing grabbing grabbing, his horse in flight, Harold's hand is on the arrow's shaft now, and the yew wood yields—William's arrowhead broken off in Harold's eye, Harold's head, Harold's wed that arrow of the Duke William and the royal child is an Abomination.

Some weaver's fingers had worried that arrow deep into Harold's eye, had really worked it in.

Some weaver had had it out against the English king something fierce.

Philippe Auguste poked his finger through the pupil-sized hole where a crossbow bolt had found home, right where the French king had willed it in with his own eye, and from where the English king's life had poured out.

Such a heart, taken down by my mere glance

* * *

And he went back to his own armor, where it now lay as an empty frame for his own portrait, and his shirt was now hard with English blood. Philippe dug into the breast pocket.

The Black Jack. Crumpled and wrinkled from a lifetime spent next to his heart, tinted with the blood of nations.

And when he held it up to the dying light at the foot of the wall, he realized: no matter how he squinted his eyes, he couldn't read the name he had written there, forty years before, so smudged it was.

This face could just as well be my own, this blood my own, this smudged ink my own name

And when he rammed his dagger through the card, and plunged it into the mortar of Château Gaillard with all his wiry strength, the dagger hung there in the stone by its point.

Nec Spe, Nec Metu

Mourir sans que personne ne le sache ;
*   Partir la nuit sans qu'on s'en rende compte ;*
*   S'infuser du sel des larmes qui montent ;*
Se repaitre de son cœur fier et lâche.

Se réveiller dans les exils qui domptent
*   Sa raison et envahissent son lit*
*   (Vivre victime de toutes les nuits)...*
Parler de son cœur, et en avoir honte.

Le malheur de mes nuits blêmes anoblit
*   Mon cœur (cette monstrueuse créature,*
*   Minuscule énormité de la nature) ;*

Mon cœur disparait. Non, il n'en a plus cure :
*   Ce radeau de chagrin veut à toute allure*
*   Sombrer, s'effondrer à jamais dans l'oubli*

To die, with no one to care any less
   And leave before dawn, no one to realize
   To drink the brine rising from my eyes
   And feast on my own heart's cowardice

To wake to solitudes that terrorize
   My listing reason and invade my rest
   To live a victim by each night distressed
   And speak of my heart, ashamed by its lies

This evil of sleepless nights lends noblesse
   To my heart (this monstrous creature,
   This minute enormity of nature).

My heart disappears. It doesn't dare endure:
   This raft of my sorrows aches, it is sure,
   To sink into seas of forgetfulness

***

'And the English fled.'

Forgetfulness is the drug that heals our sorrows, she always said in times like these, and it was true: for the life of her, Havoise could not remember how to build this simplest phrase in simplest Latin—her mind was full of memory for days gone by and seasons having changed, and there was precious little room (so she felt) for declensions and tense. *For I am no longer young, it is fine for children to remember lessons, but as for me...*

'It is a good moment.' The Abbess said this quietly.

'What, the English fleeing like rabbits before great William?'

'Yes but: that countenance of yours. You have begun to undo the weight of years, it shows on your features. No one should have to remember much more than their name and their virtue.'

Havoise concentrated. Her fingers pricked histories into her tapestry. The fire in the scriptorium chimney crackled.

***

They had thought her dead throughout the crossing: a wood and fabric bundle, down near the icy lead ballast beneath the waterline, nothing but an inch of wood planking separating her from the cold, dead waters of the Channel.

The shoremen had waded out to the ship as it ground into the Norman pebbles; they, too, had no idea that this was anything other than a stiff corpse in a colorful shroud, and *tsk*ed when they saw her ashen face and eyeless eyes staring up at the Norman sky. Quick burial unnecessary for frozen corpses, true, but at least cover their heads up will you? but then when they lift her free of the launch she is still pliable, and the corpse grunts and chuffs as they throw her over their shoulders, eyes straight ahead, face ashen. Fixed and dilated.

They seem to know which cart to put her in, are now perhaps a bit more cautious than they were before, but still whispered in tones respectful of the dead, wary of ghosts and wraiths and beings whom history has touched, whom history has wasted away.

When the rain falls again, the men leading the cart breathe easier: their whispers covered by the hush of raindrops hitting the cold steel soil.

* * *

A noble is noble because he has gifts to give. And he gives them. *Noblesse oblige.*

But no one suffers a usurper.

When they found the vast Books—so big they draped over one another like corpses at the massacre—books outlining in queerly meticulous detail William's authority over Normandy and England, they honestly had no idea what to do with them. Nervously, they whispered words like *Evidence* and *Legitimacy* and *Inspired* and *Demonic.*

'They are a record of unspeakable crimes.'

'Hush! They are a record of the Crown.'

Don't mince words in times like these: These books *are* the Crown.

* * *

Torsten the Lord Abbot of Glastonbury sat in the geometric center of those blossoming books, was their stamen and axis. When William's men weren't speaking, they could hear the scratching of his pen over parchment. It made their skin crawl.

Finally, a fist came down on the writing table, a great crack of iron against wood, and pens and knives clattered to the floor: William's Armoror, who hadn't left the side of the Lord Abbot Torsten for forty years now, thundered words they could all agree on: 'For God's sake, man, quit your scratching, it's an abomination.'

And the thundering voice guttered through the halls of the now-abandoned abbey; the King's men shuddered. Yet, the only one who *hadn't* heard was the wiry little Abbot, who never paused, never even looked up from his leaves, and the words continued flowing forth from his cut pen.

Seeing the man uncomprehending even now, Armoror snatched the pot of ink from before the Lord Abbot and heaved it with all his strength. A black lily blossomed on the scriptorium wall, and fragments of glass scattered and skittered.

Torsten looked up. He doesn't seem to see anybody in the room around him, shuffling nervously. And then, without a word, bent down beneath his table. When he straightened again, he was holding an identical jar of ink. He took care to hold his thumb over the cork as he shook it.

The men all looked on, faces as much pity as disgust.

Torsten began cutting a new pen.

And again, Armoror seized the jar of ink and flung it for all he was worth. Red this time, abbey walls wounded beyond hope.

'Take him away.'

* * *

'What are your possessions?'

Havoise had none.

'What is that you're wearing?'

It was an embroidery, a magnificent embroidery. The men had offloaded her from the cart by the gates of the convent, and when she pulled up the loose ends of the tapestry to enable her to walk, it reminded her of her youth in the little town of Falaise, where she watched the washerwomen in the dye trenches beneath the sickening gaze of Robert the Devil, raising their skirts to keep the hem dry, raising their skirts to whip the old Duke's glands into stupor, and that young harlot who raised her skirts a bit higher than was really necessary, and the day that harlot rode—so bold, so bold that Herleva was!—through the gates of the Duke's Keep at Falaise, up on the rock, and changed the course of history, the face of Normandy, and England, the course of Havoise' life and the days of her heart.

'Who gave you this tapestry?'

Havoise hadn't a word in her whole person, she held the embroidery around herself, bundled it up around her chest and her hips, turned in place to try to cover her ankles and feet.

The Abbess of Montreuil-au-Houlme lifted the loose end. 'It is... *unfinished...*' And then, beginning to comprehend: 'Are *you* the weaver of this tapestry?'

Havoise' silence, her downturned face. The Abbess interrogating her features, her words unsaid, the long raveling end of the cloth, reading the words, the images.

'Your Latin is... clumsy at times...' The Abbess' voice drifted off: there—*there*—was Duke William commanding his men to build ships, and there—*there*—was old English Harold with the arrow in his eye. The Abbess' eyes widened. '*Oh*... You're *that* weaver...'

Havoise remained silent.

'*All these griffins in the margins...*' The Abbess said this distantly, something approaching awe. '*All those corpse-pickers...*' She bent, to try to look into Havoise' downturned eyes, wondering what horrors this woman had seen, had lived.

'Philostratus,' said the Abbess, trying to break through *somehow, somewhere*, 'used to say that the castle of dreams is guarded by griffin—their role is to interrogate the dreamer-traveller: *what is your business here?* they would ask...'

Havoise' face remained impassive. The rain was falling. Abbess saw the weaver shiver.

'Milady. *What -is- thy business here?*'

* * *

Old Havoise felt a hand on her shoulder. It took her a moment to focus: the dying embers of the scriptorium chimney, her candle burned to the stump, new aches in her old spine. She looked around for her walking stick—where had that fallen to?—and her eye rose and fell to the Abbess, half-silhouetted before her, bending to try to see into Havoise' eyes. When their eyes did meet, the Abbess hove a sigh of relief.

She must have thought I had died here just now

But Havoise is reaching for her stick already, and the belfry rings distantly, bringing her back from Falaise and Glastonbury and the beachhead on the hailing English coast, and reminding her it was time for Matins—four bells—two hours before sunup, here at Montreuil-au-Houlme.

It's not like me to sleep in like this

But the Abbess is holding her walking stick now—too far away for Havoise to reach—and with another sister, has Havoise under the arms.

And where—at the scriptorium door—she would turn left to find the chapel for Matins and the *Te Deum* she loves so much, the sisters guide her to the right, toward the dormitory. And by the time she is resting in her cell, her spine flat again against her meager mattress, another pair of sisters is there, bearing curds and brandy.

But you're all missing Matins

And the Abbess sits with her till sunup, quietly chanting Matins until Havoise is asleep again.

* * *

Havoise straightens, her spine somehow longer and taller.

The valley unfolds before her, not as a wide-angle vista to dazzle the eye, but as a *val*, an open space in the deep cove forest. Her Norman eye, practiced to spot apples—*good, crunchy, fragrant Calvados apples*—sees instead, interspersed through the open *val*, great, low trees, nearly as wide as they are tall, with a bewildering array of foliages interleaved: she'll swear they bear olives and grapes altogether, and the leaves are the teardrop mink-eared leaves of ancient olives and the broad wings of the vineleaves.

This she thought *must be one of those scriptorium experiments, trefeuilles in manuscripts, drawing together margin and text, gloss and leaf and dreams... such sweetness, such savor...*

This is what it's like not to have to decide

Distantly she remembers the resonances of the word *flourish*, both a personal abstraction and a concrete reality among these curious green creations, whose branches and vines whispered secrets to one another.

For the Lord lives not in the one fruit or the other, but in the two become one, living subtly in their oneness

There are footpaths along this meandering stream. And the flash of trout within. Light in her step, her mind a wandering pathway itself. And the stream singing laughing songs, and the trees in the grove sighing their secrets, and the sweet dark fruit splitting open with their juice between her teeth.

* * *

And as the way narrows and turns; and as the chill of the air and the rush of the water in the narrow channel, thousand-year cedars here; and as the *val* is overhung with shade and cool. The sky is wild blue, and draping wings over it, branches sweep down across the narrow rushing stream and brush her hair free of its braid, and as she parts the branches here, the stream turns and the pathway is rocky and higher and free, a shared story told to the meandering water. But there on the far side there is a stone *ziqqurat*, one from another storyworld, a tale told of the ancient days, when men could build higher and nobler, and draw their blueprints from dreams and visions.

But first thou must cross over, pass across, thou maiden... Sister... Sister... Sister...

And only then did she realize she no longer remembered that old woman's name, so very far away. *Sister Whomever*. And besides, she had better things to do than recall the old dead days.

She carefully, gracefully rolled the hem of her skirts up in her hands and, straightening again to her full height, took in the view of the *ziqqurat* on the far side and: waded in.

* * *

Gates swing wide wild gyres, and lively the steps of a young girl up the curling stairs, overunder bridge and flyover arch and spire, the bright lichen on greatstone the moss of ages on rooftops, her hair a wild corona of comets swinging pinwheels spiraling free through the heavens, the stairs curling and spiraling forever upward, the lass gaining strength in her stride on long, lithe legs.

Steps two-at-a-time

Heart pounding, air roaring abundant through her broad trachea and into her pink lungs.

* * *

The Altaic peaks in sapphyric blue between spires and buttresses, *But how high have I come?* and *How much higher can I go?* and there is a high arch before her, and the rush of wings and the clatter of steel claws rampant against the stone pavers.

'What is thy business here?' the roar of wind in these words, the singing breath of archangels and cherubin. 'Is it to steal away *Pairidæza?* As if any mortal can claim such blessedness for herself... *Usus rapere* be a crime beyond sedition: would thou make of thyself a *usurper?*'

'Oh no, I would *never...* Neither to steal, nor to take anything for myself, nor even to *make anything of myself...*'

'Then what *is* thy business here?'

She won't pause an instant: 'To find my sanctuary, and sing Matins. I am late.'

The Griffin, towering over her, chuffs and flaps and shifts closer, talons metallic against stone, the rush of wings and the smelting heat of its breath blooming close range at the girl.

'Thou art *quite* late.' *(Such wise, low tones! Eyes of chrysoberyl!)* 'Matins is over for thee.'

The girl stands her ground, and speaks plainly: 'I suppose I don't need the Office of Matins in order to pray properly. So even if I'm late…'

'*This*,' thrums the Griffin, 'depends entirely on what prayer thou intendest to pray.'

'*O may I never remember, and never forget.*' The girl's voice is bold and colorful, and belies her willowy frame. Her eyes are alive with color, and they sparkle at the ease the words slip from her lips.

'*Pass across then.*'

* * *

They could spot the approach of the royal train—horses, carriages—miles before it ever came into view, if only by the way that Normans—farmers, weavers, stonecutters, cowherds, *everybody*—lined up all along the road from Caen to Falaise, and then once again all along the last fifteen miles from Falaise to the convent at Montreuil-au-Houlme. Thousands, silently, reverently on their knees at the edge of the path, and the Norman Duchess (and English Queen) Mathilde, rocking back and forth in her carriage, her veil carefully arranged to cover her face.

* * *

Surely there is nothing higher than this place

And yet the steps arc on up above the girl. At every turn in the great spiral, a landing, with a new and curious design in the pavers, with a new and different marvel carved into every door, with a new fragrance of leaf and bloom growing from each seam between the stones. The strength in her thighs and knees, the roar of her breath a great warhorse, the fire in her eyes, she could go on forever it seems...

Curiosity wins her finally, and there is a high double door, must weigh a ton on either side, scenes of rock outcroppings and dye-women striding high-kneed through dye trenches carved gracefully, and it seems made for her, for now, made to measure for this leg of her flight, and she brushes her hand against the ring and the doors glide open for her slender fingers.

It is a garden, and oh, *what a garden*, with high walls reaching into space, and vines and fountains enlacing the stones, a pool with colorful fish, are these almonds here on this side, so sweet they are almost milky?

And the sensation of immense height, the walls proud against the prevailing gale roaring around their parapets, but here all is calm and bright, and the warmth here is clement next to this little pool; overarcing the pool, there is a stout tree espaliered to the dolomitic wall, a tree with branches heavy-hanging with a strange fruit that blush sunsets at her. True, she could sit at the stone edging the pool and still reach an apronfull of them, but then she sees that the tree spreads nearly to the parapet, and *what a view there must be from up there!* and besides there is more fruit higher up, and if she has paused climbing the tall spiraling steps for a time, she can still be here, these plump, succulent fruit still beneath her hand, and still climbing upward...

* * *

'Worthy Matron, how may we serve you?' The Abbess kneeling, bent nearly face-to-earth before the Queen Mathilde.

'I understand there is the authority and legitimacy of my husband the Duke and King here, taking material shape in this very minster, in thread and ground...'

'You understand rightly, Milady.'

'I would wish to meet the Worthy Matron confectioning this treasure.'

'But Milady,' Abbess' eyes still to earth, but a bend in her shoulders that spoke volumes, 'The Archangel has borne her away already this very morning...'

* * *

Her hands find the next branch almost without reaching for it, as if the tree's geometry had unfolded with this very girl in mind, a branch right there where it would best provide handhold, foothold, and she is spiraling spiraling up and away from the earth and up toward the edge of the parapet; leaves brush her face, and whenever she pauses, there is a peach dangling, just reach out and pluck it *kissmyhand,* how so succulent and sweet.

The upper branches reaching into the gales above the parapet; she can easily get her feet into cruxes of branches and wrap her arms around the spine of this marvel, just a bit higher and she'll be able to see the infinite dome of the Blue Temple, the very throne of God rising above the sea of glass...

And climbing, caught up in the air, her heart's darkness flees away, and the worries that had darkened her features and clouded her eyes, they too flee away, and memory of old stone Keeps on Norman outcrop hills flees away, and the men all fallen down like dominos, flee away from her, and without her even noticing: the very notion of weave and warp flee away, too.

'*Et fuga verterunt angli*' she feels her heart light as a dove, caught up in the air.

And the English fled.

Qui a jamais connu un amour tel le mien ?
  Amour qui aime d'amour, et des siècles dure
  Du derrain jusqu'au suivant, constante verdure
Qui relie le jourd'hui aux trois siècles prochains

Voilà que le roi s'amadoua pour un rien
  Et que l'homme se régale d'une vidure
  Quels arts garnissaient les châteaux d'Estrémadure
Vanité des vanités, pitoyable bien

Le haut Cri terrible parmi flammes livides
  La Joconde dans un haut palais invincible
  Michelange sculpta Florence pour son David

Mais le fanatique, ayant oublié son cible
  Double ses peines pour un désir immissible
  Il n'y reste ici plus rien que le cadre vide

Whoever once knew a love quite like such as mine?
   A love to love to this cent'ry from cent'ry last
   Enduring, flourishing, gardens greening from past
   To presentday, then to three cent'ries down the line

But love of kings for empty things is holding fast
   And love of man for nobler things is in decline
   The fairytale castles we fatally design
   The utter depth and breadth of vanities amassed

The searing Scream among livid flames
   A royal palace for a smile, subtly fervid
   And Florence altogether shrines noble David

But lovers, having long since forgotten their aims
   Double their pains, their efforts all the more avid
   Leaving nothing behind but sullen, empty frames

It's been a long love affair with Temperance.

I've still been having dreams of you El, long, langorous dreams of you and me; often, it is a classic Frustration dream: an escalator casually, inexorably drawing me past the floor where you're eating breakfast or an afternoon sorbet, and I'm so close to you I can see the white of the cream or smell the tang of the coffee or spot the refractions of vapor curling from your spoon, subzero cautery, overturned, tipped up against your Toasted Almond or Crème Brûlée.

And of course the escalator doesn't serve your floor, instead just punishes me with the vision of you. Your back to me, your mane of hair variegated and cometwild, Gallia Comata incarnate, and the escalator glides on forever in Bakeresque slowmotion, there's a whole novel in the curling vapor and the way your hair falls over your shoulders, and time has dilated as I glide by, breathless, 'But El, I'm right here, just look around once, and see' caught in my throat.

I remember some other theme permeating my dreamscape, really not so very different once you scratch the surface, a great, complex building with missing floors—a hospital, a dorm, a museum under renovation—and you are there on the next floor up, some oblique transfer line between Metro stops, some white space that is neither inviting nor forbidding, but -confusing-, and you are there in the next floor up in the Winchester mansion or Escherian convent, 'all you have to do is attain me, take me to you, vicus,' in the calmest voice imaginable, low and precise, a bit of Southern Baptist drawl in those precision words, 'Attain' and 'Draw', contrary as light and dark, Yes that's all I need to do my El, there's -nothing to it- except to rewrite the laws of gravitation and light propagation through space and you will be mine, -that- was the word hanging there, in the heavens, floating between salvation and perdition: 'By this sign, Conquer.'

You are mine to lose, and my dreaming mind knows it even better than my waking intellect.

Yet 'what is happening to us' is less the point than: 'what we create'. You know I believe this in the marrowblood that animates me, in the wrinkled skin of my tired eye, in the bones of my right hand.

'To make an apple pie from scratch, you need to reinvent the Universe.' How the astronomers and cosmologists know my mind and heart, know -our- mind and heart, better than we do ourselves, is both comforting and damning.

* * *

Good God, I don't stand a chance, do I?

* * *

You've carefully dealt the cards. It is a Tuesday, and Ricus arriveth within minutes—perhaps he is already arrived, I'll never know—but it is a Tuesday, and on Tuesdays and on Thursdays and sometimes Friday and sometimes Saturday, my El disappears into some tunnel from which I'd have to dig and drill—and ping you with sonar pleadings for you to grant me some brin, some tiny mote of your mercy—to drag you. Ricus cometh to disturb your sleep, and mine now as well. And again, Tuesday imposes, and you've spent the day tiptoeing about a brilliantly-constructed house of cards, and any breath I take, even the sweetest sigh, will bring the whole edifice to a fluttering end. It is mine to lose, isn't it? Mine, to make nul. You have graciously vouchsafed me my own little fathom of rope, too short to coil, just long enough for my neck to learn the weight of my ass.

But you don't see the world as I do. That you can be assured of. If your desire is to chase me away with lacy theatrics, 'You are heartless, you are unromantic, you are dishonest, you are a sellout, you don't really want me, you just want somebody like me', then you fundamentally misunderstand me.

My world is an exquisite wind-knot in a fragile gold chain—you've shown me your jewelry box, remember, chests filled with the treasures remaining of your dear Mama, I know you know what I mean, that soft morass of fine metal given you those last fatal days—and I see you desperately trying to unwind the tangles in that rare chain, not by careful intricate loupe-work, but instead by -pulling them loose-.

And the pliable, precious pure metal deforms fatally when you pull the knots that way, and the windtangles actually weld into the chain, and the knots become new pearls, dots and dashes periodic Morse, compress in the relativistic collapse of a dying sun—and if we're lucky, the knots finish as tight, strong poppyseed neutron stars, perfect (if furnacehot) diamond stars...

But if you pull too hard, or if the knots superimpose, tangle upon tangle, last month's collapsus having been drawn tight into this month's, the poppyseed draws closed to an atom'swidth, and that fragile, irreplaceable chain will part—nothing more than a metallic thorn, a -tk-, a pop on an old record, nothing more nothing less—and the chain is now forever two...

My Darling, my Sweet El, please stop pulling so damned hard, you can't open a wind knot by pulling on it, you -do- know that, don't you?

* * *

And the world has been returned and retuned to a curious frequency, and if I could walk on water or transmute lead or make doves appear from the folds of my robes, we would not be here in close, hard orbit, trading speed for altitude or vice for versa, Love. For now you are going to Paris, and Damn You Vicus if you can't throw together a couple thou and come meet me, Latin Quarter, good God, I know St. Séverin like my own pocket, yes I know where you are, I know -exactly- where you are by point of fact, I could stand in the street and throw pebbles and wake you—just like the old movies, yes I know what to do I know what to do I know what to do—I just can't -get there- that quick on this budget.

But it is mine to lose, and if you find yourself in Paris on someone else's coin and I don't, then fatally I am the one who turned down a week in Paris with the love of my life and what fool does that if he's really in love?

But can't you wait until I can get this together on my end, can't you take time away from your life with its Tuesdays and Thursdays and sometimes Friday and sometimes Saturday? For the model is a good one: but this time, let it be my dime, let it be -my- month's salary, let me make it suchwise so that it's not an all-or-nothing, but a -vacation-, an adventure.

Pull the chain tighter on your end, El, I know you well. But as much as possible, I will give slack on my end, lest the knot deform the links yet more...

* * *

I wonder what your heart is like these days. All night—all night for a week now, your week away, this week that was mine to lose—I have this one sentence in my head, a mantra of remotest isolation, a coin from the ancient days:

Je serais peut-être sur la Lune

'I might as well be on the Moon.' You've given yourself (your heart and your body along with your mind? I'll never know) to this Ricus. I want to love him, because he is the most important man in your life, and you're the love of my life. Yet I cannot: he told me he wouldn't posture to take you away from me, that he's been nothing but respectful of our relationship, that you've been nothing but respectful of our relationship. And yet here we are: one day you've told me you love him, you're in love with him... The next that you don't really know, and that It's Hard To Say, or that We've Decided Not To Talk About It, which brings up as many questions as it answers: talk to -whom- about it? To each other?—blindly hacking away at each other in the night, forgive-them-for-they-know-not-what-they-do? Or have you decided not to bring -me- into it, ...for-you-know-not-what-they-do? For the Moon cannot but orbit distantly, watch on, watch over, 'ò invigilate watchman, tell us of the night...'

Who's been disrespectful of our love? Either you or him. Or both. I'll never know: I might as well be on the Moon. But I, in my own brand of lunacy, can't believe you would willingly hurt Us, oh no, that would be in the realm of the unreal, the unimaginable, Some Other Universe.

So my hatred and sadness fall upon him.

Yet I haven't received a word from you in days, for weeks. Sure, a downcast 'hey' on the phone—proving over and over how little you look forward to hearing from me—sure, a Scrabble move, sure, an acknowledgement that you've read my letters. But I've been brokenhearted over you and Ricus-fucking-Ricus (God, if I never heard that name ever again, it'd be too soon), about how you love him, about how you told me you love him without even saying sorry... About how you don't want to hear about it any more: 'Vicus is fucked up, Vicus has -always- been, and always will be... Vicus is suffering, Vicus feels like El's let him dry on the vine, get over it.' No, you don't want to even hear about it, you don't care to come and save my life with a word... About how you're worth sonnets and songs and words of love and longing, and not only that, but the absolute best I have in me, for I can muster the cosmos entire— crowns, treasures, the fates of nations dreamed out of nothing—just by closing my eyes and thinking of you, such universes of love...!

(And have you read any of it? How would I know? I might as well be on the Moon.)

And I'm worth what? 'Hey.' 'Som.' You sign your letters as if I could barely know who you were anymore, as if you were some stranger, as if you couldn't possibly matter to me... I hear you coddle that Love that lives like a lamp between you and him lighting you for him and him for you, I hear you protect him with your words, keeping that part of your life far from me, I hear you protect your heart from me, I hear you call me all manner of rogue when you're upset with me... I hear the cold in your voice that you reserve, lunar and changing, for me.

You don't even know my mailing address, do you? You never cared to learn it, did you...?

I might just as well be on the Moon. I might as well be on the Moon.

What does it mean when your Love, your Vicus, has now become the one whom you can see from your bedroom window, the soft glow -outside-, distant, remote, that deep blue glow in your tall quiet room, the laws of light propagation through space perversely drawing all those gentle rays to you, a light to lighten your dreams... or your nights awake, a jetlag still clutching you to itself, El and Ricus in the darkness, thank God all we have to do is draw the shades, hide our embrace from the highest rays, and only the rays oblique, the crepuscular rays a coronal glow outlining your windowframe anymore, but darkness within.

Is this what it's like to have become a fanatic in my own fashion, who, vigilant militant yet having lost his only aim, redoubles his efforts? Is this what it's like when your love has become an ornate frame without a picture?

This is maybe a bit of cognitive distance away from your wanting to 'kiss the New Year on the lips.'

Have you bothered to wrap your mind around even the tenor of my notes?—fine, I know you haven't read half of my letters, the sheaf of song and soaring word, the love of a whole life distilled into a comma-splice kyrielle, a triumphant Passacaglia of my love for you, my love for you, my love for you. Yes, I capitulate, Yes I surrender unconditional, Yes I acknowledge it now: they are worthless to you, a haystack of words you'll never read or want to read—but have you cracked them open long enough to see even the wavering hand, to say nothing of parsing them to know that yes, they are a the portrait of me, of what my heart is like, but also a mirror of -your- own person, an ornate frame of the ever-changing picture of me-watching-you, you sidling inexorably away from line of sight? If you haven't, I can let you off the hook: I know it is just charity from you to me. Yes, you can breathe easy: I concede that you've let me stumble on through, to let me call you my Muse, that you have dispensed your charity to this wretch who still wants you to complete him, to make him worth something, to make him a human being again, your charity when you condescend to me, telling me you 'like it', that you 'like' how I write you, 'like' what I write you... But have you not seen the descent, from fearless to fearful, from bold and carefree to meticulous and cautious?

I'm giving you the best of me... And I might as well be on the Moon, so little, so insignificant I am to you anymore. And so easy it is, to ignore the pebbles ticking your windowframe, the light oblique and ever-changing, the varying glow of the Moon, how easy to draw the blinds in your Paris hotel room... I will plunge fearfully ahead, losing my aim, yes; redoubling my efforts, oh yes oh yes oh yes.

I wish I knew what was in your heart, knew even if my words had reached you, known that the oblique lunar rays have illumined your night once or twice, or if they have been shaded away from your holy upper room.

I wish I knew you cared enough to help me, to endorse Us rather than endorse you-and-him, to save me from my own despair, with just a single word from you. One word.

* * *

> *Sunrise on Charlotte*
> *Jelly jars in kitchen windows*
> *Magnolia sighs and lily lies*
> *Back porch alive in morning clothes*
> *She'll brush her hair back from her eyes*
> *The coffee highs and the grey smoke blows*
> *It's time the orchids realize*
> *It's sunrise on Charlotte*
>
> *She's sunlit and starlit*
> *Starlet framed in her own front door*
> *She's sunlit and starlit*
> *She's Charlotte's child and I love her*
> *More than she knows*

The plane lays down new warpaint onto Nantes tarmac, and I wake from sweetest dreams at landing, scrub the sleep from my eyes with the hot lemon cloth they hand out remotely, coldly, for God's sake, they use tongs to bring me a little warmth?, don't touch this man he is a man condemned he is a lamb led to slaughter he's an abomination, man of sorrows.

New continent underfoot. New continent, old continent.

And you a universe away.

* * *

Like a what? Like a lost soul?

Nothing could be further from the truth.

One foot before the other, autopilot on, the brainstem knows its own map and the soul its own society, a man wearing his father's shoes—they too already know their way—and into the Vavilons, one ring of labyrinths nested within another, striding through on long, purposeful clocking strides

>'Like falling into the labyrinth' so they said
>'Like Knossos' maze,' they said, 'and Minos to defend
>Ancient victims' bones, and with the darkness to bend
>The mind and to fill the lost wand'rer's heart with dread'

>But what if: a confusion delights the mind instead
>And if the heart's own desire for darkness to mend
>It, drives it deeper t'ward the maze's heart, to blend
>Away, to play out thread upon thread, thread from thread?

>The Vavilon spiral serpentine and twist
>All 'round, but by some miracle I somehow missed
>Being at once devoured at the innermost part

>And somewhere high confusion became higher art:
>The Vavilon's reaches spiral up t'ward the mist
>And before I know it, lead me back to the start

And names are prewired in the fibers of my heart: Commerce—a poppy for my boutonnière—the bakery whose name changes every month (but whose personnel seems to know me each time, long memory, long memory, one hot chocolate croissant, one hot almond croissant with the diamond-sharp cubic sugar welded in, Wasn't that you who introduced yourself seven years ago? I -thought- I recognized your accent), rue de la Fosse and its ancient candy scents they must pump out into public spaces heaven cradled in waxed paper truth in advertising, La Brocéliande for the dessert crêpes, Heb-ken too for a chou-chenn applemead chaser, at Crébillon you make a choice of which labyrinth is really yours—the high bourgeois one, with the high bourgeoisie now living in their high little bourgeois rowhouses and the bourgeois theater the Michauds make themselves seen in their bourgeois finery in, or the lower and older one, lower and more honest, oh and so much finer? And the choice is clear once you word it that way, and then gravity wills you into the Royale vortex with its hardbaked coffee scents and here, this Christmas, ginger candy and cedar candles under the statue of Neptune pagan saint of the Nantais, oh how I miss these scents and oh how I'll miss them, and so I draw them in, all lungs.

The labyrinth is deeper the farther east now, with taller, steeper houses beginning to lean in over the avenues, old building elm boulevards cathedral arches and shrewd lights, and the Nantais know how to shoehorn a car in between in the gaptooth spaces left by the fire hydrants and the homemade Défense De Stationer signs, and they watch their reflections in the shop windows to avoid trading paint, just a kiss, just a kiss, Love.

Fifty Hostages its own hardhearted poem on Nantais history, cross at your peril, cross on a run, there's no way to -stroll- here unless you want to make it across in two or more lights, dangling from streetlamps singing in the rain midway, and so you sprint, and if Neptune protects the Mariner, Fifty Hostages protects those who know the timing of streetlights, and feet beat the machinelanguage street of the old city trying to juggle eight lanes of new traffic running chainsaws flying chaotically.

Before long, the anarithmetic interweaves of Bouffay, this is how root tangles hold forests up, even the weak get -grown in- by the strong, we'll outgrow you but at least you'll still be around to know it, and the grain of my bones spidery marrow spidery periostea know that Au Vieux Quimper will build a crêpe chapêtre to die for, and even though dessert came first, let the coroner sort it all out, The Subject Appears To Have Eaten Dessert First which brings a wrydry grin to your still-live lips can't be the end of the world, what, to leave behind a trace of still-life Epicureanism on the carbonpaper for the source scholars to puzzle over, good and hedonist like a Stendhal or a Balzac, not any of that ticklish Thoreau-oid 'shave before bathing or bathe before shaving?' *fastidiousness, and so a champêtre goes down smooth and creamy, what me have a heart attack at a time like this? and then come to think of it Make it a double chou-chenn, what me, cirrhosis?*

And the fanatic pays his check with a three-hundred-percent tip, More frame than picture n'oublions!, let the source-studies folk chew on -that- will you, and then, just a hundred yards further on, a sweet mint tea at his friend Feyk's counter, lambsteaks on the spit a sweet smell of sacrifice in the thieves' temple fillthoselungfillthoselungsfillthoselungs, and it is raining when his Dad's shoes find the pavers again.

The cathedral is closed for the night, he would've liked spending a few more minutes gazing at Temperance.

He pulls his greatcoat higher up around his neck against the rain, and he thinks if he jams his hands deep into the pockets he might better hold it up there to his ears. In they go, halfway to the elbow, and he feels with his right hand a fragment of paper—a paper letter to tack to the trees, 'I've thought about you so much, El, even dreamed about you; I've peopled my cities with you for a decade-plus'—and he feels the sharp edges and cold steel of The End Of The Line with the slender fingers of his left hand.

* * *

Rain. The rookery herons have fallen silent: what have they but to shelter and wait out the averse—it will be a long winter, and the wisdom knit into their evolution has left them with instincts to make cover in times like these: cover, find warmth, circle in.

There is a limit here, a boundary, and the fanatic crosses over deftly, having thought these last moments over in mindflight, knowing: they'll never find me in this place.

The creatures barely stir as he draws in close, picking clumsy heron steps over roots entangling and supporting his weight all at once, the ancient chestnut coppice a mangrove, the offspring of the ancient-of-days chestnut up in the close of the monastery, what are these if not his very bones, slender and angling, slender and curving, greasy with God-knows-what under the rain, and he sees how he will become immaterial with the substance of these roots and the gore they've rooted into, this is what, the most beautiful river stretch in all of France, so declareth the Francis, of the name: First, of the Faith: Defender, how better to choose than to let -that- authority act on his behalf?

And he tacks his passacaglia into the crux of a chestnut, canopied and safe.

* * *

'What is your business here?'

[...] l'Indois Griffon aux yeus estincelans,
A la bouche aquiline, aux ailes blanchissantes,
Au sein rouge, au dos noir, aux griffes ravissantes,
Dont il va guerroyant et par monts et par vaux
Les lyons, les sangliers, les ours, et les chevaux :
Dont il fouille pillard le feconde poictrine
De nostre bisayeule, et là dedans butine
Maint riche lingot d'or, pour apres en plancher,
Son nid haut eslevé sur un aspre rocher:
Dont il deffend, hardi, contre plusieurs armees
Les mines par sa griffe une fois entamees
        -Guillaume du Bartas

[...] the Indus' Griffin with the flashing eyes
The fabled Roman mouth and shining wings of white
The breast of red and back of black, claws shining bright
Warring wherewith o'er vals and mountains flying
'Gainst bear and boar, 'gainst stampeding horse and lion
Digging wherewith, too, butin from the fertile breast
Of our forefathers, tearing treasure from their chest
Bar of gold, ingot and bullion with which to line

Its nest in steepest reaches airless and Alpine
Defending, with frightening cries and tearing jaws
The precious mines it had raked open with its claws

* * *

The Griffin's silhouette, the toneless contrabasso of Antiquity.

The Fanatic's voice surprises him, nearly shouting above the weight of the rain: 'My business here is to disappear, to cross over.'

His hand hadn't left the cold steel of his left coat pocket, and the heat of his flesh and the fabric of his bones speaking secrets to the steel, and the steel speaking back to his bones and flesh, and without realizing it, the fanatic has become cold and hard, just a precious few degrees of freedom available anymore in this close forest and standing on the slipping roots: roll the chambers 'round, safety on, safety off, safety on, safety off.

No one knows how creatures of sky and earth, beautiful in their duality as this Griffin, maneuver in these lightless closed spaces, no one less than the fanatic himself who himself was entangled in his sphere, and the Griffin's talons find such sure, easy purchase among these knotting roots, and its wings folding and deploying, these branches do nothing if not delineate three-dimensional space for this beast to wend through, and You'll never find me in this space simply rings false anymore for this grand creature, who approaches the dripping man so precipitously he feels the beast's wings beat whorls into the sheets of rain, and the fanatic, fallen, knees already twisted into the roots he has destined to grow him through and the marl he has destined to become, feels the furnace heat of the Griffin's breath as it speaks subvocal:

'-Everyone's- business is to cross over, but it is not for every man to despair and disappear.'

* * *

But the complaint of the fanatic: 'See how much he -loves- her...'

But the Griffin has read his mind like a tapestry unrolled, has parsed the very pulses of his thought: the fanatic couldn't grasp the Griffin's tone as it replied in his very own words, 'See how much he loves her,' at once scoffing and ethereal, distant as history, the weight of years.

The Griffin, in the space of a thought, reads the letters tacked up to the trees, perceives through the fabric of the greatcoat cold steel in the fanatic's bony palm, and continues: 'See how much he hates... -him-.'

* * *

- I love both of you, I hear you say, El.

- But you've chosen -him-.

- I just worry that if I don't I'll lose him.

- But what then, but what then about me?

* * *

Does saying these things aloud, in the fracas pathos of a New Year's downpour in the deep of night, in the presence of the ancient gatekeeper in this sacred hidden grove that no one will ever find me in, make any of it 'real'? Could I stand it being any more 'real'? Can I somehow attenuate its impact on me anymore? I look in the mirror after a night awake—another night awake— and I see lines on my face that won't ever go away anymore. This is my face now, and it's too hard anymore to stomach this: that I've become everything I've done. And my Love in her entirety is all far and away, and her thoughts, so far from alighting upon me anymore, are all far and away, and the old days—so very very far away—are looking less like a point of pride or reason for nostalgia, and more like a very long and damned heavy burden.

The Griffin is there.

The gun is in my hand.

And tonight. A keening, complex passacaglia of ruined dreams.

-Passacaglia-

Ces fils de toutes couleurs qu'on coupe un à un
Cette Parque-là—de coup sûr, de main habile
L'œil vif, le cœur dur, le sang froid, les doigts mobiles—
Coupe un fil, puis un autre... de même pour chacun

Et l'homme—cœur transi, dans cette forêt tranquille
Tombe sous la pluie, déjà à demi défunt
On lui avait coupé les fils les plus communs
Il n'en rest' qu'un, en or, fil de sa vie subtile

Forêt, clairière, dernier art de main tremblant
Quelle défaite, quel embarras de courage
Univers inombré, une averse qui trempe

Une lettre laissée derrière mon cœur mourant
Un écho laissa tout un cercle de carnage
La balle sortit du canon trouver ma...
***
Silken sev'ral-colored threads severed one by one
The skillful Fated hand—with a swift stroke, with deft
Fingers, with alert eye, with cold blood, hard heart—cleft
One, then next, then again, the grim task just begun

This man—alone in this forest grove, heart bereft—
Falls to his knees, soaked through, already half undone
Of all those threads of his to cut through, there is none
Just one gossamer thread in subtlest gold is left

A forest, a clearing, my trembling hand's last art
My heart of hearts a broken puzzle of courage
A landscape of darkness, a whole dreamscape of rain

A single letter left behind my dying heart
A single echo left a whole arc of carnage
A single bullet left...

* * *

The hammer rises and the fanatic squints cowardice.

* * *

'Don't you dare to harm that lovely head of yours.' That dusky alto I know, my Eleanor in the rain.

The voice of my El.

This can't be real. A catch in the breath. The fanatic doesn't dare open his eyes.

* * *

'Release, my Love.'

Which part of my being wishes so hard to be near to my El again as to hear her voice in the chestnut grove in the rain, my bones ready to filigree with the chestnut roots, the blood of my veins poised to become clotting rain?, oh but El, please, for my life's sake send me your voice again, through the rush of rain, so that I can release my grip on this trigger and drop this steely death away...

'My brilliant Love—' she says to me.

Good God, her voice sounds so real, so -near-. My thumb lowers the fatal hammer—the cold and the wet make this hard to do gingerly, and there is a power curve knit into the steel springs of the mechanism to overcome, and they resist—as do the bones of my hand, having wished and dreaded and dreamed this moment for an eternity.

'My brilliant Love—' she says again. Her voice so soft, somehow in the rain itself, all around me in this grove.

> *My brilliant Love—*
> *My composer, my conductor,*
> *My Complicated Love—*

You have slain me with your words
  (And meanings of words)
You have slain me with your tongue your lips your heart
You have picked me up & taken me to greater heights and
  You have lain me down gently.
You challenge and impress me with your many talents
  And honor me with your Art
  And my body
    Sanctify, appreciate my mind &
      Treasure my soul
You are my leonine Ott, my Love

* * *

I dare, at last, to open my eyes, and I stream with rain and see nothing but the sogging grove. This is an enchantment, isn't it? I am already dead, am I not?... I hear the empty mirror speaking my words back to me, and madness interrupts madness.

'If it is you, El, let me hear you again through the rain. Call out to me in your alto voice.'

Call to me, El, my cherubim, in tones I would understand as Ours Alone. Call me back from the precipice.

And in the shadows, sure as day follows night, I hear that voice:

> *Mon Amour, mon tout-mien, ô toi ma brillante âme*
> *Mon seul maître de chapelle, compositeur*
> *De délices, de cet amour complèxe Auteur :*
> *Tant de mots, tous flambeaux pour ardre cette femme*
>
> *Tant d'étincelles dans ta parole ! O tant de flammes*
> *Pour ardre mon cœur : langue, lèvres, et ton coeur*
> *Me soulèvent jusqu'à de si hautes hauteurs*
> *Me ramènent à mon lit ou mon corps se pâme*

Enfin le défi lancé par tous tes talents
M'honore, tout comme l'art de tes Passe-cailles
Qui de mon corps entier prennent leur libre cours

En sanctifiant mon esprit—le croyant brillant—
Et en chérissant cette mienne âme sans faille
Tu restes mon Léon, mon Otto, mon Amour

***

'My Love, my brilliant Love' begins the soft refrain
Composer and conductor of my heart's delight
Maestro, my Complex Love, my Virtuosic Might:
Oh how with your words polyphonic you have slain

Me, and with their knitting tones slain me once again,
And the counterpoint of tongue, lips and heart ignite
Me, raise me up above, carry me to such height
And then, once raised up, t'war my bed so gently lain

So many gifts made me, such challenges impress
Me, such Artful passacaglias writ to honor
Me, all of me, my entire person: this body of mine

To privilege, this intellect of mine to bless
This soul of mine to treasure, this proud and inner
Being of mine, o my Love, my Ott Leonine

***

And there, in this closed sphere of rain, there are no longer Griffins to escort mortal men to the realms of the dead, nor is there death hovering around you, Mortal Man, planes of gunsmoke as yet unrealized in the grove.

Instead there before me is my El, and her hair clings to her shoulders in the rain, and the air trembles around her. Shivering El, El shivering in the rain. But then I understand her saying, 'But the dead have no life, but the life that the living lend them.'

And without pause, 'Make that damned thing safe,' she says through chattering teeth, her eyes in the rain never leaving mine, a challenge in her voice not just a challenge but a promise.

And the instinct to obey that voice, this woman I love with my whole existence, always have always will, is more than an instinct, it is a reflex: and at cue the steel in my hand releases the cartridge from its chambers, lets it tumble out of their chambers as gravity wills it to, Empty frames again, bearing neither death nor relief from sorrows: just empty again, thank God thank God thank God. Down it falls through the lattice of roots, all the arrows and the bow as well.

And there you are before me, shiveringshivering, and when my arms find you and yours find me, and my old greatcoat casts wings over you, and all I can think to say: 'My God, how cold you must feel.'

And then, with you bundling next to me, I can feel your thoughts broadcast through the ether as you rest your head against my heart, transmit from your mind to mine through magnetism, through nuclear resonance, through proximity brought to the extreme—call it intimacy, call it sympathy, call it whatever you like; and if I'm right, I would swear your shuddering is as much from the fact of having stood at the final precipice with me as it is from the cold rain having insinuated your clothes; your mind's eye, I am sure, is still following where the steel death and its leaden footsoldier had fallen. I hear your alto, reading these thoughts into real breath passing across soft tissue, the real tissues of my Love's voice:

'I was just about to say the same thing about you.'

* * *

We are alone. We are together. The forbidden grove abandoned save for us, a frame of despair aching to be made empty again.

'You're not supposed to be here.'

'Neither are you.'

Made in the USA
Columbia, SC
16 August 2019